The Story of Lilly Dawson

by

Catherine Crowe

edited with an introduction and notes
by Ruth Heholt

Victorian Secrets 2015

Published by

Victorian Secrets Limited
32 Hanover Terrace
Brighton BN2 9SN

www.victoriansecrets.co.uk

The Story of Lilly Dawson by Catherine Crowe
First published in 1847
This Victorian Secrets edition 2015

Introduction and notes © 2015 by Ruth Heholt
This edition © 2015 by Victorian Secrets
Composition and design by Catherine Pope

The cover image is Lady Isabel Somers-Cocks (1851-1921) by Oscar Gustavus Rejlander, courtesy of The Library of Nineteenth-Century Photography.

A catalogue record for this book is available from the British Library.

ISBN 978-1-906469-55-9

CONTENTS

INTRODUCTION

This introduction contains plot spoilers, so readers new to the story might want to treat it as an afterword.

Speaking Out: Catherine Crowe's Pioneering Spirit

In 1845 *The Blackburn Standard* cited Catherine Crowe as one of the six 'most popular and of course best paid' female novelists of the time.[1] During the 1840s and early 1850s Crowe was such a successful author that Colin Wilson claims that she 'was once as famous as Dickens or Thackeray'.[2] However in 1854, the year that her last novel *Linny Lockwood* was published, she suffered a devastating psychotic episode which effectively ruined her reputation.[3] This colours the way that even contemporary critics view her work, and most assume, as Roger Clarke does, that after her (extremely brief) breakdown she 'vanished from the scene'.[4] This is not quite true and she continued to write and publish up until her death. Perhaps unsurprisingly, though, Crowe's work fell into obscurity and it is only with the recent revival of interest in ghosts and the Gothic that her tales of the supernatural have been rediscovered. *The Night Side of Nature or Ghosts and Ghost Seers* (1848) is by far her most famous book and this collection of 'real' ghost tales has been attracting an increasing amount of academic interest. In *The Night Side of Nature* Crowe presents ghost stories, anecdotes and reported personal encounters with ghosts. Crowe was adamant that these vocalised experiences were worthy of serious investigation, and as the scientific community continually ridiculed the idea of the supernatural, *The Night Side of Nature* includes groundbreaking attacks on the narrow-mindedness of science and the cult of rationality. This book made her famous and secured her place as a leading proponent of Spiritualism. Aside from this text, critical attention has focussed on Crowe's first novel, *Susan Hopley: The Adventures of a Maid Servant or Circumstantial Evidence*, first published in

1 *The Blackburn Standard* , 24th December, 1845; Issue 571.
2 Colin Wilson, 'Introduction' to *The Night Side of Nature*, (Wellingborough: The Aquarian Press, 1986), p. v.
3 See Appendix A.
4 Roger Clarke, *A Natural History of Ghosts: 500 Years of Hunting for Proof*, (London: Particular Books, 2012), p. 158.

1841. This novel is now believed to be one of the very first fictional depictions of a detective figure.[5] This is of particular interest as Crowe's novel pre-dates (by just four months) Edgar Allan Poe's tale 'The Murders in the Rue Morgue', which is usually cited as the first detective story.[6] This reassessment of Crowe's part in the formation of the detective genre has revitalised interest in her wider work and this introduction to her third novel, *The Story of Lilly Dawson,* places Crowe in the vanguard of the emerging sensation genre and shows her to be a visionary and radical thinker and writer.

Lilly Dawson and the Sensation Genre

The Story of Lilly Dawson, subtitled *The Smugglers at the Inn* was published in 1847, contemporaneously with *Jane Eyre*, and is cited as Crowe's 'greatest critical success'.[7] *Lilly Dawson* is a romping tale of pirates and outlaws, murder, kidnap, mistaken identity, madness, lust and betrayal. Crowe's novels, although filled with melodrama and crime, are not of the same class as the Penny Dreadfuls or the Newgate Novels popular in the 1830s and 1840s. Indeed, they provide a quite clear bridge between these earlier lower-class texts and the middle-class sensation novels of the 1860s. Crowe is a middle-class writer who moved among the literary and scientific intelligentsia circles of the time. She knew Charles Dickens, Ralph Waldo Emerson, William Makepeace Thackeray, visited Jane and Thomas Carlyle, dined with Wilkie Collins, George Eliot and Charlotte Brontë and was very good friends with Harriet Martineau. Crowe was part of the literary establishment, and her melodramatic and sensational novels were initially published in three-volume form, intended for a middle-class audience.[8] However they were very quickly turned into cheap editions 'for the perusal of all classes',[9] and her work pre-empts the famous criticism of sensation fiction which makes 'the

---

5 For the beginning of this debate see Lucy Sussex, 'The Detective Maidservant: Catherine Crowe's Susan Hopley', in *Silent Voices: Forgotten Novels by Victorian Women Writers,* Brenda Ayres, (ed), (Westport, CT: Praeger Publishers, 2003).

6 See for example the discussion by Peter Messant in *The Crime Fiction Handbook,* (Chichester, West Sussex, UK; Malden, MA: Wiley-Blackwell, 2013), where he quotes Poe as being called 'the father of detective fiction', p. 110.

7 Quote from the Cambridge University 'Orlando: Women's Writing in the British Isles from the Beginning to the Present' online project, 'Catherine Crowe' entry, *accessed 05/11/14.*

8 Apart from *Linny Lockwood* which Crowe published in two-volume form as an experiment.

9 Quote from the Cambridge University 'Orlando: Women's Writing in the British Isles from the Beginning to the Present' online project, 'Catherine Crowe' entry, *accessed 05/11/14.*

literature of the Kitchen the favourite reading of the Drawing room'.[10] In 1980 Winifred Hughes argued that sensation literature 'had no perceptible infancy; its greatest triumph, as well as its masterpieces, coincided with its initial appearance. It sprang full-blown, nearly simultaneously, from the minds of Wilkie Collins, Mrs. Henry Wood and M. E. Braddon.'[11] More recently though, critics such as Andrew Mangham and Anne-Marie Beller do not quite see the emergence of the genre in the same way. Mangham argues that 'there is a risk [...] when we talk about sensation fiction, of overstating the suddenness with which it came and went',[12] and according to Beller 'the genre's "infancy" is clearly perceptible in the 1850s'.[13] Crowe's work begins a decade earlier in 1841, and her novels hybridise genres, cross class boundaries, and certainly move towards the sensation genre.

Crowe told Robert Chambers that she wrote 'stories of strong passion',[14] and her novels are daring and up to date. Sex, bigamy, murder, cross-class affairs and all manner of sensational scandals populate Crowe's novels and it is not difficult to see why they were so popular. The 1844 novel *Men and Women or Manorial Rights* features the sensational murder of the blackguard aristocrat Sir John Eastlake and much of the narrative is a whodunnit which unravels the mystery. *The Adventures of a Beauty* (1852) follows the fortunes of the beautiful peasant girl Agnes Crawfurd who is tricked into thinking her marriage to Sir Lionel Grovesnor of Ravenscliffe Castle is false. Agnes is led to believe that her own son is illegitimate while Sir Lionel's son from his subsequent bigamous marriage is passed off as the true heir. Finally the plot is exposed, resulting in scandal and death. Crowe's last novel *Linny Lockwood* (1854) follows the story of Linny, a poor but genteel young woman, and Lady Glenlyon, an aristocratic adulteress who abandons everything to elope Linny's husband. Both Agnes and Linny travel to the Continent in an attempt to uncover the truth and Crowe paints scenes from exotic, foreign locations. Lyn Pykett suggests that contemporary reviews in the 1860s described sensation novels as '"fast novels", "crime novels", "bigamy

10 Andrew King quotes W. F. Rae writing in 1865 in '"Literature of the Kitchen": Cheap Serial Fiction of the 1840s and 1850s', Gilbert, Pamela K., *A Companion to Sensation Fiction*, (Malden, Mass.: Wiley Blackwell Publishing, 2011), p. 38.
11 Winifred Hughes, *The Maniac in the Cellar: Sensation Novels of the 1860s*, (Princeton, NJ: Princeton University Press, 1980, p. 6.
12 Andrew Mangham, 'Introduction', *The Cambridge Companion to Sensation Fiction*, Andrew Mangham (ed), (Cambridge: Cambridge University Press, 2013), p. 1.
13 Anne-Marie Beller, 'Sensation Fiction in the 1850s', *The Cambridge Companion to Sensation Fiction*, Andrew Mangham (ed), (Cambridge: Cambridge University Press, 2013), p. 8.
14 Geoffrey Larken, *The Ghost Fancier,* unpublished text, Catherine Crowe Archive, University of Kent, Canterbury, p. 489.

novels", or "adultery novels'".[15] Any one of these descriptions would fit Crowe's novels of the 1840s and 50s and although they are not full-blown sensation novels (their basic moral stance is a little too staid), they pave the way to the more scandalous genre.

A review of *Lilly Dawson* in *The Athenaeum* notes the blending of the more respectable psychological aspects of the novel with embodied, physical sensation:

> Certain situations in this novel are evolved with a power that carries physical terror to its utmost limit. The murder of Charlotte Littenhaus by her brother, who mistakes her for Lilly, is of this kind. Such details, however, form too harsh a contrast with the psychological interest which the story most frequently excites. Mrs. Crowe, more than most living novelists, has it in her power to unite ideal purpose with its appropriate sensuous embodiment.[16]

The reviewer is not comfortable with the melding of lurid detail and the psychological realism of the novel. However, from a historical point of view, this synthesis of psychological realism with hair-raising depictions of physical terror forms an important moment in the nascent sensation genre.

Poverty and Realism

Joanne Wilkes in *The Oxford Dictionary of National Biography* gives an overview of Crowe's novels: 'The novels' interest in middle- and lower-class domestic life aligns them with mid-nineteenth-century realism, but they are also notable for crime, upper-class seducers, exotic locales, and complicated and coincidence ridden plots'.[17] This certainly chimes with the sensation genre, yet as Wilkes notes, the melodramatic elements of Crowe's work are always tempered with realism. In July 1858 an article in *The National Review* proclaims:

> The writer is a woman of genius. Her stories *Susan Hopley* and *Lilly Dawson* are models of straightforward narration. A female De Foe could not have told them better; if, indeed, such stories can be said to be told, which seem rather like the conscientious detail of real incident. [This] is not art, but characteristic of [...] minds that [...] will have reality or nothing.[18]

Crowe's more sensational plot lines tend to involve the aristocracy, while she

---

15 Lyn Pykett, *The Sensation Novel: From the Woman in White to The Moonstone*, (Plymouth, UK.: Northcote House, 1994), p. 4.

16 Review of *Lilly Dawson*, *The Athenaeum*; 13th March 1847, Issue 1011, p. 282.

17 Joanne Wilkes, 'Crowe , Catherine Ann (1790–1872)', *Oxford Dictionary of National Biography*, (Oxford University Press, 2004; online edition, May 2008), accessed, 11 July 2014.

18 'Ghosts of the Old and New School', *The National Review*, July 1858, Issue 13, p. 1.

employs realism in her sympathetic and detailed portrayals of the poor. Realism in Crowe's novels enables her to critique social injustice, and to document society from the point of view of the downtrodden and oppressed.[19] She is rigorous in her depiction of crushing poverty, of domestic abuse and the terrible physical and mental burdens endured by the *very* poor. Crowe describes their dwellings, their work and hunger with great compassion and care. Lilly's own life is full of hardship, first as a near-slave to her cousins and later in Mrs Knox's back sewing room where she is 'often kept at her work till midnight' while being paid but 'a bare pittance' (79). In *Lilly Dawson* this level of poverty is the plight of most of the main characters.

Just after its publication a review of *Lilly Dawson* in *The Literary Gazette* suggests that Crowe's

> chief merit will [...] be found in the exact descriptions of manners and feelings of the vile and lowly personages with whom she has peopled her page. Her ostlers, washerwomen, servants, beggars, villains, &c. &c., have all the semblance of realities; and we are surprised how any female in the better walks of life could learn to represent them in so vivid and apparently accurate a style.[20]

To the reviewer, Crowe's level of realism in relation to portrayals of the lowly is surprising and somewhat unedifying particularly as she is a middle-class female writer. To the contemporary reader, whilst also being surprising, the realism and detail deployed in portraying these characters show Crowe to have a sensitivity to her surroundings, a clear sense of social (in)justice and a deep sympathy for those less well off than herself. One of the most attractive characters in the book is Abel White, a blind beggar who befriends Lilly after she has accidentally but fortuitously managed to escape the tyrannical Littenhaus family. Lilly goes on the tramp with Abel and Crowe looks unflinchingly at this humble way of life, depicting it as more free and dignified than either Lilly's life of servitude before she met Abel, or the confinement of the poor house Abel has fled from. Poverty itself does not breed ignorance and her 'ostlers, washerwomen [and] servants' are often kind, sensitive and thoughtful. Abel White has been brought low by circumstance and forced to beg, but 'though he might sigh at his degradation, he had no cause to blush for it' (40). There is no shame in poverty whilst there is in the wilful brutality and ignorance that characterises the Littenhaus family. For Crowe ignorance is the greatest evil, backed by selfishness and narrow-mindedness and these vices can be found in any class of person. In the character of Abel she shows that empathy,

---

19 Crowe's novels differ from the 'Condition of England' novels also popular in the 1840s in that although they deal with social injustice and poverty, they do not directly examine the consequences of industrialisation and urbanisation.

20 'Novel in Low Life', *The Literary Gazette: A Weekly Journal of Literature, Science, and the Fine Arts*, 6th March 1847; Issue 1572, p. 187.

compassion and delicacy are to be found perhaps more easily on the road than in the drawing room.

Education

About halfway through *Lilly Dawson* Crowe's critique of social injustice moves in a different direction. She pauses the narrative, and for several pages gives a quite extraordinary and prolonged expostulation about women's education. Men, she states, have the advantage and 'if their education has been bad, it has at least been a trifle better than ours. Six hours a-day at Latin and Greek are better than six hours a-day at worsted-work and embroidery' (200). Women's education, she argues, is wasteful, useless and damaging. Crowe emphasises that an inferior and ideologically flawed education can have devastating results for women. Her main argument focuses around the concept of men and women being equal-but-different and, although she argues that women are not equal to men in some ways, not all of this is down to nature:

> man having [...] settled to his own entire satisfaction the question of the weakness and inferiority of woman, and every thing [sic] being done that training could do, to produce such results as confirmed his conclusion, it necessarily followed that she was unfit to cope with the world (199).

Men are confirmed in their opinion that women are weak, inferior and incapable because they have made sure that women are *trained* to be so. This then becomes a self-perpetuating state of affairs, which (to couch it in contemporary terms), is ideologically turned into a conception of 'nature'. Crowe argues that 'man' having educated women thus,

> saw nothing left for it but to turn the world into one large harem; perpetuating woman's slavery by perpetuating her ignorance; and teaching her, whilst he assumed a divine right to despotic sway, that it was the worst of treasons to herself – that is, that it was *unfeminine* – to dispute his claims (199, emphasis in the original).

Crowe points out the constructed nature of gender, yet she still believed in certain fundamental and biological differences between men and women. However, these could benefit women:

> If, as we believe, under no system of training, the intellect of woman would be found as strong as that of man, she is compensated by her intuitions being stronger – if her reason be less majestic, her insight is clearer – where man reasons, she sees. Nature, in short, gave [woman] all that was needful to enable her to fill a noble part in the world's history, if man would but let her play it out; and not treat her like a full-grown baby, to be flattered and spoiled on the one hand,

and coerced and restricted on the other. [...]

> From first to last, she is governed by the pap-spoon and the rod; and whilst for his own selfish ends, man kneels at her feet and flatters her with mock devotion, he makes laws and enforces customs that rob her of her free franchise (202).

Infantalising women denies them freedom and dignity, and she argues that for women, 'the fact that so many amongst them do not desire to be [free], is one of the worst symptoms of their condition' (203).

Crowe's views are contradictory, yet this hardly matters as she argues so strongly against social injustice and inequality. She acknowledges that some few women manage to escape the traps set by patriarchy but:

> Let any woman to whom circumstances have been more favourable [...] speak honestly the result of her own experience and observation in this respect. How many women could she reckon of her acquaintance who have ever dared to think for themselves; or even if they dared to *think,* would dare to *speak?* (200, emphasis in the original).

Adeline Sergeant, writing in 1897 declared that for her time Crowe's ideas on women's position and education were 'advanced' and that to air these views 'must have required considerable courage'.[21] Crowe's great contribution to the debate raging about women's education was that she did not equate it with a desired goal of marriage. Others such as her friend Harriet Martineau, while advocating improvement in education for women, still saw marriage as the object and believed that one of the main points of women's education was to make her a fit companion for her husband.[22] Crowe looks more widely to the contribution women can make to society through independence, freedom, activity and (a tempered) equality. And, although she still argues for differences in abilities and qualities for men and women, she believes that both sexes will benefit from women being free.

Conclusion

I have been working on Crowe for several years and the more I read her in the context of her time, the more respect I gain for her originality and bravery. Her

---

21 Adeline Sergeant, 'Mrs. Crowe. Mrs. Archer Clive. Mrs. Henry Wood,' in *Women Novelists Of Queen Victoria's Reign: A Book of Appreciations*, by Mrs. Oliphant, Mrs. Lynn Linton Mrs. Alexander, Mrs. Macquoid, Mrs. Parr, Mrs. Marshall, Charlotte M. Yonge, Adeline Sergeant & Edna Lyall, [1897], (Cambridge: Cambridge University Press, 2011), pp. 150-151.

22 See Harriet Martineau, writing under the pseudonym of Discipulus, 'On Female Education', *Monthly Repository of Theology and General Interest,* February 1823, Volume 18, pp. 77-81.

views on the position of women and the poor are clearly expressed in *Lilly Dawson*, and elsewhere in her writing she takes a strong anti-slavery stance, questions masculinist, rationalist science and protests against cruelty to animals.[23] Her work is pioneering and it is worth remembering that in Victorian times it was exceedingly popular. A reviewer in *The Critic*, shortly after the publication of *Lilly Dawson* exclaims that: 'It is one of the few novels that *every* circulating library, however small, may venture to order, secure of a remunerating circle of readers, and which every reader may venture to borrow, certain that he will be amused.'[24] Mid-Victorian readers were well aware of Crowe's work and appreciative of her style and subjects. With this scholarly edition of *The Story of Lilly Dawson* I hope to introduce new readers to Crowe's work. The narrative style is not always perfect, and, as we have seen, she can be didactic at times. However, as Adeline Sergeant writes:

> She left a mark upon the age in which she lived, and she helped, in a quiet, undemonstrative fashion, to mould the women of England after higher ideals than had been possible in the early days of the century. Those who consider the development of women to be one of the distinguishing features of Queen Victoria's reign should not forget that they owe deep gratitude to writers like Mrs. Crowe, who upheld the standard of a woman's right to education and economic independence long before these subjects were discussed in newspapers and upon public platforms.[25]

While her work has social and cultural significance, it is also extremely entertaining and to quote the contemporary blogger Ian Keable's take on *Lilly Dawson*; 'despite the slightly melodramatic plot it's actually a cracking good read'.[26]

---

23 See Appendix B.
24 Review of *The Story of Lilly Dawson*, *The Critic*, 13th March 1847, p. 205, (emphasis in the original).
25 Adeline Sergeant, 'Mrs. Crowe. Mrs. Archer Clive. Mrs. Henry Wood,' p. 160.
26 This quote is reproduced with the kind permission of Ian Keable: www.charlesdickens-mysteryshow.co.uk.

SUGGESTIONS FOR FURTHER READING

Please note that Crowe's novels and her ghost tales are available archive.org.

Clarke, Roger, *A Natural History of Ghosts: 500 Years of Hunting for Proof,* (London: Particular Books, 2012).

Crowe, Catherine, *The Night Side of Nature,* (Wellingborough: Aquarian Press, 1986).

Gilbert, Pamela K., *A Companion to Sensation Fiction*, (Malden, Mass.: Wiley Blackwell Publishing, 2011).

Hughes, Winifred, *The Maniac in the Cellar: Sensation Novels of the 1860s*, (Princeton, NJ: Princeton University Press, 1980).

Mangham, Andrew, (ed), *The Cambridge Companion to Sensation Fiction*, (Cambridge: Cambridge University Press, 2013).

Owen, Alex, *The Darkened Room: Women, Power and Spiritualism in Late-Victorian England*, (Chicago; London: University of Chicago Press, 1989/2004).

Pykett, Lyn, *The Sensation Novel: From the Woman in White to The Moonstone,* (Plymouth, UK: Northcote House, 1994).

Sussex, Lucy, 'The Detective Maidservant: Catherine Crowe's Susan Hopley', in *Silent Voices: Forgotten Novels by Victorian Women Writers,* Brenda Ayres, (ed), (Westport, CT: Praeger Publishers, 2003).

Wilkes, Joanne, 'Crowe, Catherine Ann (1790–1872)', *Oxford Dictionary of National Biography*, (Oxford; New York: Oxford University Press, 2004, online edition).

Women Novelists Of Queen Victoria's Reign: A Book of Appreciations, by Mrs. Oliphant, Mrs. Lynn Linton, Mrs. Alexander, Mrs. Macquoid, Mrs. Parr, Mrs. Marshall, Charlotte M. Yonge, Adeline Sergeant & Edna Lyall, [1897], (Cambridge: Cambridge University Press, 2011).

BIOGRAPHICAL NOTE

Catherine Ann Stevens was born in 1790 into a middle-class, affluent family who had made their money in the catering and hotel business. She was educated at home in Kent but not much is known about her early life. In 1822, when she was 32, she married Major John Crowe. The Crowes travelled widely and their son was born in Corfu in 1823. However, Crowe was unhappy and separated from her husband in 1833 in a rather dramatic way, asking friends Sydney Smith and his family to help her escape. Crowe moved to Edinburgh and began to make her living by writing. Over time she became very successful. She wrote five novels, many short stories, two volumes of supernatural tales, two plays and some short fiction for children. The three-volume editions of her novels sold very well and two of her novels were adapted into stage plays: *Susan Hopley: The Adventures of a Maidservant* by George Dibden Pitt (of *Sweeney Todd* fame), and *The Story of Lilly Dawson* by Edward Stirling, noted for his many adaptations of Dickens's work (some pirated and some, like his adaptation of 'A Christmas Carol', official). Although Crowe missed out on most of the royalties, the plays were generally well attended, reviewed and received.

Throughout her life Crowe had deeply held Spiritualist beliefs and she described herself as a disciple of the phrenologist George Combe. In 1848, a year after the publication of *Lilly Dawson*, her groundbreaking book *The Night Side of Nature, or, Ghosts and Ghost Seers* was published. Dickens, in a review in the *The Examiner*, calls it 'one of the most extraordinary collections' of ghost stories ever published, declaring that Crowe 'can never be read without pleasure and profit, and can never write otherwise than sensibly and well'.[1] *The Night Side of Nature* was published in January 1848 before the advent of Spiritualism which is agreed to have occurred with the Fox sisters hearing table rapping and communing with spirits in America in March. Four years later Spiritualism was brought over to England by the medium Mrs Hayden in October 1852.[2] *The Night Side of Nature* was certainly timely and it brought Crowe fame, appearing in sixpenny

---

1 *The Examiner*, Feb. 26 1848. Dickens, however, did not believe in Spiritualism and he and Crowe were to fall out about it in the 1850s.

2 Alex Owen, *The Darkened Room: Women, Power and Spiritualism in Late-Victorian England*, (Chicago: University of Chicago Press, 1989/2004), p. 19.

and three-penny editions and selling at least 65,000 copies in Britain.[3] There were French and German translations and George Routledge described it as 'a most profitable book'.[4] However, as well as acclaim, it also brought some criticism and ridicule, but Crowe was able to ride the storm.

Crowe wrote prolifically and successfully, publishing in magazines including *Chambers's Edinburgh Journal*, *Household Words* and *The Ladies Cabinet of Fashion*. Crowe described her own work as 'new school',[5] and experimented with form as well as content. Her final novel *Linny Lockwood* (1854) was published in two volumes because she said it is a book 'of a kind that people generally read but once'.[6] Crowe claimed that she 'never wrote [...] but with the view of profit and have a laudible [sic] indifference to literary fame'.[7] This is perhaps disingenuous as she courted the society of the literary elite and was mindful of her reputation.

In 1854, in a story that is possibly apocryphal (or at least exaggerated), Crowe was supposedly found wandering the streets of Edinburgh naked, carrying a handkerchief and a card case, believing herself invisible.[8] The story was widely reported in the *Zoist*, in letters written by Dickens, and Edward Bulwer-Lytton, and even repeated in a letter to Robert Browning. Dickens, who was often quite snide about Crowe, although they had been friends for a few years, wrote in a letter on 7 March 1854 to the Rev. James White:

> Mrs. [Crowe] has gone stark mad—and stark naked—on the spirit-rapping imposition. She was found t'other day in the street, clothed only in her chastity, a pocket-handkerchief and a visiting card. She had been informed, it appeared, by the spirits, that if she went out in that trim she would be invisible. She is now in a madhouse, and, I fear, hopelessly insane.[9]

Crowe strongly repudiated the claim, but that same month she tells James T. Fields that she has been seized with a fever and delirium in which she felt she was haunted by the Spirits. However, she writes, she is beginning to recover and looking forward to being 'out of the Doctor's hands' but that she is 'still weak and writing fatigues me'.[10] Lucy Sussex claims that 'her interest in the paranormal ul-

---

3 See Geoffrey Larken, *The Ghost Fancier*, unpublished text, Catherine Crowe Archive, University of Kent, Canterbury, p. 365.

4 Ibid, p. 366.

5 Ibid, p. 100.

6 Ibid, p. 472.

7 Ibid, p. 107.

8 See Appendix A for some of the reports and correspondence about Crowe's breakdown.

9 *The Letters of Charles Dickens*, Volume 7, Graham Storey, Kathleen Tillotson and Angus Easson, (eds), (Oxford: Clarendon Press, 1993), pp. 285–286.

10 Letter from Catherine Crowe to James T. Fields, 17th March 1854. Reproduced by

timately led to a mental crisis, from which she (and her literary reputation) never recovered.'[11] It appears however that Crowe did get better and in December 1854 William Thackeray writes to Dr. John Brown reporting that '[a]t Spa I saw that cheery, good-natured Mrs Crowe'.[12] Thus although many critics see her probable breakdown as the end of her career and almost as the end of her life, this is not the case. Crowe continued to travel and write, publishing the fascinating volume *Ghosts and Family Legends: A Volume for Christmas* in 1859 as well as the somewhat peculiar *Spiritualism and the Age We Live In*. Over the next decade she published numerous short stories and, when nearing the end of her life, she turned to nature itself and her writing career ends with three treatises on seaweed. Crowe died in Folkestone in 1872.

Crowe is a controversial figure, and her breakdown still affects her literary reputation and, I would argue, the amount and type of critical attention she receives. This is unfortunate as her work has great merit and is extremely entertaining. Crowe was a visible presence in the literary circles of the mid 1800s and both she and her work were known to the most famous of authors, including Charlotte Brontë and George Eliot. There is no doubt that Crowe's writing is of both interest and value and this scholarly edition of *The Story of Lilly Dawson* begins what I hope will become a comprehensive re-evaluation of her work.

Geoffrey Larken, Catherine Crowe Archive, University of Kent, Canterbury.
11 Lucy Sussex, 'The Detective Maidservant: Catherine Crowe's Susan Hopley', in *Silent Voices: Forgotten Novels by Victorian Women Writers,* Brenda Ayres, (ed), (Westport, CT: Praeger Publishers, 2003, p. 60.
12 Letter from Thackeray to Dr. John Brown, 31st December 1854. Reproduced by Geoffrey Larken, Catherine Crowe Archive, University of Kent, Canterbury.

CHRONOLOGY OF CROWE'S LIFE AND WORK

1790   Catherine Ann Stevens born in Kent on 20th September.

1822   Marries Major John Crowe.

1823   First and only child John William born in Corfu.

1828   While living in Clifton, Crowe petitions Sydney Smith for help in leaving her husband.

1833   Leaves her husband. Moves to Edinburgh (the year for the move is somewhat obscure but it is around this time).

1838   Play 'Aristodemus' published by William Tait.

1841   *Susan Hopley: The Adventures of a Maidservant* published anonymously in January by Saunders and Otley. Dramatised as *Susan Hopley! Or the Trials and Vicissitudes of a Servant Girl,* by George Dibden Pitt, The Old Vic Theatre, Lambeth, May. Meets and becomes friendly with Charles Dickens.

1842   *Susan Hopley* re-published by Tait in weekly numbers, monthly parts, and a three-shilling volume.

1843   *Men and Women: or Manorial Rights*, published by Saunders and Otley in December.

1845   Translates Kerner's 'Seeress of Prevorst', published by Moore.

1846   'A Story of a Weir Wolf' appears in *Hogg's Weekly Instructor,* 16th May.

1847   *The Story of Lilly Dawson or Smugglers at the Inn*, published by Henry Colborn. Adapted for the stage by Edward Stirling, 'Lilly Dawson or A Poor Girl's Story: A Domestic Drama in Three Acts', City of London Theatre, March.

1848   *The Night Side of Nature* published by T. C. Newby in two volumes. Story for children, *Pippie's Warning; or, Mind Your Temper,* Arthur Hall and Co.

1850   *The Story of Lilly Dawson,* Re-issued by George Routledge & Co. *Light and Darkness,* a three-volume collection of short stories, Henry Colborn. Short story, 'Loaded Dice', *Household Words,* Volume I, no 4. Short story, 'The Young Advocate', *Household Words,* Volume I, no 13. Meets Charlotte Brontë.

1851   Short Story 'The Deserted House', in *Chambers's Edinburgh Journal,* 10th May.

1852   *The Adventures of a Beauty,* published by Henry Colburn, March. Short story, 'Esther Hammond's Wedding Day', *Household Words,* Volume IV, no 96. *The Night Side of Nature* is published by George Routledge as part of the Railway Library. Meets Marian Evans (George Eliot). Moves to London.

1853   Article 'Amicable Intervention in the Question of Slavery' published in *Ladies' Cabinet of Fashion. The Cruel Kindness, A Tragedy,* George Routledge & Co. *Uncle Tom's Cabin: Arranged for Children,* George Routledge & Co.

1854   *Linny Lockwood,* January, published in two volumes by George Routledge & Co. 26th February. Crowe suffers a psychotic breakdown and is hospitalised for a short time. She is discharged and recovers.

1857   Short Story, 'The Lost Diamonds', *The National Magazine.*

1859   *Spiritualism and the Age We Live In,* T. C. Newby. *Ghosts and Family Legends: A Volume for Christmas,* T. C. Newby.

1861   *The Story of Arthur Hunter and his First Shilling. With Other Tales.*

1862   *The Adventures of a Monkey.*

1869   Moves to Folkestone.

1872   Dies 14th June.

A NOTE ON THE TEXT

This text is based on the original three-volume edition of *The Story of Lilly Dawson or Smugglers at the Inn* published by Henry Colburn (London) in 1847. A number of obvious errors have been silently corrected.

ACKNOWLEDGEMENTS

Thanks to Catherine Pope for her vision, help and support. My grateful thanks to Frosk for support and proofreading. Thanks to the members of the VICTORIA list for helpful comments and the generous sharing of knowledge. Thanks to the Templeman Library, University of Kent, for access to the Catherine Crowe archive and Jane Gallagher, Senior Special Collections Assistant for her cheerful help. And thanks always to Bill Hughes for unfailing friendship and support. I would like to dedicate this edition to Margaret Heholt, Joseph and Lilith Rhodes.

The publisher would like to thank Paul Frecker of The Library of Nineteenth-Century Photography for the cover image.

ABOUT THE EDITOR

Ruth Heholt is senior lecturer in English at Falmouth University. She specialises in the supernatural and the Gothic. She is editor of the e-journal *Revenant: Critical and Creative Studies of the Supernatural* and has published articles and chapters on various aspects of the supernatural. She is editor of a special edition of *Victoriographies* entitled 'Haunted Men' (2014). She is currently working on an edited collection, *Regional Gothic* with William Hughes and a special issue of *Contemporary Women Writers* with Fiona Peters and Gina Wisker on Ruth Rendell.

The Story of Lilly Dawson

VOLUME I

CHAPTER I

WHICH CONTAINS SOME ACCOUNT OF THE INN CALLED THE BLACK HUNTSMAN, AND ITS OCCUPANTS

Not far from the coast, in a remote and somewhat unfrequented part of one of the south-eastern counties of England, dwelt, at the commencement of the present century, a family of the name of Littenhaus. They were said to be of foreign origin; and this persuasion, which took its rise from their un-English patronymic, was confirmed by the circumstance that their house was much frequented by visitors from the other side of the channel.

Of themselves they gave no account. They had arrived there as perfect strangers from some distant part of the country, apparently in consequence of an advertisement which had been inserted in the newspapers, intimating that the inn, commonly known by the style and title of "The Black Huntsman," was for sale.

Shortly after the appearance of this notice, two young men had come to view the place; and, presently after their departure, the agent of Sir Lawrence Longford, to whom the property belonged, received a letter, purporting that Jacob Littenhaus was willing to become the purchaser. The bargain was struck and the money paid;—the sum indeed was not by any means large, for it was a house of little business; and in that respect was not considered likely to improve. In fact, none of its previous occupants had succeeded in making a living out of it; and every one wondered that a new tenant should be willing to undertake the hopeless struggle.

"But he does not know whose shoes he is stepping into," said the jolly host of the Red Lion at the neighbouring village of Combe Martin to the agent, Mr. Cobb; "they couldn't keep none of his predecessors above water. I wonder Sir Lawrence doesn't turn the place into some'ut else; it's no sitiation for an inn."

"I don't know what else it's fit for," replied the agent; "there's nothing to be made of the land, you know. It will grow nothing but heath and furze, and the house is a capital house; large and roomy—just fit for an inn."

"Why, it was built for one, I suppose," replied Lacy. "But that was in old times, when it had a trade."

"Yes," replied Mr. Cobb, "the turning away of the road, and the new pier and harbour at F., have settled its business. There'll never be anything done there again, I'm afraid. However, Sir Lawrence has got it off his hands now; and they that have taken it must make the best of it."

And this, when the Littenhaus family arrived, they seemed well inclined to do. They made no complaints of want of trade, though it was certainly but little they had; and, though the people in the village were always foretelling that they would never be able to keep the house open, yet, somehow or other, they did contrive to do that which their predecessors had failed to effect. One thing was, as our host of the Red Lion was wont to say, they had no rent to pay, as all the previous occupants had. The house was their own, so that all they had to earn was their daily bread. If they could get that, they might make a shift to live; and it appeared that they did get it.

The family, on their arrival, consisted of the father, an elderly and very infirm man; two sons; two daughters; and a little girl called Lilly Dawson, said to be the child of a younger sister of old Littenhaus; but, her parents being dead, she had become a dependant on the bounty of her uncle and cousins for her subsistence.

Of the two sons, the elder, whose name was Ambrose, was a middle-sized, strongly-built youth, with dark hair and eyes, and tolerable features; whilst the younger, called Luke, was short and thick-set, with square shoulders, light eyes and hair, and a broad, pale face.

With respect to the daughters, they were rather handsome young women, but their beauty was not of a very pleasing character: neither were their manners nor those of the brothers attractive; and their mode of life at the Black Huntsman was certainly not calculated to improve them, for it was very solitary. They were too far from the village for any constant communion with its inhabitants, even had they desired to maintain it, which apparently they did not. The sons, who were the only members of the family frequently seen, had a very anti-social air; and the daughters were rarely visible, except on Sundays, when they invariably appeared at church in considerable splendour. Nay, so unfailing were they in their devotions, that, though it rained "cats and dogs," as the worthy Mrs. Lacy of the Red Lion said, you were still sure to see Anna and Charlotte Littenhaus in their pew. On these occasions, they were wont to arrive in a covered vehicle something like the machine used for transporting pianofortes through the streets. They called it the shander-a-dan; but, as it was painted black, and was drawn by a stout horse of the same hue, it was known in the neighbourhood by the name of the *Littenhaus Hearse*.

The old man, Jacob Littenhaus, the father, had a much more pleasing counte-nance, and a more open and accessible air than the rest of the family; but he was seldom seen, his infirmities keeping him a prisoner to the house or its immediate vicinity; and if any one happened to suggest that he might come to church in the shander-a-dan, they were answered that, the vehicle not being on springs, he could not bear the motion of it.

Thus, beyond the fact of his existence, nobody knew much of old Jacob Littenhaus, nor were they much better acquainted with young Lilly Dawson. She was said to be an extremely stupid little girl; and those who chanced to see her declared that her countenance confirmed the report. Still, her features were regular; and, had they been illuminated by cheerfulness and intelligence, she might have been a pretty child; as it was, with her stolid look and squalid attire, she was a very unattractive object. Young as she was, she was made to do a great portion of the house-work, her cousins Anna and Charlotte being her only assistants, with the exception of the odd jobs done by Short Bill, the lad who drove the shander-a-dan, took care of the black horse, carried coals, did the errands, and whatever else was required of him.

He was called Short Bill from his peculiarly-stunted growth, which appeared to have suddenly stopped when he was about twelve years old, bequeathing him the stature of a child, with the form and features of a man. He was not exactly like a dwarf either, but looked more like an old boy; for, though he was in fact young, he had a shrivelled face—such a one as is sometimes seen belonging to a postboy on a well-travelled road—or, at least, used to be seen, when postboys lived and flourished; the cheeks rosy, but the skin pursing up into wrinkles, like a prematurely withered apple. Whether he had ever had a father and mother seems uncertain; there appeared no reason to suppose he had; nor was he ever known to lay claim to any patronymic, style, or title, than that of Short Bill; and, had he been able to write, such would undoubtedly have been his signature.

At the time the Littenhaus family arrived, Short Bill had been acting as supernumerary ostler[1] at the Red Lion, where Ambrose chanced to see him, and, for some merit or other, not apparent to the world in general, was so far taken with his appearance, that he immediately secured his services for the Black Huntsman, where the mode of life, which would have been insufferable to most people, seemed to suit him well enough. Being the only domestic on the premises, he had no companion: and, as he was not permitted to absent himself, except when sent on an errand, he had no opportunity of seeking any; but his natural taciturnity very much mitigated the hardship of this enforced solitude and silence. He was on very friendly terms with the black horse; and, as his duties were regular, and not extremely arduous, he spent a good deal of his time asleep in the stable; a mode of disposing of it, to which his employers made no objection, provided he was always to be found when they needed his services—and this he took care to be;

---

1 Someone employed to look after the horses belonging to guests at an inn.

Short Bill being one of those persons who are never out of the way. On the whole, he seemed very contented; and, since happiness in this life is only comparative, if he opened his eyes and looked about him, he might certainly have found great reason for self-gratulation; for he was assuredly, by many degrees, the happiest member of the family to which he was attached.

Old Jacob, the father, was not only infirm, but he was evidently a broken-down, brokenhearted man; alone, in the midst of his family; far away from his friends, if he ever had any; and gradually sinking into the grave. His sons had none of the hilarity of youth. They frequently, one or other of them, went from home, and they attended the neighbouring fairs and markets; but they sought few amusements, joined in no sports, formed no intimacies, and never invited any body to visit them. Then the life led by the daughters was inexpressibly dull; the weekly opportunity of exhibiting their fine clothes to the villagers which the recurring Sundays afforded them, appearing to be their only pleasure; except that they, now and then, made a journey in the shander-a-dan to Hotham, a town about seven miles distant, where dwelt an expert dressmaker of the name of Grosset; the mantuamaker[2] of the village not being dexterous enough for their purpose.

As for Lilly Dawson, her situation was, if possible, still less enviable. Though not more than eight years old when she was brought to the Black Huntsman, she was every body's servant, and maid-of-all-work in the most emphatic sense of the term. Certainly, Anna and Charlotte Littenhaus did condescend to some of the least onerous duties, such as dusting, making beds, and so forth; but all the dirty work fell to the share of Lilly, who, great part of her time, was little better than a Cinderella. Not that there was actually much to do; for the arrival of a guest at the Black Huntsman was by no means an event of daily occurrence; but, being unequal to her task, it was never done; and poor Lilly was always toiling after it in vain. Then she had the entire charge of waiting on the old man; but this was the most agreeable part of her duties, for he was kind to her, and she had attached herself to him, the more, perhaps, that she had nothing else to attach herself to. And even this was an instinctive, unreasoning kind of attachment, like that of a dog for its master; for her mind was subdued to the quality of her condition, and her spirit broken by hardship; so that she went through her tasks like an automaton, exhibiting only so much intelligence in adapting her means to her ends, as we often see exercised by the lower animals.

Still, there was one morning in the week in which a gleam of satisfaction might be discerned on Lilly's countenance, and that was Sunday, especially if the day were fine; for then Ambrose and Luke generally went away in their boat, and did not return till night; whilst, the young ladies being at church, she was left

2 Dressmaker.

alone with Uncle Littenhaus. This was the only opportunity she had, too, of cultivating her single accomplishment—namely, reading. On other days, when her housework was—we will not say done, for that it never was—but when it was at a standstill—she had her cousin's stockings to darn, or the house-linen to mend, till she lay down out-wearied, and already half asleep, upon her bed. But on Sundays, from ten o'clock, when the shander-a-dan drove from the door, till six in the evening, when the young women returned from church, her time was her own and her uncle's. A good part of this peaceful period she generally passed in sleep, making up for her short hours on the other six nights of the week; but Jacob Littenhaus, whose ill health warned him that he was daily drawing nearer to his end, had begun to have some twinges of affright at the prospect before him. He had always been a thoughtless, weak man, and quite ignorant of religion—he had never been taught any, never had any—and he had done many things that were very wrong in his time, more from want of reflection and want of knowledge than actual depravity; but some circumstances had happened of late, that had startled his mind awake; and when he saw himself but little past the prime of life, descending to the grave, he recollected that there was a book called the Bible, that he had heard much talk about; and he felt some curiosity to know what it was, and whether it would afford him any consolation. So he desired Short Bill, when he went to the village, to buy him one, but by no means to let his sons or daughters see it. Bill executed the commission, but so injudiciously, that the book was a dead letter to Jacob from the smallness of the print; and the only time he could derive any benefit from his acquisition, was when he could get Lilly to read to him.

Poor Lilly—who was quite as unenlightened as her uncle, read very badly, and was obliged to spell all the hard words—began at the head of the title-page, passing thence to "the Most High and Mighty Prince James, by the grace of God,"[3] and so on, to the first chapter of Genesis, till, little by little, they crept on through the Pentateuch.[4] But the Hebrew names were a terrible stumbling block in the way of the neophytes;[5] and thus, as may be easily conceived, Jacob found less comfort than he had expected from this far-famed volume; whilst the only idea Lilly had on the subject was, that if the heroes and heroines of the tale had had less crabbed appellations, she might have felt more interest in their fortunes. As the matter stood, however, the only benefit derived from these prelections[6] was, that they preserved her from the misfortune of forgetting the little reading she knew.

---

3 Prince James refers to King James whose version of the bible, translated between 1604 and 1611, became known as the 'authorized version' and the standard for English speaking Protestants.

4 The first five books of the Bible.

5 Those new to learning a subject.

6 Public lectures.

As time advanced, Lilly's duties became more arduous, for Jacob required more and more of her assistance; and, whatever else she had to do, she never neglected him; although she frequently got into trouble on account of the arrears of her other work, consequent on his increasing necessities. It was not age that rendered him so feeble; he was, in fact, not more than fifty-five; but his infirmities had been occasioned by personal injuries received before the Littenhaus family was known in the part of the country they now inhabited.

It was this premature decline—for he had previously been a hale, hearty man—that had somewhat improved Jacob's character and awakened his reflections. Had he retained his health till age overtook him, he would probably never have thought of such matters as now occasionally occupied his mind. It is sickness and sorrow that bring repentance—not old age. As it was, he yearned for that comfort which nobody was at hand to give him, and which he knew not where to seek; and, as he grew daily more and more sorrowful, he clung daily more and more to Lilly, who was his only friend; for there was no cordiality betwixt him and his children; and it was too evident that they cared nothing about him. When they spoke of him at all, it was as a burthen; and, instead of taking his place as the head of the house, he was treated as an unwelcome dependant. It would be too much to say, that this gave Lilly pain—life was to her a wholly mechanical thing; and her mind and feelings were too obtuse and unawakened to be conscious of compassion. But she was good-natured; and therefore, instinctively, the more he needed her, the more she was drawn towards him.

In this manner, the family had resided about eighteen months at the Black Huntsman, doing so little business, that it seemed difficult to believe they made a living out of it; when, one night, a man arrived, wearing a sailor's dress, who was received as a welcome guest and old acquaintance. They called him Hans Peffer; and, although he spoke English pretty fluently, it was with a foreign accent. He was moreover a rough, coarse-mannered, and sinister-looking person; and, had there been any spectator of his reception capable of observation, he might well have wondered how such an unattractive visitor should have aroused so much animation and excitement in his hosts. However, they seemed to have many old friends and recollections in common; and the inquiries on the part of the Littenhaus family were numerous. Even Jacob appeared to forget his aches and pains, whilst he listened to tidings of his former companions.

"But why didn't you come before?" asked Ambrose.

"Because I never got your letter till about three months since."

"What, did you never go to the old shop after we left?" inquired Luke.

"No," answered Hans; "we didn't know exactly what had happened, and thought it best to keep off."

"Why, what did you hear?" asked Charlotte.

"That you'd sheered off, because the place was too hot to hold you; and it was thought, if you'd stayed a week longer, worse would have come of it—so I thought we'd best give them a wide berth and keep away."

"But how came you to find the letter at last then?"

"I didn't find it; Locksley found it and brought it to me. But how are you getting on? Have you been doing any business here?"

"Very little," answered Ambrose. "Nobody has found us out but Locksley, and he's devilish cautious, you know."

"So much the better," said Jacob, shaking his head.

"And is there nothing doing in this neighbourhood?" asked Hans.

"Nothing," replied the other. "They're the most primitive people you ever saw. If you talked to them about running a cask, they wouldn't know what you meant."

"So much the better for them," again murmured Jacob, in an undertone, whilst his daughters cast a reproving glance at him.

"So much the better for *us*," echoed Hans. "Why, Jacob, what's come along o' you?"

"Oh! never mind him!" said Charlotte; "but tell us what you've got? Have you any silks?"

"No," answered Hans; "how could I venture till I'd seen the coast? I couldn't tell where to stow them away, and they might have got damaged."

"You might have brought them up here," suggested Anna.

"How could I tell that? Besides, it's a devilish long way from the shore, let me tell you!"

"Only three quarters of a mile," answered Charlotte.

"But that's a devilish long way! You may fall foul of a dozen folks in three quarters of a mile."

"They wouldn't suspect anything if you did," said Anna. "There has never been any business done here; and they know nothing about it."

"But they might learn," objected Hans.

"It *is* a difficulty," said Ambrose. "The beach is perfectly flat, and there's no great surf—capital for running in a boat—but there isn't a rock within two miles, nor even a hole big enough to stow a cask away."

"Who does that mill belong to?" asked Hans.

"Ah!" said Luke, "that's the place, if we could get it—close to the beach; and the path up to it in a gully, where nobody ever passes."

"But who does it belong to?" repeated Hans.

"A man called Ryland," returned Ambrose.

"Is it his own?" inquired Hans.

"Yes," answered Charlotte; "he spent all his money in building it, because there was no mill near at hand; and he thought he was sure to do well in it—and so he has."

"There's no buying him out then?" said Hans.

"Buy him out!—no," replied Ambrose; "where's the money to come from? Besides, he has got a boy that he is bringing up to the same trade."

"It's a pity!" said Hans. "I never saw a better place, nor more convenient, in *my* life."

"I wish we had it!" said Anna; "for, besides that, old Ryland's a regular nuisance, so near."

"What, does he molest you?" asked Hans.

"No, but he might," replied Anna; "and then that sprig of a boy of his is always prowling about the moor of an evening."

Shortly after this visit of Hans, who spent a couple of days with his friends, and then walked away as he came, two other men of the same description presented themselves, and from that time the society at the Black Huntsman was not quite in so stagnant a state as it had been. Most frequently, however, these visitors arrived in the middle of the night; and they were often away again before morning—sometimes the young men, Ambrose and Luke, with them. The effect of this stir and commotion seemed decidedly beneficial as regarded the younger members of the family; they had been vegetating before without anything to excite them—now they were alive again. They had plenty to talk of to each other; and the arrival of the strangers was always an animating event. In short, they were in their element again.

With respect to Lilly, this change of circumstances made very little difference; her routine of work was the same; and, when she had finished what she had to do, or was unable from fatigue or want of light to do more, she sat down on a little stool that was appropriated to her, took out her stocking and darned away at it, till one or other of the young women bade her go to bed. Whilst she was present, the conversation went on exactly as if she were absent—secrets of all sorts were discussed before her with perfect unreserve—Lilly was a nonentity—too dull to listen, too stupid to understand. And they were quite right;—Lilly never thought about what they were saying, or had said—all she cared for was the moment when she should be allowed to lay her head on her pillow; and, as soon as she did so, she was fast asleep. When she awoke the next morning, she thought only of what she had got to do, and indulged in no abstract retrospections. Frequently, by the state in which she found things, she knew that people must have been there in the night; but this awakened no curiosity. It might be truly said of Lilly, that sufficient for the day was the evil thereof—she never looked forward nor backward; all she had to do was to rub on.

Meanwhile, Jacob grew worse and worse; and, whilst he was wholly confined to his room, his sons and daughters frequently alluded to the approaching dissolution of their parent in Lilly's presence; but neither did this make any impression on her, for she had no precise conception of what death was; nor did she foresee that the departure of the old man would inspire her with any regret.

CHAPTER II

THE DEATH OF JACOB, AND THE INTRODUCTION OF THE RYLAND FAMILY TO THE READER

"Lilly!" said Jacob, to the little girl, one evening, "Lilly, I don't think I shall live through the night. Are Ambrose and Luke at home?"

"No," replied Lilly; "haven't seen 'em to-day."

"I heard some people here in the night—I suppose they went away with them; did they?"

"I don't know," answered Lilly.

"I should like to speak to my daughters," said Jacob, after a pause; "go and tell them so, Lilly" and Lilly quitted the room, whilst Jacob, sighing heavily, with considerable effort turned his face towards the door.

After a lapse of some minutes, the two sisters entered the room.

"Do you want us?" inquired Charlotte.

"Yes," answered Jacob—"I don't think, Charlotte, I shall live through the night."

"Pooh!" returned his daughter; "that's all fancy—you're no worse than you generally are."

"God knows, I've no need to be worse," answered Jacob; "but I'm sure I can't live long."

"So you've said these three months," returned Charlotte.

"You make yourself worse by giving way to these fancies," said Anna.

"Fancies!" echoed Jacob—"however, never mind"—and here he paused again—"but there's one thing I wish to say, before I go."

"Well, what is it?" asked Charlotte.

"I should like to have spoken to Ambrose and Luke," continued Jacob; "but Lilly says they're out."

"They're away with Hans," answered Anna.

At the name of Hans, the dying man's face contracted—but he said nothing—he knew it was useless.

"It's about Lilly that I wanted to speak to you," said Jacob.

"What about her?" asked Charlotte.

"You treat that child too harshly," continued he.

"Harshly!" echoed both the sisters. "We don't treat her harshly. Besides, how else could anybody treat such a stupid lump?"

"Remember, she wasn't born to it," urged Jacob.

"Oh, pooh!" returned Charlotte; "what does that signify now?"

"Well," said Jacob, "I'm going as fast as I can go—I only tell you—when you're where I am, you'll see things other than you do now. I was just the same myself once, and see what it has brought me to—and yet, I don't think I was, either."

"You don't! That's a good un," exclaimed Charlotte.

"I had *some* feeling even when I was at the worst," continued the old man, speaking feebly; "and, when my father was shot in the knee by the Lieutenant at St. Mary's, I carried him on my shoulders through the surf, and got him into the boat, and he died aboard his own cutter after all, instead of being swung up to the yard-arm, or rotting in a jail for the rest of his days—that *is* some comfort, at any rate."

"I'm sure talking in this way can't do you any good," said Charlotte; "we'd better go, and send Lilly up to you."

"Ah, Lilly!" said Jacob; "you *should* have some feeling for that child—remember, as I said before, she wasn't born to it."

"What's the use of bothering about Lilly at this time of day?" said Anna; "she must take things as other people do."

"Besides, Lilly's very well satisfied," rejoined Charlotte. "She knows no better. But, come, Anna, there's only Lilly below; we'd better go down."

"You'll be better to-morrow, if you don't think so much about it," said Anna, as she left the room.

"I shall be dead to-morrow," said Jacob, in a feeble voice, whilst his eyes filled with unaccustomed tears, and the white lip quivered.

"No such thing! we'll send you up a cup of tea," said Anna, following her sister—and the door closed upon "these daughters."[7]

In about half an hour, Lilly entered the room with the tea; and, with her assistance, Jacob sipped a little of it. "Lilly," he said, "I'm sure I shan't live through the night; and it's hard to be left to die alone—do you think you could keep awake, and sit up with me?"

"I'll try," answered Lilly.

---

7 Laban speaking to Jacob reminding him that he still possessed 'these daughters' even though both are married to Jacob (Genesis 31:43).

"Do," said Jacob; "come when they go to bed; and you can sit here in the arm-chair, beside me; and then, if you fall asleep, I can wake you."

In due time, the sisters retired to their chamber. We must do them the justice to say that they did not believe their father's death so near—if they had, they might possibly have paid him another visit; but he had been long ill, and they did not see sufficient alteration in him to justify his apprehensions; so they went to bed, and Lilly, without mentioning Jacob's request to them, prepared for her vigil—or rather for her nap in the arm-chair—for, though she did her utmost to keep herself awake, she had not taken up her position half an hour, before she was as sound asleep as ever she was in her life.

There lay the dying man, and there sat the sleeping child—and all the house was silent, except the dull ticking of the clock on the landing-place, at the top of the stairs, and the occasional moans of the departing spirit.

The minutes, so fleet and so slow, had thus glided on, till the hour-hand of the clock pointed at two; and then Lilly dreamed that she had overslept herself, and that Charlotte and Anna were dragging her out of bed by the arm, and yet she did not wake. To wake Lilly, the tired child, who never had her full allowance of sleep, was, at all times, a difficult task; and to wake her thus prematurely, was still more difficult.

"Lilly! wake! wake!" cried Jacob, grasping her arm. "What o'clock is it?" asked he eagerly, when, with great difficulty, the child had opened her eyes; "what o'clock is it? Isn't it yet the middle of the night?"

"I don't know," answered Lilly, quite bewildered and not recollecting where she was.

"See!" he said; "see! for God's sake! Go, look at the clock!"

"It's just two," said Lilly, as soon as she had ascertained the fact; to do which she had only to open the door of the room, as the clock was close at hand.

"I thought so!" exclaimed Jacob, in a voice of terror; "and the Lord have mercy on my soul!"

"Will you have some barley-water?" asked Lilly, who did not comprehend what he meant.

"See!" said Jacob, "they're coming to fetch me with fiery swords, and sulphur and brimstone—don't you see how they blaze?" whilst his eyes stared wildly at the window; and Lilly, now being thoroughly awake, became conscious that the room was actually lighted by a preternatural light—for it was mid winter, and yet, though they had only a feeble rushlight,[8] every object was illuminated by a lurid glare; and Lilly had ascertained the hour by this unaccustomed light alone.

"Oh, Lilly!" he said, "I've led a wicked life, and now I shall burn for it!" and

---

8 A type of candle used by the poor, made of rushes and fat.

the rickety bedstead shook with the convulsive terrors of the expiring sinner. "I'm going!" he gasped out—"I'm going! I feel I'm going!"

"Shall I call my cousins?" asked Lilly, from her natural or acquired obtuseness less alarmed than might be supposed.

"Call who?" said Jacob, whose speech grew every moment more difficult.

"My cousins," answered Lilly; "shan't I call them, uncle?"

"I'm not your uncle—they're not your cousins!" gasped Jacob. "Oh, Lilly, pray for me—it was a great sin, and now I shall burn in Hell for it, I'm afraid—I wish it had never happened—better for you if you had gone to the bottom like the rest. Do you hear what I say, Lilly?"

"Yes, uncle," replied Lilly, who heard, but obscurely understood.

"I'm not your uncle, child, I tell you—you're a stranger to me and mine—but, oh, Lord, look there! They're coming, they're coming!" And when Lilly cast her eyes to the window, certainly the sight was enough to alarm any one with less reason for fear than Jacob; the glare of light was so great, that she could distinguish every object in the cabbage-garden adjoining the house as clearly as if the sun were shining at noon-day. "Pray for me, Lilly, pray for me! you're innocent, and the Lord may hear you!" But Lilly only stood bewildered and frightened—for the extraordinary light and the expiring man's terrors had frightened her by this time—she knew nothing about praying. What she would have done, had she dared, would have been to call Charlotte and Anna; but she thought they would be angry with her for disturbing them.

Just at this crisis, a loud knocking at the door below elicited another cry of terror from the dying man, and startled Lilly out of her perplexity. When any visitor arrived after the door was closed for the evening, it was her business to open it, provided she were still up; and, forgetting that her being so now was an irregularity, she proceeded mechanically to do her accustomed duty.

"Is Mr. Littenhaus at home? Are the young men here?" inquired a youth of about thirteen, with a voice and features of great anxiety.

"My uncle is up stairs in bed," answered Lilly; "and Ambrose and Luke are out."

"Is there nobody here can help us?" said the boy; "the mill's on fire—where's your lad?"

"Short Bill's in bed," said Lilly.

"Where?" said the boy; "call him, will you? He might be of some use."

"I don't know whether I may," said Lilly; "he sleeps in the loft."

"I'll call him myself, then," said the boy; and, suiting the action to the word, he immediately proceeded to wake Short Bill—not a very easy matter either—and, having secured his assistance, and the use of the stable buckets, they set off together in the direction of the mill; whilst Lilly, having so far watched the progress of the affair, and seen them depart, ascended again to the sick man's room.

"It's the mill that's on fire, uncle," said she; "and that's what makes the light;" but Jacob did not answer. He lay on his back, with his features distorted, his lips apart, and the dim eye open. Lilly stood for a moment looking at him, and then, in a doubtful voice, again murmured "uncle!" but still there was no answer—and then a strange feeling began to creep over Lilly—she saw that that of which she had heard such frequent predictions had at length happened—Jacob Littenhaus was dead. Still she stood, as if rooted to the spot, with her eyes fixed upon his face—she could neither turn them away, nor move from the bedside. And yet it was not altogether fear that kept her there; it was rather wonder and some gleams of strange thoughts awakening in her dull brain—confused and indistinct, and yet absorbing. Gradually, however, the features of the dead man became less visible; a shadow fell over them, till little by little they faded from her view, and she found herself in darkness—the fire at the mill had burnt itself out, and the room was no longer illuminated. Then Lilly crept away to her own room, where she threw off her clothes and was presently fast asleep.

At seven o'clock in the morning, her dream of the night was realized. As was to be expected, she overslept herself, and she was awakened by the angry voice of Charlotte, calling her "A lazy, good-for-nothing thing." Heavy and stupid with want of rest, she jumped out of bed, got into her clothes the best way she could, and ran down stairs to overtake her morning's work. When she passed the door of Jacob's room, she suddenly remembered the occurrences of the night, but she did not dare stop to look in upon him, though she wished to do it; the angry voices of her cousins below, complaining that the fire was not lighted in the kitchen, warned her to make haste.

"You little good-for-nothing lazy wretch!" said Anna, "here's nearly eight o'clock" (in reality it was just half-past seven), "and not a spark of fire in the grate; instead of the kettle being on and the water boiled for breakfast."

Lilly made no answer—she never did—she only laid the wood in the grate, and gathered up the ashes and small coals to put over it; and then, having set it alight, puffed away with the bellows with all her might and main, till having got up a flame and set on the kettle, she could proceed with her other work. In the mean time, the sisters performed such little offices as they reserved for themselves; and when the table was prepared, and the water boiled, they sat down to breakfast.

"Lilly!" said Anna presently, "here, take up your uncle's tea;" for to do this was Lilly's business every morning.

Lilly left off what she was doing, and approached the table, blushing up to the eyes; she understood very well that a dead man wanted no tea; but, in the first place, she was afraid to say that Jacob was dead; and, in the next, she did not feel very certain of the fact. She might have been mistaken in the night. So she silently took the tea and bread and butter, and ascended the stairs. When she reached the room, she laid them down on the floor, whilst she opened the door and peeped in. The curtain was closed, and she stepped forward and drew it aside—there he lay, exactly as she last saw him—it was quite clear that he was dead. She felt no fear, but stood still and looked at the wan and wasted features, till there arose a swelling about her heart, and the first tears that Lilly had shed for many a day began to steal down her cheeks. She became conscious of a feeling of forlornness, which, whilst Jacob lived, helpless as he was, she had never experienced. Or, perhaps the concussion that this event had given to her nervous system had so far aroused her from the torpor which had overgrown and stifled her sensations, that she now first became in some degree sensible of her situation. She longed to stay where she was; she would have liked to sit down on the bed and let her tears flow; but she heard Anna's voice loud in the lobby; so, closing the door softly, she took up the breakfast and descended the stairs again.

"Well, what have you brought the breakfast back for?" inquired Anna, who was waiting ready to give her a thump upon the shoulders in order to quicken her movements.

"Uncle's dead," said Lilly.

"Dead!" cried Anna, and calling Charlotte they both proceeded towards his room, whilst Lilly began to wash up the tea-things.

The sisters were still up stairs, when the outer door opened and Short Bill entered, loaded with bags and boxes, as many as he could carry.

"Where's missuses?" said he.

"They're up stairs," answered Lilly; "uncle's dead!"

"Dead! is he?" said Bill, "whew! and the mill's burnt; and there's Muster Ryland and his boy, and all the things they've been able to save, which arn't much, to be sure, a coming here; and they wanted to borrow the shander-a-dan, to send away their missus to her sister's at Hotham, 'cause she's got herself burnt shocking, trying to save her bits of duds, but I told un young masters had got it away some where; and so they're bringing her along here, I believe—you'd better go up and tell 'em."

Scarcely were the sisters informed of this impending incursion, ere the cavalcade arrived—Dame Ryland on the miller's old horse, led by her son Philip, the boy who had fetched Short Bill in the night, with Matthew Ryland, the father, and his man, bearing some other articles rescued from the flames.

Their reception at the Black Huntsman was not very gracious, but, as the house was empty, there was no excuse for denying them admittance. Betwixt grief and pain, poor Mrs. Ryland was suffering so much, that her husband desired her to go immediately to bed; whilst he and his son got some breakfast. The miller was sadly depressed, but Philip, a fine, open-countenanced, spirited lad, did his best to comfort him. He was also very affectionate to his mother, taking up her tea himself, and attending carefully to her necessities.

When the breakfast was over, the father and son ascended to the sick woman's room, where they stayed some time, condoling with each other; after which, leaving her in charge of the boy, the poor miller walked to Trentisy—so the mill was called—once more to view the wreck of his little property.

So passed the first morning of their misfortunes. In the afternoon, he returned and sat down to dinner with the sisters, but, being too heart-sick to eat, quitted the table and went away to his wife. Philip, however, on whom sorrow made less impression, ate heartily enough; chatting away unreservedly on the events of the night. It appeared that the fire had broken out at about half-past one, in a little shed adjoining the mill; but the wind being unluckily in such a direction as to carry it to the main building, the whole premises, dwelling and all, were soon in flames.

"But how did it happen?" inquired Anna.

"We don't know," replied Philip. "Jem, our man, had been in there with a lantern after dark; but he declares that he never opened it, and that it's impossible he could have left any fire behind him. But father saw a man in a sailor's jacket near the mill, just at dusk, with a pipe in his mouth; and he thinks perhaps he set it on fire."

In the evening, about eight o'clock, the wheels of the shander-a-dan were heard approaching; and Charlotte went out to communicate to her brothers the events of the day, before they entered the house. "Father was dead—the mill was burnt down, and the Rylands had all taken refuge at the Black Huntsman!" This last item of the intelligence was the only one that seemed to make much impression on the young men.

"Why did you take them in?" was the first question.

"How could we help it?" asked Charlotte, "when there wasn't a creature in the house but ourselves? We should have had the whole neighbourhood up in arms against us."

"But when do they go?" asked Ambrose; "Hans and Locksley will be here to-morrow night, and they'll be confoundedly in our way."

"Perhaps they may be gone," answered Anna, who here joined the conference; "for there's Ryland inquiring if that is the shander-a-dan come back—he wants to borrow it to-morrow to carry his wife to her sisters."

"Let them have it," said Luke. "Any thing to get them away!"

"I'll go and tell them so," said Anna.

"I say, Luke," said Charlotte, drawing her youngest brother aside, "Ryland's boy says that his father saw a man in a sailor's jacket, smoking his pipe, near the mill last night, at dusk."

"He does?" said Luke.

"The boy told us so at dinner!" answered Charlotte.

"Confounded ass!" exclaimed he.

"Who? Ryland?" inquired Charlotte.

"No. Hans Peffer," returned Luke impatiently.

Charlotte's eye glanced at her brother, but she made no remark. She did not desire to know any more—indeed what need? That single exclamation revealed every thing—in ignorance was security—what she did not know, or only guessed, she could not be made responsible for.

After some further conference, the brothers entered the house; and presently afterwards Ryland came down to have some conversation with them.

"Are you insured?" asked Luke, a question he could have answered himself.

"No," replied Ryland; "no, fool as I was—I thought to save the money; and we were so careful, I thought it impossible an accident *could* happen."

"And how *did* it happen?" inquired Ambrose.

"It's hard to say," answered Ryland. "God forgive me, if I am wrong! but I can't help suspecting a man I saw lurking about just at nightfall, with a pipe in his mouth. I didn't like the looks of him somehow, at the time."

"But what motive could he have for doing you a mischief? But perhaps you think it was the pipe?"

"I don't know," returned Ryland. "There was nothing in the shed so very combustible; and a person must have taken uncommon pains to set it on fire with a pipe—he might have shaken out the ashes of twenty pipes without coming across any thing that would take fire—there was nothing but the walls, in short, for the floor was stone."

"It's very improbable any body should have set fire to your mill," said Luke. "It would need pretty good proof to make me believe that; unless, to be sure, you've been making an enemy of any body."

"I've no enemy that I know of," replied Ryland; "but there's some folks you know as is every body's enemy, because every body's theirs. I can't tell—but I've a notion there's been something going on in these here parts as shouldn't!"

"What do you mean?" inquired Ambrose.

"Two or three times, when I've been returning late from market," answered the miller, "I've seen two fellows acrossing the heath, as I didn't like the looks on; and this here chap with the pipe was one of them."

"Then, you recognised him?" said Ambrose sharply.

"And you'd know him again, I dare say?" said Luke.

"I warrant me!" said Ryland, "if he only comes in my way—and I'll lay hands on him too, as sure as my name's Mat Ryland; and make him give an account of himself!"

"That's a bold resolution of yours," said Ambrose. "Fellows of that sort are apt to be desperate—I'd rather give him a wide berth, if I were you."

"No, no! Mr. Ryland's right," said Luke gravely; "especially if he has any grounds of suspicion against this man."

"I've no further grounds than that I can't account for the fire, except it was done on purpose," returned Ryland; "and I can see nobody to suspect, unless it was that chap with the pipe. However, whoever it was, he has ruined me and my family—made beggars of us. I laid out all the money I had saved upon the mill; thinking it would be a good provision for my life, and for my poor boy and his mother after me. And now it's nothing but a heap of ashes!"

In the midst of his misfortunes and lamentations, however, the miller did not forget his wife. He wished her to be with her sister, who resided at Hotham, where she would be better attended, and in the neighbourhood of a surgeon; so he again broached the subject of the shander-a-dan. If they would lend it him, he would take her over the next day.

"It was quite at his service." This was in short exactly what they wished; and of course no difficulties were made. So, on the following day, the Ryland family, father, mother, and son, started for Hotham, in the shander-a-dan, driven by Short Bill.

"I shall leave my boy with the old woman for a day or two," said Matthew, "but I must come back myself to-morrow night, for I must try and see Sir Lawrence on Friday morning."

"By the by," said Luke, "he's your landlord as well as ours. What will he do in this business, think you?"

"I paid him ground rent, but the mill was my own, you know," said Ryland. "I wish now it hadn't been, for he's an uncommon good landlord."

"He'd have rebuilt it," said Luke. "Perhaps he will now?"

"I wish he would," answered the miller—"I'd pay him a good rent for it."

As soon as the Rylands were gone, the two young men started on foot for the village, to order a coffin for their father, and make arrangements for his funeral; which they proposed should take place on the day after the ensuing one, which would be Friday.

They had a great deal to discuss on the road, and Ambrose's first words were as they walked away,

"Suppose Sir Lawrence rebuilds the mill, what will you have got by your scheme then?"

"We must outbid Ryland," said Luke; "whatever he'll give, we'll give more. It would be worth more to us than to any body."

"No doubt of that," said Ambrose; "if there must be a mill there at all."

As they passed the Red Lion, Lacy was standing at the door. "Good morning!" said he. "So your neighbour, Mat Ryland, has met with a misfortune?"

"Yes, the mill's down," said Ambrose.

"How did it happen?" inquired Lacy.

"Nobody seems to know," answered the other.

"His man was going about with a light after dark, and I suppose he dropped a spark," said Luke.

"When there's a fire, people are always surprised and wonder how it could happen," said Lacy, "when they needn't look much further than their own noses for the cause—it's generally the carelessness of servants."

"Yes," answered Ambrose; "I'm always expecting Short Bill will set our stables on fire."

"No, no!" said Lacy; "never fear Short Bill. He's the carefullest ostler ever I had; and I wish you hadn't taken a fancy to him. But where's Mat Ryland staying?"

"He's gone to Hotham, with his wife and son," said Luke.

"He should have seen Sir Lawrence first," said the host.

"He's shockingly down about his mill," observed Luke.

"Let him go to his landlord," said Lacy, nodding significantly.

"Will he build the mill again for him, think you?" asked Luke.

"Let him try him!" said Lacy, looking as if he knew more than he wished to tell. "Ryland was always a well-doing man; and Sir Lawrence won't let him fall through, if he can help it."

It was not very difficult, by a little adroit questioning, an art which Luke well understood, to extract from the worthy host, who was proud of his familiarity with Mr. Cobb, the agent, that he had seen that gentleman, and had good reason for supposing that the Baronet's intentions were very favourable to the miller. This information was far from agreeable; and, as the brothers walked home, they discussed the question in all its bearings. In the evening, Short Bill returned with the shander-a-dan—Ryland intending to return on foot the following day.

At the accustomed hour, Lilly retired to bed, as usual; and when she descended the next morning, she perceived that there had been visitors there in the night; but this was by no means an uncommon event, and awakened no surprise in her mind.

Early in the day, the undertaker arrived from the village with the coffin, in which poor Jacob's body was placed; and it was arranged that, on the following morning, it should be driven in the shander-a-dan to the churchyard, where the Rev. Mr. Marsh would be ready to perform the funeral ceremony. The coffin was therefore screwed down at once, that there might be no further necessity for the undertaker's attendance.

Lilly had been often into the room to look at the old man, and she thought about him and felt about him, more than she had ever thought or felt on any subject before. The circumstances of his death had struck her, and the missing her daily attendance on him had awakened a chord in her heart. Not naturally a morose man, though a weak and ignorant one, and softened by sickness and sorrow, and the bitter sense of his children's neglect, he had been used to speak kindly to her; often gratefully; now, she never heard any thing but harsh and imperious commands; except indeed from Shorty, as, by way of abbreviating his name, the ostler was frequently called—he treated her as his fellow-servant, and as civilly as he would have treated any other. And Lilly felt a pang when the old man's face was hidden from her; and she descended to her work below, after the undertaker's departure, with a sadder sense of desolation than she had ever known before. Somehow, all at once, a gleam had penetrated the thick darkness that had overshadowed her intellect and feelings; and from being a mere piece of mechanism, she was aroused into the consciousness that she was something more. That night, when Lilly went to bed, she cried herself to sleep.

CHAPTER III

SOMETHING MYSTERIOUS

The room in which Lilly slept was at the top of the house; on one side of it was that where lay Jacob in his coffin—on the other, was an apartment that was never inhabited. It was full of boxes and packages, empty or full; and the door of it was always kept locked. There were two other rooms on the same floor, but they were unfurnished and never occupied, either. The young men and women slept on a lower story.

Lilly, like children in general, especially overworked ones, was a heavy sleeper; from the time she laid her head on the pillow, till custom awakened her at a precise hour in the morning, no sound ever disturbed her rest.

Many a night there were heavy feet upon the stairs; and voices and rummagings in the adjoining apartment, but she never heard them; and her bed, with herself in it, might have been placed in the shander-a-dan and carried across the common, without awakening her.

But on this night—the one preceding Jacob's funeral—Lilly found herself in a condition altogether new to her—she could not sleep. She was feverish and restless—turning from side to side—dozing a little, and then waking with a start. She was thirsty too, and would have given the world for a draught of cold water, but there was none in her room. Lilly wondered what was the matter with her, as the weary hours dragged on to the middle of the night; when at length she fell into a sounder sleep. But she had not slept above an hour, when she awoke again, more uncomfortable than ever; and, with her mouth so parched that she felt she must make a desperate effort to get some water, though she would have to fetch it from the bottom of the house in the dark. So she crawled out of bed, felt for her shoes, threw her frock which lay by the bedside over her shoulders, and softly opened the door. But suddenly it occurred to her that there was some water in Jacob's room. There had been, at least, before his death; and, as she had never thought of emptying the pitcher since, it was doubtless there still. To get it there was much easier than going below, so she turned in that direction, found the door, and entered the room. But it was pitch dark, and she had some difficulty in steering her way betwixt the bed and the coffin, so as to avoid striking against either. However, she found the water-jug; and, having taken a draught, was just preparing to carry it with her to her own room, when she saw a gleam of light and heard feet upon the stairs.

"Oh, my!" thought Lilly; "they're going to the store-room:" so the one next hers was called. "I hope they won't see my door open!" and she stood still, listening to the footsteps, intending to slip into her own chamber as soon as she heard them enter the other.

But it was not there these disturbers of the night were going; and it was fortunate for her that the bed intervened betwixt her and the door; for she had only just time to conceal herself in the scanty folds of the curtain before they were in Jacob's room. As it was, she must infallibly have been discovered, but that the spot where she stood remained quite in the shade—she could see those who entered perfectly, though they did not see her.

First, came Luke Littenhaus, carrying a candle, which he held so as to light those who followed. These were Hans Peffer, and a man called Locksley, who had frequently visited the house after nightfall; and who, as well as his associate, wore the habit of a sailor. They ascended the stairs but slowly, for they bore between them a heavy burthen; one supported the head, and the other the feet of a corpse. Behind them came Ambrose, with a slow and heavy step.

"That'll do," said Luke, as they mounted the last stair; "now, this way," he continued, pointing to the bed, and "pitch him down there, whilst we open the coffin."

The body was accordingly laid upon the bed, close to where Lilly stood.

"Did you bring up the screwdriver?" inquired Locksley.

"To be sure I did," said Luke, proceeding at once to unscrew the lid of the coffin, whilst Ambrose, pale and grave, stood back, leaning against the wall.

"Come, bear a hand, will you?" said Luke to his brother, when the lid was off.

"Hans, do it!" said Ambrose, turning away, whilst Hans advanced; and Luke, with his assistance, lifted out the body of his father, and placed it on the bed.

"Now, then," said he, as they took up the other and deposited it in the coffin; "if that isn't a neat job, I don't know what is!" and, as he spoke, he replaced the lid and screwed it down as it was before. They then wrapped Jacob's body in the rug that covered his own bed, Hans and Locksley lifted it between them, and Luke preceding them with the light, and Ambrose following them, they descended the stairs in the same order they had mounted them; scarcely a dozen words having been spoken amongst them since they entered the room.

Lilly did not faint, as heroines usually do on such occasions; but, when her ear assured her they had reached the bottom of the stairs, she took up her water-jug and stole back to bed, where she passed the remainder of the night in a restless and uneasy sleep.

It was a hard matter for Lilly to rise in the morning, for her head ached violently; and she felt, altogether, as she had never felt before in her life; but she dressed herself and went down stairs to her work, as usual; nobody observed she was ill, and she could not venture to mention it. Neither Ambrose nor Luke were there; nobody, indeed, besides Charlotte and Anna, except Short Bill.

About ten o'clock, the young men returned in the shander-a-dan; and, by their conversation, she understood they had been getting some articles of mourning for the funeral. At eleven, one of the undertaker's men arrived, and with his assistance the coffin was brought down and placed in the vehicle, which was to transport it to the churchyard. Short Bill mounted the box, and drove away at a gentle pace, whilst Ambrose and Luke followed on foot with the undertaker's man. In the afternoon they returned, and the remainder of the day passed without any occurrence.

That night Lilly slept very heavily; so much so, that she had to be awakened in the morning, to the great displeasure of her cousins; who were in unusual haste for their breakfast, as they were about to start on an expedition to visit Miss Grosset, the dressmaker, at Hotham. Poor Lilly could scarcely lift her eyelids; they seemed glued together; whilst her head felt so like a lump of lead, that she thought she could never raise it from the pillow; however, with that passive submission which she had so long exercised, she dragged herself out of bed, and hastened down stairs. But her generally pale face was now so flushed, that her illness forced itself on the attention of her cousins. They observed that she must have a cold, and agreed to bring her some medicine from the town.

When they were gone, she was in the house alone. Ambrose she had not seen all day—Luke was at home, but engaged in some outdoor work—and thus, having nobody to drive her, and feeling overcome with illness, she lay down upon the floor before the kitchen fire and went to sleep. By and by she was awakened by somebody pulling her arm.

"Lilly!" said a voice, "Lilly, girl! wake, will you?" Lilly started up, expecting a scolding—but it was Philip Ryland—the door of the house was open, and he had found his way to the kitchen in search of somebody to speak to.

"I say, Lilly," said the boy, "where's my father?"

"I don't know," answered Lilly, slowly, after staring at him for some time in silence.

"Is he out?" inquired Philip.

"I don't know," replied Lilly again, with a bewildered countenance.

"Didn't he sleep here?" said Philip.

"Sleep here!" answered Lilly. "I don't think he did."

"Did he go away to the village, then, and not come back?"

"I can't tell," said Lilly.

"Well, but he was here yesterday!"

"Was he?" said Lilly. "I didn't see him!"

"But when did you see him?" asked Philip.

"Well, I think it was Tuesday—no, it was Wednesday, when he went away in the shander-a-dan—I saw him!"

"What, hasn't he been here since?" exclaimed Philip.

"I don't know," said Lilly, with an air of strange uncertainty.

"Oh, then he must have altered his mind and gone on to the village at once, I suppose. But I say, Lilly, what's the matter with you?"

"I can't tell," answered the little girl. "I've got a bad pain in my head!"

"You look just as I did when I had the measles," said Philip. "You ought to go to bed—the doctor made *me* go to bed, and I had to stay there till I was well."

"I mustn't go to bed," said Lilly. "Cousins would be angry."

"Pooh!" answered Philip; "people must go to bed when they're ill, you know. Where *are* your cousins?"

"Anna and Charlotte are gone to Hotham," answered Lilly; "but Luke's at home somewhere—perhaps he's in the stable."

"I'll go and look for him," said Philip.

When he was gone, Lilly made an effort to rise and go about her work again, but it was with extreme difficulty she could keep herself on her feet. Meantime,

Philip sought Luke and found him, but could obtain no information about his father. He had certainly not been at the Black Huntsman since he departed thence with his wife in the shander-a-dan. It was clear he had gone on at once to the village; and thither Philip proceeded to seek him.

So the day wore on, without any other event than the arrival of a traveller, who, after baiting his horse and taking some refreshment, proceeded on his way.

At night the sisters returned; and so did Philip shortly afterwards.

"I can't hear anything of my father," said he. "He hasn't been to the village;—Mrs. Lacy hasn't seen him, and he'd have been sure to go there."

"Did you see Mr. Cobb?" said Luke. "Perhaps he'd go straight to Sir Lawrence!"

"No," said Philip, "for Mr. Cobb had been at the Lion just before I got there, inquiring for my father, and wondering he hadn't seen him. Sir Lawrence is going to rebuild the mill for us."

"Ah, ah!" said Luke. "Lucky for you!"

"But I wish I knew where my father's gone to!" said the boy, anxiously. "If I go back without finding him, mother'll be so uneasy!"

It was too late, however, to seek him any more that night, so Philip went to bed; and on the following morning he started again on foot to return to his mother.

Lilly was considerably better for the medicine her cousins brought her; and the apothecary who sent it, concluding the patient had a cold, having desired she should remain in bed, she was allowed to do so the whole of Sunday. The warmth of the bed brought out the rash—her headache left her; and it was now clear, to an experienced eye, that Lilly had the measles. Her cousins, however, did not understand this; or it is to be hoped they would not have allowed her, as they did, to rise on the second morning and go about her work as usual.

On Monday morning, a man came over from Hotham, sent by Mrs. Ryland, to make inquiries about her husband; but, after extending his search to 'the village, he returned without any information. He said that Ryland had left Hotham on Thursday afternoon, as he was to see Sir Lawrence on Friday morning. And now, in the village, a rumour arose that the miller had made away with himself.

On Tuesday, Mrs. Ryland herself arrived, with her son, in a cart, lent her by a baker. She was in great distress, and so was the boy. As she wished to go as far as the village, and the cart could not be further spared, they let her have the shander-a-dan. Her inquiries, however, were as unsuccessful as those of her son had been—no tidings could be heard of Matthew Ryland; and she returned to the Black Huntsman in extreme anguish; the persuasion was universal that her husband, in despair at the loss of his property, had committed suicide—probably drowned himself in the sea, on the evening of the day he last parted with her.

And now it occurred to her, that there had been something peculiarly impressive in his leave-taking. He had returned and embraced her a second time, and affectionately bade her take care of herself and her boy. Was this presentiment of some evil that awaited him? Or was it the tender yearning of the heart in an adieu, which he knew was to be his last?

As there was still an hour or two's daylight, Philip said he would go to the mill to look again if he could find any traces of his father having been there; whilst the poor mother, ill and broken-hearted, went to lie down, requesting that a cup of tea should be sent her. The tea was accordingly made, and Lilly carried it up stairs.

"What's the matter, little girl?" said Mrs. Ryland. "What makes your face so red?"

"I don't know," answered Lilly, in a hoarse voice.

"Why, you have a bad cold or something worse," said she, throwing back a little shawl Lilly had pinned over her neck. "Why, you should be in bed, child—you've got the measles! Bless me!" continued the good woman, rising hastily, and for the moment forgetting her own misfortunes in her compassion for the neglected child, "how very wrong to let you go about in this way! Come with me down stairs, and I'll speak to your cousins. Bless my heart! don't they see the rash out upon you?"

Not only did Mrs. Ryland's representations procure Lilly leave to go to bed, but the motherly feelings of her benevolent heart being aroused, together with some indignation at the utter indifference and neglect of the cousins, she took upon herself the tending of her; gave her a warm drink, placed barley-water by her bedside, and, after covering her up carefully, promised to see her in the morning. And she did see her; and, as her own stay at the inn was prolonged for several days, she nursed the child through the whole of her illness; and Lilly, probably, owed it to her care that she did not die of the measles.

This prolonged sojourn was owing to a slight circumstance, which, from its satisfying her that her husband had been in the neighbourhood since he quitted Hotham, inspired a faint hope that he was either not far off, or would at least return. Philip had found his father's walking-stick amongst the ruins of the mill; and Mrs. Ryland was certain that he had it in his hand when he went away.

However, this indication of his whereabout was not followed by any other discovery; and the mother and son returned to Hotham, where she had some relations; leaving the mystery of Matthew Ryland's fate unsolved.

CHAPTER IV

THE AWAKENING OF LILLY'S HEART, AND SOME ACCOUNT OF TWO RUSTIC LOVERS

Lilly had never felt so unhappy in her life as she did on the morning the Rylands left the dreary inn. She was well now, and able to resume her work; but with what a heavy heart she went about it! She had for some days had experience of what kindness and fellowship were, and what a blank it made to lose them! Mrs. Ryland, naturally benevolent and fond of children, could not nurse one through an illness, especially one who excited her compassion, without treating her with a motherly tenderness. The good woman had talked to her too, and had easily gathered from the uncomplaining Lilly that she had more reason for discontent than she was herself aware of; and, in the telling of her tale, she learnt in some degree to comprehend her own misfortune; for Lilly, like a horse whose spirit had been broken by ill-treatment at so early an age, that its fire was extinguished and its nature subdued, seemed almost to have descended to a lower grade in the scale of creation.

No play, no instruction, no sympathy, had yet fallen to Lilly's lot in the hard world that surrounded her. She could read a little, as we have said, because she knew her letters before she came to live with the Littenhaus family; and could even spell words of one syllable—and, as it was necessary for their convenience that she should be able to make out names over doors and inscriptions over shops, they had, with sharp words and hard blows, so far pursued her education, but no farther. Nobody ever made an observation to her—she never heard conversation in which she could take an interest; if anybody asked her a question, her almost invariable answer was, that she didn't know, although it might be something that with the most ordinary attention she might have known. Imperious commands, and abuse for her stupidity—and on this head neither did the few guests that frequented the house spare her—were all the benefits that Lilly derived from God's great gift of speech to man. In short, Lilly Dawson, at the period we first introduced her, was, in feeling and intellect, but one degree removed from the condition of a horse or a dog—and we here mean an ill-used horse or dog—for everybody, who has enjoyed the pleasure of an intimate and friendly association with animals, is aware that they may be as much raised in the scale of existence by an education conducted with gentleness, as Lilly was depressed in that scale by an opposite treatment.

But these few days of sunshine had swelled the bud, if not unfolded the flower, that had been nipped and withered by the bitter east wind, which had blasted Lilly's young years—she began to feel, and feeling brought thought. Her heart awoke her intellect. She became conscious that she was ill-treated; and, from being dogged, and stolid, and insensible, she came to be unhappy. But she had nobody to whom she could speak of her unhappiness, and her outward demeanour remained unchanged. Had her cousins attended to her, they might have perceived she was less stupid; but, as they did not, they were not aware even of this alteration.

One thought there was, that now constantly haunted Lilly's mind, and that was the recollection of the tender, loving, and confidential intercourse she had witnessed betwixt Mrs. Ryland and her son. Philip had been kind to herself, too; but the thing that had impressed her most was this filial and maternal love. Lilly had never seen love before, in any of its beautiful shapes; and now suddenly it had been presented to her in the most beautiful of all. It was like a glimpse of that Sun of Grace, which the ancient Pythagoreans[9] and some modern mystics describe as being the centre and grand mover of the universe; it unfolded to her some faint ideas of what human life was, or should be; and of how the world was held together—she beheld for the first time the link that binds it.

And it was curious how the sight of this mutual affection and constant interchange of tender offices reacted upon the forlorn child, filling, as if from its overflow, her desolate heart with love also. Her sympathy was imitative too—she was younger than Philip, yet it seemed to herself that she loved him with the same sort of love his mother felt for him, whilst she loved the mother with the love of the son. Poor Lilly! she was taking her first lesson, reaping her first experience in that lore of the heart, which makes up so much of the life of every human being, worthy of the form he bears.

And the harvest she reaped was the too common one; the fruit of her love was pain. Her friends were gone: they had just stayed long enough to tear the veil from her eyes, and show her her own desolation; and they were gone—probably to return no more; and not a single gleam of light did the future disclose to the forlorn Lilly Dawson.

It is not to be supposed that the disappearance of the miller excited no sensation in the neighbourhood; on the contrary, it excited a great deal. At first, the search was not so rigorous as it might have been, because it was hoped he might return; and inquiries taken up when the sensation is diminished by time are wont to be less energetic. Still the matter was not neglected; and Sir Lawrence, who had an esteem for the man and regretted the affair altogether, advertised a reward to anybody who could give information of him dead or alive. Not only was this reward announced in the papers, but bills were posted in all public situations—amongst

---

9 An esoteric sect led by Pythagoras in the 5th Century BCE.

the rest, two appeared on the stable-walls of the Black Huntsman. The sum offered was one hundred pounds; and nobody had a greater desire to earn it than Short Bill, the ostler, whose head was consequently for ever running on the subject. Every possible and impossible accident that suggested itself to his mind was turned over, weighed, and examined. He poked into every hole and corner he could think of, within an attainable distance; and many a night, when his masters believed him safe asleep in the hay-loft, he was roaming the country in pursuit of the lost Matthew Ryland; or, at least, some traces of him.

The fact was, that nature, who sometimes sets soft hearts in rude frames, had given poor Shorty a very susceptible one; he was in love; and, what was more, his love was returned. The object of his passion, too, was really a nice, pretty, village maiden; at whose taste everybody wondered. But that did not signify to her; she saw charms in her Shorty, as she called him, which, though invisible to the rest of the world, were not the less real and dear to her; and she was ready to marry him any day in the year, if they could but discover some possible means of living together: but she was as poor as he was, being employed in the most humble services; and they had little expectation of mending their condition, till the baronet's advertisement appeared. This, however, fired their hopes. No one could have greater advantages in the quest than the ostler. He knew every inch of ground and every crank and crevice in the neighbourhood; and he was living close to the spot whence, from the finding of the stick, the track should apparently be followed.

The probability was, however, that Matthew had drowned himself in the sea—to that opinion, at least, the public generally inclined—a circumstance unfavourable to poor Bill's hopes; except that there was a chance the body might be washed ashore, which had actually been the case with the remains of a lad who had been drowned whilst bathing, not long previously.

Urged by so potent a motive, the ostler's search was indefatigable; and every moment that he could steal from his sleep or his work was spent in roaming the country or wandering along the beach; but, naturally timid, quiet, and silent, he communicated his plans and projects to nobody, and had no confidante of his hopes but Winny Weston, his mistress.

Matthew Ryland had now been dead six weeks, and all search for him had been relinquished, except on the part of this rustic lover. The possibility of the body's being cast ashore still urged him to the beach; and he always hastened thither as early after the flow of the tide as he could contrive to get away; but these repeated absences being at length noticed by his employers, he had been obliged, on pain of losing his situation, to confine his expeditions to the night-time. But even here he was not secure. Some circumstance awakened suspicion; he was watched and detected; and straightway received his dismissal. A servant who employed the dark hours in prowling about the country, would certainly not be a desirable inmate in any family; but there were many powerful reasons why he should be a dangerous one at the Black Huntsman. They, too, had their midnight expeditions; and a rencontre might have been very inconvenient, and possibly have led to fatal consequences.

For certain reasons, these expeditions had been latterly discontinued; the search for Ryland, and the excitement occasioned by his disappearance, had rendered them perilous. Ambrose, too, who somewhat resembled his father—that is, was more weak than wicked—urged by feelings of his own, had been absent.

Ambrose was a smuggler—his father had been a smuggler before him—he was born and bred to the trade, and practised it without the least remorse of conscience; but he had a horror—a weak one Luke thought it—of shedding human blood; except, indeed, in the way of a fair fight—then he would not have minded it.

But Ambrose having returned, and the gossip and curiosity excited about Matthew Ryland's affair having died away, it was considered time to begin business again; especially as Mr. Fortune, the silk-mercer[10] at Hotham, hinted that the ladies were beginning to be impatient for the spring silks—"and nothing would go down with them, but they must be French."

The dismissal was a sad blow to the ostler. The Red Lion did not want him; besides, he had offended Mr. Lacy by leaving his service for the Black Huntsman; because the young men, who perceived some qualities in him very suitable for their purpose, had offered him higher wages. They had selected him because he did not appear to have a single idea beyond his business; and because he was silent and solitary, and spent the greatest part of his leisure asleep; having no curiosity and troubling himself with no man's business but his own. Indeed, he was looked upon as a sort of half-witted person, who had only just sense enough for his vocation, and no more, and therefore a very safe inmate. And they had judged him correctly. He liked his situation exceedingly; for he had good wages, with little work, and had frequent opportunities of seeing his dear Winny. For the rest, he never troubled himself to think, much less to inquire, where the young men had been, when they came home at four or five o'clock in the morning, as sometimes happened, with the horse in a sweat and the shander-a-dan covered with mud. To be sure, he had to get up to clean them; but, that done, he might generally sleep till midday, if he liked—as his masters did.

The Red Lion, as we have said, did not want him; and he saw no chance of getting a situation nearer than Hotham, which would place him quite out of the reach of his dear Winny—a great grief to both of them.

---

10 A trader in silk fabrics.

"Wouldn't they forgive you, Bill?" said Winny, "if you told 'em what took you out, and promised never to do it again—and you might promise, you know, for you'll never find him now—if he drown'd himself, he's gone out to sea, or else cast up somewhere else."

"I've a mind to go to-morrow and ax 'em," answered the lover; "for to-night there'll be a high spring tide—and if he don't come ashore this time, I'll give it up." And this plan being agreed upon, the lovers parted; for it happened to be a very busy day with Winny. Her mother was by trade a laundress, but unfortunately it was one scarcely needed at Combe Martin. The poor washed for themselves, and the gentry in their own laundries; and she got very little employment, except sometimes when there was company at the Castle, and more to do than they could get through. Then the overplus went to Mrs. Weston, and this happened to be the case now—so the old woman and her daughter were very busy, and Winny was obliged to leave off love-making and repair to the washing-tub.

"I'll go to the beach afore daybreak," said Shorty, as he took leave of his love; "and then, if I don't find nothing, I'll go to the Huntsman. If so be you don't see me here in the course of the day, you may reckon they've taken me back again; and I shall be in with the shander-a-dan, most like, on Sunday, if not afore."

CHAPTER V

MORE MYSTERY

The conversation which closed our last chapter occurred on a Thursday afternoon. On the Friday morning, when Lilly, who was always expected to be down stairs first, was opening the shutters, she saw a female figure coming hastily across the Heath, in the direction of the house; a sight so unusual at that early hour, that she paused for a moment to ascertain who it was. The rapidity, however, with which the woman walked, or ran, for her pace was something betwixt both, soon brought her within a recognizable distance; and then Lilly perceived it was Winny Weston. "She didn't know that Shorty had left, and was going to the stable to seek him"—such was Lilly's natural conclusion, as she turned away from the window and commenced her daily labours.

But she was mistaken—instead of directing her steps to the stable, as she usually did, Winny turned towards the house; and presently Lilly heard her knocking gently against the door with her knuckles; for she had seen the little girl at the window, and, being eager to speak to her, ventured on thus making her wishes known. We say *ventured*; for visitor's met with little encouragement at the Black Huntsman; and Winny's visits to her lover were always made at such hours, as gave her a chance of escaping a meeting with any of the family.

"Lilly," said the girl, breathless with haste and agitation, "Lilly, is Shorty here?"

"No," answered Lilly; "he left yesterday."

"But isn't he come back?" asked Winny.

"No," said Lilly; "not that I know of."

"Not come back!" repeated Winny, looking wildly at her, and sinking into a rude arm-chair made of twisted branches that stood before the door—"not come back!"—and with the corner of her apron she wiped the perspiration from her forehead.

"No," said Lilly; "they sent him away for staying out—haven't you seen him?"

"Yes, yes, we've seen him—we've seen him!" cried the girl, wringing her hands; whilst Lilly, too young and inexperienced in love affairs to comprehend much about her affliction, stood looking at her with perplexed sympathy.

"Are you *sure* he isn't at the stables?" said Winny.

"I don't think he is; I've never seen him," answered Lilly, "but I'll run round and see."

"It's no use! I know it's no use!" said Winny, rising however to follow the child.

The stable was locked, and they knocked and called, but no voice answered.

"He's not here," said Lilly.

"No; I knew it was of no use!" said Winny, again wringing her hands; "I knew it was of no use!"

"Perhaps he's gone to Hotham to look for a situation," suggested Lilly, whose ideas, as we have said, were very much brightened of late. *Hotham* to her had formerly been but a name; but, since the Rylands lived there, it had a sort of tangible existence in her mind, as a place, and indeed one to which she had the greatest desire to go herself.

But Winny could not find much hope in this suggestion. She was too well aware that her lover would not go to Hotham whilst a chance remained of recovering his situation.

When she had departed, which she did without entering into any explanation of the nature of her apprehensions—for, in the first place, she had very little acquaintance with Lilly; and, in the next, she looked upon her as a stupid child, who could neither sympathise with her distress, nor understand it—the latter resumed her work, wondering what could be the cause of such violent grief; or, rather, not so much wondering at the cause of the grief as the amount of it; for she supposed Winny's unhappiness arose from Shorty's dismissal; and as she was quite unable to appreciate the pangs of separated lovers, she was surprised at any body being distressed at what appeared to her so desirable a consummation. For her part, she had been envying the ostler's good fortune ever since she heard he was turned off!

How glad she would have been to be turned off!—But alas! there was no hope for her—she, as Frederick Douglas told the little boys at Baltimore, of himself, was "a slave for life!" Dreadful, dreadful doom![11]

In the mean time, Winny directed her steps once more to the beach. She had been there before she came to the Black Huntsman, for the tide had ebbed some hours ago; and she thought Shorty might have concluded his search, and have been upon his way back by six o'clock; especially, as he had expressed his determination to see his masters early, lest, in the interval, they should engage any body in his place.

However, it was possible that he might have extended his perquisitions farther than he had declared to her he should do. He had, on the previous day, resolved to go as far as Long Point, which was six miles in a direct line along the shore. It was a headland which stretched far into the sea. Beyond it, the coast veered away in another direction; the country was populous—there was a seaport not far off, and plenty of people likely to be in the way to pick up any thing that was washed in. Shorty's hopes therefore naturally terminated at Long Point; and Winny knew that he could well have been there and back, since the tide ebbed. Still, he might have been led further; besides, another thought occurred to her—perhaps he had found what he had so long sought—and, if so, he would naturally be detained. He must get people to witness his discovery, establish his claim to the reward, and remove the body. For a moment, a gleam of hope lightened Winny's heart, and she quickened her eager steps; but the hope grew faint almost ere it was born—it was stifled by the heavy fear that sat upon her soul—she was sure her lover was dead.

However, she walked on, straining her eyes forwards along the cold, flat, dreary shore, where not a moving object met her view, except indeed the ever-moving ocean, and here and there a screaming sea-bird dipping in the waves. There stood the ruins of the mill—that unlucky mill! the source of all their misfortunes—for in the misfortunes of the Rylands originated theirs. But for the miller's disappearance, Shorty would never have incurred his master's displeasure by his frequent excursions; would not have been dismissed; and the catastrophe she now apprehended would not have happened. So are our fortunes linked! And so it is, that no act we do, good or ill, or *apparently* indifferent—for it cannot be predicated of any act that it is really indifferent, since some unforeseen results may arise from the most insignificant—no act but may amongst the various ramifications of its effects produce the most important consequences to the well being, not only of ourselves and those connected with us, but of persons seemingly far

11 Frederick Douglass was born a slave but escaped and became a famous anti-slavery activist and author. Also see Appendix B for Crowe's views on slavery.

removed from our sphere.

That unlucky mill! There stood the *bare* walls of the round tower, that had borne the sails. How merrily they used to spin round in the wind, with the busy whirr and the clack-clack! Silent and still now, except for the ill-omened voices of some ravens that were croaking and quarrelling amongst the ruins. But there was nothing else to be seen nor heard—no signs of Shorty; though led on by her anxiety, she walked the whole six miles to Long Point. There she sat and rested for awhile, and relieved her overcharged breast by a burst of tears. Then suddenly her heart was stirred with the anxiety to get back again to the village—the faint hope that she might have missed him—that he might have gone round by some other way—so she arose and retraced her steps.

During the whole walk, going and coming, she had not met a human being; for, as we have said, the beach was edged by a bare unfruitful common, and there were no houses near the shore. The Black Huntsman stood nearly a mile from the sea; and betwixt that and Long Point, no habitation had existed, except the mill, which was situated on a little prominence, a small way from the beach; and the ascent to it was by a narrow ravine, or cleft, which cut the mount in two. When Winny reached this pass, she paused to decide whether she should continue her way by the water, or ascend the ravine and take the inland path to the village. While she was deliberating this point, her eye was caught by a foot-print exactly where she was standing, and, on looking more closely, she could trace several more. On one spot especially, there was a disturbance of the small shingle, that seemed to have been made by the congregating of three or four persons together; and leading from this there was a flat depressed line of about two feet wide, which looked as if something had been rolled or dragged along. It was like the mark left by a wheel; only considerably broader, less regular, and not so deep.

This discovery decided Winny on ascending the little ravine, for it was in that direction the line lay; and it was bordered on each side by indistinct marks of feet. It was clear that somebody had been there since the tide turned, for those shingle-prints were above high watermark. Could they be indications of her lover's fate? Were they the signals of his success? The foot-prints might be his, and those of others, whom he had got to assist him; the broad line might have been formed by the dragging up of Ryland's body, which he had been so fortunate as to discover. It had very much the appearance of a mark so formed. A gleam of hope and joy shot through Winny's breast as this possibility occurred to her. The vision of the £100 reward, and then the wedding, and the humble cottage they had set their hearts on, with its little garden well stocked with cabbages, and the sweetwilliams, and the tall hollyhocks, and the big sunflower that *would* peep into the window of a morning, rose up before her. How happy they should be!

For a minute or two, she forgot her fears in her hopes, and she started at a brisk pace up the ascent. When she had passed along the beach before, she had been too eagerly looking forwards to observe the foot-prints, or to turn aside at the mill, although the question had occurred to her for an instant, why so many dark-looking birds were cawing, and croaking, and hovering about it. But she wondered more now, for there they were still; and the sight and sound caused another revulsion in her breast. What was it that was gathering them together there? Her cheek turned pale and her blood froze at the thought that suggested itself.

However, she need not be long in suspense—the way was short, and she soon reached the spot. The walls of the dwelling-house had mostly fallen in; but those of the mill itself, being built of stone, were still standing; and the whole interior being consumed, formed a sort of area, into which she stept and looked around.

She breathed again; for there was nothing there to alarm her; except indeed it were the flapping wings of two large magpies who had been quarrelling and chattering in a corner, so busily, that for the first moment, they had not even leisure to be scared by her intrusion; but when she advanced a step, they flew away; leaving behind them what seemed to have been their bone of contention; apparently, a small bit of white paper.

Under general circumstances, Winny would never have thought of examining so insignificant an object further, but she was now in that state of mind, wherein nothing seems insignificant. Her lover might have been there—he might have dropped a bit of paper—there might be something written on it that would indicate to whom it had belonged—so she advanced to pick it up. But it was not paper; it proved to be a small bit of linen, clearly part of the bosom of a shirt, first torn out of the gathers, where it was attached to the collar, and there wrenched off. It was but a morsel; but the puckering of the gathers were still in it; and it was so clean that it could not have lain there long.

Indeed, it was defiled but by one small spot—but that spot was of blood.

But why should Winny's heart contract at the sight of it? She was quite sure the shirt from which the fragment had been torn was not Shorty's. The linen was white and of a medium texture—not fine, but not very coarse; the shirts he wore were of coarse blue calico. Yet it did contract with a fresh access of apprehension; and she eagerly looked about for any corroborative indications. Except some faint traces of foot-prints in the dust, however, she could discover nothing; and after examining the whole of the ruins, she pursued her way homewards, carrying the morsel of linen with her.

Till we possess the absolute certainty of a much dreaded misfortune, hope is for ever springing up afresh, suggesting this and that possibility of salvation; and now Winny found herself quickening her steps, as she drew near the village—for might she not have missed Shorty by leaving home so early? What, if she found him quietly seated on her mother's hearth? By this time, the inhabitants were astir and at their daily work, but, except to ask of one or two of Shorty's acquaintance if they had seen him pass, she did not pause till she opened the cottage door.

"Has he been here, mother?" were her first words.

"Not again," said the old woman, looking up from her ironing, and solemnly shaking her head.

"But himself—you haven't seen him?"

"No," answered the mother. "How should I? Have you heard any thing?"

"Nothing," answered Winny. "He hadn't been at the Huntsman, and I walked all the way to Long Point and back—but there's no sign of him," and here Winny sank into a chair and gave way to her tears.

"Who did you see at the Huntsman?" asked Mrs. Weston.

"I saw Lilly, the girl. She said he'd never been there since he left yesterday; and we went to the stables, but he was not there either."

"I did not expect it," said Mrs. Weston, with a significant shake of the head.

But the poor, and it is one of the advantages of their condition, cannot afford to sit with their hands before them and grieve. There was work to be done, and it was needful that Winny should dry her eyes and set about it; so she put her irons in the fire, took off her bonnet, smoothed her chestnut hair, tied on a clean apron, and took her place at the ironing-board.

"Which way did you go?" inquired the mother.

"I went by the beach and came back by the mill," replied Winny, "for just where the path turns up there were marks of feet. There had been somebody there since high water, that's certain, and they went up to the mill, but I couldn't see any thing except this bit of linen—it's a bit torn off a shirt;" and she drew the fragment from her bosom.

"Yes," returned Mrs. Weston, "it looks like it."

"Look at the spot on it," said Winny, handing it to her mother.

"It's blood," said Mrs. Weston.

"What do you think?" asked Winny.

"I wouldn't think any thing of that," answered Mrs. Weston: "it often happens shaving, you know; and that's not Shorty's shirt."

"No, it's not his," replied Winny; "only one can't help thinking of every thing now."

After a pause, Winny said, "There's a thing I should like to know."

"What is it?" said the mother.

"Whether aunt Groby saw him last night, when he passed her door? because then we should know what time it was when he went away. He said the tide would turn at half-past eleven. When the ironing is done, I'll go and ask her."

Jane Groby, however, spared Winny this trouble by calling herself. "Oh, you're busy!" said she, putting in her head.

"Never mind—come in!" said Winny, "I want to speak to you. Did you see Shorty last night?"

"Yes; he called about ten, and sat a bit with us," answered Jane.

"And what time did he leave?" asked Winny.

"Just at half-past," replied Jane; "but did you hear that they want our Bob to go for ostler at the Huntsman?"

"When did they speak of it?" inquired Winny.

"The first time was about a week ago, when he was up at the Lion, helping Jem; Mr. Ambrose asked him how long he'd been used to horses, and whether he could drive, but he said nothing about hiring him till last night. When he was going through, he called at the door, and bade Bob go up there to-day. I was surprised, till Shorty came at night, and said they'd turned him off."

"And will you let Bob go?"

"Well, I don't know," answered Jane—"it's a rise for him, to be sure; besides, it's a great thing to get regular work, instead of jobbing about here and there; but John Groby don't seem very willing for it, somehow, though I tell him it's long afore we may get such another chance, without sending him to Hotham; and sending a lad like that into a town is sending him into temptation, like."

"But why don't your husband like it?" inquired Mrs. Weston.

"Just a fancy he's got agen the folks up there, especially Mr. Luke. John can't abide Mr. Luke."

"I can't say as ever I liked the looks of him either," said Mrs. Weston; "but Shorty never made no complaint."

"No," said Jane; "I asked him about it last night. He says they treated him well enough, and that it was as easy a place as any body need wish—plenty to eat and little to do."

"But perhaps Shorty mayn't leave, after all," said Winny, who did not like to see the door shut against her lover's hopes of resuming his place. "He means to go to-day to ask them to take him back again."

"Winny," said Mrs. Weston, in a reproving tone, "how can you talk so!"

"Well, mother," said Winny, looking significantly, "you know he meant it."

"Meant it! Yes, poor mortals as we are, we mean many things that never come to pass," said Mrs. Weston.

"I dare say Shorty would not be sorry to go to Hotham again," said Jane, who did not understand the real source of Mrs. Weston's doubts. "It was a dull life up there for any body as had been used to any thing else."

"But he didn't wish any thing else," said Winny, "and Shorty's not a person that would go to put any body out of their place, if so be he wasn't sure they wished to leave it." This was meant for a hint at Jane Groby, and she took it.

"You needn't be so sharp, Winny," said she; "we've no mind to put Shorty out; but if he leaves, you know, our Bob may as well get the chance as another."

"Never mind her," said Mrs. Weston, in a quiet, decided tone; "if you and John like the place for Bob, let him go about it at once. Shorty'll never want it."

"How can you say so, mother?" exclaimed Winny, bursting into tears; and flinging down her iron, half in grief and half in anger, she quitted the room, and shut herself into the only other apartment the house contained, which was the little bedchamber, where both mother and daughter slept, and which opened from the kitchen or parlour—for it answered both purposes—where the ironing was going on.

"What's the matter with Winny?" inquired Jane, with some surprise: "I am sure I did not mean to affront her."

"Winny's no herself to-day," said Mrs. Weston, with a serious countenance, and a slight nod of the head.

"No doubt she's vexed at Shorty's losing his place," said Jane, in a tone that implied an inquiry whether that was the cause of the usually good-humoured Winny's waywardness.

"No doubt, she is," replied 'Mrs. Weston, still ironing away, and looking very grave.

"I hope there's nothing amiss between Shorty and her?" said Jane.

"No, no!" answered Mrs. Weston. "Poor things, there never was a word betwixt them. Some people wondered at Winny's fancy for Shorty; and perhaps they might, for no doubt Shorty was nothing to look at; but he was an honest lad, poor fellow, and that's better than looks."

"There's nothing happened to Shorty, is there?" said Jane, in a tone of excited curiosity; for she was not only struck with Mrs. Weston's demeanour, but also with the marked manner in which she spoke of the ostler in the past tense.

The answer to this question was only a significant shake of the head, and that folding-in of the lips, which denotes that people know more than they intend to tell.

"There was nothing amiss with him last night when I saw him," said Jane, with increasing surprise. "Did you see him after that?"

Mrs. Weston seemed to be considering for a minute or two whether she should evade this interrogation or speak out, and tell her story at once, for she remained silent whilst she deliberately finished ironing the frill of a shirt, not unconscious that Jane's eyes were fixed upon her with intense interest; for the visitor felt assured that there was some mystery to be disclosed about Shorty, though of what nature she could not imagine.

By the time the frill was smoothed, Mrs. Weston seemed to have made up her mind to satisfy Jane, and relieve herself, by communicating the secret that was oppressing her; for she placed her iron on the trivet, and seated herself in a chair opposite to her visitor.

"The truth is, Jane Groby,"—said she, wiping away the perspiration which had settled on her forehead, partly from the heat of her irons, and partly from the effect of bringing strongly before her mind the details of the event she was about to relate—"The truth is, there's some things one don't like to speak of before folks; and, may be, if I was to tell you the reason of Winny's taking on so, you'd just think we were both mad, or something worse."

"No, I shan't," said Jane.

"I'd heard of such things at different times," continued Mrs. Weston; "but I can't say as ever I believed them before—God forgive me!"

"What things?" inquired Jane.

"I mean of the dead coming back."

"Eh?" said Jane, turning rather pale.

"Ay!" returned Mrs. Weston. "You know, owing to there being company up at the castle, we've had a good deal to do this week, and last night we had to sit up, washing, till near morning. Well, Shorty had been here in the afternoon, telling us how he was turned off, and he and Winny had a deal of talk about it. You see, he'd been going about at night, trying to find Ryland's body—for there's no use in making any secret of it now, poor fellow!"

"Ah, for the one hundred pounds reward!" said Jane.

"Yes," continued Mrs. Weston, "and that's the way he got turned off; and last night, as it was a spring tide, he was to go again for the last time; and then he was to go to the Huntsman, and try to get his place again; and if he did, we didn't expect to see nothing more of him till he came in to church tomorrow. Well, it was just past one by the clock there—I was wringing out the last shirt in the tub, and Winny was standing there in the corner, with the jack-towel in her hand, wiping her arms—when we heard a foot coming up the paved walk there, from the garden gate."

"Was the door open?" inquired Jane.

"Yes, it was," replied Mrs. Weston. "The night was close, and we had set it open to let in the air."

"Well?" said Jane.

"Well," continued Mrs. Weston, "naturally we both looked towards the door, and I can't say but I felt a bit frightened to hear any body in the garden at that time of night, thinking of all the fine linen I'd got here from the castle; and then, again, I thought perhaps it might be Shorty, that had come back from the beach, and seeing by the light that we wasn't in bed, that he was coming to tell us what luck he'd had. Well, just as that came into my head, Winny said, "That's Shorty, *I'm* sure!' and indeed, as the foot came nearer, I'd ha' known it for his too."

"Then you'd time to think all this before you saw who it was?" inquired Jane.

"It was but a minute," returned Mrs. Weston; "for it's not more than twenty paces, you know, from the garden-wicket to the door, and the step was pretty quick, but thought is quicker. Well, the words were only just out of Winny's mouth, when there he stood at the door!"

"Shorty?"

"Ay! Shorty, as plain as ever I see him in my life."

"Did he speak?" inquired Jane, in a low tone.

"No, replied Mrs. Weston. "He stood there for, I dare say, the space of a minute, looking at us."

"And did you speak?" asked Jane.

"*I* didn't; but Winny just said the word *Shorty*, as soon as she saw him; and then something came over her, she says, that she couldn't say any more."

"But how do you know it wasn't Shorty, after all? Perhaps it was a trick."

"No," replied Mrs. Weston; "it's natural enough for a person that didn't see him to think so—but it was no trick."

"Well, but what did he do next? Did he go away?"

"Why, he stood there, as I told you, for perhaps a minute—we two staring at him, not able to say a word—and then he came in...."

"Came in!" exclaimed Jane, growing paler than before.

"Ay, did he. He just stept in and walked across the room, close by where I was standing; and went in at that door," said Mrs. Weston, pointing to the door of the bedchamber.

"Was that open too?" inquired Jane.

"Yes, it was; we'd all the doors and windows open for the sake of the air."

"Well, and did you go after him?"

"Winny did," returned Mrs. Weston. "I shall never forget the girl as long as I live!"

"What did she do?" inquired Jane.

"Why, as I said, as long as he stood at the door and was going across the room, we both stood like two of the stone figures on Sir Arthur's tomb in the church, staring at him—and I dare say we was as white as they are; but when he went into the bed-room, Winny, without ever turning her eyes away, went after him—I'm sure she moved more like a ghost herself than a living being—but when she'd got into the room there was nobody there!"

"Perhaps he got out of the window!" said Jane.

"The Lord himself knows that!" answered Mrs. Weston; "but if he was flesh and blood, he couldn't get out of the window—I'd defy any thing bigger than a child of five years old to get out of it—you know, it only opens one side. If it opened both sides, Shorty could never have got his shoulders through it."

"But how did he look?" inquired Jane. "What was he dressed in?"

"Justus he was dressed when we saw him in the afternoon—in his stable-jacket and trousers."

"And had he anything on his head?"

"No, his head was bare, and his hair looked very much ruffled like—and his face was very pale—and he held his left hand fast upon his throat, as a person might that had a pain there, and there was blood upon his clothes."

"And what did *you* do?"

"Well, I stood still staring at the door he had gone in at, till I heard a sound like somebody falling; and then I went in and found Winny lying on the floor, in a sort of faint. So I lifted her up and laid her on the bed, and sprinkled water on her face, till she heaved a sigh and opened her eyes."

"And what did she say?"

"She just said 'Mother, Shorty's dead!' and then she fell a-crying, and went into a sort of hysterics like."[12]

"And you didn't see any thing again?"

"No," replied Mrs. Weston. "As soon as I could get poor Winny to herself, I lay down beside her on the bed; but we neither of us got a wink of sleep, as you may think: and as soon as it was dawn, she would get up and go away to the Huntsman, to look for Shorty; but she couldn't hear nothing of him, though she went all along the beach, as far as Long Point."

"I've heard of such things," said Jane. "My first husband's mother, old Mrs. Methwin, used to declare that when her son David was drowned at sea, she had been wakened out of her sleep by hearing the splash in the water, and a dreadful cry. She knew it was David's voice, and she woke her husband and told him what she'd heard; but he called her a fool and bade her go to sleep. But soon after there came a letter, telling how, that very night, David had fell off the mast and was drowned."

---

12 This episode chimes with Crowe's belief in the supernatural and reads like some of her tales in *The Night Side of Nature* published in 1848. Crowe mentions this forthcoming book later in this text on p.243.

CHAPTER VI

WINNY MAKES FURTHER INQUIRIES ABOUT SHORTY

We have seen how, in spite of Winny's conviction of Shorty's death, hope, so slow to leave the human breast, had had power enough to drag her, not only to the inn on the heath, but mile after mile all the way to Long Point. She *knew* he was dead—but still she could not *believe* it. Everybody who has experienced any great and sudden misfortune, must have been conscious of this mental inconsistency. We each *know* that we shall die; and yet, to most persons, how difficult it is to realize this conviction, and bring it home to themselves!—

As the following day was Sunday, it was necessary that the ironing should be completed and the linen sent home, so that there was neither time for seeking Shorty nor for idle lamentations on account of his loss. Winny was too dutiful a daughter to leave her mother more than a fair share of the work; so, heavy as her heart was, her fingers lost none of their activity, and the ironing and plaiting were as neatly done as usual. It was only just finished in time to be carried to the castle that night, and Winny found she must resign all hopes of making another visit to Lilly, which she had intended, if possible, to do before she slept. But with the earliest dawn of light she was on her way to the heath again. Her mother urged her to rest longer, representing that nobody would be yet stirring at the Huntsman; but Winny said she might as well be walking, for she could not sleep.

The almost unacknowledged hope of finding Shorty at the stable urged her quickly on; whilst at one moment she condemned herself for indulging it, after what seemed so certain an indication that her lover no longer counted amongst the living; and the next, endeavoured to persuade herself that the vision she and her mother had seen had been but a dream or a delusion. But it was in vain she questioned its reality; she was too certain that they had been perfectly awake, and that, be the interpretation of the mystery what it might, they had on that occasion seen Shorty, either in the flesh or out of it; and the difficulties of the former explanation seemed insuperable. There was no possible egress for him from the little bedchamber they had both distinctly seen him enter; nor was there any possible place of concealment in it, which could have hid him from her eyes for an instant—there was neither closet, nor press, nor recess. Nothing but a small chest of drawers, two straw-bottomed chairs, a little rickety table, on which stood a cracked dressing-glass; and the bed, which, having neither curtains nor valance, was entirely exposed to view both above and beneath. Besides, poor Shorty was the last person in the world to have played such a trick, even had it been possible;

he had never made a joke, verbal or practical, in his life—nor ever understood one. Try to explain it away as she would, she was obliged to remain in the conviction that it was not Shorty alive, but the spiritual likeness of his corporeal frame that she had seen.

The door of the inn was not opened, nor the shutters unclosed, when she reached it; indeed, it was not more than five o'clock, and too early for any of the inmates to have left their beds; especially on a Sunday morning. So, Winny walked round to the stables—not with hope now; for the result of her cogitations on the way had pretty nearly extinguished the last faint spark of that; but surely there was somebody stirring in the loft!—in the loft where Shorty used to sleep, too, for the window was open and she distinctly heard the movement of some one within! Could it be he? She stood still, with her eyes fixed on the window, afraid to go forward, lest she should extinguish the bright gleam that shot through her breast. There was certainly a man in the room, for once or twice she got an indistinct glimpse of him. Should she call? Should she knock? But what if, instead of Shorty, it proved to be one of his masters? That would not be pleasant; for, besides the confusion of being obliged to avow that she came to look for her lover, she stood in great awe of the whole Littenhaus family. Uncertain what to do, she stept behind the shander-a-dan which was standing in the yard, and thence watched the window.

Exhausted by her want of sleep and anxiety, Winny was unconsciously supporting herself against the wheel, when she felt that it was wet: and, on looking at the vehicle, she perceived that it bore evidence of having just come off a journey; it was splashed with mud; and, as there had been no rain within the last day or two, the mud must have come from a distance. Certainly, this was nothing to her; except that, if the carriage had been used, somebody must have driven it, and that person was doubtless the one then stirring in the loft. If it were Shorty, it might possibly account for his disappearance; and a ray of hope once more shot through her heart. But she was not left long in suspense; presently, the stable-door opened, and Luke came out. When she saw who it was, she would have given the world to be anywhere but where she was, she was so afraid Luke would see her and ask her what she was doing there. But he did not; he passed on towards the house; and she peeped round the corner just time enough to see him enter the door, and close it after him.

She then returned to the stable, and knocked as she used to do, when she desired to advertise her lover of her presence; but there was no answer; and, as she wished to see Lilly and was now pretty sure of not being observed, she seated herself in the rustic chair that stood before the house, resolved to wait till the little girl, who was always the first to rise, should open the door. But the morning sun shone fiercely down upon her head, and ere long the weary Winny fell asleep. She had enjoyed a good hour's forgetfulness of her woes, when she was awakened by Lilly's shaking her arm.

"Oh! Lilly," said she, "how could I go to sleep here? But I wanted to speak to you, and I sate down to wait till you were up. Have you seen Shorty?"

"No," replied Lilly; "he hasn't been here!"

"And you haven't heard anything about him?"

"No," returned Lilly. "I heard my cousin Ambrose say yesterday, that he had engaged another boy."

"I wonder if they know anything of Shorty?" said Winny, somewhat abstractedly.

"Who?—Ambrose?" asked Lilly.

"Yes, and Mr. Luke!" replied Winny.

"Luke's not at home," answered Lilly. "He went away in the shander-a-dan on Friday night and hasn't been back."

"But he's back now," replied Winny; "and the shander-a-dan's in the yard. I saw Mr. Luke go into the house before I went to sleep. And did Mr. Luke himself drive it?"

"Yes," answered Lilly; "he always drives himself when he goes away at night."

"I wonder if he saw Shorty on Friday night!" said Winny. "I wish you'd ask him."

"I'll ask Ambrose," replied Lilly.

"I wish you would, Lilly," returned Winny; "for I know very well something dreadful has happened to him;" and, saying this, her tears began to flow afresh.

"Has there?" said Lilly, with some concern; for she was not only sorry for Winny's distress, but also for the ostler's misfortune, whatever it might be; for he had been civil and good-natured to her; and had many a time lent her a helping hand with her work.

"Yes," returned Winny; "I know very well he's dead; but how it happened I can't think, unless he was drowned, looking on the beach for Mr. Ryland's body; though how that should be, I can't tell; for he'd no need to go into the water."

"Did he go to look for Mr. Ryland?" said Lilly.

"Yes," answered Winny; "he used to go every night, and that was what got him into trouble with your cousins. You know there was one hundred pounds offered for him," continued she, thinking, from the manner in which the little girl looked at her, that she could not conceive the motive of the proceeding; but Lilly looked at her still without speaking; "and since he went away to the beach on Friday night, he's never come back," added Winny, with a fresh burst of tears.

"Perhaps he's gone to Hotham?" said Lilly, repeating her former suggestion.

"No, he's not!" answered Winny, mournfully shaking her head. "I know something bad has happened to him. Yesterday morning, I went all the way to Long Point to look for him, but I couldn't see no signs of him, except it was some footsteps above high water, but I don't know that they were his; but you ask Mr. Luke if you saw him any where, will you?"

"I'd rather ask Ambrose," said Lilly, "and he'll ask Luke. Here's something you dropped," added she, picking up the scrap of linen that Winny had found at the mill, and which she had now drawn out of her pocket with her pocket-handkerchief; for, being Sunday, Winny had put on her church-going gown and doffed the apron, the corner of which usually served to wipe away her tears—a pocket-handkerchief was an article belonging to her Sunday attire.

"Oh! give it me," said Winny, eagerly. "I found it at the mill yesterday morning, when I went to look for Shorty;—look, there's a large spot of blood upon it—it's a bit of a shirt."

"But it's not Shorty's," said Lilly. "He wore blue ones."

"I know it isn't his," answered Winny; "but, somehow, I can't help thinking that may be his blood!" and she looked at it, as if she thought, by her gaze, she could detect whether it were or not. "But I'm keeping you, Lilly; and I must go home to mother," added she, as she thrust the bit of linen into her bosom, lest she should lose it by a similar accident. "You be sure ask your cousins if they know anything of Shorty, and I'll come up to-morrow or next day and hear about what they say."

Winny went away, and Lilly turned to her daily labours, as usual; but, had she been capable of an act of introspection, she would have been aware that that morning was a very important one in her history. Her existence, till very lately, as we have said, had been merely that of an animal—nay, almost lower, for she had only lived her physical life without thought and without affections. The latter had never been awakened; and the former had been stifled and extinguished by her constant and monotonous labour, and the uniform hardness, coldness, indifference, and contempt which had blighted her. She had always been treated as a machine that was worked by the human voice, instead of by steam or the lever; and she naturally sunk to the level of a machine. The death of Jacob Littenhaus, and the kindness of Mrs. Ryland and her son, had first awakened her affections; and these, no doubt, prepared the way for a further development—a little more incitement, and she was set a-thinking, and this incitement was furnished by Winny's visit.

Of course, she had not forgotten, although she had never thought of, the events of the night preceding her illness. The scene she had witnessed when she went into her uncle's room, for the purpose of fetching some water to relieve her thirst, would have necessarily awakened considerable wonder, and not a little suspicion in most minds; but they had made small impression upon hers. It had never occurred to her at the time to inquire why one body had been removed from the coffin and another placed in it; nor had she any curiosity to learn whose remains they were that had been substituted for her uncle's. She was indeed too ignorant to wonder at the proceedings of her cousins and their companions—such doings might have been quite unimportant and legitimate, for anything she knew to the contrary. Then, the arrival of Mrs. Ryland and Philip, and her own illness, had effaced the scene from her recollection; and, although she had heard much discussion betwixt the mother and son, and even betwixt them and her cousins, as to what had become of the miller, it had never occurred to her to connect his disappearance with the events of that night.

But, somehow or other, Winny's account of the motive of Shorty's expeditions set the spark to a dormant train of thought in her brain. Was it Mr. Ryland's body that she had seen laid in her uncle's coffin? It was certainly very like it—from her concealment behind the curtain, she had seen enough to be aware of that. It was wrapt in no grave clothes, but was dressed, like the miller, in a coat and trowsers of some light material. She remembered, too, that Luke had carried a white hat in his hand, which had also been put into the coffin—and the miller had worn a white hat. But if it were really the miller's body, what could be the meaning of the transaction? If her cousins had found the old man dead, why did they not say so when there was so much inquiry about him? She could not imagine, and she felt that she should like to tell her dear Mrs. Ryland and Philip what she had seen, that, provided her suspicions were correct, they might be relieved from any further uncertainty.

These thoughts occupied her altogether, to the exclusion of Winny's distress and Shorty's disappearance, till her cousins were up and at breakfast; when she heard Luke ask Ambrose "if he had got that boy from the Lion," and the former answer, "that he was to be up on trial on Monday morning." No allusion, however, was made to his predecessor, nor had she an opportunity of fulfilling Winny's commission till late in the day, when, seeing Ambrose standing at the door alone, she said—

"Winny Weston has been up, wanting me to ask you where Shorty is!"

"How should I know?" replied Ambrose. "Isn't he at the village?"

"No," returned Lilly, with perfect simplicity; "she says he's dead!"

It was impossible for even Lilly, unobservant as she was, not to be aware of the alteration these few words produced on the countenance of Ambrose Littenhaus; whilst he stared at her with unmitigated surprise, the sudden paleness that overspread his features betrayed an emotion much more profound. Amazed and frightened at the effects of what appeared to her so simple a question, Lilly stared too; till, after the lapse of some moments, finding her cousin remained silent, and anxious herself to avoid the expression of his anger, which it appeared to her she had unwittingly incurred, she turned to go away.

But this movement seemed to arouse him from his abstraction; for, the moment she stirred, he seized her by the shoulder and called Luke, who was smoking his pipe in the parlour near at hand.

"What's the matter?" inquired the latter.

"Ask Luke!" said Ambrose to Lilly, in a sharp, short tone.

"Ask me what?" said Luke, seeing that the girl hesitated; for, besides being always afraid of Luke, she naturally shrunk from repeating an inquiry that had excited such a sensation.

"Ask him what you asked me!" said Ambrose, fiercely.

"Winny Weston wants to know what's come of Shorty?" said Lilly, with evident terror.

"How should I know?" said Luke, casting a look of displeasure at his brother.

"Tell him the rest," said Ambrose; "tell him what Winny told you!"

"Winny says Shorty's dead," said Lilly; so frightened that, being unable to raise her eyes to Luke's face, she was fortunately unconscious of the expression that passed over it; whilst the silence that ensued left her in doubt as to what was to come next.

"Come here," said he, after a pause; and, grasping her by the arm, he led her into the parlour and shut the door.

"When did you see Winny Weston?" was his first question.

"This morning," answered Lilly.

"When?—at what o'clock?"

"When I opened the door, she was sitting there."

"Sitting there! Then she was there before you were up?"

"Yes—she was asleep."

"Asleep! How long had she been there?"

"I don't know."

"Had she seen anybody about since she came?"

Here Lilly hesitated, and looked more frightened than before. She perceived that she had asked a question that, for some reason or other, was offensive; and she felt, from the tone of Luke's inquiries, that Winny's having seen him would not mend the matter.

"Why don't you speak?" said Luke, angrily; "if you don't speak and tell the truth, I'll flog the skin off of you."

"She saw you," said Lilly, trembling.

"She did? And what does she come spying about the house for at five o'clock in the morning?"

"She came to look for Shorty, I believe," answered Lilly.

"What does she seek him here for, if he's dead? How does she know he's dead?" inquired Luke, savagely.

"I don't know," replied Lilly; but her downcast looks and indistinct utterance left great room for supposing that she did know.

"You lie!" exclaimed Luke, fiercely; "you do know!"

"No, I don't," returned Lilly, but her terror deprived her of all firmness and appearance of veracity.

"What did she tell you?" said he; "tell me, or I'll make you repent it!"

"She told me that Shorty was dead—that she knew he was—and that I was to ask you where he is."

Luke was confounded. The manner in which Lilly stated the question was a direct implication that, the late ostler being dead, he, Luke, knew where the body was; this was the least that was implied—there might be much more. Pale and amazed, he stood with his eyes fastened on the child: whilst, with hers fixed on the ground, she trembled before him.

"Hark ye, Lilly!" said he, after a pause; "if you don't tell me everything that Winny Weston said to you, I'll lock you up in the cellar, and keep you on bread and water for a month."

But as, in fact, Lilly knew no more, no more could be extracted from her; and, after a prolonged scene of threats and interrogations, the matter ended for the present by Luke's locking her up in her own sleeping-room; where the poor child, to whom rest was always welcome, threw herself on the bed, and was soon wrapped in that blessed oblivion which enables old and young, and rich and poor, to live through their mortal woes.

CHAPTER VII

LILLY GETS INTO TROUBLE, AND LUKE BECOMES MASTER OF THE MILL

The scenes betwixt Lilly and the young men, Luke and Ambrose, narrated in the last chapter, occurred whilst Charlotte and Anna were at church; they, therefore, were quite ignorant of the cause of the girl's incarceration. When they asked for her, on their return, Luke told them he had shut her up; and, as Luke was a person who never encouraged curiosity, even on the part of his own family, his sisters made no further inquiries; especially, as they saw a cloud upon his brow, which portended nothing very pleasant to any one who was imprudent enough to importune him.

Nobody ever questioned Luke—not even Ambrose; although he was so far concerned in his undertakings and linked to his fortunes, that he necessarily became a partner, though occasionally rather a passive than an active one, in all his proceedings.

As Lilly was still a prisoner, it fell to Anna's lot to rise and light the fire, and prepare the breakfast on Monday morning; and when she opened the door, the first thing she saw was Winny Weston, seated there in the garden chair. It was lucky for Winny that Anna knew nothing of the offence she had committed the day before, or she would have met with a sharp rebuke; as it was, she simply asked her what she was doing there.

"I only came up to ask for Shorty," said Winny.

"He's gone from here," replied Anna; "didn't you know that?"

"Yes, ma'am," answered Winny; "but Lilly Dawson said she'd ask Mr. Luke about him, for me."

"Ask Luke what about him?" inquired Anna.

"Where he is, ma'am," replied Winny.

"How should we know where he is?" said Anna. "He has been away from here these three days. He's gone to Hotham, to look for a place, most likely;" and, shutting the door in order to put an end to the colloquy, she left Winny to go home as unsatisfied as she came.

In the mean time, the ostler's disappearance began to be talked of amongst the villagers; and the gossip about him even reached the Castle. But poor Shorty was a person who belonged to nobody, except to Winny—he had no enemies, but he had no friends; and as he was not considered to have any abiding-place, his being missed from one spot only led to the conclusion that he had gone to another—it was not a circumstance calculated to raise any question or curiosity. Nobody but Winny and her mother, who were acquainted with the amount of his attachment, and the humble hopes and plans founded on it, could estimate the improbability of his voluntarily absenting himself, or the significance of his disappearance from the neighbourhood of Combe Martin. To everybody else it seemed a very ordinary event, and it was certainly one which would have excited no notice at all but for the rumours which had got abroad about the apparition.

Jane Groby circulated the story; and, as the interest which had been excited by the miller's misfortunes was, by this time, pretty well exhausted, a new subject of conversation was not unwelcome, especially such a one as this; for, let people laugh as they will, there is a chord in almost every human breast, though pride seeks to conceal it, which is instantly stirred by the conception that the dead do sometimes, as Isaac Taylor suggests, "actually break through the boundaries that hem in the ethereal crowds; and so, as if by trespass, may, in single instances, infringe upon the ground of common corporeal life."

The tale was variously received; the women generally believed it, and the men as generally laughed at it; some honestly, others to avoid being laughed at themselves. In the due course of circulation, the host of the "Lion" told Mr. Cobb, the agent, of it, and the agent told Lady Longford, who, from having heard of a similar circumstance in her own family, was not altogether disinclined to credit the testimony of the two women. Sir Lawrence, on the other hand, thought it quite absurd to give heed to them, and forbade her lending her countenance to so silly a rumour, by sending for them to the Castle, as she wished to do. "If you want to question them about it," said he, "take an opportunity of doing it some day, when you meet them accidentally."

Lady Longford took an early opportunity of meeting them accidentally, by calling at the cottage, where she heard the whole particulars from Mrs. Weston and her daughter, as they had been related to Jane Groby. The tale was so simple and so direct, that the lady came away thoroughly satisfied that one of two things must be true; namely, that the women had, on that occasion, either seen the ostler himself or his apparition.

But when she declared this conviction on the same evening at dinner, she found Sir Lawrence perfectly impervious to the evidence she adduced—"he could but wonder how she could be so silly as to believe such a story." It was in vain that Lady Longford insisted on the known honesty and veracity of Deborah Weston, and the extreme candour of Winny, and that she put it to him, whether he would not believe them on any other subject that simply concerned the evidence of their senses. He could not deny that he would; but still he laughed. Then, she turned to the rector, Mr. Moore; but he smiled, and said that the common people of all countries were apt to be believers in witchcraft and ghosts; but that an enlightened education was the remedy for such superstitions.

Lady Longford asked how we could be sure that the belief in such things was merely a superstition, and not founded on some ill-observed facts; whereupon, he told her, that the word superstition was derived from the Latin *superstitio,* and meant vain fears, &c., &c.

The agent, who was, of course, a lawyer, then remarked, that few people are capable of observing facts or giving evidence; an assertion which Lady Longford willingly admitted; maintaining, however, that the fact in question was of so simple a nature, that since both witnesses combined in affirming it, there was no alternative but to suppose that, if it were not true, they had agreed to assert a falsehood. The agent thought the last hypothesis would, in all probability, turn out to be the real explanation of the mystery. The man had got into some scrape, and wished to stifle inquiry, by persuading the world he was dead; so, he had either played them a trick, or they had mutually agreed to *désorienter*[13] the public, by circulating this tale of a ghost; after which he related the particulars of the Cock Lane ghost[14] and some others, equally to the purpose. The doctor next took up the subject, and informed the company that ghost-seers were merely the victims of spectral illusions,[15] a by no means uncommon disorder; and, after a learned dissertation on hysteria and *delirium tremens*,[16] he of course concluded by relating the case of Nicolai, the bookseller of Berlin.[17]

As it did not, however, appear to Lady Longford that any of these objections or explanations met the point in question, with true feminine pertinacity she retained her own opinion still. Nevertheless, the ostler's fate was not investigated, because it was nobody's business to trouble themselves about it, except the Westons, who had not the means. For the rest, it was only the women who avowed their belief that poor Shorty had come to an untimely end; and, of course, the more weight they attached to the evidence of the ghost, the more the men laughed at them. To institute any inquiry upon such grounds, was out of the question.

In the mean time, as Lilly's services could not be conveniently dispensed with, she had been released from her confinement, after receiving a severe reprimand from Luke, who threatened her with fearful consequences if she dared to repeat her offence. But, as poor Lilly did not clearly understand what her offence was, she was manifestly in considerable danger of incurring the menaced vengeance

---

13 Disorient.

14 The Cock Lane ghost first manifested at 21 Cock Lane in 1759. The property was disturbed on and off for a number of years, but the haunting reached a crisis in 1762 when the ghost was identified as Fanny Lynes who, it was said, had been poisoned by her husband. Séances were held almost nightly and Roger Clarke estimates that 'well over two hundred' people must have witnessed the ghost (or at least attended the séances), while 'hundreds more massed in the streets', and Clark terms it the first 'media circus'. (Roger Clarke, *A Natural History of Ghosts*, Penguin Books, 2012, pp. 129-146).

15 False impressions or perceptions created by the senses. A person may think they see a ghost through mistaken visual cues or through disease. Also referred to as 'waking dreams'.

16 The effects of alcohol withdrawal on those with a chronic problem. Symptoms can include delirium and hallucinations.

17 Shane McCorristine notes the following: "In 1799 Christoph Friedrich Nicolai, a Berlin bookseller and philosopher of a sceptical disposition, read a paper to the Royal Society of Berlin entitled 'A Memoir on the Appearance of Spectres or Phantoms occasioned by Disease, with Psychological Remarks'. Nicolai had seen the apparition of his wife. However he refused to believe what he saw and documented his sightings of the apparent ghost, noting his physical condition at the time and also exploring the idea of 'spectral illusion' or dreaming whilst awake". (McCorristine, 2010, 'The case of Nicolai and Spectral Illusions Theory', Wellcome History, wellcomehistory.wordpress.com).

without knowing it; and so she felt—neither was it long before she found herself trespassing. One cause of her release had been, that it was washing-day; the lavatory process being always performed conjointly by the two sisters, with such aid as Lilly was able to give them. They were all three thus engaged, when Charlotte Littenhaus, drawing a shirt out of the tub, said to her sister, "look here, at one of Luke's shirts! What a shame it is! One of the last new ones, too!"

"What is it?" inquired Anna.

"A great piece torn out of the bosom; see!"

"It must be joined," said Anna.

"Winny Weston's got the piece," said Lilly.

"Winny Weston!" echoed the sisters in a tone of surprise.

"Yes," said Lilly; "she found it up at the mill."

"How do you know?" inquired Charlotte.

"She told me so yesterday morning," returned Lilly.

"Told you so! Why, how came *you* to see Winny Weston yesterday morning?"

"She came up here to look for Shorty," answered Lilly.

"And was it for speaking to her that you were shut up?" asked Anna, with evident interest.

"Yes," replied Lilly. Here the two sisters looked at each other, and Anna approached Charlotte, who was more narrowly examining the shirt.

"See!" said the latter to her sister, as she pointed to some stains upon it.

"And where is the piece?" asked Charlotte. "Did she give it you?"

"No," replied Lilly; "she said she should keep it."

"Keep it," said Anna; and again the eyes of the sisters met; and Lilly, now grown more observing, remarked that the countenances of both expressed considerable uneasiness.

"But how do you know, Lilly," said Anna, speaking with more gentleness than was customary to her, "how do you know that it was a bit of Luke's shirt that Winny Weston found at the mill?"

"I know it was," said Lilly; "because, when I took up the shirt to put it in the tub, I saw it was just that piece that was out; and because there were some spots of blood upon it, and there was a spot of blood upon the bit Winny found."

"Luke cut himself when he was shaving, the other day," said Anna.

"Go, Lilly, into the garden, and cut some cabbages," said Charlotte, and Lilly went.

When she returned, she found the two sisters in close conversation, and the washing at a stand-still. However, they resumed their places at the tub, and no more was said about Winny Weston or the shirt, till Luke came in to dinner, when he was privately informed of what had passed; and Lilly, to her terror, found herself once more *tête-à-tête* with him in the parlour. He led her in and locked the door; and then, with the calmness that he felt necessary to his purpose, he interrogated her more particularly than he had hitherto done, about Winny's visits and communications; gradually leading to the finding the piece of linen, and endeavouring to ascertain what Winny knew, or had said, with respect to it.

But it was not easy to come to any conclusion on this subject. Lilly's alarm and the fear of saying something that would cause offence, rendered her confused, and gave her the appearance of evasion; so that the colloquy at length concluded, without affording him any satisfaction; whilst it left Lilly a great deal more frightened than before; so terrific were the denunciations he uttered against her, if she ever dared to interfere with his concerns, or speak to Winny Weston, or even pronounce his name.

Just when she was leaving the room, he called her back, and told her that the piece of linen Winny had shown her did not belong to his shirt; and that if she ever dared to tell such a lie again, he'd make her repent of it. Lilly determined she never would; indeed, she had no desire or inducement to do it. Curiosity in her case was but feebly developed, still less that degree of reflection which gives birth to ready suspicion. All she sought was to escape punishment, and to avoid, if possible, this new class of offence into which she had so unwittingly fallen. Her life had been so entirely confined to this isolated family, of which she herself was an isolated member, that she was as ignorant of the world, either in its good or evil aspects, as if she had been brought up in a forest, and had been fed by a she-bear. Her food had been about as graciously given to her, and she had experienced about as much tenderness, as, under such an hypothesis, she might have expected: and if it had not been for the recollection of Mrs. Ryland and Philip, she would scarcely have aspired to any more exalted happiness than such an education might have fitted her for; but the ameliorating effects of their kindness, transient as it had been, were not yet effaced; and although Lilly entertained no notion but of entire submission, and did not venture to hope for anything better than an exemption from punishment or extraordinary severities, she could never hear the word Hotham pronounced without a certain awakening of the heart, for there dwelt Philip and his mother. When her cousins, male or female, made an excursion there, it seemed to her that they must be very happy; and if she ever did venture to do what youth is so prone to do, namely, to build a castle in the air, her little edifice was confined to the possibility of some future visit from these, her only friends.

The next bit of gossip that took possession of the village of Combe Martin, was concerning the rebuilding of the mill. Mr. Cobb, as usual, told the news to Mr. Lacy, with whom he had a great habit of chatting as he passed through the village; and Mr. Lacy, no less communicative, told it to his customers. Sir Lawrence had always entertained a friendly feeling to Matthew Ryland, who was indeed a very worthy, honest man. He had lamented his misfortune, and but for his disappearance would have rebuilt the mill for him. As it was, he had afforded some assistance to the widow, and had Philip been old enough, he would have placed him in his father's situation. But the boy was too young; and the mother, whose health and spirits were sadly broken by her late misfortunes, felt unequal to undertake the management of the concern. Nevertheless, a mill was much needed; there was none within a convenient distance; and the neighbourhood felt the want of it. Sir Lawrence, therefore, sent a builder to survey the premises, and make an estimate of the costs of a re-erection.

No sooner had this news got abroad, than there were two candidates in the field, eager to be allowed to rent the new mill. One was George Taylor, the owner of the rival mill, which lay some miles on the other side of the village. Ryland's mill had done him great disservice, drawing off a great part of his business; and he was now desirous of either monopolizing both mills, or of exchanging the one he now occupied for the new one to be built. He offered a very sufficient rent, and was certainly not an undesirable tenant.

The other candidate was Luke Littenhaus, whose offers were equally liberal. The wishes of the people were in favour of Taylor, for Luke was no favourite with any body; and, as opinions in the nightly *sederunts*[18] at the "Lion" ran very high on the subject, it was expected that this focus of public sentiment would not be without its influence, since, through the host and the agent, the channel was direct to Sir Lawrence Longford's ear.

Great was the disappointment, therefore, when it was understood that Luke was the successful candidate! and till the cause of this arrangement was understood, and the terms of the agreement made known, the Baronet did not escape without animadversion.[19]

"Doubtless," it was said, "the Littenhaus people might give the highest rent, but that ought to be no object to a gentleman like Sir Lawrence; and it was very shabby, for the sake of a few pounds a year, to prefer these new comers to such an old tenant as George Taylor."

However, ere long, the truth came out, and fully justified the Baronet, since it appeared that the interest he took in the Rylands was the real cause of the disappointment. He wished to secure a future provision for Philip, by making an agreement with whoever rented the mill, that he should, in the first instance, take the boy as his apprentice, in order that he might thoroughly learn the business;

18 Meetings, usually of a court or ecclesiastical assembly.
19 Censure or criticism.

and that, secondly, when Philip reached the age of twenty-one, the mill should be given up to him, if he liked to take it; so that, in point of fact, it was only to be let for a few years, and with the incumbrance of Philip on the premises; for an incumbrance both Taylor and Luke considered him. In consideration, however, of these disadvantages, the rent demanded was extremely moderate, and Sir Lawrence engaged to rebuild, and entirely fit up the mill at his own expence. Nevertheless, Taylor would not agree to the terms. He was not sure of being able to keep both mills at work successfully, and it would have been very imprudent to shut up his own, for the sake of so short a lease. Besides, he had a boy of his own, and would not be troubled with Philip.

Thus Luke got the mill, disliking the short lease quite as much as Taylor did, and the incumbrance much more. The difference between them was, that Taylor would have considered the terms of agreement binding, whilst Luke hoped to evade them. Besides, the importance of keeping the mill, either empty or in their own possession, was paramount to the interests of the whole Littenhaus family, and, indeed, to their safety too; so that, however disagreeable the conditions might be, there was no alternative but to accede to them.

The agreement signed, the building was straightway commenced, and in a moderate time finished, whereupon Luke made his *début* in the character of a miller; for it was, in reality, little more than a dramatic assumption of the part. In the first place, he knew nothing about the business; and, in the second, he did not want to know any thing about it. He had only taken the mill to keep any body else out of it; and the absence of his customers was to him more agreeable than their presence. And indeed he was troubled with few, for his disagreeable manners and ill-done work soon disgusted them; and people preferred carrying their corn[20] to George Taylor, though it was a good deal further, rather than submit to the rude indifference and carelessness of the new miller of Trentesy.

One consequence, however, arose from this arrangement, very important to Lilly, and that was the establishing of Philip Ryland as a member of the family. His mother brought him too, and stayed a couple of days—interesting days to poor Lilly; for as mercy blesses the giver as well as the receiver, her own former kindness to the girl had made an interest for her in the good woman's heart; and Lilly's gratitude, humble and inexpressive as it was, was not lost upon her. When she went away, nothing would have pleased Lilly so much as an opportunity of being useful to Philip; but for this few occasions offered. He was kept at the mill all day; and in the evening, when he came home, after eating his supper, he was sent to sleep in a room fitted up for him over the stable.

---

20 Taking your wheat to the mill for it to be ground was common practice in the nineteenth century.

"New brooms sweep clean," says the adage. At first, though the life was a sadly dull and monotonous one—the more so, that there was so little to do—Philip had not much fairly to complain of; but, gradually, when every body had got used to the arrangement, and the eyes of the little public of the neighbourhood were no longer occupied in observing how it worked, the complexion of affairs began to change, but by slow degrees, so that for some time it would have been difficult to advance any palpable cause of dissatisfaction; nevertheless, the whole amount of annoyance together formed a large sum of discomfort. The boy was ill fed and ill lodged, and, though not overworked, he was constantly confined; no recreation of any sort was allowed him; and he was treated with as little respect and consideration as if he had been a dog; neither was it long ere this sort of contemptuous neglect degenerated into extreme harshness, though this was never exhibited before a stranger.

Lilly, however, whose interest in Philip brightened her faculties and quickened her observation, saw it; but, except in one respect, she could do nothing to alleviate the annoyance. What she could she did; she had always had plenty to eat herself; but for this she never could have got through the work, and endured the fatigue she had done at so early an age. The truth was, there was no lack of good living in the house; economy or privation formed no part of the Littenhaus ethics—they seldom do amongst persons who prefer to subsist by irregular means, rather than by honest industry.

Previously to the affair of Winny Weston, she had always ate at the same table as the rest of the family; subsequently, that privilege was withdrawn, and she was made to take her dinner in the kitchen, after the rest had finished theirs. She had formerly been looked upon as a creature without eyes, ears, or understanding—the tendency, and perhaps the purpose of her bringing up was to render her so; but by that offence she gained credit, not only for as much observation as she had, but for much more. She had become, in some degree, an object of suspicion, and was therefore kept more apart from the family. She gained one advantage, however, by her solitary repasts; namely, that she had it in her power to save some of her portion for Philip. She used to give it to him in the morning, when he went away to the mill, before any body else was up, and glad enough the hungry boy was to get it. This little kindness on her part also bred a confidence and intimacy betwixt them. Philip was very unhappy. Whilst his father lived, he had been accustomed to a cheerful, comfortable home; and, both before and since, he had always found himself the object of affection and tender consideration. The change to him was a very sad one, and his situation was not improved by his having no one to speak his sorrows to, so that Lilly's sympathy was a real consolation; not only that material evidence of it which was demonstrated in the shape of cold meat and bread and butter, but the spiritual part also—it was a relief to be able to complain.

"I wonder how *you* bear it, Lilly?" he said.

"I've plenty to eat," said Lilly.

"Well, but you've no comfort of it; they treat you like a dog," said Philip. "It's not as hard to you as it is to me, though," he continued, perceiving that Lilly did not exhibit the indignation he thought her entitled to feel, "because you're used to it; but I'm not, and I don't like it; and my mother wouldn't like it, if she knew it."

Then, as their acquaintance improved, he confided to her that, but from the fear of grieving his mother, he would complain to her; but he was conscious that the knowledge of his unhappiness would make her very miserable. Besides, he did not see how she could help him. Luke would not mind any thing she could say; and it would not do to throw away the prospect held out to him at the end of the term for which the mill was let. "No," said he, "I must bear it till I am twenty-one, and then I shall be master of the mill, and have a house for my mother; and then, Lilly, you shall come and live with us."

Lilly said she was afraid her cousins wouldn't let her; but, nevertheless, the bare idea of such a beatitude gave her great pleasure.

In this way, time advanced till Lilly was near fifteen, and Philip a year older; when a circumstance occurred that ultimately changed the current of her fortunes.

CHAPTER VIII

A PAGE OUT OF LILLY'S EARLY BIOGRAPHY—SHE IS REMOVED TO HOTHAM

One day, Bob Groby, who since the disappearance of poor Winny's lover, had succeeded to his situation, having been sent to the village on a message, returned with the announcement that he was followed by two gentlemen, that were coming to lodge at the Huntsman. The strangers were at the Lion, when he passed, and Mr. Lacy had called him up, and bade him show them the way.

"There they be!" said the boy, "coming across the Heath, and the butcher's cart is to bring up their luggage in the evening."

There was such scanty inducement of any kind to stay at the Huntsman, that the house was singularly little troubled with customers, and it was a marvel to everybody how the Littenhaus people could make it answer. Indeed, to get rid of the difficulty, the little clique which constituted the public had been obliged to invent, or adopt, for the story was probably set afloat by the family themselves, a convenient fiction regarding some property on the other side of the channel, which helped to eke out their scanty profits. An oddish, foreign-looking man, who had been occasionally seen at the house, was said to be an uncle, and the master of a ship; and also the agent through whom the funds came; though some persons took it upon themselves to affirm that the money was his own, but that, being childless, he bestowed his superabundance on his nephews and nieces.

However this might be, the arrival of two such customers as now approached the Huntsman was a rare event. They were evidently gentlemen; and, although in plain clothes, had the appearance of officers, naval or military. Why they should wish to locate themselves at that solitary inn seemed, at first, an enigma; but when the butcher's cart arrived with the portmanteaus,[21] the driver solved it in some degree by the information that he had "heard folks saying at the Lion, that they were officers come down to survey the coast."

The first effect of their arrival was the disappearance of the two young men, Ambrose and Luke. They at no time interfered with the management of the house, nor ever attended on the guests. These duties devolved wholly on the sisters and Lilly; so that strangers, who lodged there, seldom saw them. Now, however, they both decamped, taking up their abode at the mill, *pro tempore;*[22] whilst the new lodgers quietly took their tea and retired early to bed.

On the following morning, they went out immediately after breakfast, and did not return till night. When they returned, they found cards and an invitation from Sir Lawrence Longford to dine at the Castle on the third day, which they accepted. On the intervening one, they dined at home. Up to this time, in consideration of their rank, Anna and Charlotte had waited on them themselves, keeping poor Lilly, who, as we have said, was little better in appearance than a Cinderella, in the background; but the necessity of providing a more than ordinarily good dinner on this occasion rendered it impossible to dispense altogether with her services; whilst Charlotte officiated in the kitchen, and Anna in the dining-room, Lilly went backwards and forwards between them, carrying the plates and dishes.

"Did you observe that girl?" said one of the gentlemen, whose carpet-bag and portmanteau bore plates inscribed with the name of *Captain Adams*.

"No," replied the other, whose name was Markham; "I did not look at her."

"Do then," said the first, "when she comes into the room again, and tell me if she's like anybody you know?"

"Oh, certainly," said the second, when Lilly returned; "I see what you mean. She's the very picture of poor Nancy," continued he, as Lilly left the room with a dish in her hand—"as far, at least, as such a creature as that can be like one so different. She has just the features and just the eyes and hair."

"And something in the expression, too," said Captain Adams, "in spite of her

---

21 A leather suitcase or bag.
22 For the time being.

looking so stupid. What's that girl's name?" said he, turning to Anna, who stood behind his chair, listening to the conversation.

"Lilly Dawson, sir; she's a cousin of ours," answered Anna.

"If Cropley and my cousin got hold of her," said Markham, laughing, "they'd produce her in court as the lost Isabel Adams, and claim the estate on the strength of the likeness."

"And call us as witnesses," said Captain Adams.

"And we certainly could not deny it," returned Markham.

"It's an inexplicable thing to me, how your cousin can persevere in that suit!" said Captain Adams. "He never can hope to gain it; if any one passenger out of the Hastings had been saved, it must inevitably have been known."

"Of course; he knows that very well; but, in the mean time, as long as he can keep alive a doubt about the child's death, he shuts your brother out of the estate; and that's all he wants."

"But the loss of character," said Captain Adams. "It's so discreditable!"

"Revenge is blind and deaf to all such considerations," returned Markham. "He never could forgive the marriage; and I am sorry to say, that I do believe he was not sorry for poor Nancy's death and the tragedy in which the union termi-nated altogether; because it vindicated his prediction that they were to be miser-able."

"Yes, only that their misery was of a very different kind to that he foretold. According to him, they were to be miserable together."

"They were but too happy together, poor souls!" said Markham with a sigh. "If their over-anxiety had not induced them to send the child home in that un-lucky ship, poor Nancy would probably have been alive now; and their happy *ménage*[23] contradicting his malignant prophecy—for, though he is my cousin, *malignant* I must call it."

"Malignant! To be sure it was," said Captain Adams; "odious. There never was a kinder heart in the world than my brother Charles has; nor was there ever a man more devotedly attached to a woman than he was to your sister. I never could properly understand the source of General Markham's hatred—nor, indeed, how anybody could hate Charles."

"It was an old Eton friend," said Markham; "but the cause always appeared to me so inadequate to so much enmity, that, upon my soul, I never had the patience to hear my brother John's account of it!"

"It's a great pity, at all events!" returned Adams. "And I fear my brother will be a good deal embarrassed to give Freddy an adequate education."

"We must try to get him into one of the Military Colleges, when he's old

---

23 Household.

enough," replied Markham. "But surely the suit can't last much longer?"

"I don't know;" returned the other. "Once in Chancery,[24] the Devil may get it out again!"

Anna lingered at the sideboard till the conversation took another direction; and then, quitting the room, she related to her sister what she had heard.

"Lilly must not go into the room again," said Charlotte.

"Certainly not," answered Anna; "and Luke must be told of this directly;" for Luke was the governing spirit of the family; his strong will and fearless temper gave him the mastery over all, who, from weakness or wickedness, had once joined in his schemes. As for Lilly, she was glad to escape waiting on what appeared to her such grand gentlemen, not to be perfectly obedient to the prohibition; so, unseen, she was soon forgotten by the strangers; whose short visit terminated without any other occurrence connected with the thread of our story.

As we have mentioned above, Lilly was now turned of fifteen years; she was small of her age and did not look more than thirteen, her growth being nipped by hard labour and insufficient rest. From the same cause, her cheeks were colourless and her eyes dull. The features, naturally regular and delicate, had a pinched expression, and the language of the countenance altogether was that of a slave—a hopeless, unawakened spirit. She had always been treated as a chattel,[25] and never had a will of her own on any subject whatever; nor was it thought necessary to consult her in an arrangement, which was now hastily formed, for disposing of her for life. She was to be married forthwith to Luke Littenhaus.

Now, marriage was a thing about which Lilly had the obscurest notions possible; so that being married or otherwise was a matter of indifference to her; but she both feared and disliked Luke, and she could not but entertain a horror of any event that seemed likely to bring her into closer relations with him. Her feelings towards the rest of the family were merely passive; but towards him both her natural instinct and his brutality to herself had inspired her with positive terror and aversion. However, her opinion on the subject was not asked; the thing was mentioned as a great honour and favour designed for her; and she was too feeble and subdued to give expression to her sentiments; and too ignorant to be aware that doing so could be of any avail. She wished Mrs. Ryland was there, that she might ask her about it; and she did communicate to Philip what awaited her; and Philip told her that if he were her, he would not marry Luke on any account; but Lilly did not know how to set about resisting.

"Run away!" said the boy; "I'd run away to-morrow if it wasn't for my mother!"

---

24 An English and Welsh court of equity, well known and often parodied for its slow proceedings, most famously in Charles Dickens's *Bleak House* (1853).

25 Personal property. Lilly is treated as the Littenhaus's property.

And this advice of his was very honestly given. There was nothing in the world he wished so much as to run away from his apprenticeship; he thought of it day and night; and it was only his filial duty that withheld him from indulging his inclination. He had always had a great desire to go to sea, and that desire, daily augmented by the disagreeables of his situation, sometimes almost amounted to a frenzy. The truth was, Luke earnestly wished, and pretty confidently expected, that he *would* run away; and he did every thing he could, or, at least, every thing he dared, to goad him to it.

But Luke, who had never been conscious of any domestic affections himself, was unable to calculate the force of the resisting power; and he accordingly found his project of less easy execution than he had expected. However, he succeeded so far as to inspire his victim with a restless anxiety to break his chains; and as Philip was ever painting to himself the joys of liberty, he described them to Lilly in the same glowing colours; but her conception of the elysium[26] he drew was necessarily much less vivid than his own, her experience being more contracted and her imagination very unexcitable. Indeed, she was in her present state of feeling and intellect altogether incapable of forming such a project, so that, whilst he spoke, she only listened and admired; without any thought of applying the advice to herself.

As to will and to do were pretty generally simultaneous processes with Luke Littenhaus, it was settled that their marriage should take place immediately; but, wishing to get the thing done as quietly as possible, and to avoid any observation and gossip that such an unexpected event might excite in the village, he thought it advisable to be married at Hotham. With this view, he engaged a lodging there, in order that the bans might be published; and as Lilly had never been in possession of any decent attire whatever, she was sent there with Charlotte, for the purpose of fitting her out; it no longer consisting with the family views to have her in the state of dirt and destitution in which she had hitherto lived.

If Lilly had ever had a wish in the world, it was to go to Hotham. The energy of this desire had somewhat abated since the translation of poor Philip; still, his mother lived there; and Lilly thought that to go to Hotham was necessarily to see her; so that on the morning they started in the shander-a-dan, she really felt an emotion very like pleasure. She had been rather better treated, too, since this new project was on foot; and Lilly, whose mind was merely that of a child, easily forgot the past and the future, in the present.

Hotham was a large town, and the lodging she was taken to was in an obscure suburb of it. Lilly thought it very grand as they drove through the streets in the shander-a-dan, and was sorry when she found herself located in a back room, which only looked into a dull yard, that she could see nothing of what appeared

---

26 Greek mythology: A wonderful place where the blessed dead enjoy a happy afterlife.

to her such a gay and busy scene. As soon as they were settled, and Bob Groby dismissed with the vehicle, Charlotte went out, leaving her companion to amuse herself as she could. For the first afternoon, this did very well; for Lilly, to whom sleep was always in arrears, found no difficulty in slumbering away the rest of the day.

But Charlotte had several acquaintances in Hotham. There was Mr. Fortune, the silk mercer; Mr. Bright, the spirit merchant; and Mr. Walker, the tobacconist; with all of whom the Littenhaus family carried on some secret mercantile trans-actions; and who, one and all, thought it to their own advantage to be civil to Charlotte; so that she received daily invitations to their houses. She also amused herself with improving her own wardrobe, whilst she refitted Lilly; but all this be-ing done without Lilly's participation or assistance, the poor girl found her life at Hotham no better than it had been at the Huntsman—indeed, it was worse; as it is, in fact, less painful to have too much to do than to have nothing. Mrs. Hobbs, who kept the lodging, frequently sent her own child into the room to keep her company, as she called it; because she was extremely glad to get her out of her own way; but the little girl was a noisy, riotous, troublesome creature, and nothing but the desperate solitude and want of occupation could have fortified the quiet Lilly to bear with her. Mrs. Hobbs recommended her to go out, and offered to send the child with her: but, as Charlotte had strictly forbidden Lilly to show her face out-side the door, she answered that she "dare not—her cousin would be very angry;" an instance of tyranny that filled the breast of the liberal Mrs. Hobbs with con-siderable indignation. Lilly also wished, as earnestly as she could wish any thing, to see Mrs. Ryland; but even that was denied her. She knew that if she expressed such a wish, Charlotte would ask her "what *she* could want with Mrs. Ryland?"

Altogether, these preliminaries of marriage did not tend to raise Lilly's ideas of the state itself. However, the preparations for the wedding, amounting, as far as she was personally concerned, to a few new habiliments of an ordinary descrip-tion, advanced daily; and Luke Littenhaus and Lilian Dawson had been asked twice in church;[27] when there arrived a letter from Anna to say, that the two gentlemen had returned, accompanied by two others; and that, as the cooking and attendance together exceeded her abilities, and her brothers did not choose to make their appearance, that Charlotte must return to officiate in the kitchen. This was Luke's desire; and, as the ostler could not be spared to drive over for her, she was to make the journey the best way she could, and be at home early on the fol-lowing morning. It was supposed the strangers would not stay more than a couple

---

27 Otherwise known as Banns. This is a custom whereby a couple announce their inten-tion to marry during three consecutive church services. The idea is to give anyone who knows of a legal reason why the marriage should not take place a chance to speak out.

of days, and then the marriage could be proceeded with. In the mean time, Lilly was to be left at Hotham, under the care of Mrs. Hobbs; as her appearance at the Huntsman was, for various reasons, at present not desirable.

CHAPTER IX

LILLY MAKES A NEW ACQUAINTANCE

"I shall most likely be back to-morrow night," said Charlotte, as she left the door; "and remember, you are on no account to go out till I come."

"What a shame!" cried Mrs. Hobbs. "Does she want to shut up the girl all the days of her life? If I was she, I wouldn't put up with it!"

But Lilly had not the slightest idea of rebelling, though she wished extremely to go out; and the first day she stayed at home, in spite of all Mrs. Hobbs's advice to the contrary. But the second found her weaker. It happened to be washing-day: little Sally was terribly in the way on these occasions, and her mother wished nothing better than to get rid of her for the morning.

"Come! nonsense!—go along out and amuse yourself!" said she to Lilly. "Why shouldn't you, I should like to know? Who has a right to prevent you?"

"My cousin will be angry," objected Lilly.

"Angry!—Fiddlesticks! How should she know it? Besides, if she does, I'll say I sent you."

As Lilly's obedience to her cousin's precepts had hitherto been merely mechanical, it was not very difficult to change its direction, by the application of a new force. She had no arguments with which to rebut the advice of Mrs. Hobbs, and her inclination was all on the side of the seducer; so she put on her bonnet and started with the child for a walk.

Sarah Hobbs was just seven years old; a sharp, independent, forward creature, who knew her way very well about the greatest part of the town; being in the habit of roaming abroad whenever she could escape, unperceived, from the threshold; sometimes, much to her overfond mother's alarm. She was extremely spoiled, and thoroughly ungovernable. Poor Lilly was no match for such a companion; and, although she had been sent out in charge of the child, the latter very soon took command of the expedition; dragging her on from street to street, and through one lane after another; listening to no expostulations, and annoying Lilly exceedingly by not allowing her time to look in at the shop-windows. Still, she was amused; and, if Sarah would have suffered her to lounge along as she liked, she would have enjoyed the novelty exceedingly. At length, the child fell in with some of her own acquaintance, and they formed a ring and began to play at "thread-my-needle"[28] and games of the like sort; and, as she was now as determined to stay where she was as she had before been to go forward, Lilly, who had no alternative but to submit, amused herself with looking at the shops.

Presently, her attention was attracted by the sound of a horn, and the London mail dashed through the streets, dispersing the noisy children who were playing in the middle of it; who, together with Lilly and other idlers, collected about the inn-door, hard by, where it stopped, to observe the descent of the passengers, and the unloading of the luggage. When this little drama was concluded, Lilly looked about for Sarah, with the intention of inviting her to go home; but she could not see her; the child had moved off with one of her companions into another street.

Lilly felt a little uneasy, but she thought she would come back again; so she seated herself on a door-step to wait; but Sarah did not come, and, as time slipped on, she began to be very much alarmed; she was afraid to go back to Mrs. Hobbs without the child; besides, she did not know her way, nor even in which direction the house lay, so many turnings they had made since they left it; neither was she acquainted with the name of the street. Added to this, she was getting very hungry, and, as she had no money, her only prospect of procuring anything to eat was by finding the lodging; so, after much screwing of her courage, she entered a shop, and asked the people if they could tell her where Mrs. Hobbs lived. But they had never heard of such a person.

In another shop, she was told that there was a Mrs. Hobbs in West Street; and she found West Street; and even the house that had been indicated to her betwixt a butcher's shop and an ironmonger's; but Mrs. Hobbs had removed thence, and nobody knew whither she was gone; nor did it appear that any one else could give her the information she wanted.

Finding her inquiries vain, Lilly again sought the spot where she had last seen Sarah, hoping the child might yet return thither. She discovered this by means of the ostentatious crown and sceptre that hung over the door of the inn, and seated herself on the same step she had occupied before. But the afternoon passed and the evening drew on, and no Sarah appeared; then Lilly became dreadfully alarmed; so she rose once more with a desperate resolution to walk straight on for a considerable distance, in the direction she thought most likely to prove the right one: and, as she advanced, she began to have great hopes she was approaching the spot she sought; the streets and houses bearing a considerable resemblance to those which Mrs. Hobbs inhabited. She had, in fact, reached a suburb at the other extremity of the town. After wandering about and inquiring for Mrs. Hobbs for some time, till, betwixt hunger and fatigue, she was quite exhausted, she seated

---

28 A children's game where some children join hands while other children pass underneath the arch.

herself once more on the only resting-place she could command, namely, a door-step, and began to cry. The people passed backwards and forwards before her, but her tears excited no attention; crying girls being no uncommon phenomena in the suburbs of any town; and Lilly's very youthful appearance rendering her sorrows little remarkable.

She had sat there about a quarter of an hour, when there came out of the door behind her a very humbly-dressed old man and a small, rough-looking red terrier. The dog seated himself on his hind-quarters, and the man leaned against the rail that divided that step from an adjoining area. Presently, he sighed heavily and muttered some words to himself. Lilly thought he spoke to her, and, looking up at him, she perceived he was blind; she perceived also that he had not addressed himself to her; but, probably from an instinctive feeling that this forlorn-looking being might pity *her* forlornness, she ventured to ask him if he knew of a Mrs. Hobbs that lived thereabouts.

"No," replied he, "I'm a stranger here. You should ask at the shops."

"I have, sir," said Lilly, "but I can't find anybody to tell me the way."

"Why not!" said he; "do you know the street?"

"No, I don't know the name of it," returned Lilly. "I should know the house, I think, if I saw it."

"If that's all, you'd better go home and look for it to-morrow!" said the old man.

"I don't know where to go," said Lilly.

"How's that?" said he, becoming aware, by the tone of her voice, that she was weeping.

"I live at Mrs. Hobbs's, and I don't know anybody else in Hotham, except one person," she added, as she recollected Mrs. Ryland; "and I don't know where she lives, either."

"Poor child!" said the man. "Come along with me, and we'll ask about it next door;" and, with great patience, the old man accompanied her to several shops in the street, where she repeated her inquiry; but it was to no purpose. Mrs. Hobbs in West Street seemed to have been heard of by various people; but the fame of so obscure a person as Lilly's Mrs. Hobbs, living in a second floor in a back street of a suburb, was not likely to have spread beyond her own immediate neighbourhood.

"I'm afraid you won't find your home tonight," said the old man at length, as he turned his steps towards the door he had come out of. Lilly did not answer, but a convulsive sob conveyed the sense of her distress to his ears, though his eyes could not see it. "Have you no place to go to?" said he.

"No, sir," answered Lilly.

"Come in here," said he, "and I'll ask the woman of the house if she'll lodge you for the night."

But the woman of the house, who was in a little shop close by the door, was not disposed to take in a stranger under such circumstances: the girl might be a thief; and she would have nothing to do with her.

"You may take her into your room, if you like, Mr. White; but you must be answerable for her."

The old man placed his hand upon her head, probably seeking to ascertain something about her age and height.

"Come along," said he, after a little reflection; "I won't turn a child like you into the street—some mischief may come of it. You may stay in my room, if you like, till to-morrow morning. That is, if you can't do anything better."

"Thank ye, sir," answered Lilly, glad enough of the offer, and exceedingly unwilling to part with the only protector she seemed likely to get.

"Come along, then," said he, feeling his way by the wainscot[29] of the passage.

"Is it up stairs, sir?" inquired she.

"Yes," said he; "at the top of the house."

Whereupon, Lilly spontaneously took hold of his hand, and led him in the direction he wished to go. When they reached the upper story, he pushed open a door to the right with his stick, and she found herself in a small chamber, containing a bed, a rickety table, and two wooden chairs.

"Now sit down," said he, "and presently I'll give you the rug off the bed; you're young, and will be able to sleep upon the floor—children can sleep anywhere. I suppose you are a stranger in Hotham?" he added, after placing his stick in a corner, and seating himself upon the bed.

"Yes, sir," answered Lilly; "I've only been here ten days."

"I wonder you haven't learnt to know the street you live in, in that time!" said he.

"I never heard the name of it," returned Lilly.

"Can't you read? The names of the streets are to be seen at the corners of them, generally."

Lilly said she could read, but that she had not looked at the name of the street; which confession gradually led to further interrogations, till the old man found that till that morning she had had no opportunity of acquiring the knowledge, from the want of which she had suffered so much inconvenience.

"And have you no mother?" said he.

"No, sir."

"Nor father?"

"No, sir."

---

29 Decorative wood panelling on the lower part of an interior wall.

"And you've always lived with your cousins?"

"Yes, sir."

"And are your cousins good to you?"

Here Lilly hesitated: she was not capable of estimating the amount of ill-treatment that had been inflicted on her from over-work and the slavery to which she had been submitted; yet she felt that she could not say her cousins were good to her.

"And what did you come to Hotham for?' said he.

"To be married to cousin Luke," returned Lilly.

"To be married!" reiterated the old man, in amazement. "Why, how old are you?"

"Fifteen and a half, sir."

"Fifteen! I thought you were a child; but that's very young to be married. And do you like being married?"

"No, sir."

"You don't! Don't you love this cousin Luke?"

"No, sir."

"You don't love him?"

"No, sir; I don't like him at all."

"Then what do you marry him for?"

"I don't know, sir."

"That's very extraordinary," said the old man. "Are they making you marry him against your will?"

"Cousin Charlotte said I was to come to Hotham to marry cousin Luke."

"Do you know what being married is, child? I don't think you do," added he, observing that Lilly made no answer. "You can't be married against your will, you know. Have you nobody to stand up and speak for you?"

"No, sir."

"Have you no friends that you remember, besides these cousins?"

"No—I don't think I have," said Lilly, with some hesitation. "There was uncle Jacob—but he's dead; and grandpapa—"

"And is he dead, too?" inquired Abel White.

"He was drowned in the ship," said Lilly. "Cousins told me so."

"What ship?"

"The ship we came over in."

"Where did you come from?"

"I don't know, sir. I was a very little girl."

"And were your mother and father drowned too?"

"No, sir; they stayed behind, I believe; I don't remember about them."

"And you've lived ever since with these cousins?"

"Yes, sir."

All this seemed natural enough, except the marriage; but why this cousin Luke should be going to marry this ignorant, simple child, who, from what he extracted from her, had evidently only been treated as a servant in the family, he could not conceive; and the conclusion he came to was, that there was probably no marriage intended, but that cousin Luke was a libertine, who designed to take advantage of the girl's innocence and ignorance. He felt very sorry for her; but what could he do to help her? A desolate, sightless beggar! He could give her nothing but advice, and that it was quite clear she was incapable of following.

The interest of the conversation had so beguiled the time, that it was far beyond the old man's usual hour of rest, or Lilly's either, before the rug was stretched upon the floor for her night's repose. He threw himself upon the bed, with his dog beside him; and she, in spite of her hunger, her sorrows, and her hard couch, had no sooner lain down, than she was fast asleep.

When she opened her eyes in the morning, her protector was already up and seated on the side of the bed, eating a piece of bread, and supping some weak coffee out of a tin mug.

"Sleep is so sweet to the young," said he, "I did not like to wake you; but now we must be stirring; for Pipes and I must set out upon our tramp again. I should think you'll be able to find your home, now that you have the whole day before you."

Lilly rose from the floor, and stood looking at him, but made no answer.

"If I had my eyesight," he said, "beggar as I am, I'd try to help you; for I'm afraid you've nobody to save you from this man that you say you're to marry! but—" and he sighed heavily—"I can't help myself now. But listen, child: try and find somebody to protect you; and if the worst come to the worst, tell the minister, when he's going to marry you, that you have not given your consent—do you hear?"

"Yes, sir."

"You could do that, couldn't you?"

"No," said Lilly; "Luke would be so angry!"

"Then you are very much afraid of him?"

"Yes; Luke's very angry often."

Abel White sighed again.

"Well," said he, "God help the helpless! Come, Pipes," he added, rising from the bed, "we must be off. Here's a drop of water for you, before we go," and he felt for a brown jug that stood on the floor, but it was empty. "They haven't filled it," said he; "so you must go without, my dog."

"I'll fetch some water," said Lilly, with alacrity; and she quickly ran down stairs with the jug and was up again in three minutes.

"Light of foot, light of foot," said he, "poor child! but not light of heart, I fear. Come now, then, let us go down stairs;" and silently Lilly followed him.

When he had reached the bottom, he went into the little shop and paid for his lodging.

"Sorry to see you on the tramp alone, Mr. White," said the woman.

Abel sighed and folded in his lips, as if to shut in the lament that hovered on them, and which he felt it was vain to waste on this hard sympathy.

"Times is bad, too, for all trades, and yourn's no better than the rest, I doubt."

"I've no trade now," said Abel; "I beg;" and though his voice shook when he made the avowal, it was with other recollections, not with shame; for hard necessity forced him to beg. And though he might sigh at his degradation, he had no cause to blush for it.

"And how do you get along?" asked the woman. "Don't you find it hard?"

"Hard enough," said he; "I've only my dog and my stick."

"You should try to get some child to lead you," said the woman. "Mrs. Mackenzie let out her boy Tommy to a blind man, and he paid her threepence a day for the use of him; but to be sure the child came home half starved. I think, for my part, it stopped his growth, for he has never grown since."

"I shouldn't like to be responsible for another person's child," said Abel; and wishing the woman "Good day," he came out to where Lilly was standing within hearing of this conversation.

"Little girl," said he.

"Yes, sir," said Lilly.

"Good by to you now, and try and find your home; ask at all the bakers' and butchers' shops, and don't marry that man; he'll ill-treat you, child." And then, with the string that was attached to Pipes in one hand, and his stick in the other, he stepped into the street and wandered on, saying ever and anon, in a melancholy voice, "Remember the poor blind."

For a minute, Lilly stood upon the step looking after him, and then she too quitted the door; and partly because all ways were alike to her, who did not know which was the right one, and partly from an unwillingness to lose sight of the old man, she turned in the same direction he had done, slowly following his footsteps through the street.

As she went along, many thoughts and feelings awakened by her distress of yesterday and the conversation with Abel White were floating through her brain. Recollections of "grandpapa," and some faint, faint reminiscences of a former state, of something anterior to her residence with her cousins, and different to it, like those evanescent gleams of unknown scenes and persons, which make us fancy we have lived before—recollections which were nearly effaced from her dulled brain; but which, under these quickening influences, shaped themselves again to memory, as the invisible inscription on a sympathetic tablet is revived by the appropriate re-agent.[30]

Then the interrogations of the old man, and the observations he made upon her answers, suggested to her more vividly the idea that she was ill-treated and oppressed; and that it was not necessary for her to marry Luke, when she did not like it. But, at the same time, whilst she awoke to the obscure consciousness of her being an individual who had some rights and claims of her own, and who ought not, therefore, to be the mere slave and tool of others, she felt an entire conviction of her own incapacity to resist. To say *no* to any of her cousins was a thing that had never entered her mind. To say *no* to Luke was utterly impossible—she felt as if his eyes would strike her dead, if he could only read her thought.

Then, how was she to go home and meet Charlotte, after the extraordinary disobedience she had been persuaded to commit, and the dreadful aggravation of staying out all night? She did not doubt but her cousin had returned, as she had said she would, on the preceding evening, and how angry she must be! And who could tell but that Luke might be with her! How could she face them? She actually turned pale at the mere idea of it, and trembled as she walked through the streets, lest she should run against one or the other of her tyrants.

Meanwhile, the old man groped his way on, sometimes stopping to ask a question, or to receive charity, till Lilly saw that they were approaching the extremity of the town. The houses began to be farther apart, the way was unpaved, and green fields shone before her in the sun's light. She was certainly, therefore, not going in the right direction to find her cousins; and yet, though conscious that she was doing that which rendered her offence still more unpardonable, she felt cheered and relieved by the prospect before her; and with every step she took, her disinclination to return augmented. So she continued to follow the old man, with the instinctive feeling of a dog, till they had got a good way from the town, and he sat down on a bank, by the roadside, to take a rest. Lilly sat down, too, at some distance. Not that she felt tired, or even hungry; for, although she had had nothing since the previous day's breakfast, she was not conscious of any appetite, and when Abel patted his dog and gave him a bit of crust from his pocket, she felt no desire to partake of it. She was in fact wholly engrossed with her anxiety not to lose sight of the old man, and by her momentarily increasing terror at the

---

30 Crowe might be referring to Greek mythology and the idea of 'sympathetic magic'. This is representative or imitative magic, for example using a poppet or doll to represent a person.

thoughts of going back to encounter her cousin's wrath. When Abel had rested a bit, he arose and continued his journey, and Lilly crept on after him.

It was now, for the first time, that the blind man became aware that he was followed. He had doubtless before heard the light footsteps behind him, but without being awakened to any curiosity with respect to the passenger, who might chance to be going the same way as himself. But the cessation of the sound when he sat down, and its renewal when he resumed his journey, naturally attracted his attention. So he stopped, and, turning half round, leaning on his stick, with his sightless eyes in the direction of the footsteps, waited for the traveller to come up. But when he stopped, the sound ceased, for Lilly stopped too. Could his ears have deceived him? Could it be the echo of his own footsteps? Surely it must be; so he went on again; and as soon as he moved, the sound recurred. But his attention being now fixed on it, he felt quite satisfied that it proceeded from other feet than his own. So he stopped and waited again, but with exactly the same result; and, although he spoke, and asked "Who's there?" there was no answer. After trying the experiment several times, he came to the conclusion that he was followed by some animal, whose attachment to humanity, or a necessity of one kind or other, was urging it to keep near him. So he held on his way, though not without curiosity with respect to his silent companion.

The day was bright and fine, the birds were singing in the hedges, and, as they were advancing inland, the country was getting more beautiful every mile they trod. Lilly felt that if she could only have walked with the old man instead of behind him, she should have liked the journey very much—far, far better than toiling in the kitchen at home. The further she went, the less disposed she felt to return. About mid-day they came in sight of a village; and, as they entered it, the voices of the children playing in the road seemed to advertise Abel of the point he had reached. He kept his way on the right side of the little street, till about the middle of it, when Pipes seemed disposed to turn off at a right angle. Abel then struck his stick against a signpost that stood before a very humble place of entertainment; and, finding the dog was right, he followed him into the house.

CHAPTER X

LILLY CONTINUES HER JOURNEY

"It's old Daddy White, mother!" said a child, who had been standing at the door.

"Ah, Mr. White!" said the woman; "come in. I didn't expect to see you this way so soon. Why, it bean't your time for being this way yet, sure! Eh?" added she, as she looked in his face, "what's this has happened? Where's your girl?"

"Gone, Mrs. Martin," said the old man, in a tone of hopeless resignation.

"Poor little Matty's under the sod; she lies in Frampton churchyard; and I gave her a decent burial—poor as I am."

"Matty dead!" exclaimed the woman. "Lord! Mr. White, do sit down! Well, to be sure! Who'd ha' thought it! but, as my good man used to say, we're here to-day and gone to-morrow!"

Abel dropped into the seat the woman placed for him, and again there was the folding of the lips, the shutting in the lamentations that would under such circumstances have profaned the memory of her he mourned—they could not understand *his* grief!

"Well, Mr. White, and now you'll take something, I'm sure, after your walk. What shall it be! Ah, poor little Matty! It was always a bit of bread with her. I don't know as ever I see that child eat anything but a crust. 'Twas 'A bit of bread, please, ma'am,' whenever one asked her."

"She ate bread, that I might eat meat," said Abel, in a low tone.

"Ay, I believe she did," said Mrs. Martin. "Many a time I said to our Betsy, says I, 'I do believe that child denies herself, for sake of her grandfather.' 'Yes,' says Betsy, 'she's just the most patientest little creatur as ever I see.'"

Abel's lip quivered, and the corners of his mouth were convulsed; but he could not trust his voice to speak.

"We've got a nice bit of cold bacon, and the beer's quite fresh, if you'd like a draught," said Mrs. Martin.

"I'll take a pint, if you please," said Abel.

"And a mouthful of the bacon too, won't you? Come, come, you must. What's the use of grieving?" for the flash of recollections that had overwhelmed poor Abel, on reaching a spot where he had last been with his beloved one, had made him feel unable to eat; and the woman saw what had taken away his appetite.

However, she placed the bacon and beer on a small table, and having cut him a slice or two with some bread, she laid them together and handed him the food.

"I see you've got your dog yet," said Mrs. Martin, throwing Pipes a bit of the rind, and wishing to facilitate poor Abel's slow mastication by saying something consoling. Abel patted the dog which sat at his feet.

"By the by," said he, "some animal, I believe, has been following me all along the road; unless it's some poor deaf and dumb creature; for I could get no answer when I spoke to it; but I heard its foot behind me all the way from Hotham, as far as your door, I believe, or nearly."

"Look out," said Mrs. Martin, to her little boy, who was standing at her elbow; "see if there's anything there."

"No," answered the child; "there's nothing but Bop, lying next door."

"That's our neighbour's dog," said Mrs. Martin, going to the threshold to take a peep out herself.

Meanwhile, Lilly was sitting on a stone, on the opposite side of the way, uncertain what to do, and whether to go back or forward; for though the idea of the former became every moment more dreadful to her, yet the apprehension of the old man's displeasure, when he discovered that she had followed him, alarmed her very much, also. So, without being able to determine what she should do, she sat watching the door; for, observing that the house was an inn, she thought he would probably come out ere long and continue his journey; in which conjecture she was not mistaken. After a couple of hours' rest, she saw him standing on the threshold, in conversation with the woman and the child, whose head he patted, as he bade them good by, and continued his way. Lilly waited till he had gone forward about a hundred yards, and then, without questioning with herself any further, she obeyed her instinct, arose, and followed him.

As there were several persons moving to and fro in the village, till they had got beyond it, the sound of her footstep was not observable; and even when they reached the highway, she kept further in the rear than she had done before, warned by the old man's repeated endeavours to discover who was behind him. However, on a road where they were only now and then passed by a carriage or a passenger, it was not long before the footstep became audible to Abel's excited ears. For there was a growing mystery and a strange interest beginning to creep about him with regard to this unseen companion. What light foot could it be, that had tracked him thus all day?

Without holding any fixed belief on the subject, Abel White had never wholly rejected the beautiful faith that those who are gone before may be the guardian angels of the loved ones left behind; and now he could not dismiss from his mind an idea that this might be his lost Matty, still watching with tender care over her poor old grandfather.

How he wished, if it were so indeed, that she would enter into more free communion with him! and ever and anon he paused and looked back, and even ventured to murmur her dear name; but there was no answer, and when he stopped, the sound ceased.

"She will not be questioned," thought he; so he resolved to make no more efforts, lest by too much boldness he should banish his protecting spirit. So on he walked, with Lilly behind him, for a couple of hours more, when he again sat down by the wayside, to rest. All this while, Lilly had had no refreshment; nothing but a drink of water now and then from the clear springs they passed had entered her lips; and hitherto, her anxiety and fear had kept off her appetite; but now, in spite of these, the fine air and constant exercise began to have their influence, and Lilly felt hungry. How she was to get anything to eat she could not imagine: she had no money; indeed, she had never had a halfpenny in her life. She was getting tired too; and what was to be the end of it? The evening was approaching; the old man would rest somewhere, but where was she to rest? She had no prospect of getting a bed: and, bad as Lilly's fate had hitherto been, to starve in the street would be far from an agreeable termination to her woes.

The sense of her desolation came over her; the tears rolled down her cheeks; and whilst she wept within a few yards of him, the thoughts of the blind man were divided betwixt his Matty's spirit, which he believed was hovering near him, and the unfortunate little girl whom he had sheltered on the preceding evening. He wondered if she had found her home, and sighed over the melancholy fate that seemed to await her when she was married to "Cousin Luke."

Whilst he and his unseen companion were thus employed, the wheels of a carriage were heard approaching with great rapidity, and Abel had scarcely made his usual appeal of "Remember the poor blind," when a voice from the vehicle cried "Here!" and hastily threw into the road some pence which had been received at the last toll. Poor Abel's apprenticeship to the art of taking care of himself was yet but of late date; he had before had his Matty's eyes to rely on; and, although he had been long blind, he had not yet fully acquired that other sense which sometimes seems to serve the sightless almost as well as eyes. Thus, on the present occasion, in his attempt to catch the money, he rose so hastily that he almost fell forwards. He escaped this calamity; but, in the struggle, he not only dropped his stick, but Pipes got his foot crushed by the wheel of the gig. A loud cry from the poor animal advertised Abel of this misfortune—a grievous one to him, both as regarded his own convenience and his sympathy for the dog; and in great distress he sat down again, taking Pipes in his lap, and trying to ascertain, by feeling, the amount of the injury; whilst the dog expressed at once his pain and his gratitude by whining and licking his master's hand.

"Oh, Pipes! Pipes!" exclaimed the old man, "what is to become of us now?"

What, indeed! How could he go forward, without his dog to lead him? or how should he, who could not take care of himself, carry the lame animal? Poor Abel's case was bad enough before: but it was desperate now; and, absorbed in the contemplation of his distress, he forgot even the guardian angel that he had almost persuaded himself was watching over him. But Abel did not know the worst yet. Lilly, who had involuntarily drawn near when the accident happened, suddenly saw him stretch out his arms and feel about, before, behind, and on each side of him. He had just recollected his stick—where was it? It had rolled away into a ditch. Abel laid down the dog and rose.

"Oh, Pipes, Pipes!" cried he, "this is worse than all!"

At that moment, the stick was silently placed in his hand. It would have been strange to have beheld the countenance of the old man as he received it—the flush that overspread his pale face—the glow of sublime joy that illuminated his countenance.

"Matty!" murmured he, very low.

Lilly durst not speak.

"Lord, forgive me!" said he, in a tone of great reverence, joining his hands, and turning up his sightless orbs to Heaven. "Lord, forgive me that I feared! Come, Pipes," he added, stooping to lift the dog. "Come, let us go on! The Lord himself will guide us!" and, with Pipes in his arms, he attempted to move forward. But, however great his faith and his will, it was a difficult matter to guide himself without the dog. He veered from side to side, and, the sense of insecurity rendering his step uncertain, he stumbled frequently. Then, not having a hand at liberty, he repeatedly knocked his head against the branches of the trees that overhung the road; to avoid which, he stepped off the path and walked in the middle of the way, at the risk of encountering some careless horseman or driver.

The poor old man tried to keep up his spirits amongst all these difficulties; for, after so signal an instance of the favour of Providence, he thought it a sin to doubt; but the perspiration stood upon his forehead, and the hand that held the stick shook with nervous anxiety. And the difficulty of walking was not all. How was he to ascertain when he had reached the little inn where he intended to pass the night? He had travelled the country for four years, with his grandchild and Pipes; and the dog, who was well acquainted with all the houses he stopped at, regularly led his master to the doors; but now there was great danger that Abel might miss his night's lodging. In spite of his faith and his gratitude, poor human nature quailed; the helpless wanderer became every moment more confused and tremulous; and when, at this crisis, he was suddenly startled by the sound of four galloping horses and the rattling wheels of a stage-coach, and was advertised, by the loud cry of "Hoigh! hoigh!" that he was in danger, he could only stand still in his amazement, and leave them to run over him if they liked.

"Hoigh! Hoigh!" cried the coachman, again; and the scream of a female voice which proceeded from the roof warned him of the imminence of his peril; but, just at the critical juncture, a little hand was placed within his, and he was drawn aside.

The coach passed on; and Abel, overcome with wonder and gratitude, fell upon his knees, crying, "Lord, what am I, that thou shouldst care for me!"

CHAPTER XI

LILLY'S FORTUNES SHOW SYMPTOMS OF IMPROVEMENT

Abel rose from his knees, brushed the dust from them, again took Pipes in his arms, and, with a reverent heart, was just about to step forward, when the same little hand was thrust into his, and a timid voice whispered, "Let me lead you."

Abel's first, momentary idea was, that it was the voice of an angel, but the delusion was as quickly dispersed—the hand that held his was assuredly of flesh and blood.

"Who are you?" said he.

"Lilly Dawson, that slept in your room last night," replied she.

"But how came you here?" asked he, now completely recognising her voice.

Lilly hesitated, afraid to confess the truth, lest he should be displeased.

"Is it you that have been following me all along the road?" said he.

"Yes," answered she.

"Then it was you that gave me my stick, and saved me from the coach?"

"Yes," said Lilly.

"But why didn't you answer, when I spoke?" he inquired.

"I was afraid you'd be angry, and send me back," answered Lilly, gathering courage, as she perceived no symptoms of displeasure.

"Lord, thy ways are wonderful!" exclaimed Abel, almost as much amazed at this *dénouement*, and as much disposed to believe it a direct interference of Providence, as when he imagined himself protected by the spirit of his grandchild.

"But why have you come so far, child?" said he. "What is to become of you in this strange place; and how are you to find your way home again?"

Lilly hung down her head, and was silent; she scarcely knew herself why she had come so far; and she was afraid to avow that she did not wish to go home again.

"Is it because you wish to avoid marrying your cousin?" said Abel.

"Yes," answered Lilly.

"But how can I keep you?" said he; "I have no home to give you, my child; I'm but a beggar myself—a beggar and a wanderer on the earth."

"I could lead you," said Lilly, wishing to induce him to let her stay, by suggesting the service she might do him.

"But you wouldn't like to wander about the country with a blind beggar?" said Abel.

"I should like to keep with you," answered she.

"But what will your cousins say when they miss you?"

"I hope they won't find me," said Lilly; and Abel felt that the little hand which he still held trembled with terror at the idea he had raised.

"Then you don't wish to return to them?"

"No," answered she.

"What, never! Have you no love for them?"

"No, none," she answered, speaking with more decision than before.

"And you really wish to stay with me?"

"Yes," said she.

"Then God's will be done!" said Abel; "for I believe it is he that has put it into your heart to do this. If you had a father or mother, I should think it my duty to take you back again; but, since nobody seems to have any claims on you but these cousins, and they, I'm afraid, have done *their* duty badly by you, I don't think it's mine to reject the blessing the Lord has sent me; so, come along."

Abel was naturally very anxious to learn as much of his new companion as he could extract from her. He first asked her about her adventures of the day; what had put it into her head to follow him, instead of trying to find her home; and how she had sped during the journey. Lilly could not tell herself why she had followed him; for it was instinct rather than design that had guided her foot-steps—one reason, however, she could assign; and that was, that she preferred to go any way rather than to meet her cousin Charlotte, who she expected would be at the lodging before she could get there. As for the journey, Lilly said she had got on very well, except that she was rather tired and hungry. Abel was quite shocked when he learnt that she had been fasting so long, and immediately insisted upon her sitting down and relieving the exigencies of her appetite by a bit of bread, some of which he always carried in his pocket for the use of himself and Pipes.

Lilly enjoyed the bread very much, especially now that her heart was light-ened of its great care. "I haven't been hungry long," said she, "because I was so frightened, for fear you'd send me back again."

When she had rested and refreshed herself, Abel proposed continuing their walk; "for we have not much farther to go to-night," said he; "and then you shall have some supper and a good night's rest. She's a decent woman at the house we're going to, and she'll be good to you—she was always good to Matty."

Lilly wondered who Matty was, and where she was; and could not help feel-ing half afraid that she would come and supersede her; for, now that she had hold of the old man's arm, and that, so far from being angry, she found that he was extremely glad of her company and assistance, she felt a fulness of content that she had never known before; and, forgetful of her previous fatigue and exhaustion, she trudged on with a step as light as her heart.

There was something in Abel's countenance and manner, too, that loosed her tongue and inspired her with an ease and confidence quite unusual to her. He did not treat her with contempt, nor call her a "stupid fool," as her cousins were wont to do. On the contrary, he spoke to her with gentleness, and questioned her about her past life, as if he supposed he was addressing a rational being, whilst his thin pale features, and the gray hair that floated over his shoulders, inspired her at once with pity and reverence. Here was no chilling fear to freeze up her young heart; Abel was as helpless as she was; and she had seen how much he needed her services; so that their relation at once assumed the character of mutual dependance.

As for the old man, the more he questioned her, the more he felt that he was doing her no wrong in permitting her to follow her inclinations, or in accepting services so needful to himself, in exchange for the little protection he could afford her. Hardship and poverty certainly awaited her in the line of life she was choosing to embark in; perhaps want; but he had no assurance that the marriage with her cousin was to exempt her from these evils; whilst he was quite certain that it would entail others quite as bad. Added to which, unable to divine any motive for Luke's wishing to marry this destitute oppressed child, he very much doubted the honesty of his intentions with respect to her. In short, the advantages both he and Lilly derived, and the evils they both escaped by their junction, were so manifest, that he could not help believing that it was the providence of God that had brought them together, to help each other; and he felt scarcely less fortified and exalted by this evidence of heavenly superintendence, than he would have done, had his first notion been confirmed, and the spirit of Matty proved to be the ministering angel sent to watch over him.

"Let me carry Pipes a bit now," said she, after they had proceeded about half a mile.

"You're not afraid of him," said Abel.

"Oh no," answered Lilly; "I love dogs. We'd a great big dog at the Huntsman; he was always chained up, for he was very savage, and nobody durst go near him."

"Who wouldn't be savage that was always chained up?" said Abel. "Most frequently man himself makes the cruelty he suffers by."

"I dare say it was being tied up that made Nero savage," said Lilly; "for he wasn't savage when he was young."

"Some animals are naturally malicious," said Abel; "but I believe it is generally man that makes them so. He is the tyrant and the curse of the races below him; but I question much whether he will not be hereafter accountable for their perversion, as well as for their sufferings."[31]

This was the first humane or rational sentiment that Lilly had ever heard

---

31 See Appendix B for Crowe's views on dogs and cruelty to animals.

clearly and distinctly enunciated in her life. If by chance a reflection of this nature had been dropped by the passing guests she waited on at the Huntsman, she was too much absorbed in attending to her business, and her intellect was too much blunted to heed it. Her ears were open now; but she had, nevertheless, but a very obscure conception of Abel's meaning—of his allusion to man's future account-ability she had not the least. She did not, however, admire him the less for not understanding him. On the contrary, she looked up at him with both wonder and reverence, whilst she silently patted and stroked poor Pipes, as a practical acknow-ledgment of that much of Abel's homily that her natural sympathies enabled her to appropriate.

Thus, each lightened of much of their cares, they trudged cheerily along the road; Abel questioning and Lilly answering; a process as instructive to her as to him; for, whilst he gathered information with respect to her past life, she, in some measure, learnt to review it and to comprehend it. She, at least, began to perceive that such a life as hers had hitherto been was not a necessity, and that her igno-rance had been abused and herself ill-treated. She felt every moment more happy that she had followed Abel, and this self-gratulation inspired her with an anima-tion that transformed her into quite a different person to "the stupid little girl at the Huntsman;" whilst, at the same time, it lent an alacrity to her services, that stood well in the place of the affection that was yet undeveloped. Matty herself could scarcely have been more ready and attentive, and certainly not more hum-ble.

No longer afraid of missing his resting-place, which was a very lowly inn standing somewhat back from the road, and anxious not to over-fatigue his com-panion, Abel frequently indulged in a little repose; so that it was eight o'clock before Lilly announced that, from his description, she thought they had reached the spot. The exclamation of the good woman of the house soon announced that she was right; and then came the usual inquiries after Matty; and, by the answers, Lilly learnt, for the first time, that this rival whom she had begun to fear was dead.

"Well, to be sure!" exclaimed Mrs. Wylie, "is Matty Lintock dead, with her fair hair and her pretty blue eyes! Who'd have thought it! Well, I'm sorry, to be sure! And you must be badly without her, Mr. White—but I see you've got an-other girl."

"Yes," replied Abel, gravely. "God sent her to me in my need."

"Well, to be sure! Matty Lintock dead!" pursued Mrs. Wylie; "I don't know how to bring it to my mind; she was such a fresh, wholesome-looking little crea-tur; one would never have thought it."

"She took a fever," said Abel, speaking with difficulty; "the scarlet fever—it was raging in the place, and it was His will to take her from me."

"And it's that has brought you back this way so soon, I suppose?" said Mrs. Wylie.

"Yes," replied the old man; "I'm going back to tell her mother that Matty's gone;" and thus through the whole way they travelled there were lamentations for the child.

From various motives, Abel entered into no explanations about Lilly, who, weary with her long walk, was glad to get some supper, and go to the tidy bed that was provided for her; for Abel was not treated as a beggar—having never before been seen on the road exactly in that character. He had, indeed, often received gratuitous relief from the charitable, who were moved by his blindness and his gray hairs to offer it; but he had hitherto travelled as a merchant of tapes, and pins and needles, carrying the basket that held his wares, slung before him by a strap, passing over his shoulders; whilst Matty had charge of the merchandize and conducted the sale. But it was impossible for him to pursue this trade alone; and, when death deprived him of his grandchild, he had disposed of his basket and determined to beg his way home again—if home he could be said to have.

CHAPTER XII

THE HISTORY OF ABEL WHITE

Abel White was the son of a very poor curate in the West of England; but, poor as his father was, his childhood had been well cared for. A heavy sufferer himself by the anomalous position he was placed in—that of a gentleman with seventy pounds a year—Gilbert White resolved not to ruin his son by the same mistake; so he put his pride in his pocket, and, instead of setting Abel to study the classics, he gave him a good plain education, and endeavoured to shape his views to an humbler but less anomalous line of life.

Abel, however, without any particular talent, had a considerable taste for books, and was rather averse to his father's prudent project; although he complied so far as to allow himself to be apprenticed to a haberdasher and hosier in the county town; and from his own good principles performed his duty in the situation selected for him. Still, he did not like it; and his love for books, augmenting with the difficulties necessarily in the way of his obtaining them, became a passion, to indulge which he deprived himself of that degree of rest that the maintenance of his health required. The books he borrowed of whoever would lend them; but his means of obtaining light being very limited, he endeavoured to train himself to read with scarcely any; straining his eyes night after night, during the hours he should have passed in sleep, to decipher the page by the faint gleams of the moon or a rushlight; persuading himself that habit was everything; and that in due time he should see, like a cat, in the dark; till he at length produced a disease in his eyes, which, after incapacitating him for any such pleasures for the future, finally, at a later period of his life, terminated in total blindness.

Before this misfortune overtook him, however, Abel was a husband and a father. The first thing that reconciled him to measuring tape was love. The object of his passion being almost as poor as himself, it was only by complying entirely with his father's views that he could hope to maintain her; the visionary projects he had formed of finding some more clerkly vocation being entirely dissipated by the weakness of his sight. His father, foreseeing the calamity that awaited him, and content with the character of the young woman, eagerly promoted the match; dreading lest his son should be cast upon the world in his darkness, without any hand of duty or affection to guide him. He therefore strained every effort to aid the young couple; and, by the co-operation of her friends, who looked upon her union with the son of the curate as an ascending step in life, they were ultimately established in a respectable small shop, sufficiently stocked with haberdashery to make a fair beginning. Orderly, prudent, self-denying, and strictly honest, Abel White and his wife carried on their little trade with small profits but with great content. They did not desire much, and, as they had only one child, they did not need much; and, had it not been for Abel's failing sight, they would have lived almost without a care. But his eyes were always growing worse, till at length poor Abel was blind: and he could no more behold the ever comfortable face of his affectionate wife, or sun himself in the bright eyes of his little Martha.

As misfortunes never come singly, it was not long before this calamity was followed by another. In reaching a box from an upper shelf, Mrs. White overstrained herself, and, from some consequences of the injury, fell into bad health. As soon as this occurred, her first thought was for Abel—what was to become of him if her services failed him, or if she died?

Alarmed for her much-loved husband, she immediately set about endeavouring to alleviate the threatened misfortune, by providing a successor to herself in the person of their little girl. She commenced immediately teaching the child, not only to wait upon her father, but to manage the shop; and, being a docile and intelligent creature, little Matty made such progress under her tuition, that when at fourteen she lost her mother, Abel's inextinguishable regrets at the departure of his wife were not materially aggravated by other evils—so well did Matty supply her place. She was the most affectionate of daughters, the most prudent of housekeepers—ever cheerful, active, and loving; and for the first four years of his widowhood Abel had daily cause to rejoice and be thankful.

But, besides her other recommendations, Matty was very pretty, and this, added to the many valuable qualities she possessed, procured her several offers of marriage from the young tradesmen of the neighbourhood. They looked upon Matty as a fortune in herself; but, as all their proposals involved the necessity of a separation from her father, she unhesitatingly rejected them, although one or two of the more eager aspirants offered to pay a small stipend for the old man's board and subsistence. But to leave her father to the mercy of strangers, Matty could not consent, and the suitors were therefore nonsuited; till at length one presented himself who won Matty by what was, at once, her strength and her weakness— namely, her affection for her father.

The name of the successful candidate was Giles Lintock. His father had been in the same line of business as Abel, though on a rather more extensive scale; but, being but an indifferent tradesman, he had never been a successful one. He had just made a living out of his shop, and that was all. When he died, his only son Giles succeeded to this inheritance, such as it was; and, on more accounts than one, Giles was desirous of obtaining the hand of Matty White. In the first place, her beauty pleased him; and he entertained a sentiment towards her that he digni- fied with the name of love; in the next, he was no more fond than his father had been before him of being nailed to his own counter; and such a wife as Matty would be invaluable to him, inasmuch as her trustworthy diligence would release him from confinement, without any risk to his pocket; and thirdly, he considered that Abel White's custom and stock, small though they were, would be no bad addition to his own.

Aware of the rock on which the other suitors had split, Giles went more cun- ningly to work, and won Matty's affections through her devotion to her father. Promises cost him nothing; the old man was to live with them; and the com- forts that were to surround his declining years formed the subject of many pretty pictures. Neither did Giles do this with a deliberate intention to deceive; but he wished to marry Matty White, and he seized the most ready way to gain his object, without thinking or caring how far he might be able or willing, hereafter, to fulfil his promises. They answered his purpose for the time perfectly. Whether Matty might have ever given him her heart, had he not thus blinded her through her affections, is extremely doubtful; for, although he did not want some of those qualities which are apt to win women, it is probable that her just mind would have been repelled by his want of principle. As it was, she shut her eyes to his faults, believing that his kind heart and his regard for herself would soon correct them. He had had an indifferent father and a disreputable mother; "and it was only a wonder that poor Giles was as good as he was." Such was Matty's view of the case; and, as Abel both literally and metaphorically saw only with her eyes, it was natural that he should make no opposition to the match.

So they were married. Poor people make no settlements; and, as soon as the ceremony was performed, Giles stepped into possession of all his wife's little havings and holdings; for what was Abel's was hers; the old man being like a child in their hands, and never thinking of interfering or objecting to any thing that was proposed. In accordance, therefore, with Giles's plan, the little house and shop which had been bought by the friends of the young people at the period of Abel's marriage was sold; and, whilst the proceeds of the sale went into Giles's pocket, the stock was removed to augment his own. It is true, that Abel came with it, and was ensconced in a tidy room which his daughter had furnished with every comfort for him; and at first matters went well enough. But the poor young wife soon saw cause for alarm. It was not that her husband left the management of the business entirely to her—that she did not mind; but his draughts upon the till became daily more disproportioned to their receipts; and she soon had reason to know that the company he kept was not likely to improve his morals. She concealed her apprehensions from her father as long as she could; and, although Abel did think his son-in-law was too much abroad, it was not till his daughter was confined of her first child that he became in any degree aware of Giles's extravagance and irregularities; for even then the husband could not stay at home to take care of the shop; whilst the domestic funds ran so low, that there was actually a deficiency of ready money for the incidental expenses of the occasion. Now, as Matty was a frugal housekeeper, and they had a tolerably good business, it was not difficult to guess the source of the deficit. However, Matty begged her father to say nothing on the subject to Giles, for, of all things, she dreaded any disagreement in that quarter. Abel obeyed her; and, when she recovered, matters went on as before.

But it was a hard struggle for the young wife to keep the business afloat, and only by means of the greatest caution and self-denial that she succeeded; and even these would not have sufficed for the six years that she fought through her difficulties, had not her merits and sufferings excited the sympathy both of her customers and her creditors. The former adhered to her, and the latter spared her, often to their own inconvenience. But Giles's evil genius was too strong for them; and, in spite of their indulgence and her struggles, every year saw her embarrassments augmenting; till at last she sank altogether, and the shop was shut up. But even then her friends did not fail her; they engaged two rooms for her, and her father, and her children; and exerted themselves to furnish her with needlework. But the reckless libertine, whose habits and tastes had sunk with his fortunes, poisoned the atmosphere of even this humble abode; and at length drove Abel out of it; and the son of the curate was obliged to take refuge in the poor-house, where he pined in sorrow for his daughter's misery and his own separation from her.

This last blow was the heaviest of all to Matty; but it was one she had long

foreseen and tried to provide against. With such a husband and a young family
of children, she knew that she must, ere long, resign all hope of being her poor
blind father's guide and comfort; and she had early set about preparing a substitute, as her mother had done. She had accustomed her eldest child, who was
called Matty, after herself, from her infancy, to attend upon her grandfather; and,
as the little girl was a counterpart of what she had been in her own childhood,
her instructions were perfectly successful. Matty the second became Abel's good
angel; and, the attachment being mutual, she almost broke her heart when the
old man was withdrawn from her care, and sent, or rather when he retired, to the
poor-house; for, to the last, his daughter sought to avoid the separation. But it was
inevitable. Whilst they resided in the shop, although the blind father had many
rebuffs to encounter, yet, as the family had a decent house over their heads, and
Giles was rarely at home, Matty contrived to prevent a disruption; but, when they
were circumscribed to two small rooms, their remaining together was no longer
practicable. Not that the husband was often at home, either; but his visits were
uncertain; and, when he did come, his behaviour was intolerable.

Abel pined in the poor-house, and little Matty pined out of it; but how they
could be brought together it was not easy to see, till a friendly neighbour suggested the plan that had afterwards succeeded so well.

"Why couldn't Abel go about the country with little Matty, and grind an
organ, as I saw a blind man doing to-day?" said Mrs. Jones. "She's such a steady
little thing, that she could lead him well enough, although she is so young; and
Mr. White is hale and hearty, and could walk well enough."

"I don't know that," said Mrs. Lintock. "My father is not so strong as he was."

"To be sure not," replied the other; "how should he be, shut up from week's
end to week's end in a workhouse? Besides, any body may see he's breaking his
heart there, poor old man, and well he may!"

The mother at first recoiled from the idea of letting her pretty little Matty
travel about the country, exposed to so many perils, and with no other protector
than an old blind man; but there were various inducements, on the other hand,
that at length induced her to hint the proposal to her father; and his eagerness
for the realization of the project soon bore down the remaining objections. It was
evident to herself also that she should be obliged, ere long, to part with the child,
who must needs get her own living, and be sent into the world to encounter the
evils and difficulties that bestrew the path of the very poor; for besides that, the
mother could not maintain her—the home visited by that reckless father was not
a home for a young girl.

Then, the confinement she necessarily endured was as injurious to the child
as the atmosphere of the poor-house was to Abel; and finally difficulties were

considerably alleviated by a few of Mrs. Lintock's former friends coming forward, and agreeing to fit out the old man, by subscription, as a small merchant in threads, tapes, pins, and needles—such wares, in short, as he had formerly been accustomed to deal in; and with these, neatly arranged in a basket, and with a volume of instruction and advice stored in her little head, Matty and her grandfather were launched into the world, in this new character; and so well did the child fulfil the expectations that had been formed of her, that all parties had reason to congratulate themselves on the success of the enterprise. Not only did Abel contrive to earn a living, but, when he made his annual visits to his daughter, he had generally something to spare in aid of her hard-earned and slender means; whilst the constant change of air, exercise, and contentment kept the travellers in better health than they had ever known before.

And thus for four years had Abel White and his little companion roamed the world, when an attack of malignant fever snatched her from his arms, and left him alone to grope his way back as best he could, with his sightless eyes, to communicate the sad news to his unfortunate daughter.

CHAPTER XIII

THE TRAVELLERS REACH THE END OF THEIR JOURNEY

No words can depict poor Abel's woe at the death of his grandchild! Everything combined to render his loss inappreciable. There was not only the inexpressible love he had felt for her, and the anticipation of her mother's grief, but there was also his own utter desolation. He must grope his way back, and, having poured this additional drop of bitterness into his daughter's already too bitter cup, shut himself up in the poor-house again for the rest of his days. It was when he was overwhelmed with this weight of affliction that Lilly came to his aid; and it was natural enough that he should look upon her as the especial gift of God. Certainly, no two persons could need each other more, and they had met in the very nick of time—each helpless and forlorn, but capable of incalculable service to the other.

When Matty died, Abel had sold off his basket and its contents, knowing he should not be able to carry on his trade alone; so that he was altogether in flourishing circumstances as regarded pecuniary matters, and was able to supply his new companion's necessities without inconvenience.

Never had Lilly waked with so cheery a feeling as she did after her first night's rest at Mrs. Wylie's; and no wonder! For, however poor a lot it may seem to travel the world as the companion of a blind beggar, certain it was that her condition was immeasurably improved by this change in her fortunes. The very sense of freedom was much in itself; and the escaping from her harsh cousins and the dreaded Luke was a blessed emancipation from a hated slavery, hitherto indeed endured with dull submission, because not understood; but which, seen by the light of a single day's liberty, became abhorrent. Then, Abel White was such a contrast to the Littenhaus family. The curate's son had not forgotten his gentle blood and early breeding; moreover, he was by nature a kind-hearted, reflecting man; and the soft tones and (compared to what she had been accustomed to) polished language, in which he addressed her, fell musically on her ear, and soothingly on her heart; arousing and awakening the sympathies that had languished in the cold atmosphere that had hitherto surrounded her. Besides, Lilly was to him an angel—a God-given help and aid—and therefore doubly to be cherished; so that, from the neglect and contempt to which she had been formerly subjected, she found herself all at once translated into an object of the tenderest care and almost reverential regard.

This was just what her nature needed, and, under the warm sun of kindness, it unfolded with astonishing rapidity. It was so cheering and encouraging to find her little offices requited with gracious acceptance instead of ungracious sufferance; she began to feel what it is to live in the sweet service of love; and the old blind beggar, growing from hour to hour in her affections, exciting her wonder by his remarks and conversation, and her gratitude by his thoughtful kindness, became a deity to her, as she was a ministering angel to him; whilst every day's intercourse, by convincing him of the bodily subjection and mental blindness in which she had been held, tended to release his conscience from any uneasiness with respect to the propriety of facilitating her escape, and keeping her with himself.

So they begged along the way, from day to day; for, although Abel was not wholly penniless, his funds were not so large as to preclude the necessity of replenishing his purse; and he had, at present, no other means of doing so, except by asking charity. But, whatever evil the initiation into so idle a life might be likely to do Lilly, he endeavoured to counteract by the instruction he administered: and in this manner, they advanced by easy journeys, till they reached the South West of England.

It was not till they were approaching the town where Matty Lintock and her husband lived, that Abel White began to feel in its full extent the embarrassments that awaited him. Though the memory of his little grandchild was as warm in his heart as ever, the interest excited by Lilly, and the excitement produced by the singular circumstances of their meeting, had considerably relieved his affliction, and raised him from the "slough of despond"[32] into which he had previously sunk;

---

32 A deep bog in John Bunyan's *The Pilgrim's Progress* and an allegory for deep depression, hopelessness and despondence.

so that he had not sufficiently measured the difficulties that were before him. But now they presented themselves in their full proportions. There was not only the pain of appearing before his daughter without her child, but there was the embarrassment of intruding a destitute stranger into the poor family that were unable to support themselves.

The idea of abandoning Lilly he could not bear; yet, unless friends came forward and fitted him out with a basket again, what could he do with her? Or what prospect was there for himself but the workhouse? To be sure, he might beg; but, although necessity had reconciled him to the temporary expedient, he recoiled from the degradation as regarded himself, and the corruption that would ensue as regarded Lilly, if he relied on charity as his permanent resource. Oppressed with these anticipations, he became gradually silent and abstracted; whilst Lilly, aware of the change, though unconscious of the cause, toiled on wonderingly and timidly by his side; for she had been so subdued by her early training, that the least reaction or apparent withdrawal of kindness banished her new-found confidence, and threw her back into her former feelings of subjection.

It was on a cold, wet, dismal September evening that the poor travellers entered the city they were bound to. The wind blew in gusts through the streets, extinguishing the lamps, turning people's umbrellas inside out, and sending their hats skimming through the puddles and streaming kennels. As it was Saturday night, too, the streets were more than ordinarily thronged, and the poor blind man and his inexperienced guide found themselves in everybody's way and everybody in theirs.

Heartily glad was Lilly when they turned in at an open door, and Abel, with a heavy step and slow, led the way up stairs, till they reached the upper story. Here he stopped; and, bidding Lilly remain where she was, he laid his hand on the latch of a door to the right, and then, after pausing for a moment, to summon courage for the scene that awaited him, he lifted it and entered. One dim candle burnt within, but that was enough to show Martha Lintock who it was; and never doubting that her child was behind him, she started from her seat and rushed to the door, crying, "Oh, father! Oh, Matty!" and, before he could prevent her, she had taken the astonished Lilly in her arms and dragged her into the room. Abel comprehended, though he did not see, her mistake.

"Why, it's not Matty!" she exclaimed as soon as the light fell on Lilly's face. "Why, father, who's this? Where is Matty? Oh, father, has anything happened to Matty?" she added anxiously, seeing the old man standing with his stick shaking in his trembling hand, unable to speak. "Is Matty dead, father?—and have you brought home a stranger instead of her?" said she, thrusting Lilly from her.

"Matty's gone!" said Abel, with a quivering lip and voice; "the Lord has taken her from us!"

"Oh, Matty! Matty!" cried the mother, sinking into a chair and covering her face with her apron. "Oh, Matty, my child!"

"It was God's will," said Abel. "You know, Martha, I would have given my life for hers, and blessed him for taking it."

"But where was it? How was it?" asked Mrs. Lintock, when her tears had in some degree relieved her heart. "She that was so strong and healthy!"

"She died of a fever," said Abel, "nearly three hundred miles from this."

"Three hundred miles!" exclaimed Mrs. Lintock, the current of her feelings diverted for a moment; "then how have you ever got along?"

"Badly enough, at first," said Abel, "till God sent me help."

"What help?" inquired his daughter, looking for the first time with some interest at the stranger.

"This child," said Abel, laying his hand on Lilly's head; for, alarmed at the first outburst of the mother's grief and confused by the instinctive consciousness that she was an intruder, she had crept close to his side for countenance and support. "This child, Martha," said he. "I had lost my stick, and the dog was lame and could not lead me; and I stood in the middle of the highway, sightless, helpless, and alone. But God saw my distress——and sent this child to be my guide."

"And has she led you all the way?—all the three hundred miles?" inquired Mrs. Lintock, with surprise.

"Two hundred and fifty of them," said he, "and more."

"Sit down," said Martha, showing Lilly a seat, whilst the tears streamed down her cheeks. "Father, you're still standing—forgive me! But you know how I loved Matty!"

"Everybody loved her!" said Abel, as his daughter led him to a chair: "there wasn't a house we stopped at along the road, where the good woman wasn't fond of Matty. But how are Lizzy and the boys?"

"Lizzy's in bed with a cold, and the boys are not come in yet," answered Mrs. Lintock, still sobbing, as her heart swelled with the recollection of her favourite child.

"And Giles?" said Abel.

"I haven't seen him for these ten days," was the reply. "But you'll be hungry, father?"

"No," answered Abel, turning out the contents of his pockets, which amounted to four or five shillings; "I am not hungry;" for the pain of this melancholy meeting had banished hunger; "but poor Lilly has had nothing since the morning. Here's something to buy food."

"I'll go below and get something," said Martha, quitting the room.

Abel sat with his forehead resting on his hands, that were crossed on the top of his stick; Pipes, stretched out with his head betwixt his fore-legs, and his nose close to his master's feet, lay in an attitude of expectation rather than of repose, feeling instinctively that there was a want of harmony in the mode of their reception, and, consequently, not quite assured that they were at the end of their day's journey; whilst Lilly, actuated by the same feeling, sat in an attitude of doubt and timidity on the edge of her chair, as if she were preparing to start up and evacuate the premises on the shortest notice. Her very breathing was so low and suppressed, that Abel's quick ears, intensified as his hearing was by the want of sight, could not detect that she was in the room; and for an instant the doubt crossed him whether she had not been fluttered away by Martha's surprise and emotion, and the sense of her own strangeness and intrusion.

"Lilly," said he.

"Yes, father," answered Lilly; for he had taught her to call him so.

"Don't be frightened, my child; poor Martha's not herself yet."

"Shall we go away again to-morrow?" asked Lilly, already dreading some reverse of fortune, and anxious to resume her previous happy life.

"Not to-morrow," answered Abel, himself oppressed with fears for the future.

"But soon, father? Shall we go soon?"

"I hope so," said Abel; "but we must trust in God, Lilly, and be patient."

But poor Lilly's faith was yet in its infancy. She knew nothing of God but the name, before she met Abel; and, although he had lost no opportunity of enlightening her ignorance since, he had not been able to awaken in her any lively feeling of devotion or trust in the unseen. Lilly discerned nothing about her but the material world, and had yet no glimpse of the airy spirits that guide us through its labyrinths. Her meeting with Abel, which he, in his child-like faith, looked upon as a special interference of Providence, appeared to her simply the result of her seating herself on the step of the house he lodged in. In short, Lilly had not arrived at seeing that "there is a Divinity that shapes our ends, rough-hew them as we may."[33] So that her heart sunk within her; and for the first time since she was Abel's acknowledged companion, she felt very unhappy; so unhappy, that although she had had no food for several hours, she could not eat, and out of this circumstance gleamed the first little ray of comfort since she had entered Martha Lintock's door. The good, motherly Martha was distressed at seeing that neither of her guests could partake of the food she had purchased; and beginning to forget her own grief in their dejection, she tried to cheer them, and efface the effects of their painful reception. She questioned them about their journey; and, addressing herself chiefly to Lilly—for to be kind to Lilly was to be kindest to Abel—she

---

33 From *Hamlet*, Act 5 Scene II.

endeavoured to restore her to confidence, and not without some success; for Lilly was very susceptible to external influences. She had been easily subdued, yielding without resistance to the oppression that extinguished her; and she was as easily won by kindness, and quick to forget past storms in present sunshine.

At a late hour, Mrs. Lintock's boys came home; two wild lads of ten and eleven, who had been helped to some employment by the mother's friends, but who, it was feared, had too much of the father's blood in them to make much of it. They and the grandfather slept in one room, whilst Lilly shared the other with Martha and her little sick girl.

CHAPTER XIV

LILLY MAKES FRIENDS

The following morning being Sunday, whilst Martha stayed at home to nurse her sick child, Abel took Lilly and the two boys to the Cathedral. The latter, however, preferred amusing themselves outside the doors; but Lilly and the old man went in, and found seats on a bench appropriated for the poor;[34] and here, for the first time, Lilly became sensible to the effects of music. The solemn grandeur of the interior, too, impressed her; and the chanting of the choristers in their white surplices, together with the loud swell of the organ, filled her with a strange sensation of awe and wonder. Till she joined Abel, she had never been in any place of worship; since that, she had been in several, of various denominations, for none came amiss to him—he was ready to pray with all men; but neither the decent routine of the establishment, nor the more energetic appeals to Heaven of the dissenting churches,[35] had ever penetrated Lilly's understanding, or touched her heart, through which her understanding was to be reached. She was there an unmoved spectator of a drama she did not comprehend; and which had no meaning for her. But now the lofty nave, and the dimly-lighted aisles, and the prayers flung up to Heaven in such appealing tones by those young voices, awakened her imagination; and when she saw the dean move slowly up the aisle to the altar, preceded by the verger, she felt inspired by a vague reverence for she knew not what—an undefined consciousness that there was something out of, and beyond, this world, and an obscure notion of the purport of this pompous and solemn worship.

In this Cathedral Abel's father had been a minor canon, and the blind man,

34 Rich parishioners were able to rent or appropriate pews and there was a movement towards setting aside free pews for the poor.
35 The Established Church was endorsed by the State and religion was ordered and mediated through ordained ministers. Dissenters did not approve of state interference in religious matters and felt that religion and faith were individual and personal matters.

when a boy, had been acquainted with every nook of the edifice, and with every monument it contained. There, in the north transept, lay the ancestors of the blind beggar; and he showed Lilly the tomb of Rupert de Witte, with its knightly emblazonments; and the flat stone that covered the remains of Dame Margery White, Abel's great grandmother.

Lilly was very silent that day, and she wished exceedingly that the next had been Sunday too, that she might hear that music and see those "long drawn aisles again."[36]

In the mean time, poor Abel's mind was engrossed with the very important consideration of how he was to keep out of the workhouse, and how contrive to subsist without parting with Lilly. Remaining with his daughter was out of the question, unless he and his *protégée* could have done something to support themselves; nor even then would it have been practicable, if Giles Lintock came home; which he might do any day. His darling project was, again to start on his travels, with a well-furnished basket of threads and tapes; but where was he to get it? The whole afternoon Abel sat racking his brain for some expedient that would enable him to resume his previous mode of life. Silent and abstracted, with his forehead resting on his stick, as was his usual attitude when depressed or perplexed, he forgot Lilly, or appeared to forget her, when he was thinking most about her: whilst she, shrinking into herself, with her feelings of strangeness and timidity, found herself all at once, and most unexpectedly, translated from the free air and roving life she had so much enjoyed, to close confinement in a dull, dark room, the very atmosphere of which seemed heavy with sorrow; and, instead of the easy confidence and tender watchfulness that, during their journey, had been gradually transforming her from a dull serf to an animated human being, with consciousness and affections, she felt herself a burthen and an intruder—a neglected alien, in an unhappy family, who had too many wants and sorrows of their own to have any sympathy to spare for hers. So she sat crouching in a corner, unwilling to obtrude her existence on any body; whilst Abel was buried in his cogitations, and Martha busied herself in nursing her sick child.

In this way passed the Sunday, and Lilly went to bed extremely unhappy; but the sorrows of childhood—and Lilly, though nearly sixteen, was a mere child— do not banish sleep; so she slept soundly, unconscious that Martha had been up all night with Lizzy, whose illness had taken a sudden turn for the worse. When she opened her eyes, she saw the child tossing on the bed with crimson cheeks, and the poor mother kneeling beside her, looking pale and worn with her night's watching; and with her own throat and head bound up with a handkerchief, as if suffering from cold.

---

36 From Thomas Gray, "Elegy Written in a Country Churchyard", 1750-1.

Lilly arose, and dressed herself in silence, and whilst she was doing so, Mrs. Lintock asked her if she thought she could light a bit of fire in the next room and boil a little water for breakfast. She said she could; and set about it, with the readiness prompted by her desire to do something that should make her situation in the family less uncomfortable, and with the adroitness acquired by long practice. The fire was lighted, the water boiled, and the humble breakfast served, with an alacrity that surprised Mrs. Lintock, in whose eyes she had hitherto exhibited herself as little brighter than the stupid little girl of former times; and, being once set to work, and seeing that she gave satisfaction and could make herself useful, Lilly kept herself astir; setting the rooms in order, preparing the dinner for the boys, and making the barley-water for the sick child; and as for all she did Martha thanked her kindly, she became hourly more capable, resuming her former habit of diligence, enlightened and directed by her lately-acquired intelligence.

Thus passed the second day; and, on the third, her services were more needed still; for now Martha was also very ill, and unable to rise; so that Lilly had all the household duties to perform, and to nurse the sick into the bargain. Yet, the more she had to do, the happier she was.—Away went all the timidity and embarrassment, and the stupidity with it. She was a free and voluntary worker now. Martha said, "What she should have done without her she could not tell, and she believed it was God's providence that had sent her to help them in their need;" and Abel nodded his head significantly, implying that he did not doubt it. She could sit up at night, too, and keep awake, as it became very needful she should, from the condition of the patients; for of late she had had plenty of sleep and easy days and nights, instead of being overwatched and overwrought, as she was at the Huntsman. And then, her heart was in her work; for it was Abel's child and grandchild she was attending; besides, we easily grow to love those we serve, when our service is thankfully accepted.

Meantime, however, want was beginning to steal in at the door. Poor Martha's needlework lay unfinished; and, although Lilly took it up, and did a few stitches when she had time, she could make but slow progress. Neither was she very dexterous at this kind of work; hers had been of another description. Abel, humbled by his daughter's distress, would have gone out with Pipes to beg; but she entreated him not to do so, in a place where they had once been known to live so respectably; so, finding himself but a useless burthen, he once more took refuge in the poor-house. A small relief from the parish was also sent to the family, but very inadequate to their wants; whilst they had latterly been a good deal lost sight of by those former friends, who had assisted them in their early difficulties; not from any decrease of desert on the part of Martha, but because it was pronounced useless to attempt to serve her, whilst Giles remained a clog upon her industry; it was only giving her money for him to squander. Besides, the world gets tired of people who persist in being unfortunate; when it sees that a few efforts do not suffice to lift a poor wretch out of the slough, it loses patience, and allows him to sink into it, over head and ears. So that great was the desolation of this poor house in which Lilly had found shelter; and, in the midst of it, came home Giles Lintock.

Giles had treated his wife so ill, that by this time he had grown to mortally hate her; and he never came home at all, except when his usual expedients for living failed, and he found it convenient to sponge upon her little means. As he was at the present moment greatly in need of money, he had returned with the intention of raising it on whatever goods and chattels of hers he could lay his hands on; but her illness, and that of the child, interfered with his plan. She had herself pawned whatever she could spare; and, if he had taken the bed from under her just now, he would probably have been mobbed, or have brought the parish officers[37] about his ears; so he forbore; but, as he had nowhere else to go, he remained at home, eating up the tables and chairs, and whatever else he could turn into money; even to his wife's silver thimble, and the linen that had been entrusted to her by her employers.

At length, things being so bad that they could get no worse, they began to take a little turn for the better. The doctor who had attended the patients becoming aware of their distress, interested his wife and some other ladies in their favour; and the fever, from which they were both suffering, having reached its critical term, began to subside. Giles, too, tired of staying at home, and finding he could make nothing of it, as the little aid given to Martha was so managed that he could not get hold of the money, relieved them of his presence; which was, in itself, a great improvement.

It may easily be conceived that, by this time, Martha Lintock's feelings towards Lilly were very different to what they had been previous to her illness. The forlorn little stranger had proved herself a most valuable and efficient aid in her great need; and now, to use a Scotticism, "she could not think enough of her;" and what she thought she said, to everybody that would listen to her story. The consequence of which was, that the ladies began to take an interest in Lilly; and one amongst them offered to receive her into her service, as under nursery-maid, at six pounds per annum. By the advice of Mrs. Lintock, she accepted the proposal; and, after due purification, and the lapse of such a period as was thought sufficient to preclude the danger of infection, she was installed in her new situation; where we will, for the present, leave her; whilst we return to inquire into the effects of

---

37 The first police force was established by Robert Peel in 1829. However, it was very small and many parts of the country had no police protection. In 1842 the Parish Constables Act was passed and there were more officers, but many were part-time and very poorly paid.

her mysterious disappearance on those she had left behind.

Mrs. Hobbs had sent Lilly forth, partly out of good nature, thinking her con-finement cruel and unreasonable, and partly in order that, during "the thick of the washing,"[38] she might keep her own troublesome child safely out of the way. As order and regularity were not the distinguishing characteristics of the Hobbs fam-ily, little Sarah's not returning to dinner excited neither curiosity nor displeasure in the mother's breast; nor was it till the afternoon that she began to express any surprise at the child's continued absence. Then she did begin to "wonder what had come of Sarah!" and ever and anon, betwixt the rubbing and the wringing, she went to the door, and looked up and down the street, in hopes of seeing her. As the evening advanced, the wonder became mingled with uneasiness; her visits to the door were more frequent, and she asked the neighbours and every passen-ger that she happened to be acquainted with, if they "had seen any thing of her girl." But nobody being able to give her any intelligence, her anxiety augmented so much, that she finally abandoned her tubs, and started forth herself in search of her darling. But, by this time, the children that had been playing with Sarah in the morning, had retired to their homes, and Miss Hobbs was too diminu-tive and unimportant a personage to have attracted the notice of the public in general; so that, after an hour spent in seeking her, Mrs. Hobbs was returning, with no more information of her daughter than could be extracted from some evanescent glimpses of a yellow frock and green pinafore, which one or two of her acquaintance averred to have seen in company with several other girls, in the Market Square, some time during the day, when, at the corner of a street, she met the identical Sarah, with her finger in her eye; weeping like Niobe,[39] with a torn bonnet and a very dirty face.

"You nasty little thing, you!" exclaimed the mother, who, having been very frightened, was, of course, very angry; "where the dickens have you been all this while? Here am I obliged to leave my work to come and look after *you*—where's the girl that went out with you?"

"She went away and left me!" sobbed out Sarah, rubbing her eyes still harder with her dirty fingers.

"Left you! when did she leave you?" inquired Mrs. Hobbs, the current of whose wrath was quite ready to change its direction.

"This morning," sobbed Sarah.

"And where's she gone to?" again inquired Mrs. Hobbs.

"I—don't—know," sobbed Sarah.

---

38 Right in the middle of the work.

39 In Greek myth Niobe's children were killed by Apollo and Artemis to repay her for ar-rogance. She was turned to stone and formed a stream from her ceaseless tears.

"You don't know! Why, didn't she tell you where she was going?"

"No; she went away, and didn't say nothing," sobbed Sarah, with a fresh burst of grief, or rather of passion; for, in the first place, she was tired and hungry; and, in the next, she had been ill-treated and teased by some children bigger than herself, which catastrophe had terminated her day's amusement, and sent her home in a very ill temper; and, accordingly, very well disposed to lay the whole blame of her misfortunes on her absent companion. As for Lilly's desertion, it was a fact she took for granted, without being disposed to inquire too curiously into its historical accuracy. She had, in reality, never sought her, or thought of her, till she needed her aid to defend her against her tormentors—then she was not forthcoming, and Miss Hobbs naturally felt herself exceedingly ill-used and neglected. It is needless to say, that Mrs. Hobbs adopted her daughter's opinion; and, whilst she sympathizingly led her home, she did not fail to descant eloquently on the enormity of Lilly's offence, and to "bless herself for ever sending the child out with such a stupid good-for-nothing dawdle."[40]

When Sarah, however, was safely lodged, and her afflictions mitigated by the application of a good supper, Mrs. Hobbs began to think a little more seriously of Lilly's absence, and how she should answer for it to Charlotte Littenhaus. The meaning of it she could not divine. That a girl of Lilly's age, "with a tongue in her head," as she said, should be lost in a town no larger than Hotham, she could hardly conceive; neither from what she had seen of her could she imagine that she had formed a deliberate design of absconding. The most probable hypothesis was, that she had found some acquaintance, or been enticed away by somebody, and would return the next day.

"And, please the pigs, she comes before Miss Littenhaus returns, there'll be no harm done!" was her final orison[41] for that night, as she closed her eyes to sleep.

But Lilly came not; and the resentment of Mrs. Hobbs was naturally in proportion to her consciousness of being herself the cause of the misfortune, and to her apprehensions of what might ensue when Charlotte Littenhaus returned, which she did not do, however, for nearly a week. To do her justice, Mrs. Hobbs had neglected no means that she was mistress of to find Lilly in the interval; but, as her departure had been unobserved by any body, she had little chance of success.

The anger and astonishment of Charlotte, when she found the bird flown, it would not be easy to describe. Of course, Mrs. Hobbs, with a due instinct of self-preservation, took care not to criminate herself; and, according to her representation of the case, Lilly's going forth had been an act of her own will.

---

40 Someone who loiters or hangs around.
41 Prayer.

"Young folks will have their own way, you know, Miss Charlotte; and it wasn't no business of mine to interfere with her, as I'd no orders so to do. When you was away, she had no need to say with your leave, nor by your leave; and she isn't no such a chicken, but she would have found her way back if she'd chose to come;" and, so saying, Mrs. Hobbs nodded her head significantly; leaving the angry Charlotte to draw what conclusions she liked.

CHAPTER XV

SYMPTOMS OF DANGER

The displeasure of Charlotte, however, was far exceeded by that of Luke; who came over immediately on the receipt of the unwelcome intelligence, in a state of extreme consternation and suppressed wrath; for Luke could always restrain the exhibition of his passion, when he thought it advisable to do so. The alarm he felt at Lilly's disappearance and the importance he attached to recovering her, were greater than it would have been prudent to display. She was gone just at the crisis when he had begun to learn her value and to fear her power; and from the very circumstance of her going—for he never doubted that she had done so designedly—he drew the conclusion, that though she might not be acquainted with the first, she was with the last—she undoubtedly knew too much, and might use her knowledge, sooner or later, to his destruction.

Luke's motive for the sudden resolution to marry the despised and neglected Lilly was a complicated one. His objects were, wealth and advancement, on the one hand; and security on the other. Jacob's dying words, which had fallen unheeded on the little girl's dull ear, were not without their significance; but till the conversation overheard by Charlotte, whilst attending the two officers at dinner, they did not know exactly who she was. They, and some comrades of theirs, had found her on board a wreck, which, in one of their nocturnal expeditions, they had accidentally fallen in with and plundered, in company with a gentleman who told them that the rest of the crew and passengers had put off in the boats; but that he had refused to accompany them, confident that they would never reach the shore—which they did not. For the sake of the money and valuables this stranger had about him, they took his life; in opposition to the wishes of old Jacob Littenhaus, who, though a smuggler, and not averse to the robbery, objected seriously to the needless shedding of blood. The party, however, maintained that their own safety demanded the sacrifice; at least, their only alternative was to resign their booty, a thing not to be thought of. They even wished to murder the child also; but, on this question, Jacob's opinion prevailed, and she was consequently spared, and brought up to believe that she was their relation.

In spite, however, of the precautions they had used to prevent detection, when it was discovered that the wreck had been visited and plundered, some suspicion fell upon the Littenhaus family; and it was this circumstance that had ultimately determined them to quit that part of the country. Too much observation cramped their exertions; and in the lonely inn on the coast of Sussex, they found exactly the conditions they required; a wild stretch of barren common, thinly populated; and a house which had once carried on a flourishing business, but which the making of a new road and the sudden rise of a fishing-village into a watering-place had ruined.

The life of the Littenhaus family was a curious instance, not only of that perversion of morals which makes people prefer wrong to right, but also of that not uncommon mistake which induces them to lead a life of continued sacrifice for the sake of acquiring that which they can never enjoy. Their illicit practices constrained them to a dull and solitary mode of existence; nor were their gains sufficient to justify a hope that they might some day spend in peace and pleasure the money earned in peril. The situation of the sisters was peculiarly unpleasant; for they had not even the excitement which seasoned the life of the brothers. "Six dull, idle days, with now and then a guest to attend to; and a visit to church on the seventh, dressed far above their condition," might have been stereotyped as the standing record of their weary existence. Astonishing the eyes of the rustics with their rich silks and laces, and inspecting the stores of those their drawers contained, seemed their only pleasure, excepting their occasional visits to Miss Grosset, the dressmaker; and their other acquaintances at Hotham.

But infatuated mankind have such a strange love of money for its own sake, that very frequently those who are the most entirely incapable of using it, in such a manner as to purchase pleasure for themselves or any body else, are not the less eager to acquire it; whether it be to confine it under lock and key in their strong box; or to muddle it away in ungraceful, unsatisfactory profusion; and so it was with these people, more especially Luke; who united with an utter want of principle an intense selfishness and an iron will. He was the demon of the family; tyrannizing over his infirm father whilst he lived; and since his death, though the youngest son, domineering equally over the other members of it: availing himself of the vanity of the sisters and the weakness of his brother to gain his own ends; which were, after all, only such as a more rational human being would have looked upon as *means;* for of ends, properly so called, he had none—not even present enjoyment; for he pursued no pleasures nor indulged in any recreations; nor had any ultimate views whatever. The first gleam of any such appeared in this project of marrying Lilly; but even this might have been resolved into a desire to clutch a large sum of money; for he had no idea of the enjoyments of a more exalted station, nor any taste for them. His second motive, as we have hinted, was to ensure his own safety by having her in his power. The circumstances connected with Shorty's death, Winny's visit, and the bit of linen, had led him to the conclusion that she was more observant and reflective than he had imagined; and that she knew more than was consistent with his own security. A wedding-ring, however, is probably not the instrument he would have selected to silence her, had it not been for the light thrown upon her birth and fortunes by the officers. The name of the ship, as well as that on some of the property they purloined belonging to her protector, together with other corroborative circumstances, left no doubt in their minds that the despised Lilly was the lost heiress, Isabel Adams. She had, indeed, whilst her recollections of her home and her previous life were fresh in her infantile mind, told them that her name was Isabel; though, at other times, she said it was Lilly; which last they adopted, concluding it to have been used as a diminutive. Her surname they never clearly ascertained from her. When they questioned her, she would sometimes say she was called Miss Lilly, and at others Isabel Addin—at least, so it sounded to their ears—and as they were rather desirous that she should forget it than otherwise, they soon ceased to make any attempts at recalling it to her memory.

The poor little girl was, at first, not insensible to the change that had taken place in her fortunes—she felt, though she could not understand it; but too young to reflect, or to collect, arrange, or methodize her thoughts, they gradually became confused and slipped from her grasp, leaving on her mind such a faint image of all that had happened to her before she came to live with her cousins, as she called them, that her previous life, if it ever occurred to her memory at all, seemed more like a dream than a reality. By nature, a lively and impressionable child, accustomed to the greatest indulgence and tenderness, her mind became stultified and her spirit broken by continued harshness and unremitting labour; her growth was nipped, her fair skin assumed an unhealthy whiteness, her eye was heavy and her countenance stolid; whilst absorbed in the mechanical routine of duties imposed on her, she neither saw nor heard any thing that did not refer to them; and felt neither interest nor curiosity in what was passing before her eyes. Such was Lilly, till the kindness of Mrs. Ryland and Philip struck a chord in her heart; and, by arousing her affections, somewhat awakened the dormant faculties which subsequent occurrences were destined to further unfold.

But to return to Luke. When he found Lilly was really gone, and that such inquiries as he instituted through the town brought him no intelligence of her, he became seriously uneasy; and, according to the old adage that "conscience makes cowards,"[42] he anticipated alarming consequences to himself from her evasion. Designedly, or otherwise, she would be led to reveal the circumstances of her past life; and there was no telling how much she remembered, nor how much she knew. Her departure, so cleverly managed—for in order to exonerate herself, Mrs. Hobbs gave the whole proceeding the colour of a deliberate design on the part of Lilly—her departure alone was sufficient to prove that she was not the stupid, unmoved, unobserving tool they had thought her. It indicated that she had been playing a part, that she had been actuated by some distinct motive, and had only been waiting for an opportunity to put her plan in execution.

Now, Luke was one of those unhappily organized human beings in whom any injury, real or fancied—any crossing of his own plans, however they may have interfered with the rights of others—are wont to arouse an insane desire for revenge. For the rights of others he had no respect; indeed, he had no sense or consciousness of them—he saw nothing in the world beyond himself—he was the very incarnation of selfishness. Selfishness is always blind; and inevitably takes the wrong way to its own ends, if its ends be happiness and enjoyment—but Luke's was the blindest of the blind; for he not only spent his time, his cunning, and his labour, such as it was, in the dishonest acquirement of small gains, exposed to present peril and future ruin, without earning as much as he could have done by fair trade—most persons who take tortuous modes of getting money do this—but when he was crossed in any of the projects this self-love had framed, it became so angry with the smart of disappointment, that it ran away with him into the most perilous and profitless paths in pursuit of the revenge that it thirsted after, to restore its self-complacency; and in this pursuit, seeing still nothing beyond the immediate gratification of his passion, he stopped at no crime, nor was arrested by any considerations.

When he found, therefore, that Lilly had actually made her escape from his clutches, every passion of his soul was stirred; his fears and his vengeance were fully aroused; the hitherto despised little girl assumed in his eyes an immeasurable importance; and to entrap her again in his toils immediately became the object which superseded all others.

That he should succeed in recovering possession of her, he did not doubt. Little more than a week had elapsed since her departure, and without money or friends she could not have gone far; his first essay, therefore, after he had made his inquiries in the town and given notice to the parish officers to be on the look out for her, was to make a circuit round the immediate environs. But, as his perquisition did not happen to reach the ears of any of those few persons whom Lilly had requested to direct her to her temporary home, and as she had

---

42 From *Hamlet*, Act 3 Scene I.

passed along unobserved whilst following Abel, he gained no information. Still he found it difficult to believe that she was not sheltered in the neighbourhood; and, fortunately for Lilly, he lost the time which would have enabled him surely to overtake her, in seeking her where she was not. Several times he was about to start on a more extended circuit, when this persuasion on the one hand, and the difficulty of deciding which road to take on the other, deterred him; but so far from the delay mitigating his vengeful feeling or shaking his determination, the one was aggravated and the other re-enforced by the irritation of disappointment, and the mortification he felt at what, he supposed, must be her triumph at the success of her project.

Still there was no raging or storming; that was not Luke's way. He said little; but those sinister gray eyes and that broad, white, cadaverous face looked more demoniac than usual, whilst, maintaining the coldness of his external demeanour, he privately gnashed his teeth, and silently swore deep oaths of a bloody vengeance when he clutched her again.

He had good cause for his wrath; for, during this interval, the object of his pursuit was advancing happily along the road, little heeding the past, and never dreaming of the turmoil she was creating in the family she had abandoned; and at length, when he did extend his quest further, he missed the track by one of those slight oversights that render unavailing so many pursuits. He did inquire for her at the village where Abel had first baited, which was about ten miles from Hotham; but as the old man had not then been aware that she was following him, and as she had not entered the house, but merely sat down on a stone in the little street, till he came forth again, nobody had observed her. Mrs. Wylie's, where Abel and she had passed the first night, was only five miles beyond; and, had he advanced so far, he would inevitably have heard of her; but this small, lone house was not thought of; and the idea of advertizing her having suddenly entered his head, he turned his steps back for the purpose of carrying this resolution into effect, and so missed his game. He, however, inserted the advertisement in two of the local papers, offering five pounds reward for any information respecting her, and anxiously waited the result; but none was elicited. He then renewed his search personally, but with no better success; and week after week and month after month passed, without bringing any tidings of Lilly. Ambrose, and even his sisters, advised him to think no more about her: but his obstinate nature was only indurated by opposition, and he swore he would never give up the point, and that he would "catch her yet."

It was not till nearly a year had elapsed that he one day returned from Hotham, triumphantly holding a letter in his hand which had been delivered to him at the office of the editor, who published the "Sussex Weekly Chronicle."

"Here," said he, "didn't I always tell you I'd get hold of her?"

"Is it about Lilly?" eagerly inquired the others.

"Where is she?" said Ambrose, holding out his hand to take the letter.

"Never mind," said Luke, seeming to recollect himself, and drawing it back; "I know where she is—that's enough!"

"You'd better let her alone, Luke," said Ambrose, significantly.

"You'd better mind your own business," answered Luke, drily; at the same time folding the letter and putting it in his pocket.

CHAPTER XVI

LILLY COMMITS A MISDEMEANOUR

We left Lilly installed as under nurserymaid in the family of a respectable solicitor; where she was well treated, well fed, and well clothed. Assuredly, since the hour the good ship Hastings was wrecked in the channel, Lilly Dawson had never been so well provided for. Her labour was light, and her situation altogether, for a young girl in her condition, unexceptionable. Moreover, she gave satisfaction to her employers. She had been trained to obedience and activity; and they found her honest and steady. The only fault they complained of was, that she was not lively. She was a dull companion to the children, and could not amuse them or enter into their sports.

This was natural enough; she had had no childhood herself, and had known no sports nor plays. Like the children of the very poor, who become prematurely thoughtful about pence and halfpence, and the price of meal or the quartern loaf,[43] she had been as prematurely involved in a routine of monotonous labour that had worked all the sport and play out of her. She was like a young horse that had been under a harsh breaker[44]. This was a fault that could not be mended; but, for the sake of her other good qualities, it was overlooked; and Lilly might have kept her place, had it not been that, in spite of all these appliances, she was not happy. She pined for Abel, and she knew that Abel was pining in the poor-house. She loved the old man with the most tender and reverential affection; she had acquired a taste for his conversation and instruction, which was to her the teaching of a sage and a philosopher; she found nothing around her that could compensate for the loss of his society, whilst her heart yearned to think he was wasting his latter days in sadness and sorrow. There were no companions for Abel in the poor-house; he had nobody to talk to, nor nobody to instruct there, for they did not care to hear him. He had no occupation, either. They tried to teach him to make baskets, but

43 Bread made with exactly 3.5 pounds of wheaten flour.
44 Referring to the practice of 'breaking' or training horses.

he was too old to acquire any dexterity at it; feeling his work was worthless, he could not do it; and time hung heavy on his hands. Then he sighed for the free air of heaven, the daily journey, that was at once his business and his pleasure; the road-side chats with other travellers, the variety furnished by his nightly stations, and the friendly recognitions of his hosts and hostesses. Above all, he sighed for his independence; and he mourned for the days when, humble as was his calling, he was honestly earning his bread, and even able to save a trifle to bring home to his daughter. Lilly knew all this, for she went to visit him as often as she could; and she saw how pallid and thin he looked, and how the expression of his features was changing, from that of cheerful resignation to one of hopeless dejection.

"I don't sleep, either, Lilly," said he; "the want of air and exercise that I've been so long used to keeps me wakeful; and then I lie on my hard bed, with my old bones aching, and thinking of past times—perhaps my bones used to ache, too, when we were travelling, but I was tired at night and slept soundly; and I'd no time to think of them—now I've nothing else to think of. Ah, Lilly! sorrow is a sorrowful thing when we're old, for then we've no hope to help us to bear it—no hope—no hope!"

"But, father," said Lilly, anxious to find some source of consolation, "you told me that good people had always something to hope."

"Ay, my child, beyond the grave," returned Abel.

"Well, father, then that's something."

"Yes," replied he, gravely; "it should be—but somehow, Lilly, I feel further from God here than I did when we trod the highways and the green lanes, where the birds sang in the hedges and the grasshoppers chirped in the fields. When I heard the bees buzzing amongst the wild flowers, I knew He was near me; but there's no joy, no gladness in a poor-house—no gathering of honey here, Lilly. Those joyous sounds of God's own free scholars were *my* light; they were eyes to me, as well as ears; and, whilst they preached to me of His goodness, they showed me His works. But all is dark now, Lilly; I breathe nothing but the thick air of this dank yard, enclosed within four brick walls; I hear nothing but complaints—sometimes curses—and I think the Lord has forgotten me!"

And poor Lilly's theology not being prepared to sustain the argument any further, she could only sigh and wish it were otherwise; and, after these conversations, she would walk slowly home, pondering on what had been said to her; and less disposed than before to attend to the prattle of the children, or mingle with their sports.

Thus, slowly and heavily, passed the first six months of Lilly's service at the solicitor's. It was the month of May; fine, genial, bright weather; and she had found Abel, whom she had been visiting on the Sunday evening, more desponding than ever.

"Bring me a branch of hawthorn, Lilly," said he, "when next you come—a sweetsmelling hawthorn! Are the lilacs and laburnums coming out yet? Next month the bean-fields will be in flower;—what I would give for the full perfume of a bean-field now! Lord! how little we value thy blessings whilst we enjoy them! I used to think I was thankful—but, God forgive me! I often repined at the loss of my sight, when I should have been singing hallelujahs for what was left me."

"I'll cut some hawthorn to-morrow, father, when I go out with the children," answered Lilly, "and I'll bring it you at night, if I can get out before your gate's shut; and we have some laburnums and lilacs at the front of the house, and I'll bring you some of them, too, when they're in blossom."

"Do, my child," said Abel. "Your visits are my only comfort. Poor Martha cannot spare time to come often; and, when she does, I know by her voice how unhappy she is, though she doesn't complain; and she leaves me more unhappy than before; and I'm sure she goes away more unhappy herself, at seeing her old father ending his days in the workhouse."

"Martha has got a great job of work now," said Lilly, "and she's very busy."

"Ay, so much the better—but it's toil, toil, and no hope of anything better, while Giles Lintock lives. He hasn't been home, has he?"

"No," answered Lilly. "I called this morning, as I went past from church, but he hadn't been there."

"So much the better," said Abel. "It would be a mercy of the Lord if he never came again. You see, Lilly," continued he, "I've more comfort in your coming to see me, because I have been of some use to you, one way or another, by the help of God. Poor as I am, it's through me and mine, partly, that you're better off than you used to be; but, when I hear the sad tones of poor Martha's voice, that was once so cheerful, and feel her thin hand, and stroke her hollow cheek, I can't help reproaching myself. I should never have let her marry Giles Lintock. Many a better man offered; but she sacrificed herself for me—and the end of it is, that she's wretched, and I'm in the poor-house."

The tears stood in Lilly's eyes, as she listened to this mournful chant, seated beside Abel on a wooden bench in the workhouse-yard; but she was too inexperienced to detect any source of consolation, and too timid to suggest a hope of any amendment in his daughter's situation or his own. That night Lilly went home with a heart unusually saddened.

On the following morning, when the family-breakfast was over, she was summoned to the dining-room. Mr. Ross and the children had already left it; and Mrs. Ross was seated at a side-table with a pen and ink, and her housekeeping-books beside her.

"Lilly, is that you?" said she; "come here—nearer!—I want to speak to you! What makes you look so grave, child? You're not like a young girl—you've no spirits—no animation. Are you dissatisfied with your situation?"

"No, ma'am."

"I'm sure you've not too much to do, have you?"

"No, ma'am."

"And there's nobody unkind to you, is there?"

"No, ma'am."

"Well, then, do try to look a little more cheerful, will you?"

"Yes, ma'am," replied Lilly, looking as grave as if she had been following a hearse.

"Well, that's a bad beginning, Lilly," said Mrs. Ross, unable to resist laughing at the incongruity between the girl's countenance and answer; "but mind, Lilly, I am not dissatisfied with you. On the contrary, I think you are a very good, steady girl; and certainly it is better in your situation to be too grave than too gay. I think you have now been with me six months, haven't you?"

"Yes, ma'am."

"And you have, therefore, half a year's wages due to you. You know, I was to give you six pounds a year—wasn't that our agreement?"

"I don't know, ma'am," answered Lilly; for she had never had any money in her life; and, having no idea whatever of what was meant by six pounds, she had paid no attention to that part of the bargain.

"Don't you remember that I said I would give you six pounds a year?"

"Yes, ma'am," answered Lilly, beginning to recall the circumstance.

"Well, then, your half-year's wages amount to three pounds. As I am satisfied with you, I'll make it three guineas[45]—here they are!"

"Thank you, ma'am," said Lilly, taking the three pieces of gold, and looking at them with wondering eyes.

"And now you've got your money, take care you don't lose it," continued Mrs. Ross. "Where will you put it?" Lilly blushed, but made no answer. "Perhaps you don't know where to keep it? Shall I take care of it for you? You can have it whenever you like, you know! "Lilly's blush grew deeper. "I think it would be safer with me than with you, Lilly, unless you want to buy something with it—do you?"

"No, ma'am," answered Lilly, looking down, but still grasping the money as if she did not intend to part with it.

"Perhaps you had rather keep it yourself," added Mrs. Ross, observing her attitude. "Would you?"

"Yes, ma'am," murmured Lilly, shily casting down her eyes.

---

45 A guinea was the equivalent of one pound plus a shilling.

"Oh! very well—then keep it, my good girl; only take care of it," said Mrs. Ross. "And now you may go and send up Elizabeth;" and Lilly quitted the room, with the money in her hand, and pervaded by a strange feeling, made up of wonder, joy, and perplexity.

Surely, she thought, those three bright pieces must be very valuable. But, if so, that they should be hers seemed very extraordinary. But then again, if they really were hers, and, at the same time, so valuable as she supposed, what might she not do with them? Might she not relieve Martha Lintock's distresses and set Abel free? What a joyful idea! She felt quite bewildered and intoxicated with it; and, forgetting the message to Elizabeth, she went straight up to her own chamber, and there remained sitting on the side of the bed, with the money in her hand, till the upper nursery-maid, missing her from her daily duties, came to inquire what she was doing.

She put the money in her drawer, and went below; but how she longed for the evening, and how she wondered whether she should be permitted to go out when it arrived! a privilege that depended wholly on the humour and generosity of her superior; whom it was therefore her interest to please. But Lilly had hitherto had so little to think of, and was so unaccustomed to think at all, that now that she had actually got something important in her head—now that an idea had taken possession of her brain, she was quite bewildered and unable to manage it. It ran away with her; she did not know what she was about—did everything wrong, and forgot everything she should remember; whilst the grave Mrs. Janet, quite unable to comprehend Lilly in this abnormal condition, kept quietly watching her out of the corner of her eye, for the purpose of deciding whether she had not been making too free with the ale-jug.

Thus, not without several rubs and crosses, passed the day; and, as the evening approached, Lilly's excitement and abstraction only became the more observable. Her cheeks, which, from leading a more healthy life and being much in the open air, had lost their former pallor, were now crimson; her eye was bright and unsettled, her hand was unsteady; and she actually had the appearance of being either under the influence of some stimulant, or in a state of incipient fever. Mrs. Janet was perfectly confounded.

Lilly was permitted to go out to visit her friends on every alternate Sunday evening; that was her established privilege; but her extra excursions were all, as we have said, under favour of Mrs. Janet, after the younger children were gone to bed. She thought, to-night, they never would go to bed. How wearisome their plays and prattlings were! How long they were bidding their papa and mamma *good night!* How Miss Caroline dawdled over her bread and milk! And how many times Master Henry threw off his nightcap, after she had tied it on! Then, there was no getting them through their prayers. Miss Lucy would persist in praying for the cat; and, let Mrs. Janet do what she would, little Johnny would not pray God to bless his brothers and sisters." And when they *were* in bed, they would not go to sleep, they were so full of fun and mischief! till, at length, Johnny got peevish with being too long awake, and began to cry. Then he had to be pacified; but now, the matter becoming serious, Mrs. Janet set her veto against any more fun for that night; they would all be ill next day, and papa and mamma would be very angry; so, after one or two expiring efforts at rebellion on the part of Henry, they closed their laughing eyes; their soft cheeks sunk into their downy pillows, and they lay lapped in their rosy sleep.

Now was the moment that, when Lilly wanted to go and see Abel or his daughter, she was accustomed to request permission to do so. But this only happened occasionally, as she was expected to employ her evenings in general in mending the children's stockings, and so forth. In the present instance, her anxiety to go, on the one hand, and her consciousness of Mrs. Janet's dissatisfaction, on the other, rendered the request a difficult one.

"You'll find plenty of work in the basket," said the nurse, pointing to that which contained such articles of the children's clothes as needed repair; "and there are some frills to be hemmed for Miss Caroline's new nightcaps." Lilly approached the table where the basket stood. "You had better do the stockings first," added Mrs. Janet, "and try if you can't darn them more neatly. You made such a lump in one of the heels of Master Ross's blue stockings, that he complained it hurt his foot."

Lilly took out the stockings, sought for her needle and thimble, and sat down behind the nurse. Her head was in a whirl, betwixt the desire to get away, and the dread of asking; especially as she had an entire conviction that her request would not be granted. She felt like a newly-caught bird in a cage; and, whilst her body was fixed to the nursery-stool, her spirit was flying through the window and on the road to the poor-house. This agony had endured about half an hour, when Elizabeth came to the door to say, that if the children were asleep, Mrs. Janet was wanted below. So Mrs. Janet rose and left the room.

She had no sooner closed the door behind her, than Lilly flung down her stocking and rose from her seat. For an instant, she hesitated; but time pressed. There was the nursery-clock pointing to the half hour past eight—at half-past nine the gates of the poor-house closed, after which, without interest, no visitor could be admitted. There was not a minute to lose, so she softly opened the door and listened; nobody seemed near. Her own bonnet and shawl hung on a hook on the landing-place, that they might always be at hand when she had occasion to accompany the children to the garden. She took them down, and, without putting them on, descended the stairs. An instinctive caution led her rather to carry them in her hand than wear them; though, had she met Mrs. Janet, which was what she feared, the mere appearance of them in her possession would have betrayed her. But fortune favoured her, and she met nobody, except the kitchen-maid, who was not entitled to interfere with her proceedings. Mr. Ross was in his office; Mrs. Janet was with Mrs. Ross, in her bed-room, discussing some nefarious designs against the liberty and freewill of the unsuspecting slumberers above; and the other servants, when they saw Lilly slip out at the back-door, had no reason to suppose that she was going without leave. So she effected her escape without opposition; and, once clear of the house, she made the best of her way, for the distance was considerable, and she trembled lest she might not arrive before the gates were shut, and the object of her expedition be defeated.

"I wish," said Mrs. Ross, just as the subject of her remark was climbing over a wicket[46] at the bottom of the garden, that happened to be locked—"I wish we could get Lilly to exert a little more energy with the children. She's a steady, good girl as can be; but she's so dull!"

"I don't quite understand Lilly, ma'am," said Mrs. Janet. "Sometimes, I think she's got something in her head. I'm sure, all to-day she hasn't known whether she's been standing on that or her heels."

"But that's not generally the case, surely," returned Mrs. Ross. "She always appears collected enough. Perhaps she's a little excited at receiving her wages."

"I don't know, ma'am; I should be sorry to think she'd been taking anything, but, really, I don't know what to make of her."

"Where is she?" inquired Mrs. Ross.

"In the nursery, ma'am."

"I'll go up and look at her," said the lady; and, suiting the action to the word, she ascended the stairs with the nurse.

"Heavens and earth!" cried Mrs. Janet, who went first with the candle, as she rushed to the table, whilst Mrs. Ross cried loudly for help. They were but just in time. The stocking Lilly had been mending had caught the candle, as she hastily flung it down. In a minute more, the flame would have reached the work-basket, and the room would have been on fire!—perhaps the children burnt in their beds!

There was no question as to who was in fault; but where was the culprit? Gone out without leave—and nobody knew whither!

END OF VOLUME I

---

46 A small gate.

VOLUME II

CHAPTER I

AN ALARM

Forgetting everything she had left behind, and thinking only of the friend she was hastening to, Lilly flew along the streets, and succeeded in reaching the poorhouse, just as the clock struck the quarter past nine. Abel was still in the yard; his long habit of outdoor life rendering even that joyless place of exercise more agreeable to him than the interior. He had resigned all hopes of Lilly and the hawthorn for that night, and was sitting in sad solitude, ruminating on his troubles, when the bell rang.

"Father!" said she, breathless with the speed she had used, "look here!"

"Is it the hawthorn?" inquired Abel, holding out his hand to take it.

"No, it's money," answered Lilly; "I forgot the hawthorn! Feel, what a deal! They're gold, father! Ain't they worth a great deal?"

"Is it your wages?" asked Abel.

"Yes," replied Lilly; "Mrs. Ross gave them to me this morning."

"You must take care of them," returned Abel; "mind you don't lose them, Lilly. Where will you put them?"

"What would they buy?" inquired Lilly; "wouldn't they buy a basket?"

"Yes, a great many baskets; but, do you want a basket?"

"I mean for you, father; a basket such as you had before, with things in it to sell."

"But what could I do with a basket alone?" inquired Abel, whilst a flush overspread his pale face, as he caught a glimpse of her meaning.

"Couldn't I go with you, father?" said Lilly.

"But would you, Lilly?" said Abel.

"Oh, yes," answered Lilly; "I should like it so much."

The old man's heart swelled with gratification at this proof of his *protégée's* regard and gratitude, and, for a moment, with the hope of being released from his present cheerless abode; but the latter feeling quickly subsided, and his face resumed its mournful expression, as he shook his head and said gravely, "No, Lilly, that must not be. You are in a respectable situation, and you must try and keep it. All your future welfare may depend on your remaining in Mrs. Ross's service, and conducting yourself so as to win friends. You know you have no friend in the world except me and Martha, who can be of no more use to you; and you must try and make some for yourself. Going about the country with me was very well, when you could do nothing else—but now you can; and you must stay where you are."

Poor Lilly! If Abel could have seen her face, he would have had some idea of the amount of disappointment he was inflicting; but, as he could not, he had no conception of it; for Lilly, who had been trained to an unreasoning obedience, never disputed any body's commands; still less his, whom she had every disposition to obey. She only stood silently beside him, with her features and form relaxed from the tension of elated hope; whilst he, never dreaming how much her heart was set upon the project, or, indeed, that it was set upon it at all, and believing that in doing his duty towards her there was no sacrifice but his own, advisedly changed the subject, and reverted to the hawthorn, in order to curtail the pang that the conscientious extinction of this glimmer of hope was costing him.

"Bring it the next time you come, Lilly, will you?" said he.

"Yes," answered Lilly faintly.

"And be sure you take care of that money. I think it would have been better to have left it with your mistress. You don't want it; do you?"

"No," replied Lilly, speaking more firmly; for the question was quite pertinent to her thoughts. She felt very clearly that she did not want it now.

"Then give it her, my child; and ask her to keep it for you."

"They're going to shut the gates," said Lilly.

"Then you must go," said Abel.

"Good night," said Lilly.

"Good night, my child! and don't forget the hawthorn," said Abel, as she slowly moved towards the gate she had a few minutes before entered with so much alacrity.

"There, off with you! Move a little quicker, will you?" said the man who was waiting to close them; and, in a moment more Lilly was in the street.

She walked slowly on, unconsciously retracing her steps towards Mrs. Ross's, too suddenly let down from her exaltation to have yet recovered the fall or her own recollection. The possibility of Abel's declining her proposal had never occurred to her, nor had she any appreciation of the motives that led to the refusal. Oppression with her had begun at so early an age, and been so unremittingly exercised, as to nearly extinguish desire; or, if she had ever wished for anything, it was for the recurrence of Sunday, when her cousins would be out, and she would have rest. She had, therefore, had no temptation to rebellion, having no will of her own to oppose to that of others. Since her emancipation, all her wishes had centred in Abel; and, as her ideas of duty and respectability were as yet in a very rudimentary state, she could not conceive any reason why both he and she should remain unhappy, when they had the means of being otherwise. It is true, that she had much improved under Abel's society and tuition; but it was not so much her understanding as her feelings that had been cultivated; though, doubtless, the exercise of the last had not been without its effect on the first. Still, she was a mere child, though she was sixteen years old; and she was nearly as ignorant of duties and conventionalities as if she were only sixteen months. Even Abel himself was by no means acquainted with the extent of this ignorance. She had always complied with his wishes and intentions; she had shown herself active, obliging, and useful, at Martha Lintock's; and she had given satisfaction by the regular observance of her routine of duties at Mrs. Ross's. But, in the two first instances, her affection for him had been her prompter; and, in the last, the motive was little different. He had wished her to accept Mrs. Ross's proposal; and, as she could not remain with him, she had no motive for objecting; whilst her naturally good disposition and early habits of obedience led her to do what was required of her whilst she was there. But, as soon as the prospect of something she would like much better was opened to her, being neither under the dominion of fear, as formerly, nor conscious of having undertaken a duty, or of being a party to an agreement, she had dropped her chain, and joyously set herself free, without hesitation or remorse.

But now that Abel had so briefly and decidedly awakened her from her dream, there was a complete re-action. The strings of the harp were all relaxed—her step was languid, her spirits depressed, her mind confused, by the blow that had extinguished her hopes; and it was only instinctively that she kept her way towards her home; nor was it till she arrived within sight of the house, that the idea of what she had done, and of Mrs. Janet's displeasure, presented themselves to her in any thing like their true colours. There was the wicket she had climbed over; beyond it was the back door of the house; and, although it was eleven o'clock, the family were not gone to bed, for there was a light in the pantry window. But Lilly felt herself quite unable to encounter Mrs. Janet's surprise and wrath; and she stood hesitating what she should do, till she saw the shadow of John the footman against the blind; and presently afterwards the light in the pantry was extinguished; by which she understood that all the servants had retired to their beds.

What was to be done now? It was nearly midnight, and there was Lilly standing at a garden-gate in the outskirts of the town, without an idea of where or how she should pass the remaining hours till morning. Martha, her only friend, lived not far from the poor-house. She might certainly find her way thither; but Martha would be in bed, too; and Lilly's timidity and depression quite unfitted her for such an enterprise as first disturbing her friend, and then explaining the cause of her doing so. Besides, from what Abel had said, she had become aware that her abandonment of Mrs. Ross's service would grieve, if not incense them; and she felt afraid to meet them, not because she was conscious of having done wrong, but because she could not bear the pain of their displeasure. In short, with the best intentions in the world, Lilly had got into a terrible scrape; what she was to do next she could not imagine; and, for want of being able to make up her mind on the subject, she remained where she was, leaning against the little garden-gate, and expiating her mistake by showers of tears.

By and by, she heard the distant church clocks strike the hour of one; and, just as they had ceased, she distinguished the sound of footsteps and voices approaching. Mr. Ross's house, as we have said, was on the outskirts of the town; it was, in fact, situated in a suburb, on the London road, amongst other villas of the opulent gentry. The persons approaching were coming towards the town, and as the hum of the population had ceased, and the night was extremely calm, their voices reached Lilly from a considerable distance. That she should be alarmed was natural. Every woman has an instinctive dread of encountering strange men in lonely places; and, without a moment's reflection, she followed her first impulse, which was, to jump over the gate and conceal herself under the hedge, which extended on each side of it.

Meantime, the travellers drew nearer and nearer; and as, from the lateness of the hour, they probably considered themselves quite secure from being overheard, they did not stint their voices. The first sentence, however, that distinctly reached Lilly's ears, was uttered by one exceedingly familiar to her; it was no other than Giles Lintock's.

"It's the next house we come to," said he.

"They seem fine buildings," observed his companion.

"Very," returned Giles; "they all belong to rich people. This Ross, I suppose," and, as he said this, the two men drew up at the little wicket, standing with their arms resting on it, exactly where Lilly had stood a few minutes before, "isn't worth less than fifty thousand pounds. He has the best business of any man about this part of the country."

"And it's here she lives?" said the other.

"Yes," replied Giles: "they've got several children, and she's under nursery-maid. But, I say, will she go with you for asking?" added he. "You know I can't answer for that. What I undertook was, to bring you to her—and that I've done; at least, I will do it to-morrow, or when you please; and then I'm entitled to the five pounds. But, if you don't take care, Mr. Ross will be inquiring into what right you have to claim her—that is, if she disputes it—and I doubt whether your being her cousin gives you any legal right over her person; unless you can prove you are also her guardian!"

"I am aware of all that," returned the other; "but I don't think she'd dispute my will, if I was face to face with her—she'd better not."

"Perhaps not, if she'd nobody to back her," answered Giles; "but, with Mr. and Mrs. Ross at her shoulder, it may be very different."

"I suppose she comes out alone sometimes," said the other.

"No doubt of it," replied Giles. "She comes to my wife's—I've seen her there. You might nab her then, and nobody a bit the wiser."

"With your help," returned the stranger.

"You shall have that," answered Giles.

"How late does she stay out?—do you know?" inquired the other.

"Probably, ten o'clock; it's the usual time servants have hereabout."

"If the nights were darker," said the stranger, looking up at the sky, "it would be easy enough, along this road."

"Not so easy, if she made any resistance," replied Giles. "There are always people walking about here on a fine night, especially Sundays, when she's most likely to be out alone. Besides, the footmen stand lounging at the gates, looking about them, and gallanting with the maids next door, as late as eleven o'clock, very often."

"Humph!" said the stranger, as if cogitating on this information; "couldn't you get your wife to send for her some evening, and then offer to walk back with her?"

"I might perhaps," replied Giles; "but my wife and I don't draw very well together.[47] I don't know whether she'd do it for me, unless I could give her some good reason for it."

"We may think of a reason," returned the stranger. "The thing is to get her away from this house—the rest is easy enough."

"We must talk it over to-morrow," said the other, moving from the gate.

"What's the name of this place?" inquired the stranger, following Giles.

"It's called Cardigan Terrace, and Mr. Ross's is No. 5," were the last words that reached Lilly's ears, as the two men walked away towards the town.

Poor Lilly! Here was the verification of the old adage again, "that misfortunes never come singly." The stranger was no other than Luke Littenhaus, who, in consequence of the answer to his advertisement, had followed her track; whilst Giles, neither knowing nor caring anything about their relative situations, nor Lilly's motive for abandoning her relations, was quite willing for so handsome a remuneration as five pounds, to facilitate the stranger's recovery of his captive.

At the same time, all he cared about was the promised reward; and he privately entertained considerable doubts of Luke's effecting his object. First of all, he would have to prove what claim he had to her; and, with so powerful a defender as

---

47 They do not get on very well.

Mr. Ross, it was not likely he could establish any that would entitle him to carry her off, against her will. But this was nothing to him; nor did he intend to endanger his own safety by aiding his new acquaintance in any perilous enterprise. Anything he could do to serve him in the way of quiet stratagem, he had no objection to; whilst, in the mean time, he had so worded his bargain, that as soon as he had actually brought Luke and the young girl face to face, he was entitled to the recompence; and of doing this, he entertained not the most distant doubt. How should he, when he had left Lilly a few weeks before, quietly ensconced in so excellent a situation as Mrs. Ross's, and was aware that only six months of the year for which she had been engaged had yet expired?

CHAPTER II

AN UNEXPECTED JOURNEY

We will not attempt to depict poor Lilly's terror and amazement, whilst, crouching beneath the hedge within three yards of the speakers, afraid to breathe lest they should discover her, she listened to this conversation. She was actually paralyzed with fear; and, for some time after they had passed on, she remained as motionless as if she had been turned into stone. It was not till the echo of their voices had long died away, that she ventured to creep out of her hiding-place, and take a side peep at the gate, where she almost feared she should still see them standing. But the faint beams of the waning moon showing her that there was no one there, she ventured, with as little noise as possible, to rise to her feet; and, after cautiously listening, for the purpose of making sure that her enemies were not returning, she climbed over the wicket again into the road.

Had Lilly not been a child in understanding and experience, there would have been nothing easier now than to have escaped all her difficulties. If she could have summoned courage to have presented herself before Mrs. Ross, and explained the motives that had led to her offence, and the danger that was impending over her, she would have probably found both pardon and protection; but this she did not know. She could not imagine, that after going away in the manner she had done and staying out all night, she could ever be forgiven or admitted into the house again; and she had no conception that Mr. and Mrs. Ross either would or could have defended her against those to whom she imagined she belonged. Added to which, an instinctive feeling, derived from the past, vague and undefined as her notions had been as to the real interpretation of what she had witnessed at the Huntsman, made her look upon Luke with the same sentiment that a child might look upon an ogre. An undefinable terror of something—she knew not what—pervaded her at the idea of falling into his hands; and she had his own word for it, that he would scruple at no means that might serve to entrap her. All she thought of, therefore, was immediate escape; and, without considering where she was to go, or reflecting on the probable consequences of so rash a proceeding as setting out alone, in the middle of the night, on a journey, which might conduct her to greater perils than those she was flying from, she took to her heels and ran along the road in an opposite direction to the town, till she was fairly out of breath, and obliged to relax her speed for want of it.

With the slower pace came something like reflection; and, though urged forwards by the eager desire to get out of the reach of those she feared might pursue her, she did now begin to wonder whither she was going, and what was to become of her. But, unable to form any reasonable plan of escape, and afraid to return, she still walked on; with her heart yearning towards Abel, her only friend, to whom she would have given the world to explain her dilemma; though not without some fears of his displeasure, too; for she was sure he would be very sorry, if not very angry with her, for the imprudence which had lost her so excellent a situation.

The night was very fine, and it was not long before the forlorn traveller was cheered by the dawn of morning, and then she could venture to sit down by the wayside to take a little rest. But the voices of some men approaching started her to her feet; for she could not divest herself of the apprehension of being pursued, and she fled forwards again with somewhat of her former speed, till she reached a village; and, as she was very hungry and had plenty of money in her pocket, she would have very gladly purchased some food; but the shops were not yet opened; and, afraid to linger, she walked through. And now the early travellers and the labourers in the fields began to be afoot, and ever and anon she was saluted by the observation that it was a fine morning, or with a rustic compliment upon her early rising; and thus she proceeded without any particular adventure, till, exhausted by hunger and fatigue, she seated herself on a low stone post, which stood at the gate of a neat little villa, enclosed in a garden.

She had sat there about half an hour, with somewhat of the feelings of a hunted hare, alarmed at every foot she heard approaching from the west, and so confused and perplexed with the strangeness of her situation, that she was entirely incapable of determining on any step that might diminish her difficulties, when she heard, first, the door of the house, and, next, the gate unlocked behind her; and presently a man came out, bearing in his hand a small trunk and a large blue bandbox,[48] which he set down on the pathway, and then retreated into the house, leaving the gate ajar. On the trunk were the letters A. T. in brass nails, and on the bandbox was inscribed "Mrs. Treadgold, passenger."

---

48 A large round cardboard box for hats.

Presently the man came out again and looked down the road, as if expecting something. Then he looked at Lilly, and seemed about to address her; when a voice within, calling "James," caused him suddenly to reenter the gate.

A third time he made his appearance; and now, after listening for a moment, Lilly heard him say, "I think she's coming now!" and then, turning towards her, where she was still sitting on the post, he added, "You're waiting for her too, I suppose?"

"Sir!" said Lilly, not understanding what he meant.

"James!" cried a voice from within, "isn't that the coach?"

"Yes, ma'am, she's coming up now," answered James, re-entering the gate; out of which he presently issued again, accompanied by a lady; upon whose appearance Lilly rose from her seat, and at the same moment the coach swept round a curve in the road, and dashed up to the gate. In a moment, the coachman was off his box, arranging the luggage in the boot, whilst James opened the coach-door and handed in the lady.

"Now, my dear," said the coachman, taking hold of Lilly's arm, and drawing her to the coach. "Come, come, don't be frightened—put your foot there—the other there—that's right!" and, before she knew where she was, between the driver on one side, and James on the other, Lilly found herself at the top of the London coach, spanking away at the rate of ten miles an hour.

The truth was, that the coachman, seeing a respectable looking servant-girl standing with the lady, set her down at once for the maid; whilst James had taken it for granted she was there waiting for the coach. The mistake was not unnatural in either party, for Lilly was very well dressed, with a neat bonnet and shawl, and a gown that had formerly been worn by Mrs. Ross herself. For, as the under nursery-maid had to walk out with the children, that lady had recruited her wardrobe with various articles from her own. The strangest feature in the affair was Lilly's consenting to mount the coach, without any attempt at an explanation; but this arose, in some degree, from the suddenness of the thing, which gave no time for so timid and inexperienced a person to collect her wits, till she was actually hoisted up; and by that time a vague notion, that since she was flying in that direction, riding was both a more speedy and a more agreeable way of attaining her object than walking, prompted her to submit in silence to what fate seemed to have ordained for her.

There is something very exhilarating in dashing along with four horses, whilst the free air is blowing in your face; and Lilly was by no means insensible to so novel a pleasure. At eight o'clock they stopped to breakfast, and then, having done ample justice to the ham and toast, she presented one of her guineas in payment, and received nineteen shillings in change, which seemed to her to be worth more than the gold that she had given.

When people start on a journey at four o'clock in the morning, they are seldom very communicative till they have had their breakfast; and, accordingly, everybody on the outside of the coach had hitherto possessed their souls in silence. But now, warmed by the tea and comforted by the toast, there seemed a general disposition to talk; with the exception of Lilly, whose early habits of enforced silence still clung to her; and her next neighbour, who was the only person of, apparently, a similar grade to herself on the coach. This was a pale, thin, somewhat sickly-looking woman, with a baby in her arms, that, by its whining and crying, seemed to be suffering from its teeth, or some other infantile malady. The mother wore a dress of black stuff,[49] a shawl of the same colour, a white straw bonnet, a good deal the worse for wear, tied down with a single bit of black ribbon, and a pair of black cotton gloves. She had altogether the look of respectable poverty; and a life of sorrow, suffering, and trial, had left its records engraven on her face. She sat behind the coach, with her back to the horses, as did Lilly; and the latter had observed that she had not made her appearance in the breakfast-room, with the rest of the passengers. When they returned to the coach, she had found her eating a biscuit, a bit of which she now and then drew from her pocket for the child, whose uneasiness was temporarily allayed by sucking it.

On the other side of this poor traveller, who occupied the centre seat, was a well enough dressed, but coarse-looking, and very coarsely-mannered man, who, from his conversation with a gentleman in a white hat and green shooting-coat, opposite him, appeared to be a stable-keeper. This personage was by no means an agreeable neighbour. He had taken a dram[50] where they stopped to change horses, before breakfast, and another as soon as he had swallowed his meal; and, from the manner in which she turned away her head, the fumes of the liquor seemed to be annoying the sickly woman; but, by and by, when he took out a short pipe and began to smoke, without any regard to the convenience of those about him, she became positively ill; and was under the necessity of asking Lilly if she would hold the child for her, for a minute or two. Lilly took the child willingly, and nursed it as well as she could; and when the mother, on feeling somewhat recovered, offered to take it again, she expressed her readiness to keep it longer.

"It doesn't tire me," said she. "I can hold him very well."

"He's teething, poor little fellow," said the mother, "and it makes him so restless that I don't get any sleep o' nights with him, and that keeps me ill all day; for I'm not overly strong, at the best."

This commencement naturally leading to further communication, the

---

49 Coarse woven wool fabric.
50 A small amount of alcoholic liquor.

stranger asked Lilly if she were going all the way to London; and Lilly, who did not know where she was going, answered that she believed she was.

"I have been down to the country," said the stranger, "seeing about my husband's brother, as is just dead, though it was very inconvenient to me to travel with a young child, and he sickly too, and not very well myself: but Mr. Watts—that's my husband—couldn't leave his work, so I'd need to go, whether or not." Here she sighed as if the results of the journey had not made her amends for its fatigues. "Travelling by coach is very expensive too," she added. "I've paid sixteen shillings for my place to London, and as much when I came down—that's one pound twelve shillings, which is a great deal for a poor person;" and here another sigh furnished the commentary to the text.

"How much shall I have to pay?" inquired Lilly.

"About fourteen shillings, I should think, from the place you got up," answered Mrs. Watts. "But your missus pays for you, I suppose?"

"No," said Lilly, looking at her with some surprise; and wondering how she knew any thing about her mistress.

"Then she gives you the money to pay, yourself; that's the same," said Mrs. Watts; and as this was an axiom that Lilly could not dispute, she made no answer.

"My husband had a cousin lived in your family," continued Mrs. Watts—"he comes from this part of the country—it's a very good family to live in, isn't it?"

"Yes, very," answered Lilly, not a little frightened at this unexpected recognition.

"I know who Mrs. Treadgold was too, afore she married Mr. Treadgold," added Mrs. Watts.

"That's she inside the coach," said Lilly, still not comprehending the quid pro quo;[51] "she's got her name upon her box."

"Oh, yes, I know her very well," said the other. "She was a Miss Allison—there was two of 'em—and this here one was the handsomest, and married Mr. Treadgold, and the other married Mr. Knox, and she keeps a milliner's shop, in Oxford Street; and Mrs. Treadgold goes up once a year to see her. Tom Watts—that's my husband's cousin—knew well enough where she went, though she always gave out something different, and that's where she's going now, no doubt. But she was never used to take a maid, and I wonder she does now."

"I don't think she has any maid," returned Lilly. "I didn't see one."

"I thought you were her maid," said Mrs. Watts, looking round with some surprise.

"No," answered Lilly.

---

51 Something given and something received. Here meaning Mrs. Watts's assumptions based on what she thinks she perceives.

"But you're with her, ar'n't you? You came to the coach with her?"

"No," said Lilly; "I was only sitting there to rest."

"Oh," said Mrs. Watts, still not suspecting Lilly's involuntary Hegira,[52] "then you live somewhere near there, I suppose?"

"Not very near," returned Lilly. "I had walked a great way."

As this last piece of information suggested no new question, the conversation rested there for some time; and presently after this, they stopped to change horses.

"That has been a fine horse in his day," remarked the gentleman in the green shooting-coat to him of the pipe; as the ostler led out the beautiful remains of a bright bay hunter.

"Ay, sir," returned the other; "I know him well; he's been a famous un in his time. I sold him myself five years ago to General Markham. He was then just rising four."

"He's been terribly hard run," observed the gentleman whose name was Thornley.

"Yes," said Elliott, the stable-keeper. "The General's a bad horse-master; he'll run any horse off his legs in five years."

"He lives somewhere hereabouts, doesn't he?" said Mr. Thornley.

"We've passed his place some time back," replied Elliott. "He owns a great deal of land about Weldon; and has a deal of property one way or t'other."

"Is he married?" inquired Thornley.

"Yes, he is, worse luck for him," returned Elliott. "He married out of spite, and a bad business he made of it."

"How so?" inquired Mr. Thornley.

"Why, you see, sir," said Elliott, "he was the son of old Markham, the rich East Indian."

"I remember," said Thornley; "he left an immense fortune."

"Yes, sir, and he left it all betwixt this here General Markham—he was Colonel Markham then—and his daughter; they was his only children—he never had but them two."

"She's dead, I think," said Mr. Thornley; "a brother of mine met her in Calcutta, and used to speak of her as a very sweet creature."

"I believe she was, sir; I've heard say so. Well, sir, you see, by the old nabob's[53] will, if she died unmarried, her share of the fortune was to go to her brother and his heirs; and wice wersa; if he died unmarried, his share went to her. Well, you see, nat'ral enough, he wished to keep the girl single; but she wasn't by no means o'

---

52 Escape or flight.

53 A very wealthy person. Most often used to refer to someone returning from India with a fortune.

the same mind; and what does she do, but falls in love with a Captain in a march-ing regiment—Charlie Adams, he was called—an uncommon fine young fellow! We sold him the first horse he ever owned—it was a roan mare, nearly fourteen hands, and a capital one to go—she won him several handicaps[54] before he went to India; then he sold her to Colonel Gordon; and what came of her after, I don't know."

"And Miss Markham married Captain Adams, didn't she?" said Mr. Thornley, more interested in the biography of the Markham family than in that of the roan mare.

"Yes, sir; she married him, worse luck for her; before she was of age too, and against her brother's consent."

"Was the marriage an unfortunate one, then? Didn't they agree, she and Adams?"

"I believe they agreed well enough, sir; but you see, her brother, who was disappointed—for she was but a delicate creatur, and I suppose he was in hopes she'd die and leave all the fortune to him—did every thing he could to cross 'em, and kept 'em as poor as he could."

"But he couldn't keep her fortune from her," said Mr. Thornley.

"Well, even there, luck was against 'em. You see they'd a child, a boy I be-lieve it was—no, by the by, now I think of it, it was a girl—well, sir, they doted upon the child, and they were very unwilling to take it to India with 'em, when they were ordered out there; but it seems they'd nobody to leave it with, it being but an infant; so they took it. However, they intended to come home as soon as she—that's Mrs. Adams—was of age and got her fortune; but by that time her husband, Charlie Adams, had got to be a Major; and he didn't like leaving the service; so, instead of coming themselves, they sent home the child under the care of a relation; but the ship they came in was lost in the channel, and every soul on board perished."

"Then did the fortune revert to the brother?"

"No, sir; it should have gone to the husband by rights; for whether the old nabob meant it, or not, isn't clear; but the will ran so, that in default of heirs, the money went to her husband."

"And didn't he get it?"

"He has never got sixpence of it, sir, though it's now, I dare say, a dozen or fourteen years since the loss of the Hastings—that's the ship the child was sent home in—and, I believe, the mother did not long survive the news. She died of a broken heart, they say, at the loss of her child."

"But how could Major Adams be kept out of it?"

---

54 A type of horse race.

"Why, sir, if the lawyers are backed by a long purse, it's my belief they can keep any body out of any thing."

"But on what plea do they keep him out?" inquired Thornley.

"Why, sir, the General first disputed the will. He declared it never was the nabob's intention that the money should go out of the family—perhaps it wasn't; however, the will ran so; and Charlie Adams won that suit against him. But now he disputes the death of the child—which he says can't be proved; and as he's got plenty of money, and Colonel Adams, for he's a Colonel now, spent all he had in the first suit, he can't make no head against this one."

"I see," said Mr. Thornley; "though the General can't get the money himself, he can keep the other out of it."

"Exactly so, sir; and I believe the Colonel—that's Colonel Adams, I mean—is but badly off for want of it. The more so, as he married again about a year after the death of his first wife."

"And had his second wife no fortune?" inquired Thornley.

"Not a rap, sir, as far as I know; she was the daughter of a brother officer of the Captain's, I believe; a beautiful creature, but no money."

"And are there any children by this second marriage?" asked the other.

"One son, a fine lad about eight years old; and I don't think they've got much besides the Colonel's half-pay for the three to live on; for, when he found the first suit was to be decided in his favour, he left the regiment and came home."

"It's a great pity that the law can be made such a weapon for envy and malice!" said Mr. Thornley. "But who did the General marry himself?"

"Why, sir, he was in such a hurry to get a wife when he found his sister was re-solved to marry Charlie Adams, for fear he might die himself and leave his fortune behind him for them to enjoy, that he never stopped to look before he leaped, but married his own dairy-maid! An uncommon fine girl to look at, as you'd wish to see, but...." and here Mr. Elliott nodded his head in a manner that implied noth-ing very complimentary to the character of the General's ménage.

"She makes him pay for his folly, I suppose?"

"I fancy she does, sir. You saw that lady as breakfasted with us—she we took up at the willa this morning—her husband is the General's agent, and manages his estates for him—and they say he's obliged to manage the wife too; for though everybody's afraid of the General, the General's afraid of his own wife—at least, so folks says."

"Well, I don't pity him," said Mr. Thornley.

"Few people does, I believe, sir," returned Elliott.

CHAPTER III

A FRIEND IN NEED

It seemed a pity, as far as Lilly was concerned, that the journey to London should have ever come to a termination; at least, as long as she had money enough to pay her fare and her score at the several inns where they might stop to breakfast, dine, and sup. She had never had experience of any thing so agreeable as this careering through the air, for the sheer purpose of getting an appetite, which she had an opportunity of luxuriously satisfying exactly at the proper intervals. Could she have refrained from wondering what was to become of her when the coach stopped for good and all, she would have been in a state of real beatitude.

But even this anxiety did not oppress her as it would one who knew mankind and the world better. She did not, in short, sufficiently comprehend the peculiarities of her own situation to be very unhappy; and out of the hundred and one dangers that necessarily environed her, she saw but one, and that was the pursuit of Luke Littenhaus, from whom every mile was farther removing her.

"Is this London?" inquired Lilly, for the third time, as they drove through Kensington.[55]

"No; but we're close to it now," answered Mrs. Watts. "I suppose you'll have somebody waiting for you at the Coach Office?"

"No," replied Lilly; "I don't know anybody in London."

"How will you do then?" naturally inquired her new acquaintance.

"I don't know," said Lilly.

"Perhaps you've got a letter to somebody that will look to you?" said Mrs. Watts.

"No, I haven't," replied Lilly.

"My goodness!" exclaimed the other. "What makes you go to London, then?"

This was a question more easily asked than answered. Lilly blushed, and, not knowing how to explain her situation, remained silent; and the suspicion that she was a fugitive naturally suggested itself to her companion. But a fugitive from what cause? She appeared to have plenty of money—for, whenever the passengers descended to take refreshment, she had accompanied them; where they dined, she had paid her fare; and she had once drawn a guinea from her pocket for the purpose of amusing the child. It was not easy to avoid some suspicion of a person

---

55 Although Kensington was beginning to be developed in the mid-nineteenth century, there were many market gardens and it was still largely an agricultural area which supplied London with fruit and vegetables.

so oddly situated. Had she robbed somebody, and was escaping from justice? or, was she a girl of bad character, going to ply her evil trade in London? But so quiet, so humble, so apparently simple and inexperienced a creature surely could not be the last! The first supposition seemed the most probable, for very simple-looking girls are sometimes found guilty in this kind.

Nevertheless, an interest, compounded partly of curiosity and partly of good-nature, urged Mrs. Watts to further inquiries, which she could put without any danger of being overheard, as they sat side by side, and the rattle of the wheels drowned their voices.

"But where do you mean to go to sleep?" she asked, resuming the inquiry.

"I don't know," replied Lilly. "Do you know any place?"

"People don't like to take in strangers at this time of the night—that's *respectable* people don't," said Mrs. Watts, with an emphasis on the word *respectable*; a piece of intelligence that Lilly thought must be erroneous; since, when she travelled with Abel, they had never experienced any difficulties of that nature. "And you wouldn't like to go to any place that isn't respectable, I suppose?" continued Mrs. Watts, by way of sounding her.

"No," said Lilly, "I should be afraid;" for in the course of their travels such resorts had been pointed out to her by Abel, with remarks on their insecurity.

"And if you have much money you'll be very like to be robbed," said Mrs. Watts.

"Shall I?" said Lilly, beginning to be alarmed—for her day's adventures had taught her the value of her money.

"London's full of thieves," said Mrs. Watts.

"Is it?" said Lilly, looking somewhat amazed.

"Yes," returned Mrs. Watts; "they just lie in wait for country people, and if you don't take care, they'll be sure to strip you of every thing you've got."

"What shall I do with it?" said Lilly, pulling out of her pocket the piece of brown paper which contained her fortune; at that moment consisting of one guinea in gold, and the greatest part of another in silver.

"I can't tell," replied Mrs. Watts. "How much have you got?"

"Here's a guinea, and all this silver—I think its eighteen shillings," said Lilly, innocently laying open her store to the stranger's inspection.

"She can't be a thief," thought Mrs. Watts. "I've half a mind to ask her how she got it," a question which Lilly's simplicity rendered less difficult than might be imagined; so she put it.

"It's my wages for half a year," said she. "There were three guineas, but I changed two to pay the coachman and the dinner."

"Perhaps you're going to London to try to get a situation?" said Mrs. Watts, very much disposed to believe what she had told her.

"I should be very glad to get one," answered Lilly.

"But you'll want a character from your last place," said Mrs. Watts.

Here Lilly's blushes betrayed her again.

"Won't they give you a character?" asked Mrs. Watts.

"I don't know," murmured Lilly, looking very much ashamed, for now for the first time in her life she began to feel the importance of what she had so thoughtlessly flung away, and the inevitable disgrace and mortification of wanting it.

"Were you sent away for anything?" said Mrs. Watts.

"No, I wasn't sent away," replied Lilly; "but I went out without leave."

"And they wouldn't take you back again?"

"I don't know—I didn't try," answered Lilly.

"Did they ill-treat you, then? Didn't you like your place?"

"I liked it well enough," answered Lilly; "but I went to see somebody, and when I came back it was so late; and I was afraid the head-nurse would be very angry and tell Mrs. Ross about my going out without leave."

"But what made you come off to London? Hadn't you any friends to go to?"

"No," said Lilly. "I've only two friends, and one's in the workhouse, and the other's very poor, and her husband wouldn't let me stay there." And this was true; for Giles, little dreaming what a prize he was chasing away, had formerly objected to Martha's sheltering Lilly under her roof.

"But what made you come to London?" finally inquired Mrs. Watts; and then, for the first time, she discovered that Lilly's expedition, at least as far as the coach was concerned, was altogether involuntary.

"My goodness! I never heard of such a thing!" exclaimed Mrs. Watts; and well she might be astonished, since the real cause of Lilly's flight was yet a secret to her, and the ostensible one seemed a very inadequate motive for encountering such a "storm of fortune." But Lilly's dread of Luke was so great, that she would have found it difficult even to mention his name, much less tell the history of his persecution. Besides, as, in spite of what Abel had said to her on the subject, she could not divest her mind of the idea that her cousins could and would claim her if they knew where she was, and force her to return to them, an instinctive caution closed her lips.

"I can't think what you're to do!" continued Mrs. Watts, staring at her, and wondering whether she was mad or foolish; "and you don't know Mrs. Treadgold?" for she still supposed that Lilly had not been far from her home when the coachman had caught her up and carried her off; "else she might help you."

"No, I never saw her before," said Lilly, getting very much alarmed from seeing the impression her situation made on her companion; and as she began to cry, the attention of the passengers near her was attracted, and the gentleman in the green coat inquired what was the matter. Lilly was silent, but Mrs. Watts said that the young girl had foolishly left her place in the country, and was going to London without any acquaintance there to help her.

"Why don't she go back again to her friends, then?" said Mr. Thornley.

"Very true, sir," said Elliott; "why don't she go back again? We have passed half-a-dozen coaches going down, that would have taken her, and thank ye." But as, though they pressed Lilly with this question, she did not choose to give her motive for not following their advice, she incurred their suspicions too; and they privately agreed that she had doubtless very good reasons for the step she had taken. However, it was no business of theirs; and as they had now reached the end of their journey, and the coach was driving into the inn-yard, they addressed themselves to their own affairs; namely, the identification of their luggage, paying the driver, and procuring vehicles to convey them to their several homes.

Meantime, Mrs. Watts and Lilly had also descended; and as the first had only a bundle, and the last nothing, their transactions with the coachman were very soon terminated; and there remained nothing for either of them but to walk away in any direction she pleased; but Lilly stood still, because she did not know where to go; and Mrs. Watts did the same, from a different reason. She was herself not altogether unknown to Mrs. Treadgold; and, during the last quarter of an hour of their drive, she had formed a plan of addressing that lady, when she descended from the coach, on the subject of their forlorn fellow-passenger. But the plan was not so easily executed as formed. Two gentlemen were waiting with a coach ready to receive the lady, and they carried her off with such rapidity, that, without impertinently interrupting her first greetings with her friends, it was not possible to speak to her; so the poor woman stood still, watching Lilly, to see what she would do next.

"Come! get out of the way, girl!" cried a man, with a weigh-bill[56] in his hand; "there's no room for you here;" whereupon Lilly moved about three yards from the door of the office, and then stood still again. "Get out of the way!" said he again presently, giving her a push; "here's another coach coming up, and you'll be run over, I tell you!"

"Are you waiting for me, my dear?" said a vulgar-looking young man, who had been standing on the step and had overheard the clerk's address; and as he spoke he attempted to throw his arm round Lilly's waist.

"No, sir," said she, disengaging herself, impatiently.

"But that's very unkind," rejoined he, persevering in his unwelcome attentions; "I'm sure you wouldn't say no, if you knew me better. Are you a stranger in

---

56 An official document describing goods.

London? Come, I may be a friend to you."

"Please to let me go, sir," said Lilly, bursting into tears.

"Come along with me!" said Mrs. Watts, advancing and taking hold of her arm; I can't find in my heart to leave you here alone!"

CHAPTER IV

THE POOR ARE THE FRIENDS OF THE POOR

Lilly needed no second invitation to induce her to accompany her good Samaritan; for she was beginning to have some idea of what it was to be a helpless stranger, without a friend, in a great city.

"We're but poor folks," said Mrs. Watts, as they made their way through the then dimly-lighted town, "but I couldn't answer it to my conscience to let you walk the streets at this time of night. We've no spare bed; but I'll spread a rug on the floor for you; and you'll be out of harm's way, at any rate; and to-morrow, you'd better go back to where you came from, before you've spent your money."

This was a heavy doom to Lilly; for to go back was to run into the jaws of the monster that was waiting to devour her; at least, thus she considered it. However, it was no time to make objections; so she tramped on through street and lane, crying, ready to break her heart, but saying nothing, till they reached a mean neighbourhood, betwixt Holborn and the Strand, where Mrs. Watts and her husband rented two upper rooms.

Though it was not far from midnight, there were little signs of repose either in the house or the street. At one part of the latter two men were fighting; the lights of a gin palace flared brightly in another; a poor creature with the remnant of a melodious voice was singing "Crazy Jane" in the middle; and at the door of the house Mrs. Watts entered stood a sturdy woman, damming up the entrance against a miserable-looking little man, who appeared to be her husband, and whom she was accusing of not having seen his home since the previous Saturday morning. She was luckily too much occupied with her own squabble to attend to Mrs. Watts, who slid past her as quietly as she could, (for various reasons very glad to escape unnoticed) and, followed by Lilly, ascended the stairs to the top of the house. Her husband was already in bed, but, on recognising her voice, he arose, and let her in.

"Ah, Jane!" said he, "is it you? Well, what luck?" but perceiving Lilly, he added, "what! is this my brother's girl?"

"No, no," said Mrs. Watts. "This is a poor thing that came up on the coach with me, and she hasn't no where to sleep; and I didn't like to leave her to walk the streets all night."

"No, sure," said John; now that he had recovered his surprise, remembering his dishabille,[57] and modestly retreating behind the door; "she can lie down on my bed, and I'll get a rug into the next room for myself."

"No, no, you'd better keep to your bed, John," returned the wife; "she's young and healthy, and can sleep any where."

But John's hospitality wouldn't hear of such an arrangement; and, finally, Lilly found herself inserted between the sheets, beside a pretty little girl of six years old, whose sleep was undisturbed by her mother's arrival, or the change of bedfellow; whilst John, having hastily drawn on his clothes, retired to the next room to hear the detail of his wife's adventures.

Alas! there was nothing good to tell.

John's brother Abraham, who had lately died, was believed by his poor relations to have got together what they called "a good bit of money," which he had not the heart to spend; and, as he was known to be unmarried, although there were vague reports of his having an illegitimate daughter, poor John hoped to find himself the heir of his wealth. But there was no wealth to inherit; Abraham had been thought a miser, and he prudently encouraged the report; the truth being that he was very poor and had nothing to hoard. However, his reputation for wealth had stood him in good stead whilst he lived, exempting him from many of the evils of poverty; and when he died and people discovered their mistake, they might digest their disappointment as they could.

So thought Abraham Watts; and even with respect to his brother he was equally indifferent; not unfrequently laughing in his sleeve at what he called "John counting his chickens." But it was no joke to John and Jane; and indeed it was with the greatest difficulty that the former in his honesty and simplicity could be brought to believe that his brother had so cruelly deluded them. He had a little packet of Abraham's letters in an old trunk; and to these he now referred for self-justification; and there was enough in them certainly to authorize all the expectations he had indulged.

There was scarcely a letter without some sentence alluding to his own property, and to the circumstance of his having no heir but his dear brother John. In short, he had played "Sham Abraham"[58] upon poor John, who, placing implicit faith in all he said, had sent off his wife on the receipt of a letter announcing his brother's death; devoting to the expenses of the journey, at a period when their fortunes were at the lowest ebb, all the money he could get together, amounting to about three pounds; one of which was at that very moment due to their landlady, Mrs. Thom, for rent. Thus, as is too often the case with poor people, this delusive

---

57 Being in a state of undress or dishevelled in appearance.
58 Someone who tricks or deceives.

gleam of hope was good for nothing but to plunge them into deeper distress than they were in before.

For some time, the poor husband and wife sat up talking over their misfortunes; but people who have to work for their bread cannot afford to lose their night's rest; and fatigue, by procuring them that sleep which forsakes the pillows of the rich Unhappy, is a medicine, and considerable counterbalance, to their woe.

Lilly was awakened in the morning by the cries of the little girl, who on opening her eyes was frightened at seeing a stranger in bed with her; but the sight of her mother soon dried her tears; and the poor family arose and prepared for their humble breakfast. It was during this repast that for the first time John was made acquainted with Lilly's story, so far as his wife knew it. An overworked, patient, gentle-spirited man, he had no harsh remarks to make upon her folly—to him there was nothing incomprehensible in the fear of reproof that had deterred her from going back to her situation, after the offence she had given; but he united with his wife in recommending her immediate return; and proposed himself securing a place for her on the top of the night coach, as he passed to his work.

"I see you don't like the thoughts of going back," said he, for, though she ventured no objection, Lilly looked very down-hearted every time she heard her doom reiterated; "but you'll never get on here without friends, or any body to give you a character. If we could help you, we'd be willing enough; but we can't help ourselves, worse luck! And London's no place for a stranger; especially a young woman like you." And John's *like you* was not without meaning; the truth being, that Lilly was now rather a pretty girl. The thick white complexion, that had formerly disfigured her, had given place to a clear red and white; and every body knows how much roses and lilies have to do with female beauty; whilst the heavy, stolid expression her features had acquired from hardship and over-work had changed to one of extreme simplicity and good nature; which were really, at present, the distinguishing characteristics of her mind.

They had finished their breakfast, and John was just preparing to depart for his daily labour, when the door opened, and in walked Mrs. Thom, the virago who had been apostrophizing her husband at the door on the previous evening when the travellers arrived. A more unwelcome visitor could not have appeared; and the expression of the two faces that met her view did not tend to sweeten the tone of her subsequent discourse. However, Mrs. Watts offered her the chair from which she had herself just risen; whilst John dropped again into his, on the opposite side of the table, nerving himself, as well as he could, to meet the brunt of the battle. Had Lilly had more *savoir vivre*,[59] she would naturally have retired into the adjoining room on perceiving that the visit was one of business; and if she had,

---

59 Knowledge of life.

probably the whole current of her future life might have changed its direction; but, as it happened, her timidity and ignorance kept her where she was—that is, sitting on a wooden box, in a corner of the room, with the baby in her lap, which the mother had just before requested her to hold.

"I suppose I needn't say what brings me up so early?" said Mrs. Thom, in a tone of dry decision. "Nothing but being chock sure of the money when your missus came back could have got me to wait so long; for I've been very badly off for it, I can tell you. That drunken scoundrel ha'n't been home till last night—and then I wouldn't let him set his foot inside the door—since he got his wages."

"But I wouldn't drive him away when he did come, if I were you," said Mrs. Watts.

"Not drive him away!" exclaimed Mrs. Thom, indignantly; "do you think I'd encourage such a drunken beast! Why don't he bring his money home to his poor wife and children that want it. Suppose I went on as he does, where should we all be? If it wasn't for my lodgings, we might all want bread for *him!*"

"It's very bad," said Mrs. Watts; "only, driving him away must make him worse, you know."

"Make him worse! Let it make him worse, then! It's only what he deserves! A man that has no feeling for his wife and young family!—and I'm sure, though I say it that shouldn't say it, I've been as good a wife to him as...." here Mrs. Thom's eloquence being impeded by the want of a simile, as too frequently happens to orators, her mind naturally reverted to the occasion of her visit. "As I was saying, if it wasn't for my lodgers, I should like to know how I should pay the baker's bill? If it wasn't for your money that's coming in, and has been due this fortnight, we might sup upon our fingers, for anything he'd care."

"I'm very sorry," began John, who during this discourse had sat with his head leaning on his hand, in the attitude of the poor farmer in Wilkie's "*Distraining for Rent*;"[60] "I'm very sorry, but...."

"But me no buts, now, Mr. Watts, if you please!" said Mrs. Thom, interrupting him. "I want my money, and I must have my money. It's not a little that 'ud have kept me out of it for a fortnight, and me and my children wanting bread; but as you'd got a fine fortin left you, it wasn't me that 'ud bar your getting it for the matter of a week or two—though it isn't every body that 'ud ha' waited as I've done. But waiting's waiting, and paying's paying; and now I'll thank you to come down with the money, which is just one pound five shillings, being one quarter's rent for these two rooms—and cheap they are at the price! There isn't two better nor more respectabler rooms in the street!"

---

60 A painting by Scottish artist David Wilkie portraying the distress for a farmer with a large family who is threatened with eviction as he cannot pay his rent (1815).

"It's very unlucky," said Mrs. Watts, who, partly because she did not like to encounter Mrs. Thom's fierce eye, and partly that she might be at hand to sustain and second John, had placed herself behind the landlady's chair, on the back of which she leaned,—"it's very unlucky indeed! But it wasn't only us, but everybody that knew Abraham Watts, thought he had a lot of money hoarded up somewhere; and he always told John in his letters that we were to have it."

"And who's got it?" inquired Mrs. Thom, diverted from her own interest, for an instant, by her sympathy with the lucky person, whoever he might be.

"There was none to get," said John, with a heavy sigh. "It was a cruel thing of my brother to deceive us. I could show you letters, Mrs. Thom..."

"It isn't letters I want, Mr. Watts," interrupted the landlady. "I comes here for my money, one pound five shillings. There it is, on a bit of paper, and a receipt to it all ready. I brought it up on purpose—twenty-five shillings—gold or paper, it's all alike to me, so I gets it."

"We haven't got it," said John, sadly, but firmly. "You know, Mrs. Thom, that illness I had in March has thrown us back terribly; if it hadn't been for that—"

"Mr. Watts," said Mrs. Thom, "if me no ifs; it wasn't for to hear *ifs*, nor *ands* neither, as I left my tub to come up here to you this morning. What I want is my quarter's rent, one pound five shillings; that's what I comed for, and that's what I'll have!" and as she announced this determination, she clenched it by an expressive thump of her fist upon the table.

"I can't pay it," said John, in the same firm but dejected tone—a tone which, whilst it betrayed the deepest sorrow, and a consciousness that to petition for longer delay would be useless, seemed to forswear all attempts at subterfuge or evasion. "I can't pay it," said he; but at that moment a timid hand was stretched forward from behind Mrs. Watts, and the twenty-five shillings were laid on the table before the landlady.

"No, no!" cried Mrs. Watts, trying to arrest the arm.

"No!" cried John, rising from his chair; "we're not going to rob the stranger that has taken shelter with us," and he extended his hand to push back the money. But he was too late. No sooner had Mrs. Thom's eye fallen on it, than she had scraped it into her pocket, whilst, with a hearty laugh, and a countenance glowing with satisfaction, she congratulated John and his wife on this timely assistance, not forgetting a compliment to their benefactress.

"Upon *my* word, miss," said she, to Lilly, who had slunk back to the corner, blushing crimson at her good deed, "upon *my* word, if that isn't behaving like a lady, I don't know what is! I'm sure I wish I'd such a friend!"

"It's very wrong, indeed!" said John, whilst Mrs. Watts wiped her eyes with the corner of her apron. "We've no right to take what we don't know how to pay back."

"What's that to you!" said Mrs. Thom. "Ha'n't you a right to take what folks gives you, without asking? Thank ye, miss," she added, addressing Lilly, as she pushed back her chair, and prepared to take her leave. "Such friends as you's always welcome: and all I can say is, that I hope there's plenty more where that comed from!"

CHAPTER V

LILLY OBTAINS A SITUATION

As soon as Mrs. Thom had closed the door, John Watts laid his head upon the table, covering his face with his hands, and his wife dropped into the chair the landlady had left, and relieved her feelings by tears; whilst Lilly still sat nursing the baby in the corner, and the little girl, who during Mrs. Thom's visit had been amusing herself by playing with a rag doll, now crept to her mother, and laid her curly head in her lap, instinctively sympathizing with the feelings of her parents.

"I shouldn't mind it," said John, "if I saw how I could pay it back."

"Perhaps, if you keep your health, we may do better next half," said Mrs. Watts, who did not like to see her husband so depressed.

"But how's the young woman to find her way to the place she came from?" said John. "And what can she do here?"

"Perhaps we may get something for her to do," said Jane, wishing to console him; "but I say, John, do you know what o'clock it is? you'll be late at your work!" At which intimation, John, who for the moment had forgotten his duty in his sorrows, started from his chair, and, taking his cap from the nail where it hung, hastily quitted the room. Then Jane sat down beside Lilly, and having taken the baby, who was beginning to whine for its mother's bosom, she entered into conversation with her about the future.

Nothing could have been more entirely disinterested than Lilly's timely assistance; for she had acted wholly on the impulse of the moment, as it was her nature to do when her impulses were not forcibly suppressed by her fears: but, had she calculated the result, she could have done nothing better for her own interest; at least, for her own object—for what line of conduct might prove most conducive to her interest no one could yet forsee. She had, at all events, put it out of her own power to follow that advice, which she could scarcely have rejected, however disagreeable it was to herself; she must needs have allowed John to secure her a place on the coach; and, unless she chose to throw herself, a houseless wanderer, on the streets, she must have travelled back to whence she came, and thus probably have run into the jaws of Luke Littenhaus. Now, she must stay where she was;

and it had become the duty as well as the desire of John and Jane Watts to do all they could to help her to some means of getting her bread. Jane herself was a clear starcher, and, till John's illness, which had thrown them behind in the world, they had always contrived to make both ends meet, though they could not do more; but now, as we have seen, they were very poor, unable to maintain their own family, still less any addition to it.

"Can you do needlework well?" she asked of Lilly.

"I can hem and sew pretty well," answered the other; "but I can't stitch well, nor make button-holes."

"Then you won't do for the plain workshops," said Mrs. Watts.

"I could do house-work, or take care of children," said Lilly. "At Mrs. Ross's, I was under-nurserymaid."

"But people are so particular about character for that," objected Mrs. Watts—"I mean for nurserymaid; but I'll speak about it at the places I work for; and, meanwhile, if you'll take care of my baby, it will give me more time for my business;" and, accordingly, Lilly became at once nurse and maid of all work; whilst Mrs. Watts went forth amongst her customers to obtain employment, and then set herself to execute their commands.

Amongst the persons she worked for was that Mrs. Knox, whom she had mentioned as Mrs. Treadgold's sister. These ladies had been the daughters of a small farmer, but marriage had somewhat divided their subsequent careers. When the eldest married Mr. Knox, who kept a straw bonnet-shop in Oxford Street, it was thought a very good match for a portionless girl;[61] but when Christina, the youngest, who was handsome, was selected for a wife by Thomas Treadgold, Esq., the humble fortunes of her sister were wholly eclipsed; and although the good understanding and family friendship that had previously subsisted between them still survived, their further intercourse was subjected to considerable restrictions.

Mr. Treadgold had been brought up in the office of Mr. Ross, who reckoned amongst his clients most of the principal gentlemen of the county; and, amongst the rest, General Markham. Quickwitted and industrious, young Treadgold speedily rose to be first clerk; and, being brought much into communication with his master's clients, some of them, with General Markham at their head, advised him to set up for himself, and promised him the agency of their estates.

He followed their council; and, so rapid was his progress, that he was soon in a fair way of making an ample fortune, and could afford to indulge his inclinations by marrying the pretty Christina Allison, whom he had half fallen in love with in his boyhood, when they attended the Dame school together in their native village. Thus, the young bride rose at once into another sphere of society;

---

61 A girl without a dowry or any money.

for, besides the most opulent of the middle classes, her husband, and occasionally herself, were received at the tables of the proud county aristocracy; and with any of these it was impossible to bring the milliner of Oxford Street into approxima-tion. Very glad indeed Mrs. Treadgold would have been to have given her sister a little country air now and then; but, alas! she had not the courage. And yet her neighbours knew as well as she did herself who and what her sister was, though they had been born in another county; such delicate little secrets always creep out. Nay, they knew the very shop; and would buy a bonnet there, when they went to London, for the sake of seeing Mrs. Treadgold's sister behind the counter—they were the wives of the doctors, and lawyers, and so forth, who did this—as for the real aristocracy, the whole affair was beneath their notice; the agent's wife and the milliner being so far below themselves, that to their optics they appeared both on a level. Every body knew, too, where Mrs. Treadgold went when she visited London; so that, in fact, she gained nothing in the world by these sacrifices to her own gentility and the folly of mankind—or rather of womankind—except more or less of the contempt of those whose prejudices she stood in awe of; for, though probably not one of them would have had the courage to do otherwise—nay, some were, in one shape or another, doing the very same thing—yet they all saw the weakness and cowardice of the oblation,[62] and would have respected Mrs. Treadgold much more if she had not made it.

Lilly had been an inmate of the Watts family some three or four days, when John's brother, who had formerly been a cleaner of knives and shoes at Mr. Treadgold's, and since promoted to be an errand-boy at Mr. Knox's, arrived with a packet of lace, and some fine muslin caps to be clear-starched. They belonged to Mrs. Treadgold, who always seized the occasion of these annual visits to refresh her wardrobe.

"I don't think she knew me," said Jane; "but I came up by the same coach that she did."

"She's come at a bad time for us," said Tom; "for we're all at sixes and sevens at our house."

"It's just the busy time," observed Jane.

"Yes," said Tom; "the ladies runs so upon straw bonnets this month; and mis-sus can't get sewers enough."

"Can't she," said Jane, whose thoughts instantly reverted to Lilly; "I wonder if it's work any body can do."

"No, I don't think it is; I believe they have to learn it," answered Tom; "why? would you take it?"

"Not I; I couldn't leave John and the children," returned Jane; "but I've a

---

62 A solemn (usually religious) offering.

friend I should be very glad to get in, if I could."

"Can she do it?" inquired Tom.

"Well, she's young and she could learn," said Jane; "every body must have a beginning. I've a great mind to go to Mrs. Knox and speak about it."

"Well, do," replied Tom; "I know they want sewers, terrible."

Upon the strength of this hope, Mrs. Watts immediately set to work at the clear-starching; and having by a little extra diligence completed the job by the next day, she started for Oxford Street, leaving Lilly to take care of the children.

"I mustn't say anything about the running away, nor how she came up," thought Jane, "or they'll take a bad opinion of her at once;" so, accordingly, she merely mentioned Lilly as a young person wanting employment, and willing to turn her hand to anything.

"But does she know the business?" inquired Mrs. Knox.

"No, ma'am, I can't say she does; but she'd be quick at learning it," answered Jane, at a venture; "and she's the most good-tempered, obliging young person I ever saw."

"That's something, certainly; but is her conduct respectable? for we get so many that are not."

"Oh, yes, ma'am," answered Jane, with great confidence; for she really thought herself quite safe upon that head; and, for the rest, she considered herself bound to venture something for one who had served her so opportunely. "Lilly didn't stop to think how she was to do without her money," thought she; "and I must risk something to help her to earn her bread decently; or else who can tell what may come of her."

Fortunately, Mrs. Knox *was* in very great want of hands at the moment; and, as she had an excellent opinion of Jane, and was exceedingly afraid of getting dis-honest or disreputable girls into the house, she consented to give Lilly a trial; and Jane returned home quite overjoyed at her success.

That night they sat up late, washing and ironing Lilly's habiliments;[63] for she had not an article of clothing but what she wore; and, on the following morning, Jane conducted her to her new situation. "You'll come back to sleep," she said; "for none of the girls are allowed to sleep in the house—no wonder they're so apt to turn out ill, poor things!" And presently Lilly found herself seated amongst some ten or a dozen young people of her own age, and of various degrees of skill. For her part, she was set to the coarsest preliminary work; and awkward enough she was, at first; but she was urged to success by strong motives; and, in the mean time, her unabating diligence and quiet deportment told much in her favour. Her wages, however, were but a bare pittance, but they were enough to furnish

---

63 Clothes.

her breakfast and other small necessaries; whilst she slept under the roof of John Watts; and got her dinner and tea where she worked.

For the first few nights, John fetched her; but, as the young people were often kept at work till midnight, this was necessarily given up, as soon as she knew her way, and declared herself able to thread the throng alone. But in the beginning, for his brother and sister's sakes, and afterwards from another motive—Tom, when he could manage it, would offer to escort her. So that, on the whole, considering the apparent hopelessness of her prospects on the night she arrived in London, matters had taken a better turn than could have been well expected; so, for the present, we will leave her making straw bonnets, and return to those she left behind her.

CHAPTER VI

LILLY IN LOVE AGAIN

Having conducted Luke to a house where he could be provided with lodgings for the night, Giles turned his steps homewards, and rang up his wife.

"Have you seen that girl, Lilly Dawson, lately?" was one of his earliest questions; "is she still at Mr. Ross's.

"Yes," replied Martha; "she's doing very well, and they are quite satisfied with her—it's a lucky thing she got the situation, poor girl, wasn't it?"

"Very," returned Giles, with unusual sincerity; for he naturally reflected that, if she had not, he might have lost sight of her. "Does she come here often?" he inquired.

"Sometimes, of a Sunday evening—indeed, generally, after she has been to see my father."

"Is it always of a Sunday she comes?"

"Almost always," returned Martha, beginning to wonder at this sudden interest in the despised Lilly; and, when Giles proceeded so far as to inquire the hour at which she usually made her visits, she felt so assured that he must be actuated by some selfish motive, that she said, "Why do you ask?" He gave her no reason, however, but turned the conversation.

On the following morning, he went out to look after his new acquaintance, Luke; and, presently after he was gone, one of the servants from Mrs. Ross's called to inquire if Mrs. Lintock had seen Lilly.

"No," said Martha; "why?"

"Because she ran away last night after setting the house on fire, and has never come back."

"What!" exclaimed Martha, turning pale. "You don't say Lilly's gone!"

"She's gone from us," returned the man; "haven't you seen her?"

"No," returned Martha. "Lilly gone!"

"They don't think she has taken anything away with her; but if missus hadn't gone up to the nursery, the children would have been all burnt in their beds," said he.

Martha folded her hands and sunk into a chair, staring at the man, really incapable of receiving as fact intelligence which appeared to her out of the range of possibility. Her acquaintance with Lilly was certainly but of late date; but her father's opinion of the girl was so fixed, and had been so countenanced and corroborated by her own experience, that to believe all at once that she had been cunningly persevering in an assumed character for so many months, was a sort of conversion that would have undermined her whole code of faith. If Lilly were not what she had seemed, she must be the most finished hypocrite that ever lived— and all for what? For the mere pleasure of deceiving.

Martha was too honest and sincere herself to believe this very readily. She asked, "Had she been reproved? Had she been scolded?" Not that the man knew of; missus had paid her wages in the morning; and he believed Mrs. Janet thought she had been drinking. Martha could have almost laughed at this; it was so out of all keeping; but if anybody knew anything of Lilly, it would be her father; so she resolved to go to him.

It was a dreadful shock to Abel to learn that Lilly had not been home since she left him; what he feared was, that the possession of the money had brought her into danger. Or, could it be possible that, captivated with the wandering life she had led in his company, she had resolved to pursue it alone, on finding he would not go with her. Finally, they rather inclined to this opinion; since it was more accordant with Lilly's character—her impulsive nature and her entire ignorance of the world—than any other supposition.

Martha went next to Mrs. Ross's, in order to ascertain the truth with respect to the girl's departure, but she could learn no more than the man had told her; only that Mrs. Ross was not disposed to adopt the opinion that Lilly had purposely set fire to the stocking, which the zealous and indignant Mrs. Janet rather inclined to; but wherefore and whither she had gone nobody could imagine.

"Can Giles's inquiries be in any way connected with her disappearance?" thought Martha. She could not see how that could be, nor could she conceive the motive of his curiosity; but, nevertheless, those very inquiries were the cause of her not mentioning the subject of her departure to him, which she would otherwise have naturally done.

The week passed on, and there were no tidings of Lilly; nor did Giles ask any more about her till the Sunday, although his frequent visits at home of an evening somewhat surprised his wife. But, when Sunday arrived, he became anxious; he was fidgeting in and out of the house all day, and at length could not forbear asking Martha whether she thought Lilly would come, and at what hour.

"I am afraid she will not come at all," said she.

"Not at all!" exclaimed Giles. "Why, I thought you said she generally came on a Sunday."

"So she did," returned Martha; "but she's left Mrs. Ross's, and nobody knows what's become of her."

"Left Mrs. Ross's, and nobody knows what is become of her!" exclaimed Giles. "What the devil do you mean?"

"I mean just that," answered Martha.

"She went away last Monday evening, after leaving my father."

"And why the h—ll didn't you tell me so before?" said he.

"I didn't know you cared about Lilly," returned Martha, raising her eyes to his face.

"Gone away!" he reiterated. "What made her go?"

"That's what nobody knows," answered Martha. "She'd received her wages in the morning; and, sometimes, I'm half afraid some mischief is come to her."

At first, Giles suspected that his wife had, somehow or other, penetrated the plot formed against the girl, and had helped her to escape; but he was obliged to believe Martha's assurance to the contrary, for her truth was unimpeachable. The next idea was, that Lilly had discovered it herself, and to this supposition Luke inclined, when he heard the ill news. "She has somehow caught sight of me!" he said; but how, it seemed difficult to conceive, as he had not entered the town, or even approached the suburbs, till so late an hour on the Monday evening.

But what was to be done now? Giles was no less disappointed than Luke; and his anger at his wife for not having communicated Lilly's departure earlier, when there might have been some chance of tracing her, was excessive. However, he swore he would find her; for, besides the motive furnished by the money, his spite now supplied a second. But accident had contrived Lilly's escape so ingeniously, that Jack Shepherd or Louis Mandrin[64] themselves could scarcely have managed it better; neither her friends nor her enemies could discover what route she had taken.

Luke had, in some respects, the disposition of a bulldog; what he once fastened on, he never let go. Most people would have thought the hope of finding

---

64 Jack Shepherd was an eighteenth-century highwayman renowned for escaping from prison. Louis Mandrin was a French smuggler. Both figures became folk heroes and seeming champions of the poor.

Lilly, even at the first, much too faint a gleam to follow. Not so Luke. His determination was strengthened by opposition; and the compound of fear and avarice, which had formed his first motive for pursuing her, was now reinforced by revenge at his disappointment and defeat. He was like Othello;—what he would do, he knew not; but something he was resolved to do,[65] that should gratify his vengeance or replace her in his power.

But what? There was the question; and, whilst he and Giles are debating this point, we will see what Lilly is doing in London.

The difference that a few weeks' residence at Mrs. Knox's made in her appearance was quite remarkable: Luke might very well have passed her in the street without recognising her. The healthy life she led with Abel, and subsequently with Mrs. Ross, had first brightened her eyes and cleared her complexion; and to these improvements were now added a certain grisette-like[66] neatness that became her exceedingly. She had quickly observed the difference betwixt herself and the other girls; and, being abashed by it, she endeavoured to repair the disadvantage by dressing her hair more neatly, and adding a few articles to her wardrobe.

Previously to this, Lilly had never thought of her person; and she had had as little inclination as means to adorn it. It was the *de haut en bas*[67] manner of the young people she worked with, that first turned her eyes upon herself, and awakened something like shame at her own mean appearance. Not but the clothes she had worn when she quitted Mrs. Ross's were quite respectable; but, in the first place, she did not know how to wear them; and, in the next, they were rapidly growing shabby. The first was the greatest disadvantage of the two; her companions could have excused her poverty; but her want of taste was contemptible. The first day Lilly put on a new pink spotted linen frock, made by a cousin of Jane Watts; and a cottage bonnet, tied down with a pink and brown checked ribbon, was a very important period in her life; for, when she saw herself in the bit of glass that served the Watts family for a mirror, a vague notion dawned upon her mind *that she was pretty.*

She was extremely surprised; but she really could not help suspecting it. The idea had never struck her before; and the glow of satisfaction that thrilled through her nerves at the unexpected discovery brought a brighter colour to her cheek, and a decided confirmation of the pleasing suspicion; which even the attentions of Tom Watts had not awakened, though she sometimes wondered at them. Now she began to understand his motive; and, as the truth gleamed on her, she blushed again; and, somehow, the recollection of Philip Ryland recurred to her mind.

---

65 Crowe is referring to *Othello*, and Othello's jealousy, anger and misery.
66 A pretty, French, working-class girl.
67 Superior or supercilious, literally from high to low.

Not that she had ever forgotten him; on the contrary, she thought much more frequently of him and his mother than on any subject whatever connected with her past life. They stood boldly out from the dull uniformity of her daily drudgery, which itself had so little to mark its course, that it was fast fading from her memory; her short intercourse with them was almost her only landmark.

But the recollection of Philip had never stirred her heart, or brought the colour to her cheek before—now it did both. In short, for the first time, Lilly felt she was a woman; and the consequences of this important revelation were by no means gratifying to her humble admirer. She comprehended that she must not encourage hopes she could not fulfil; and, as precautionary measures of this description are seldom executed with due moderation, Lilly, as her betters too frequently do on such occasions, rushed into an excess of coldness that confounded all Tom's calculations, and well nigh drove him frantic; and as this circumstance produced some unpleasant scenes and caused some dissatisfaction in the bosoms of John and Jane Watts, Lilly found it advisable to relinquish the shelter they had hitherto afforded her, and seek a lodging elsewhere.

Amongst the young people that worked at Mrs. Knox's was a girl called May Elliott. She was, or at least had been, one of the prettiest young creatures that man's eye ever looked upon for evil. She was the daughter of Elliott, the stable-keeper, in whose company Lilly had travelled to London; and, having lost her mother in her infancy, she had been permitted by her father to grow up as wild as an untamed colt. She ran about the stable-yard, joked with the grooms, and rode astride on the horses' backs, without saddle or bridle; and her principles did not escape the forfeit which seems attached to all who have much to do with those seductive animals. When she grew older, she became her father's clerk; and, seated in a little office that looked into the yard, with the books before her, she kept the accounts, and noted down the orders of his customers, whilst he attended to other branches of his business. A less desirable situation for a pretty young creature of fifteen could scarcely have been contrived;—exposed to all sorts of companionships, and left wholly to her own guidance, it was to be wondered that she did not do worse than she did; which was to form an attachment to a man of very indifferent character, called Maddox, who, for matters of business, frequented her father's stables. He was what is commonly called a gentleman; but he was a sharper who frequented horse-races and gaming-tables, and lived by them. His manners and appearance, however, fascinated May, who idolized what she called *style*; and, as Maddox knew old Elliott to be rich, he saw no objection to indulging his fancy for his lovely daughter—the only child he had.

Elliott, however, much as, through ignorance and want of reflection, he had neglected his daughter's education and superintendence, did not choose to give her or his money to a man he looked upon as a scoundrel. He accordingly forbade the match, and withdrawing May from her office in the stable-yard, shut her up in the dull house, at the back of it, under the care of his sister; a bitter Christian, who was extremely pious, and hated everybody that was not, except her brother, whom she never resigned the hope of converting.

The consequence of this scheme of reform may be easily foreseen. May, wretched, and wearied out with the preaching, and the scolding, and the confinement, watched her opportunity, and ran away to her lover, who, she never doubted, would receive her with open arms. But she had reckoned too hastily on his attachment. May Elliott, with her father's consent and without it, was a very different person. With it, he was still ready to marry her; without it, he would have nothing to say to her. But Elliott, enraged at the step she had taken, was not only inexorable with regard to the marriage, but actually refused to receive his daughter again under his roof; and there is no telling to what evil she might have fallen, had not her mother's sister offered her the shelter of her humble home.

May was, at first, extremely unhappy. She blamed her father, and sometimes blamed herself; but, as it was rather the consequences of her error than its commission that she bewailed, she soon sought a little distraction in an attachment— or rather a flirtation, for he never touched her heart—with Giles Lintock, who had been an acquaintance of her early years. But Giles was just then on the point of marriage with poor Martha; and, in order to separate May from him, and enable her to provide for herself, her aunt had induced an acquaintance in London to teach her the straw-bonnet business, and thence she had risen to be employed at Mrs. Knox's, where she was looked upon as a very valuable coadjutor; not so much for the work she did, as for the use that was made of her pretty face. Every bonnet that May put upon her head was a becoming one, however dowdy and ugly it might look in the hand; and people were apt to fancy that they had only to buy the bonnet to look like her. Her beauty, therefore, which had marred her fortune, might almost have made it again, if she could have been prudent; but she could not. She had a good salary, but she spent it all in dress and frivolities; and, whilst she had a wardrobe quite unbecoming her condition, she was generally in arrears with her rent.

Nobody had felt more contempt for Lilly, when she first appeared at Mrs. Knox's, than May Elliott; she had looked upon her indeed as quite beneath her notice; a circumstance that had exceedingly pained Lilly, who was entirely captivated by May's beauty and *tournure*,[68] and her gay offhand manners. Attired in silks, with her beautiful hair most becomingly and even fashionably arranged, she appeared to Lilly a sort of princess; and, when the poor girl was sent into the

---

68 Style or figure.

showroom with a message, she not unfrequently forgot what she had to say, whilst she lost herself in admiration of May Elliott's beauty.

Though the modest Lilly "never told her love," it was not long before the young people discovered it; and, as they were not aware that the enthusiastic love of one human being for another, although misplaced, is yet a sacred thing, they did not spare ridicule, which, shy as she was, distressed her exceedingly. But now May herself came to her aid. She saw nothing absurd in Lilly's admiration, and would not permit her adorer to be laughed at—for it was a real passion in its way; and May Elliott was to Lilly as much an impersonation of the ideal as if she had been a Venus or a Minerva.[69] Thus there originated, we will not say a friendship, but a sort of league, betwixt the two girls, in which protection was yielded for devotion. May would not allow Lilly to be teased or laughed at, and Lilly obeyed and waited upon May as if she were a goddess; and thus it arose, that when Lilly was forced to seek for a new home, May offered to let her share her lodging.

Setting aside the ethical view of the question, this was a wonderful step for Lilly; May's lodging being very superior to any thing she could have herself commanded; besides, as she had only her breakfast to purchase, her little wages enabled her to dress respectably; and, as with her means grew her ambition, so, in proportion to the development of the latter, low as were its aims, did her intellect brighten. She began now to see herself; and, from seeing herself, she proceeded to look around her, and see other people and things; and, whereas, nothing had had a meaning for Lilly before, she now began to discern what was passing under her eyes, and to comprehend something of the world and of the human beings that inhabit it. She was like a person that had been born blind, and was now beginning to see and to be acquainted with objects with which she had always been familiar, but which she had not understood. We do not mean to imply, however, that she comprehended May Elliott. May was a riddle far beyond Lilly's guessing—indeed, she would not have presumed to try; she was too happy in being permitted to adore her, and in believing nobody was so clever, and so wise, and so good, as well as so handsome, as May Elliott.

CHAPTER VII

LILLY MEETS AN OLD ACQUAINTANCE

There was not a more constant attendant at church than May Elliott—there she saw fine people, and the fine people saw her; at least, she thought they did; and, no doubt, her pretty face did sometimes attract the eyes that looked down from

---

69 Roman Goddesses of beauty and wisdom respectively.

the well-lined gallery-pews. Lilly, who had never been to church since she left Mrs. Ross's, would have liked very well to go too, but she had not courage to enter such a place alone; and May, not considering the pink-spotted frock sufficiently in accordance with her own toilet, did not invite her to accompany her, and yet, aware of Lilly's wishes, she did not like to leave her at home and alone. "I'll tell you what you shall do, Lilly," said she; "go, and take a walk in Hyde Park; did you ever see the park?"

"No," said Lilly.

"Well, you shall go, then, and I'll show you the way—it's just straight along the street, so you can't go wrong; and I'll come round that way for you, as I come out of church;" and Lilly, having her own little ambition, too, and being as proud of her linen frock as May was of her silk one, willingly accepted the offer.

As there seemed to be nobody in the park but nurses and children, she was neither noticed nor molested; and, having strolled about till she thought the service must be almost over, she seated herself near the gate, that she might be ready for her friend. She had not sat long, before a young woman came and sat down beside her. Lilly thought she knew her; but the girl not appearing to recognise her, she did not like to speak. Still, she could not take her eyes from the stranger; and at length, the other seeming to notice this scrutiny, turned round and stared her full in the face. Then Lilly was sure—it was certainly Winny Weston—a good deal altered for the worse; perhaps, as much as Lilly was altered for the better; she was pale, thin, and poorly dressed; but still it was Winny; and almost involuntarily Lilly pronounced her name.

"Don't you remember me?" said she.

"No," answered Winny; "I never saw you before, to my recollection."

"Don't you remember me up at the Huntsman?" said Lilly.

"What!" exclaimed Winny, "are you Lilly Dawson, that lived up there with them devils?—God forgive me for calling them so! Why, how you *are* altered!"

"So are you," answered Lilly; "I wasn't sure it *was* you, at first."

"Well I may be," replied Winny; "but only think of your being in London all the while! For my part, I always thought you was dead; and I said so."

It is very odd, but people always laugh at the idea of being thought dead—whilst one's alive it seems so absurd! And yet, as the day will assuredly come when we shall think it a very serious matter, one might be tempted to wonder where the comedy lies; but it is probably in the contrast. Howbeit, Lilly laughed. "What made you think I was dead?" said she.

"I thought they'd murdered you," said Winny, "as they did poor Shorty;" and at the name of Shorty she burst into a passion of tears; her grief was as fresh as the day she lost him.

"Did they kill Shorty?" Lilly asked, looking very much amazed.

"I'd lay down my life upon it," answered Winny.

"Who told you?" inquired Lilly.

"Every thing told me," answered Winny.

As this was an assertion Lilly could not apprehend, she remained silent—not unaffected, but surprised and puzzled.

"But how, in the name of goodness, did you get away from them?" inquired Winny. "They said you had gone to see some friends you had, where they lived before they came to the Huntsman; but them might believe them that could. I never believed a word they said, for my part."

"I wouldn't have cousin Luke know where I am for the world," said Lilly, suddenly remembering the danger that might accrue to her from the recognition.

"You needn't be afraid he'll know it from me," answered Winny. "But now you're out of their clutches, perhaps you won't mind telling me what you know about Shorty."

"I don't know any thing," answered Lilly, "except that he was sent away for being out o' nights—and cousin Luke said he stayed out drinking."

"Drinking! Shorty drink!" cried Winny, indignant at the imputation on her departed lover; "Shorty never took a mug of beer more than was good for him in his life! He went out to look for Mr. Ryland, and nothing else. Did you ever know what came of old Mr. Ryland?"

"No," replied Lilly, blushing from the consciousness that she was not telling the whole truth. She certainly did not *know* what had become of the miller; but she very strongly suspected that she knew where his body might be found; but not for the world would she have breathed this thought to any one; not even to Philip himself.

"It's my belief you know more than you like to say," continued Winny. "However, never mind; it 'ill all come out some day, you see if it don't."

"What'll come out?" inquired Lilly.

"It's natural for a person to stand up for their relations, to be sure," remarked Winny; "though I don't see that you was much beholden to 'em, either. I'm sure you don't look like the same person you was when you lived up there."

"I'm a great deal happier, now," observed Lilly.

"No wonder! Who wouldn't?" answered Winny, in whom the feminine instinct, quickened by her affection, had bred an absolute antipathy to the Littenhaus family.

"Well, it's well for you you're out of their claws," she continued, perceiving that Lilly was not disposed to be communicative. "I wish poor Philip Ryland was away from them, too."

"Philip! Is he there still?" inquired Lilly, blushing again.

"Ah," said Winny; "many a time when he came into the village he spoke about you, and asked if we could guess where you were; because one day he overheard them saying you had run away. But I said I was sure you hadn't the spirit to do it. I'm sure I wonder *he* don't run away, for they lead him a shocking life, *I* know."

"But how came you to London?" asked Lilly.

"I never could be happy there, after what happened to poor Shorty," said Winny. "Every time I saw them people come into the village, my blood boiled so, that I used to tell poor mother, that if I'd been a man, I'd have done something to them—I'm sure I couldn't have helped it."

"And is your mother in London, too?" inquired Lilly.

"No," said Winny; "what should she do here, poor old soul! No; I came up to be servant to a family that wanted a strong, healthy girl, from the country; but, what with the hard work, and the fretting, and one thing or another, I fell ill, and they put me into the hospital; and I'm just come out of it."

"And are you going back to your place?" said Lilly.

"No; they say I'm not strong enough for them, and they've got another servant," answered Winny; "so I've been to an office where they recommend you to places, and I am to go and see a lady to-morrow."

As now Lilly saw May Elliott approaching, she rose and took leave of Winny, after telling her where she might hear of her.

"Who was that you were talking to?" said May.

"It's a girl from the place I come from," answered Lilly; and then she related Winny's story, omitting, however, the charge brought against her cousins; and ending with a request that May would recommend her to a place, if she could.

"I can recommend her to a very good one," said May. "There was one of our customers asking Mrs. Knox to get her a servant only yesterday."

"Shall I go and tell her?" said Lilly.

"Yes, do," said May; "and tell her to come and call, and I'll speak to her this evening."

Poor Winny, who had come out of the hospital with scarcely a shilling betwixt her and destitution, gladly accepted the offer; and, in the evening, she called at May's lodging at the time appointed. "The family only keep two servants," said May; "and I believe there is a good deal to do, because the gentleman is nearly blind. He's a colonel on halfpay; and they have only one son, and they live at No. 6, Elm's Row, Lambeth. If you go there to-morrow, and say you were recommended by Miss Elliott, at Mrs. Knox's, Mrs. Adams will see you."

As the girls were at tea, Winny was invited to take some with them; and, before it was over, May was in full possession of every particular regarding Winny's

history and her lover's disappearance, which, being the subject her heart was always full of, she required little inducement to talk about it. May, whose acuteness
and knowledge of the ways of the world far exceeded that of the other two girls,
found her curiosity a good deal excited by the story; and by her questions she
elicited from Lilly an account of the proceedings at the Huntsman, which excited
it still more.

"Depend on it, those cousins of yours are a bad set, Lilly," said she, after
Winny was gone.

"Do you think so?" said Lilly.

"I've no doubt of it," said May; "I shouldn't like to lodge with them, I can
tell you! I shouldn't wonder a bit if they robbed and murdered the travellers, as
Jonathan Bradford[70] was going to do. Was any body ever missing that lodged
there?"

"There was one person," answered Lilly; "and people never knew what became of him—but I think I know."

"You don't say so!" exclaimed May. "Why, Lilly, you're as bad as they, if you
don't tell."

"I don't mean that they killed him," said Lilly; "I don't think they'd do such
a thing as that."

"I dare say they did," said May; "but there's a ring at the bell; go and see who
it is;" and the conversation being thus interrupted, the subject was forgotten.

"Does Miss Elliott live here?" inquired the person who had rung at the bell.
The voice was that of a man; but in the dim light of the evening, Lilly could not
distinguish his features; however, she bade him walk in; and as he passed through
the door into May's room, where there was a candle, she saw that it was Giles
Lintock. Unacquainted with the intimacy that had formerly subsisted betwixt her
friend and Martha's husband, she naturally concluded that he had come in pursuit
of her, till she understood by their familiar salutation that they were old friends.

"Well, May," said he; "I've found you out at last; I've been looking for you
these two months."

"Have you?" said she; "what for?"

"I'll tell you presently," said he. "But what are you doing? How are you getting on?"

"I'm getting on very well," said May. "I'm show-woman at Mrs. Knox's, in
Oxford Street."

"And who's that girl that let me in?"

---

70 Jonathan Bradford was an inn keeper who was accused of a murder he did not commit. He had intended to kill one of his guests but someone else murdered them first.
Bradford was executed for the murder erroneously.

"She's a girl that works there, that I let live with me."

"Well, just send her out of the way, will you? I want to speak to you about something particular."

"Speak on; she won't hear you," said May. "I heard her go into the next room and shut the door."

"Well," said Giles, "as I said before, I've been looking for you these two months. Mr. Cropley, the lawyer, wants to see you."

"Wants to see me?"

"Yes; but it's to be a great secret, whatever it is—so to begin, you must not mention to any body that he wants you, nor that I came to look for you."

"But what can he want me for? Is it my father that wants me?"

"I don't know; but I don't think it is. It's two months now since Mr. Cropley sent for me; and when I went, I found it was to ask me if I knew where you were. I said I didn't; and he bade me try and find out for him. I didn't dare go and ask your aunt myself; but at last I got somebody else to ask her; and when I told Mr. Cropley I had discovered you, he desired me to come up to London and find out what you were doing and how you were living."

"What's that to him?" said May.

"That I suppose he'll tell you himself," said Giles; "only I was to make out as much about you as I could and let him know; so I shall write to him by the post tomorrow."

When Giles was gone, Lilly emerged from the bedchamber, not a little alarmed. Of her previous history, her present benefactress (and a benefactress she really was) knew scarcely any thing, for May was too entirely occupied with herself to have much curiosity to spare for other people's affairs. That Lilly had had unkind relations and an unhappy home was nearly all she knew, till Winny's story had led to some further explanations; but Lilly now felt it advisable to enter into other particulars, since it was necessary to secure May's silence. She therefore narrated her past adventures; and pointed out the danger she apprehended from Giles Lintock should he recognise her. "If he knew who it was that opened the door to him, I'm sure he'd tell my cousin," said she, after concluding her story.

"I dare say he would," said May; "but, of course, I sha'n't tell him who it was, you know;" and May meant what she said.

CHAPTER VIII

SELFISHNESS AND DEVOTION

It is a trite thing to say, that many good qualities may harbour with many bad ones; and May Elliott, with all her imperfections, had yet her virtues too. She was good-natured, good-tempered, and benevolent. Even her extravagance was not altogether selfish, for she was as ready to give away money, when she had it, as to spend it on herself; but then she very seldom had it to give, except it was on the day she received her salary; by the next, it was generally gone for some superfluity quite inconsistent with her condition.

Her intentions towards Lilly were, in the first instance, really generous and kind. She required her to pay nothing for her lodging; the only outlay demanded of her was, that she should furnish her share of the breakfast and the Sunday's provision; and on this footing they began.

In return, Lilly worked like a slave for May. She lighted the fire, prepared the breakfast, cleaned the rooms, dressed the Sunday's dinner; and sat up at night to mend her stockings and do whatever jobs of work she needed; and this she did with the greatest delight, and thinking she was doing nothing. But it was not long before her devotion was further taxed. When a loaf or half a pound of tea was wanted, Lilly was sent to fetch it; and May would say, "pay it, Lilly, will you? for I've no change;" till, gradually, Lilly paid every thing for May, as far as her money would go, and had nothing left to lay out upon herself. Still, not a suspicion crossed Lilly's mind, nor a thought degrading to her idol. As long as the money lasted, it was paid without a murmur or a regret.

But unfortunately Lilly's small wages could not long furnish May's necessities. May could not eat salt butter, but must have fresh, at sixteen pence a pound; then she liked a drop of cream to her tea in the morning, and must have it sweetened with white sugar; and as her wants were all according to the same scale, Lilly's means soon became inadequate to supply them. Inexperienced in matters of economy, she had not foreseen this difficulty, and had commenced by partaking of the same fare that was provided for her friend; but, as soon as she perceived that their funds were failing, she began to curtail her own share of the indulgences that there might be the more for May. She ate her bread without butter, and drank her tea without sugar. May was much too quick-sighted not to observe this, and she would really rather that Lilly had fared the same as herself; but her generosity went no further; it could not reach the length of self-denial; and she very soon became used to it; and then it seemed quite a matter of course that Lilly should breakfast on a crust of dry bread, whilst she had a new roll and butter; and that she should have cream and sugar, whilst Lilly had none.

Then, Lilly never grumbled, but always seemed so satisfied, that there could be no occasion to pity her privations; besides, she considered that it was a great thing for Lilly to have a lodging on such easy terms; whilst Lilly thought that to lodge with May, on any terms, was happiness enough. Nor was her gratitude at all diminished by May's selfishness and want of principle. Practically, Lilly's ethics were unexceptionable, but she was utterly devoid of theory; nobody had ever taken the trouble to teach her any.

Abel White might perhaps have done so, had he been fully aware of her uninstructed state; but her love for him, her habits of obedience, and her naturally good disposition, stood her in stead of principles, and prevented his discovering the amount of her ignorance. A savage from the wilds of Australia could not have less ideas of duty than Lilly had. Obedience was the single virtue she had been taught; and when she was not acting under its influence, instinct was her only guide. Thus, the faults of May's character did not repel her, for she did not see them as faults.

But the little *ménage* could not long be supported upon Lilly's savings, and the hour of difficulty drew nigh; she blushed crimson the first time she had occasion to tell May she had no money to pay for the butter.

"Very well," said May; "tell the man you forgot to take the money with you, and that you will bring it to-morrow," and Lilly obtained the butter and whatever else she wanted, by a promise of payment on the following day; but without saying she had forgotten the money. She fully expected May would have given it her the next morning; but, as nothing was said on the subject, she supposed it had escaped her memory; or that, as usual, "she had no change."

The young people at Mrs. Knox's were paid either by the week or the month. Those of the higher class, like May, were paid monthly; the subordinate ones, like Lilly, received their money every Saturday night. When Lilly received her little salary at the end of the week, she called on her way home, at the shops where she was a debtor, and discharged the accounts; but, as she had only six shillings a week, and there had been a late purchase of tea and sugar, she arrived at home with an empty purse.

"What have you got for dinner to-morrow?" inquired May. "I declare I'm starving, with those nasty mutton-hashes we have every day at Mrs. Knox's!"

"I haven't got any thing yet," answered Lilly.

"Well, I should like a bit of something very nice," said May; "a nice tender beefsteak would do; but mind, it must be cut from the best part."

"He won't cut it from the best part, unless I take the money with me," answered Lilly.

"Well, then, take the money," said May.

"I haven't got any more," returned Lilly. "It took it all to pay the things we owed for."

"What things?" inquired May.

"What we've been having this week," returned Lilly. "You know I owed for the tea and sugar, and every thing."

"How could you be so stupid, Lilly?" said May; "when you know I'm so particular about having something for dinner on Sunday, and I told you only yesterday that I was sick at the sight of Mrs. Knox's dinners."

"I thought we must pay," answered Lilly, innocently.

"Well, but there was no such hurry! Couldn't you wait till the month's up? and then I shall have plenty of money myself."

Lilly saw that she had been extremely stupid, and that she had deprived May of the good dinner she had relied on to make amends for the hashed mutton. However, she promised to go and see what could be done with the butcher.

"Tell him, you'll pay him on Monday," said May; and Lilly obeyed, and on this promise obtained the meat and the other things she required, and brought them home to May; who, as soon as her wishes were gratified, was perfectly contented, troubling herself not at all about how the promise was to be fulfilled.

But though to please May was Lilly's first object in life, yet her satisfaction on this occasion was very much alloyed; for she now comprehended that her friend had no money, and she had made this promise whilst perfectly aware that she could not fulfil it; and do what she would, she could not shake off the uneasiness this consciousness occasioned her. Yet, what could she do? She could not let May go without such a dinner as she could relish—that was impossible! May's wants and wishes must be complied with; yet her natural integrity was painfully wounded by the deception she had practised. On the following day, however, when she saw how much May enjoyed the dinner; and (there being more than she could eat herself,) how kindly she made Lilly share the steak with her, instead of allowing her to dine on a bit of cold bacon—a relic of the previous Sunday's repast, as she had intended—she consoled herself. On the ensuing Saturday, May would receive her money, and then these little difficulties would cease; and, in the mean time, Lilly was so happy, and May was so kind!

"I saw such a lovely shawl in Bond Street, to-day,"[71] said May. "I'd have bought it directly if I had had the money with me. It would suit my new lilac silk so beautifully!" Lilly wished she had enough to buy the shawl for her friend; and

---

71 A street in London's West End famous for high-class, expensive shops.

regretted very much that the money, when it came in, must go for provisions and rent instead of being devoted to the adorning of that pretty person. She felt also rather embarrassed by a little need of her own, which would oblige her to spend her week's wages on herself, instead of devoting it to May, as had been the case for some time back. Her shoes were so worn, that she could scarcely keep them on her feet, and she was getting quite ashamed of appearing in them at Mrs. Knox's; whilst, for the last Sunday or two, she had actually refrained from walking out, on account of their dilapidated condition.

Feeling, therefore, that the shoes must be purchased, though sorry to appropriate the money to her own use, when she left work on Saturday night, she proceeded at once to a shop in the neighbourhood of Leicester Square, for the purpose of providing herself with what she needed. It was a small "Emporium,"— such was the name with which it was dignified—kept by a man and his wife, he selling shoes on one side, whilst she sold gloves and haberdashery on the other. It was a busy night, and a busy hour; and Lilly had to wait whilst several persons who were previously there were served. Amongst the rest was a respectable-looking elderly woman in mourning, who was buying a pair of black cotton gloves, and who, when she was served, instead of leaving the shop, seated herself on a stool, as if she were waiting for some one. Lilly had just got her shoes, and had laid down her money for them, when the woman, whose back was towards her, rose and moved to the door.

"Are you ready?" said a voice.

"Yes," she replied. "Have we anywhere else to go to-night, Philip?"

"You dropped this, ma'am," said Lilly, who was waiting for sixpence out of her two halfcrowns.

"Thank you, my dear," said the stranger, taking a little parcel that had fallen from her lap. "I'm not used to this bustling place, and it will be well if I don't lose myself before I'm out of it."

All the blood in Lilly's heart seemed to rush into her cheeks as those words were uttered. Should she speak? Should she let them go? It was Mrs. Ryland and Philip; he so grown, so altered, that she would not have recognised him, had not his mother called him by his name; her earliest friends, whom she had never ceased to love—they who had first shown her kindness, and awakened her heart out of its death-like sleep. They had looked at her and not spoken; perhaps they did not know her? Perhaps she had forfeited their good opinion by running away? and whilst she hesitated they had disappeared.

The opportunity of addressing them no sooner seemed lost, than Lilly felt desperate; and, pushing through the throng, she rushed after them the way they had gone; but they had turned into some shop or street, for she could not find them, and after vainly seeking them for some time, she went home, overcome with grief and vexation at her own stupidity.

When she reached the lodging, May, who was generally allowed to leave Mrs. Knox's at an earlier hour than Lilly, was there before her. She had got two candles lighted, and was standing before an old dim looking-glass, in a carved frame, whose spotted face but indistinctly reflected her pretty figure, trying on a new shawl.

"I say, Lilly, isn't this a beauty?" said she, as her companion entered.

"It's beautiful!" answered Lilly; "what a handsome border it has! Have you bought it?"

"Yes: I could not help it," replied May; "it will look lovely with my lilac silk, won't it?"

"How well you look in it!" exclaimed Lilly, contemplating May with admiring eyes.

"Do you think I do?" said May. "I'm so glad I bought it! But it cost a world of money!"

"Did it?" said Lilly.

"I believe it did," said May, with a smile and a significant nod; "but la, Lilly, what's the world worth, if one can't indulge one's fancy now and then?"

Lilly had no disposition to dispute this implied axiom, for she thought May had every right in the world to indulge her fancy; whilst May was so supremely happy in the possession of the shawl, that, for some time, she quite forgot that it was necessary to prepare for the next day's dinner. But she remembered it at last, and asked Lilly what she had provided.

"I did not know what to get," said Lilly.

"Oh, get anything!" said May, still too much occupied with her new acquisition to care much for what generally interested her considerably.

"Will you give me some money, please?" said Lilly, putting on her bonnet to hide her blushes.

"Haven't you got any?" said May, turning sharply round.

"No!" replied Lilly; "I've only a shilling; for I was obliged to buy a pair of shoes; and I forgot to bring away the sixpence change."

"How unlucky!" said May, impatiently; "and there's the woman wanting her rent. I'm sure I don't know what's to be done!"

Lilly felt quite distressed, and wished her shoes back in the man's shop.

However, the rent was paid, and the dinner was bought, and they went on again as before; that is, living on such credit as they could get, and on Lilly's small wages, for May had not sixpence left of hers, so large a portion having been spent upon the shawl.

CHAPTER IX

OLD FRIENDS

Lilly scarcely hoped it would be of any use, but, as in the present state of her finances sixpence was a sum by no means below her consideration, she bethought herself of calling at the shoe-shop on the Monday morning to tell the man that she had not received her change. Fortunately, he had observed her sudden exit, and had replaced the money in his till. "It was your own fault," said he; "I put down the sixpence, but you ran out of the shop as if you was frightened."

"It was to speak to somebody that had left a parcel," answered Lilly.

"The parcel would have been safe enough," said the man. "We should have sent it in to her—she lives next door."

"Does she?" said Lilly, eagerly turning back. "Does Mrs. Ryland live next door?"

"Yes, she does," replied the man. "I saw her pass out two minutes ago."

Here was news for Lilly, who had been grieving ever since Saturday over her own want of resolution. Now, she resolved she would see them. She would call at night as she came from work, and she was quite happy and excited all day in the expectation of the visit. But, when the evening came, her heart almost failed her; and, when she reached the door, she had not courage to open it. Perhaps they would not be glad to see her; perhaps they would not remember her at all.

It was a shop where meal, and seeds, and bread-stuffs were sold; and Lilly stood on the step, looking in through the glass door, to reconnoitre the interior. Behind the counter stood an elderly sickly-looking woman, wearing the dress of a widow; and a young lad near the desk was just taking off his jacket and apron, and putting on a black coat;—but these were not her friends. Could the shoemaker be mistaken? She feared so, for, on looking at the name over the door, it was not *Ryland*, but *Dewar!*

"Allow me to pass?" said a young man, moving her aside, whilst a hand was placed on the latch of the door.

"Now or never!" thought Lilly, and, with a faltering voice, she murmured "Philip!"

"Did you speak to me?" said he, looking her in the face, but evidently not knowing her.

"I'm Lilly Dawson, that you knew at the Huntsman," said she.

"What?" said he, taking hold of her arm, and drawing her into the light, "you're not Lilly Dawson!"

"Yes, I am," she answered. "I saw you and Mrs. Ryland at the shoe-shop next door; that's the way I knew you were here."

"Come in!" said he. "How you are altered, to be sure! I should never have known you if you had not spoken. Mother!" cried he, leading her into a little room behind the shop, "who do you think this is?"

"Lork knows, my dear! Who is it?" said Mrs. Ryland, putting on her spectacles, and peering up at Lilly.

"It's Lilly Dawson, the little girl that used to live at the Huntsman."

"You don't say so!" said Mrs. Ryland. "Well, I should never have known her, I declare!"

"So you took my advice, and ran away, Lilly?" said Philip. "Well, you were quite right. I should have followed your example, I believe, if I couldn't have got away by any other means."

"But what are you doing, child, and how do you live?" inquired Mrs. Ryland; and, thereupon, Lilly told them how she was situated; and was gradually led to narrate the history of her adventures, which created no little interest in the breasts of her auditors; but what puzzled them most was the strange desire manifested by Luke to marry a person for whom he had always evinced the greatest contempt, and from whose alliance, it seemed to them, no advantage was to be gained.

"If he saw you now, Lilly," said Philip, "I shouldn't wonder at his wishing to marry you; you are so much improved!" and as, when Philip made this remark, his eyes appeared to survey her with considerable satisfaction, Lilly blushed, and felt a little stir about her heart, accompanied by a sudden wish that she had had on her Sunday frock.

"Philip was very unhappy there at the mill," said Mrs. Ryland.

"And I was much worse off after you were gone, Lilly," said Philip, interrupting his mother; "for then I had no friend; and often and often I wished you back again, I can tell you, when I was obliged to go to bed with a scanty dinner and no supper."

"But he bore it all for my sake," said Mrs. Ryland, "and without complaining too; for I never knew how badly he was off till my brother died."

She then proceeded to inform Lilly, that the late Mr. Dewar, the owner of the shop they were then in, was her brother; that he had a very comfortable business, and was doing extremely well, till an unfortunate accident had caused his death. When he found his end approaching, he had advised his wife, who was very sickly, to send for Mrs. Ryland and Philip, to come up and assist her with the business; his own son being only fourteen, and not fit to undertake the management of it.

"As I always hoped to end my days at the mill," said Mrs. Ryland, "and never could abide London when I came up to see my brother, I was very unwilling to hear of this; but when I mentioned it to Philip, and I found how unhappy he was with them Littenhaus folks, and how glad he'd be to get away, I got Mr. Cobb to mention it to Sir Lawrence; and very well he behaved about it, to be sure. He got Philip off his apprenticeship with Mr. Luke; and he says, for all that, he shall have the mill when he's twenty-one, if he likes to take it."

Lilly went home happier than she had ever been in her life after this interview. The Rylands were so kind and friendly, and all her former love for them was so vividly reawakened in her heart! And her intercourse with them now was so different to what it had been formerly, when she had been the poor drudging Cinderella. Now, she was a smart, pretty girl, to whom Philip felt naturally disposed to be gallant; and whom his mother treated as an old friend; inviting her to dine with them on Sunday, and to call frequently and see them. Betwixt her idolized May Elliott, on the one hand, and the Rylands, on the other, how rich she was in friends! She, who for so long a period had never seen a single gleam from the light of love on her path. Amidst all this joy, however, there was one little dark spot, and that was the mortification she felt at not being able to make a better appearance when she went to dine with her friends on Sunday. She had got a pair of new, strong, clumsy shoes, certainly; for she had bought them for use, and not for ornament; but her bonnet was none of the best; and the sun and the washing-tub had considerably tarnished the lustre of the pink gingham.[72]

Before she joined housekeeping with May, she had been laying by money for the purpose of indulging herself with a little finery; but her savings had all been dissolved into fresh butter and white sugar for her friend; and she had never been able to purchase an article for herself. Mrs. Ryland and her son were so well dressed, too, that it was the more mortifying to appear before them in such shabby attire. If she could only buy a frock, there was plenty of time to get it made, and, by forestalling a couple of weeks' wages, she might have done it perfectly; but then what was May to do for her luxuries? How could she ever confess to having bought a frock when there was nothing for the Sunday's dinner? She felt she could not—it would be so unkind to May, and so selfish!—so she did not do it; but contented herself with her old clothes, or rather submitted to them; for the consciousness of them never left her all day; diminishing her confidence, and marring the completeness of her satisfaction.

Mrs. Ryland, however, was very kind; she thought nothing about her dress; whilst Philip admired her smooth hair and soft, blue eyes and delicate features; and thought her a great deal prettier from contrasting what she was with what she had been. Her modesty and timidity pleased them too; they wondered to

---

72 Dyed cotton.

find her not at all spoiled by living in London and growing pretty. But Lilly was always thinking of somebody else—seldom of herself; and was, therefore, not easily spoiled.

As May had always her own engagements and diversions for a Sunday afternoon, and as she never invited Lilly to accompany her on these occasions, the latter was at liberty to spend the day with her friends, after she had cooked May's dinner, which she did with unfailing punctuality, before she thought of her own pleasures. Thus, her intimacy with the Rylands improved rapidly, and everybody who knows the charm of meeting an old acquaintance in a strange place will easily comprehend this. Sometimes, too, she ran in of an evening, as she came from her work; and not unfrequently she met Philip taking a stroll at that hour, when the business of the day was done; and then he would give her his arm and walk home with her; and they would talk over past times, and laugh at the recollection of the "stupid little girl," and the half-starved boy; and the hunches of bread and the lumps of pudding she used to secrete for him. In short, they grew, from day to day, more familiar, more unreserved, more affectionate with each other. For all that passed between them, they might have been brother and sister; but the animated countenances, the sparkling eyes, and the bounding hearts with which they met, were evidences of a sentiment not purely fraternal. However, they did not trouble themselves to analyze their own feelings; they were happy—that was sufficient.

Philip's situation too was a pleasant one enough. Under the instructions of the widow, whose ill health rendered her personally inactive, he carried on the business, which furnished him both with employment and a small remuneration for his services. Lilly also was promoted to a salary of ten shillings a week, which, with her own limited wants and quiet habits, would have made her rich, could she have retained her money for her own use. But May, who was ever in arrears, still kept her purse empty, and her wardrobe ill furnished; whilst Lilly's idolatrous love scarcely permitted her to feel the wrong she suffered.

CHAPTER X

BREAKERS AHEAD!

It is not to be supposed that Lilly's intimacy with the Rylands could continue without the repeated occurrence of May's name, and frequent dissertations on her beauty and merit; and when Philip was inclined for a jest, it was generally at the expense of this unknown idol. He would select some particularly ugly, ill-dressed girl in the street, and ask Lilly if that was not May Elliott; or he would tell her that, at last, he really had seen her; he had been to Mrs. Knox's with an acquaintance who went to buy a bonnet, and May had served them; and then he would proceed to laud her in the most hyberbolical manner, to Lilly's great delight, till she found he was quizzing[73] her.

But, as Philip had insight enough to comprehend that Lilly's enthusiastic attachments were the results of her own character, rather than the consequence of other people's deserts, his curiosity was, in reality, not the least excited about May, any more than hers was excited about him. Indeed, for her part, the idea she entertained of Philip was anything but flattering. "Some country hobbitihoy[74] of a miller's boy" was the way she designated him in her own mind, rashly concluding that poor Lilly's friends were not likely to be very interesting to her. But she was mistaken. Their acquaintance at length originated in the accident of Lilly's being confined one Sunday by a bad cold and sore throat, which obliged her to remain in bed, instead of paying her accustomed visit to her friends. She had been unwell when they had last seen her; and, apprehending that augmented indisposition was the cause of her absence, Philip called to inquire for her. He had never visited her hitherto; but, as he had often walked home with her, he knew very well where she lived; and, ringing at the door, he inquired for Miss Dawson. The woman who answered him said she believed she was at home, and, bidding him ascend to the third story, and "take the door facing him," she left him to find his own way.

"Who's there? Come in!" said a voice that was not Lilly's.

However, Philip obeyed and entered. "I beg pardon," he said; "I came to inquire for Lilly Dawson."

"Oh! Lilly's in bed with a cold," said May, turning upon him her bright face; for she had got a new bonnet, and was trying it on at the glass; and, being conscious that it was extremely becoming, her features were, just at that moment, illuminated with pleasure.

"Can this be May Elliott?" thought Philip, whilst he proceeded to say that he had called, fearing Lilly was ill, as they had not seen her for some days.

"Come in," said May. "You needn't be frightened at me;" for, somewhat surprised at what he saw, he stood with the door in his hand, ready to retreat. "If you'll come in and sit down," said she, "I'll tell Lilly you are here."

Philip did sit down, but he felt more confused and bewildered than he had ever done in his life. May Elliott appeared to him a lady of the very first water.[75] The elegance of her attire and the easy self-possession of her air and manner quite dazzled him, and threw him aback. In short, if he had been suddenly introduced into the presence of Majesty itself, he could scarcely have been more impressed.

---

73 Teasing.
74 Crowe's spelling of 'hobbledehoy', an awkward, clumsy or uncouth young man.
75 Highest quality or class.

"Lilly's right this time, certainly," thought he, as May stepped into the adjoining room.

Lilly would have been very glad to have risen to see her friend, but that was out of the question; she was too ill; so May had the charge of entertaining him—a charge which, however, she cheerfully performed, and indeed voluntarily incurred; for Philip's modesty would have prompted him to take an immediate leave, had she not given him marked encouragement to stay. But, although flattered himself, and admiring her, he found it impossible to recover his self-possession. The tone of May's manners and conversation were so entirely different to those of any woman he had met before, that he felt as if he were in the presence of a being of another race altogether. Certainly, his experience had been extremely limited; whilst such a phenomenon as May Elliott might have startled an older man from his propriety. Nevertheless, the consciousness of his confusion mortified him extremely; and he was never less pleased with Philip Ryland, than at the moment he closed the door of the lady's apartment. But for this self-dissatisfaction, it is probable that, however much he admired her, he might never have made any further advances towards her acquaintance. But, unfortunately, his pride was wounded; he felt that she must look upon him as a shy, shamefaced boy; and, for a youth of eighteen to be so thought of by a pretty woman, is a severe trial to his self-love. It was, therefore, rather resentment at her superiority, than a desire to see her again, that determined him to take the earliest opportunity of repeating his visit. He would show her that he was not the awkward, stupid clown she doubtless took him for! and, with this manful determination, he returned on the following evening, Lilly's indisposition furnishing a sufficient excuse for his visit.

May was always well dressed; but this not being Sunday, her attire was less dazzling, and her demeanour consequently less imposing, than it had been the day before; so that Philip's project of vindicating his manhood, and recovering his own self-esteem, was of more easy execution than he had expected; whilst May, who in the morning had thought it a pity so handsome a young man should be such a booby, began to suspect that it must have been the power of her own charms that had occasioned his confusion. It is true, she supposed him to be Lilly's lover; but that was no reason he should not admire her, nor that she should abstain from making herself agreeable to him; and thus each, under the influence of gratified vanity, showed themselves to the best advantage. It is true, their conversation was little varied; for, apart from Lilly, they had no subject of any interest to discuss, except themselves; for in those days books were expensive articles; and Philip had little reading, and she less. But that one subject, *ourselves*, is an inexhaustible one, provided we can get a good hearer—there is the only difficulty.

Strange that it should be so!—What do we study metaphysics for, or read novels—which should be metaphysics in action—but to get a peep into men's minds and motives? and possibly, if we were quite sure they would tell us their minds and motives, we might be more patient. But there is the rub—who dare be candid, except to some rare soul to whom we can speak as to our conscience! Men flee the Truth, and are so unaccustomed to her face, that it affrights them. We live in a continual seeming, and they are considered the safest and surest in society, who practice this seeming with the most unvarying fidelity. The outspeakers are all sufferers by their honesty; they are not "dwellers in decencies;" and, whilst they rend their own veil, every man trembles for the integrity of his. Time and experience teaches them prudence; till, at length, they learn to accommodate themselves to the climate; like some poor tropical plant, that is obliged to modify its nature to new circumstances, and cease to shed its flowers and fruits in an ungenial atmosphere.

But, in the present instance, the incitement to listen was sufficient to procure each speaker an attentive auditor; for each was an object of lively curiosity to the other. When May related her own history and adventures, after her own manner—that is, with variations—representing herself as the victim of parental barbarity and an unhappy passion, Philip was moved with pity and indignation; and the effect the story produced upon him was not at all to be wondered at. He had never read a novel or romance in his life, and May's story was a romance to him; narrated, too, by the lovely lips of the heroine! Then her confidence was so flattering!—the transition from the previous embarrassment to the present ease and familiarity, so gratifying! No wonder he forgot Lilly as he bent his arms on the table before him, and with flushed cheeks sat looking into May's bright eyes.

Then she questioned him about himself, and inquired the history of his heart. "Had he never loved?" And Philip scarcely knew how to answer. When he entered that room, he had fancied he loved Lilly, but now he began to doubt it. Lilly had never flushed his cheek, or sent his blood careering through his veins as May did. They had met with pleasure, and parted in kindness; and he went home and slept easily on his pillow; but this night there was no sleep for Philip; he had drunk of the Syren's cup,[76] and was in a state of intoxication! May's eyes had said such things to him—to him, a young country lad, who had been scarcely acquainted with any women, except his mother and Lilly. He seemed to have awakened into a new world, and what a bright world it seemed!

But Lilly! what was to become of her? Fortunately, he had never mentioned the word *love*; but still, as he had fancied himself attached to her, he feared he must have betrayed something of the sort by his manner. But probably she had

---

76 Siren from Greek mythology. Dazzlingly beautiful water maidens who lured sailors to their deaths with their irresistible songs.

not understood it; so simple, so humble, so inexperienced; it was not likely that she should; and still less likely that she should have entertained any corresponding sentiment. Her feeling for him was, doubtless, entirely that of a sister; and he would always be a brother to her, and do all he could to serve her. So he consoled and cajoled himself; not quite easy, the while, however, about her; but, whenever Lilly's pale lamp sought to put forth its modest ray, May Elliott's flaring torch would start up instantly and put it out.

Meantime, May slept calmly, and awoke refreshed; not that she was much less pleased with Philip than he was with her; but the feeling was different. The effect she had produced upon him appeared to her the most natural thing in the world, and it occasioned nothing beyond a pleasing excitement. It would be very interesting to observe the progress of her influence; as to what might be the result of their acquaintance it did not occur to her to consider. Neither did the thought of Lilly's probable pain give her any concern; for, with all her good nature, she never saw any body that stood in her own way; if they had that misfortune, she invariably ran them down, without mercy. Her good nature, which had gained her much good liking amongst her companions, was never practised at any personal expense. She would willingly do a kind thing, if it cost her nothing; but her benevolence never extended beyond this. It is true, that she would give away her money occasionally, when her purse was full, but this was only from her natural recklessness and extravagance; for she would give it to one, whilst she owed it to another; and she would not have refrained from purchasing a new shawl that took her fancy, though her dearest friend had been starving. For her, there was no individuality but her own; she only conceived of others as in relation to herself; and out of these relations they had no existence whatever for her.

In short, May Elliott was a thorough specimen of a certain class of women; dazzling and dangerous; with a sufficient veneering of pleasing qualities to fascinate, and a sufficient alloy of bad ones to destroy, her victims—victims of her character, not of her designs. She did not mean to harm them; only, whilst galloping on to her own ends, she could not help running over them.

CHAPTER XI

AND LILLY'S FRAIL BARK SWALLOWED UP IN THE VORTEX

On the ensuing Sunday, Lilly, considering herself well, resolved, as soon as she had prepared May's dinner, for her own was a small matter, to go, as she had frequently done before, to the Rylands, accompany them to the afternoon service, and spend the evening with them. These Sundays, so spent, were the happiest days she had ever known. We are drawn by a singular tie to those whom we meet far from the locality of our first acquaintance; and to this bond in the present instance were added others. On Lilly's part, gratitude for early kindness; affection for the mother, and incipient love for the son. On Mrs. Ryland's, a motherly feeling, engendered by pity and approbation; for she thought the way this forlorn young creature, cast upon the world without a friend, had contrived to earn her bread, was very creditable to her; and on Philip's there had been altogether a tender interest, compounded of gratitude, pity, and a lively sense of her ingenuous character and eager affections, together with the private opinion, that she was really a very sweet-looking girl. And so she was; much prettier than May Elliott to a wise eye; for May's beauty was merely physical; Lilly's shone out from within.

So, having given May all she wanted, scarcely stopping to eat her own morsel, she set off to join her friends. Philip was standing at the door, with his hat on. She saw him before he saw her, and she observed that he was looking somewhat annoyed; but the moment his eye fell upon her, his features lighted up with satisfaction, and hers reflected the joy.

"Ah, Lilly, I'm so glad you're come!" he said. "My mother's just putting on her bonnet for church, and you'll go with her."

"Yes," said Lilly.

"That's a good girl," replied Philip. "There, just go up and tell her so, will you?"

"Yes," answered Lilly; and she entered the house immediately for the purpose; "and Lilly!" cried Philip, calling after her, "tell my mother that, as she has you to go with her, I needn't; I want to go somewhere else."

"Yes," answered Lilly, in a flatter key, for this last addition to his commands let her down at least a semi-tone.

The truth was, that Philip had reckoned on being free that afternoon, by having engaged his cousin, young Dewar, to accompany his mother, which he did not usually do, as they belonged to different denominations. The Rylands were Dissenters, and the others attended the Established Church. But his mother, being somewhat of a bigot, had objected to the boy's fulfilling his promise. Her health did not admit of her going to church herself, but she insisted on the strict orthodoxy of Peter.

"I can't think where Philip wants to go!" said Mrs. Ryland, whose views on these subjects were rather exclusive also. "He never missed going to church with me before, since we have been in London!"

When they went down stairs, Philip was gone; and they saw no more of him that evening. Lilly would not have believed she could have been so dull in the company of her dear Mrs. Ryland; but the time did pass so heavily! And when she went home there was no Philip to escort her. May was not come in either; and the woman of the house said she had gone out after tea, with the young man who had been there several times during the week. Lilly knew of no young man having been there but Philip; and this set her wondering strangely. However, of course she should hear all about it when her friend came in. But no such thing! May was dressed *à ravir,*[77] and looked radiant; but she said no word of where she had been, nor by whom accompanied.

For the first time in her life, Lilly felt something like jealousy. She was aware that Philip had called every evening to inquire for her, and that he had sat some time with May; how long, she did not know; as at first she had really been extremely unwell; and latterly, though better, she had, in accordance with May's behest, only risen for a few hours in the middle of the day. But candid and unsuspecting as she was, she could not help being surprised at this sudden intimacy; and still more at the mystery they were making of it. However, she was too much in subjection to May to make any inquiries about what the other did not choose to tell her; so she said nothing. But it influenced her conduct; for she did not call on the Rylands all the week; and when Sunday came she did not feel courage to go, either. In the mean time, May continued much as usual, only that she was out most evenings, and Lilly saw less of her than she was accustomed to do.

On Sunday morning, May made an elaborate toilet, whilst Lilly cooked the dinner; which being eaten, her friend asked her if she were not going out. Lilly said she did not think she should; whereupon, May, having arranged her bonnet and shawl with the greatest care, took her departure.

Lilly sat at the window and followed her with her eyes to the end of the street, where she lost sight of her. She did not doubt but that she was going to meet Philip, and she had never felt so melancholy before; she was, in fact, oppressed by a new sensation. Her previous sorrows had been of a very different kind to this; and she had been very different at the time they afflicted her. She felt bereft now. There was a cloud rising up betwixt her and May; she was sure there was; and Philip was forgetting her; and she should lose both. Inexperienced as she was, her woman's instinct enlightened her; Philip had liked her, but May's charms had dazzled and bewitched him; and she must expect no more kind looks, or playful endearments, or gentle squeezes of the arm as he walked home with her at night, when, after laughing at her extravagant encomiums of May, he would say, "Well, I do love you for your good heart after all, Lilly!" And she should never be able to earn this praise any more, for, though she still loved May, she knew that she could never again expatiate on her perfections as she had done; and, least of all, to Philip. Indeed, she felt that she would rather not see him; she was sure he would

---

77 Ravishingly, delightfully.

read her heart in her face, for Lilly had no powers of concealment; she could forbear saying what she felt, but she could not forbear looking it.

But it was very dull sitting at home all the afternoon with her own sad thoughts, so she put on her bonnet and shawl and went out. It was too late to go to church, so she strolled on towards Cumberland Gate, where she had met Winny Weston formerly, with a sort of vague wish that she might meet her again; not that she cared about Winny particularly; but she was an old acquaintance, and she wanted something to cling to; besides, Winny would talk to her about Philip, and although she could not have spoken of him now to any body who might have divined her feelings, she longed to hear the sound of his name from one who could not.

However, as was to be expected, Winny was not there; and as she found strolling about in the Park alone as dull as staying at home, she directed her steps towards the gate again; walking dreamily on as one without motive to stay or to go. Although it was not the fashionable part of the Park, the turf was dotted with groups of various character: conscious and unconscious lovers, nurses and children, parents and their progeny, some lounging about, some sitting in the shade of the trees that bordered the gardens; for, although it was autumn, the weather was mild and the sun shone cheerily on the green earth.

Lilly was threading her way amongst them, feeling the more lonely from the contrast of her late happy Sundays, when she suddenly perceived Philip and May Elliott coming towards her, at a right angle. They were also making their way to the gate, but from a different direction, and they were very near before each observed the other. Lilly's heart was in her throat; but, before she had time to think what she should do, they had turned away and passed her. They had both seen her, for there was so little distance between them, that she was fully sensible of the effect her sudden apparition had produced. Philip was startled, and had instinctively made a movement towards her; but May had drawn him away, and he had turned his face from Lilly and yielded to the charmer.

What a bitter moment it was! Philip who, previously to the last fortnight, had been so kind to her! nay, so loving! For, although he had never mentioned the word *love*, and though the humble Lilly had scarcely dared to embody the thought that he entertained such a sentiment for her, yet she had felt it and pastured on it in her innermost soul. The unconscious consciousness had wrapped her around like the sweet airs of Heaven, comforting, and cheering, and intoxicating her with a bounding joy, that, though untold and unanalyzed, made her young heart leap with delight. And now he turned his face from her and would not see her; and May, the idolized May, was the cause and abettor of his dereliction. "Perhaps it was because she was so shabbily dressed!" May was attired in the height of the fashion; and Lilly's faded gingham and coarse straw bonnet, which had delighted herself so much when they were new, were certainly but sorry companions for the lilac silk and Bond Street shawl. But Philip had been very well contented to take her, hanging on his arm, to church in no better habiliments; and May knew very well why she *had* no better.

But they had turned away and were gone; so Lilly with a grieved heart pursued her path; and now a wish arose in her breast to go to Mrs. Ryland. She felt a yearning love towards her; she fancied that she too must feel deserted, and that there would be a silent sympathy between them. But would it be silent? What if Mrs. Ryland asked her if she had seen Philip. She could not say *no*; and her instinct told her that to say *yes* would be betraying him. She was sure that he did not tell his mother with whom he was passing the many hours he was away from her, and therefore *she* must not tell; and, since she must not tell, she must not go there; so she went home; and as she shrank from seeing May, she took care to be in bed before she returned.

On the following morning, they went together as usual to their work; but May's manner towards her was now wholly changed. She made no observation on the occurrences of the preceding day; indeed, she scarcely spoke to her at all; and during the remainder of the week, she maintained the same cold and distant demeanour. A spectator would have imagined that Lilly had given her some heavy offence—the offence was, that she was in her way. Can there be a worse? For that offence how many a one has died—man and woman too!

CHAPTER XII

LILLY'S FAITH IN DANGER

Amongst the persons employed at Mrs. Knox's was a very poor girl, called Betsy Barton. She was not used as a worker, except in cases of great exigency; commonly, her office was to carry to the customers at night the articles purchased in the course of the day. She was a plain, coarse, shock-headed child, with black hair, and black eyes as sharp as needles, very poorly clad, and with hands, into the cracks and crevices of which the dirt had made such a lodgment, that no washing could by any possibility ever extract it. Her parents were the poorest of the poor, and from her earliest childhood, till now that she was twelve years old, Bet, as she was commonly called, had been obliged to earn her own bread—or go without; and, much to her credit, she had contrived to avoid the latter unpleasant alternative.

Great natural energy and acuteness, combined with a healthy frame, had enabled her to struggle through the sea of troubles and difficulties that environed her; and though, like Lilly, her work had been of the hardest, yet, as it had been very various, and she had been thrown much upon the resources of her own wits, they had been rather sharpened than blunted by the process. She had been so accustomed to go of messages, that she was acquainted with every street and lane in London, and knew where every body lived; and she was so trustworthy, that nothing committed to her care had ever failed to reach its destination. On the whole, Bet was rather a favourite with the establishment; and they had latterly had occasion to give her an evidence of their good will.

Bet had arrived at Mrs. Knox's one day in a state of very unusual disorder. She was without the old bonnet and shawl that she ordinarily wore; her head looked as if it had been drawn through a furze-bush; her eyes were red, and the hard, fixed, brick-dust coloured cheeks were variegated with white. On inquiring the cause of all this discomposure, it appeared that her father, who was a journeyman bricklayer, had been killed by falling from a ladder, and that this calamity would necessarily involve a great increase of poverty and distress to the family. She had, moreover, a little brother very ill, and in order to procure him some medicine Bet had parted with her bonnet and shawl to a girl for sixpence; it was certainly as much as they were worth—but, as she had no means of replacing them, the loss was considerable to her.

This circumstance chanced to occur at a time that May Elliott happened to have a little money, and her good nature led her to present Bet with five shillings, and an old bonnet and shawl of her own; whilst she moreover suggested that there should be a general subscription for the benefit of this poor family. The young people acceded to the proposal, and each put her hand in her pocket; some drew out half-a-crown; others, with lower wages, blushingly laid a shilling on the table. But Lilly gave nothing; for she had nothing to give. May, seeing this, subscribed for her, and of course obtained the credit of extraordinary liberality, whilst every body wondered what Lilly could do with her wages; for she was known to have no friends needing her assistance—and her toilet bore witness to her spending nothing on dress.

May heard all the comments lavished on the apparent parsimony of her friend, but her generosity did not carry her so far as to exculpate her, because she must have done that at her own expense; so Lilly remained under the imputation of withholding the bounty that others, no better off than herself, had bestowed, whilst May rose twenty per cent in every body's estimation. As for Bet, who had witnessed the whole scene, her gratitude knew no bounds; and from this time she became May's sworn slave and serf—for there was a wild energy in the girl's nature, that, untutored as she was, rendered her passions, when they were awakened, as intense as those of a savage.

It was but a few weeks after this, that Mrs. Knox, with rather an excited air, entered the work-room, where Bet was employed at the time, to make inquiries concerning a box which she had been charged to deliver on the previous Saturday evening, at the house of a Mrs. Wilmot.

"I took it," answered Bet.

"Took it! Yes; but what did you do with the blond fall[78] that was in it?"

"Was the blond fall to go there?" inquired Bet.

"To be sure it was!" answered Mrs. Knox. "What did you do with it?"

"I don't think it was in that box!" said the girl.

"Don't tell me that!" returned Mrs. Knox, "when I put it in with my own hands. It was at the bottom of the box, in a bit of silver paper."

"The maid took the things out of the box—I didn't," answered Bet.

"Well, and did she take that out? Mrs. Wilmot positively declares it never came."

"I didn't see it," answered the other.

"But what became of it?" insisted Mrs. Knox—"that's what I want to know. You could not have dropped it out without dropping out the bonnet; besides, there was a string tied round the box!"

Bet stood silently looking at Mrs. Knox, with a firm and fearless countenance, that betrayed no consciousness of having done wrong; but she made no answer to this last interrogation.

"I say, I want to know what became of it?" repeated the lady. "That fall was worth three guineas; and that I put it into the box myself I am positively certain. Where is it?"

"I don't know," answered Bet.

"You don't know!" reiterated Mrs. Knox, with rising passion; "what do you mean by *I don't know?* Don't you know that I gave it you?"

"Yes," replied Bet.

"Then where is it?"

"I don't know," reiterated the girl.

"Did you lose it?"

"No," said Bet.

"This is very extraordinary!" exclaimed Mrs. Knox. "You know I gave it you, and you did not lose it, and yet you can't tell where it is. Did you see Mrs. Wilmot's maid take it out of the box?"

"No," answered Bet.

"Did you see it when she was taking out the bonnet?"

"No."

---

78 A decoration for a bonnet made of blond lace.

"Then you must have opened the box before you got there: for I am as positive that I put it in, as I am that I am standing here!"

"No, I didn't open it," answered Bet, stoutly.

"There's some mystery in this," observed Mrs. Knox; "and if you don't choose
to tell me what it is, you must take the consequences. I have always believed you
honest, and though I can't afford to lose three guineas, I should be more likely to
forgive you for telling me the truth, than for standing there looking in my face in
that way and telling me you don't know. Do any of you know anything about the
fall for Mrs. Wilmot's bonnet?" said Mrs. Knox, turning towards the table, and
addressing the young people, who, one and all, lifted their eyes from their work
and answered, "*No.*"

But amongst these, there was one *No* of a totally different character to the
others; that was Lilly's: she looked up and moved her lips, but her face was observed to be very much flushed, and her *No* was inaudible.

"Do *you* know anything about it, Miss Dawson?" inquired Mrs. Knox, observing her confusion, as she ran her eyes round the table and perused the different faces.

"Lilly must have left some time before you sent away the boxes," observed
May; "hadn't you, Lilly?"

"Yes," replied Lilly.

"She had cut her thumb, if you recollect, and you told her that as she couldn't
work she needn't stay," remarked May.

"Very true—I remember—that was Saturday," returned Mrs. Knox. "But
what *is* become of this fall? That is what I want to know."

But Bet either could not or would not tell; and the final conclusion arrived at
was, that the distress of her friends had overcome her honesty. The consequence
was, that she was dismissed from her place—a cruel misfortune to herself and her
family, especially as the reflection on her character was likely to incapacitate her
for another.

No words can possibly describe the strange confusion of Lilly's mind during
the course of this examination and after it. When Mrs. Knox had commenced
her inquiries respecting the missing article, she had raised her eyes to May's face,
fully prepared to hear her say that she knew where it was; but May had continued
diligently pinning flowers into a bonnet she was finishing, without taking the
slightest apparent notice of the question. It was therefore not for Lilly, in her subordinate situation, to speak; and she waited, every moment getting more anxious
and more puzzled; nor did anything occur to clear up her difficulty.

Bet was dismissed, and went forthwith, without making any representations
or expostulations; and naturally the occurrence led to a great deal of discussion

at the worktable. Lilly said nothing, and May little—except that she believed the girl was perfectly honest; and that she dare say she had met with some accident.

Now, the truth of the matter was this: Bet had been charged with two boxes on that Saturday night; one was for Mrs. Wilmot, and the other contained a new bonnet of May Elliott's. Just as Bet was starting, Mrs. Knox, who had forgotten the fall, ran into the shop, hastily raised the cover of the box the girl had in her hand at the moment, and, lifting up the bonnet, laid the parcel under it. Of this second other box she knew nothing, that being May's private concern; and both bonnets being of straw, and the shop not lighted, she had in her haste not remarked the difference.

Lilly knew nothing whatever about all this; but she had been at home, when the girl had brought May's bonnet, and had seen her lay both that and the parcel on the table. May was out at the time; but, when she came in, she had carried both articles into her bedroom, without making any observation on the occurrence, and Lilly had thought no more of the matter; but, having seen a corner of the blond protruding from the paper, she now felt assured that Bet had left the fall with May's bonnet, instead of with the other. But Bet must have known this as well as she did, whilst May could not have forgotten the circumstance. Why they did not each declare the truth, she could not conceive.

The reason May did not declare it was that she felt it was too late. It was now Thursday; she might have brought back the fall on Monday morning, with a perfectly good grace; but, after so many days, it was difficult to account for not having produced it before. The reason Bet did not speak out was, that, though but a child, her manner of life had shown her a great deal of a certain part of the world, and that not the best. Her parents were harmless, ignorant people; and she had no vanities, no desires to tempt her to do wrong; but she had been in situations where she had witnessed plenty of dishonesty; and it had neither shocked nor surprised her—it was a way of life like another.

When therefore she perceived that May did not own to the possession of the blond, she comprehended at once that she had her own reasons for not doing so; and her vivid gratitude kept her silent. She saw clearly that to have said where she left it, would have been to accuse her benefactress. She had witnessed many little things that were not strictly right, even at Mrs. Knox's; and her mind was too much familiarized to small peculations to be astonished or disturbed at the present event, further than as it affected her own prosperity; and this she sacrificed. Had May not been present at the examination, she would have probably declared the truth at once—but there she sat; and Bet's savage allegiance closed her lips.

Now, with respect to May's retaining the blond fall, it had been, in the first instance, an action wholly unpremeditated. She had carried it into her room with her bonnet, supposing the paper to contain some washed lace of her own. When she opened the parcel and perceived what it was, she comprehended that it had been put into her box by mistake; and she intended to take it back, when she went to work on Monday.

May's favourite diversion on a Sunday morning before church time was to figure before the glass, trying on her finery, dressing her beautiful hair, and studying the becoming; and when she put on her new bonnet, she could not forbear trying the effect of the fall. How well it looked, and how much she wished it was hers! It was indeed an article of dress she had often wished for. She had half a mind to wear it that afternoon; only the possibility of meeting any of the Knox establishment deterred her. Mr. and Mrs. Knox usually went out of town on Sundays, but the girls might recognise it and "peach;"[79] so she forbore, and laid it in one of her drawers.

On Monday morning, she forgot it at the moment of starting; her head being, at that particular period, very much occupied with the growing interest of her acquaintance with Philip. When she recollected that she had left it behind, she was half way to her destination, and had no time to return. The human mind is very subtle, and motives are sometimes scarcely recognisable to those whom they are influencing; for, although May had formed no design of retaining the lace, there must have been some latent reason for her not mentioning the subject to Mrs. Knox immediately, which she did not, and the day elapsed without any allusion to it.

"*Ce n'est que le premier pas qui coûte,*"[80] as the French proverb says; but, unfortunately, the cost of this first step is apt to be considerable; and it was so in the present instance; for the first day passed in silence rendered the production of the fall on the next somewhat difficult. Still, it was practicable; but by this time certain visions had arisen in May's mind of the possibility of this white blond fall being converted into a black one, by the aid of a dyer—in which case it would not be so easily recognisable; so Tuesday and Wednesday passed, and still nothing was said of it.

Though every day augmented the difficulty, a restitution was yet possible, had the movement originated with herself; but, when the inquiry came suddenly upon her, she felt that she could not have owned to the possession of the lace without betraying her guilt in her countenance. When the examination commenced, she trusted that Bet might have forgotten where she had left it; and, when it terminated, she thought that was the case; for, incapable herself of the generous motive

---

79 Inform against, or betray.

80 It is only the first step that costs, or in other words it is only the first step that is difficult.

that had actuated the girl, she did not suspect it in another.

As for Lilly, May was not sure that she knew anything about it, till she observed her confusion on being appealed to; but Lilly she knew would not speak where she was silent. Only to arrest further question, which might have rendered the embarrassment more evident, she diverted inquiry from her by mentioning that she must have left work early, on that Saturday; and so could know nothing of the boxes nor of their contents.

Thus, the danger was averted for the moment; but May was far from feeling easy on the subject. Bet might come to her recollection, or Mrs. Knox might learn from some accidental observation that the girl had left the house with two boxes on that evening. She wished sincerely that she had returned it at first; for she doubted now whether she could ever venture to wear it, even though disguised by the dyer.

Then she was annoyed that Lilly should be aware of her dishonesty. She felt pretty sure she would not betray her to Mrs. Knox—but might she not to Philip? Besides, the mortification of feeling herself in the power of one she considered so much her inferior wounded her exceedingly.

Altogether, May was a very considerable sufferer by this indirect experiment in the art of illegal appropriation; and, added to this, she really felt extremely sorry for poor Bet.

CHAPTER XIII

WHO MR. CROPLEY WAS, AND WHAT HE DID FOR MAY

In the mean while, Philip and May had been making daily progress in their acquaintance, and every moment each had at command was bestowed on the other.

Philip was just at that age when a man is extremely liable to be caught in the snares of a woman a little older than himself. At this period, boys are aspiring to be men, but, wanting courage, confidence, and experience, they are arrested in their career by *mauvaise honte*,[81] and are consequently subject to a long train of mortifications. A youth at that age is like an actor, full of ambition that, having sublime conceptions of the character he is to fill, finds, when he steps upon the boards, that the sight of the audience has disabled him for its representation. A woman, at the same period, is much more advantageously placed; her part is to be quiet and wait; and her *mauvaise honte* takes the graceful name of modesty. An accomplished, well-bred man, knows how to accommodate himself to this phase

---

81 Bashfulness.

of femininity; and the society of such gradually dissipates the confusion and forms the manners. But, when the shy boy and the shy girl come together, the situation of the former is extremely painful. She can do nothing towards helping him to overcome his difficulties; on the contrary, she adds to them the amount of her own.

Then, when girls are older, they are still looking upwards; they are aspiring to the notice of some man who has black *moustaches* or an estate; and if a youth in his teens addresses them, they snub him without mercy.

This is the usual position of the sexes, in regard to each other, during a certain period; but, now and then, there is an exception; and there is no intoxication greater than that of a youth who finds himself the object of regard to a woman whom he would never have dared to address, had she not smoothed the way for him. Gratitude, pride, and the sense of relief from the nightmare that oppressed him, all swell the tide of his passion; and his love for her is augmented by the whole sum of his love for himself.

In Philip Ryland's case, to all the weight of the above influences was to be added those of the excitements of wonder and surprise. Till he came in contact with her, he had not conceived of such a woman as May Elliott—perhaps the women he saw whirling through the streets in gilded equipages, or going in feathers and trains to St. James's, might be like her—but, within his own sphere, he could not have dreamt of such a prodigy: and that this bewitching creature should condescend to love him, awakened in him a ravishing joy that seemed beyond this world.

For Lilly he had felt the calm love of a brother, that, from the contemplation of her ingenuous, candid, devoted nature, was gradually ripening into something more tender: but for May his passion burst into full flower at once, the moment the sun of her favour shone upon it. To walk with her of an evening, pressing with eager grasp the hand that was passed under his arm; to look in her eyes, and hear her, a dozen times in an hour, respond to the as oft-repeated question, "May, do you love me?" seemed a foretaste of all heavenly joys; and for them he forgot not only poor Lilly, but almost his mother and his business too. Still, the thought of these at times gave him great pain. Old Rachel had been the tenderest of mothers to him, and her affections were centred in him with as much devotion as his were in May. Well organized, and, in his childhood, well trained and nurtured, he had never given her a moment's uneasiness till now; but, since his acquaintance with May, it was easy to read in her eyes how she was searching into his for the key to his mystery; which he dared not give her—he could hardly tell why; but his instinct forbade him. He felt that she could neither understand May nor his passion for her; and that the disclosure of his engagement would be the signal for a struggle that he dreaded to encounter.

He had other troubles, too. The small stipend he received was not sufficient to allow him to dress in a manner conformably to his new ideas; nor did it enable him to offer his mistress such little gallantries as he saw she expected. But he could not hope for so much happiness without alloy; and that May should love him, in spite of all these disadvantages, was only the greater proof of the sterling reality of her affection.

May, meanwhile, had her troubles, too. Not to mention the unpleasant affair alluded to in the last chapter, and her growing aversion to Lilly, she was also distressed for money, and hourly dreading being called on for what she could not pay. If Philip had but been rich, he would have been perfect; but his poverty really annoyed her; and sometimes she could not forbear making him feel it. But, just as her difficulties were threatening to get the upper hand of her devices, an unexpected re-enforcement came to her aid.

The suit carried on by General Markham against Colonel Adams, which amounted to nothing more than an embargo on the property, which the other could not take off for want of money, was not conducted by Mr. Treadgold, who managed his affairs in general, but by a person of the name of Cropley, whose notions of right and wrong were anything in the world but precise. To him, the justice of a cause he took in hand was so far from being an object, that he rather preferred one in which the whole exercise of his scheming intellect was required to make out a case at all. He considered everything fair in law; and, if he could not obtain a verdict for his client, he prided himself on the ingenuity with which he had frequently succeeded in preventing the successful suitor deriving any benefit from his failure. Thus it was in the present instance; but, for this fatal and unprincipled ingenuity, Colonel Adams and his family would not have been pining for ten or twelve years in poverty and disappointment.

Born to pride and splendour, nursed into selfishness and ill-temper, and educated into habits of controlling everybody within the sphere of his influence, except himself, General Markham had looked upon his sister, who was several years his junior, as an intruder in the family, and had treated her accordingly. Whilst she lived, he had opposed and oppressed her; and, after she died, he persecuted her husband more out of hatred than avarice; for he could not get the fortune himself; but, to keep his enemy out of it was a great consolation. He was, in short, an aristocratic Luke; the one took lives, whilst the other broke hearts; it was merely the accident of fortune that caused their malice to take different directions.

It was just whilst suffering under the pangs of his disappointed malice, when the first verdict was given in favour of Colonel Adams, that Mr. Cropley came to his aid. They had not been previously acquainted; for Mr. Treadgold had conducted the first suit, which was considered a legitimate one enough; it being the general opinion that the wording of the will was obscure; and that, in fact, the old nabob never had intended the fortune to go out of the family. On learning the General's vexation, Mr. Cropley thought he saw an opening for himself; and, accordingly, he presented himself before the great man, and disclosed his plan.

At the time the Hastings was lost, it was universally understood that every soul on board had perished. Colonel and Mrs. Adams were in India; the General, if he even knew the child had been in the ship, had felt no interest in her fate; so that no especial inquiries had been made on the spot; and no suspicion that she had survived existed in any quarter. But Mr. Cropley saw at once that her death remained legally problematical, and on this he built his hopes. A better client for his purpose than the General he could not have found. The long indulgence of violent temper and malignant passions, partly consequent on, and partly promoted by, an unfortunate physical constitution, had rendered him nearly insane; indeed, he was as reckless of consequences, and as indifferent to honour and principle in the attainment of his ends, and the gratification of his revenge, when once his fury was excited, as if he had been quite so.

Owing to the inability of Colonel Adams effectively to maintain the Chancery suit, it would have been generally at a stand still, had not that state of quiescence been extremely adverse to the interests of Mr. Cropley. As far as the court itself was concerned, no money being ever demanded of the Accountant-General, the thing might have remained in *statu quo*[82] till the day of judgment; but Mr. Cropley had his annual bill of costs to look to; and something must be done to cover, at least, a couple of folio sheets. Accordingly, when he had no other opponent, it was his custom to fill that part himself; and regularly, twice or thrice every year, he would present himself before the General with a face of importance, to tell him, that some friend of the Colonel's had taken up the affair, and was about to move the court, or file a bill; and that they must be stirring, and so forth; and the General, who had not patience to read the papers he laid before him, believed, and paid.

As this game had now been played several years, and as, in fact, the suit *was* at a stand still, Colonel Adams having no money to spend upon it, it became annually a matter of greater difficulty to Cropley to maintain his influence with the General, or to make out a handsome bill at Christmas; added to which, he feared that, for want of opposition, his patron might become indifferent on the subject; and that this important source of profit, which he considered himself entitled to look upon as part of his income, might fail him altogether. Unbounded, therefore, was his satisfaction, when, from some hint that reached him, he found an excuse for riding over one day to the General, and telling him, with a very long face, that

---

82 Status quo. Preserving the current state of affairs.

Colonel Adams was about to procure an order that the girl, Isabel Adams, should be produced in court, "which will dish us entirely," said he; "unless we could get somebody to personate her."

"Why," said the General, "I would certainly rather anybody had the fortune than that fellow, Adams; but it would be a most provoking thing to give it to an impostor, too!"

"There's no danger of that," said Cropley. "The other party will take care we don't give her the fortune. No; all that is to be gained by the stratagem is delay. They will not admit that the girl we produce is the real Isabel Adams; but how are they to prove she is not?"

"But, could anybody be trusted to act the part?" inquired the General.

"Why, I think I know a girl that would do it for a couple of hundred pounds or so;" said Cropley. "She's a little past the age, but she looks young, and is up to anything."

In this description, Cropley had May Elliott, whom he had known from her childhood, in his eye; not that he thought it might be absolutely necessary ever to mention the subject to her at all; and still less did he intend to give her the two hundred pounds; but it was advisable to have some one in view, and she was the most likely person for his purpose that he was acquainted with.

But the freaks of malice and idleness are unaccountable; the idea of the pain and vexation this substitution would occasion his adversary was so gratifying to the General, that he entered warmly into the plot; declared his readiness to pay down the two hundred pounds, and desired the girl might be sought for, and instructed in her part without delay; and Cropley, after putting the thing off as long as he could, at length found it advisable to speak to May Elliott on the subject; lest by some strange chance or caprice his patron should require to see the girl himself.

By this time, however, he had mislaid the letter in which Giles had sent him her address, and he now wrote to him requesting it again. But Giles, who had quitted town, had also forgotten the number of the house she lodged at; added to which, she might have removed in the interval; so he wrote to his son George, who was then apprenticed to a shoemaker in London, desiring him to inquire in such a street for Miss Elliott, and if she had moved to ascertain whither she had gone.

The answer to this letter contained a piece of intelligence that was much more welcome than the number of May's lodging. "Miss Elliott lives at No. 2," said George, "and who should I see there when I called, but Lilly Dawson. I knew her directly; but she did not know me, as I suppose I am so much bigger than when she saw me. She is very much altered too; but I asked the woman that opened the door if that girl's name wasn't Lilly Dawson, and she said it was; so I'm sure it was she."

On receiving the necessary information, Cropley took the earliest opportunity of calling when he went to London, and, without mentioning names, he told May what might be required of her. He was under no apprehension of shocking her principles, which he rightly judged accessible to a bribe. She would probably never be wanted; all that was required of her was, that she should be ready to say whatever he told her, should he have occasion to call upon her.

"But what am I to have for doing this?" inquired May.

"That will depend on what we demand of you," returned Mr. Cropley.

But May pressed for a retaining fee; she said she was badly off, and that she would rather have a little money in hand, than the promise of a much larger sum; and Cropley, willing to keep well with a woman who might do him future service, ended by giving her twenty pounds; and one of the first uses she resolved to make of it, was to change her lodging; for by doing this she would be able to shake off Lilly. To turn her poor companion out of doors was a step that neither accorded with her character nor her interests; it was not her nature to do harsh things—at least, when she did them under a sufficiently strong incentive, it was rather by stratagem than by open violence. She preferred to spare her own feelings as well as those of the person who was to suffer.

Still, she was perplexed; she would not that Philip should think her unkind to his old favourite; and she would not, on any account, that complaints should reach Mrs. Ryland. She ardently wished Lilly could be provided for at a distance; and she began to form a project of persuading her to quit Mrs. Knox's, or of getting her discharged.

It was scarcely a surprise to Lilly, though a pang shot through her heart, when May first hinted to her that they must part. She had foreseen that this must happen; but without some sudden impulse to urge her into action, she was incapable of making the first movement towards the separation herself.

None but those of a like nature to Lilly's can tell, what a rending of the soul it is, when the bonds that bind the lover to the loved are rudely snapped; and the poor heart is sent adrift on the dark, cold ocean of indifference, with not one friendly harbour to cast anchor in.

CHAPTER XIV

PHILIP IN TROUBLE, AND A FEW WORDS ON AN OLD SUBJECT

"What shall you do?" inquired May.

"I don't know," replied Lilly, with a pale cheek and subdued voice.

"Do you mean to stay at Mrs. Knox's?" asked May, in a tone implying the expectation that she would not stay.

"I suppose so," replied the other; and at that question she *was* surprised; for she did not yet understand the hardness of selfishness; nor how obnoxious she had herself become.

May was silent for a minute or two, but her countenance was unrelenting when she rejoined, "If you mean to remain there, you'll have to look for a lodging for yourself, you know;" a difficulty which, to the penniless and inexperienced girl, she was aware would appear gigantic.

Lilly could scarcely tell what made her say it, but she answered, that she "could ask Mrs. Ryland what she should do."

The first effect of this rash communication on her auditor was to bring the colour to her cheeks and make her eyes flash fire; but, as the flush subsided, she became paler than she was before.

"You had better not be in a hurry to do that," she said, raising her eyes to Lilly's face and compressing her lips, with an expression that seemed to say, "I understand the threat." "*I'll* look for a lodging for you."

Lilly coloured, but she had no courage to assert her own rights further; the impulse was not strong enough; her veneration and not yet wholly extinguished love for May forming a counteracting force to her jealousy, distrust, and sense of wrong.

Upwards of a month had now elapsed, since she had seen Philip and his mother, except on the occasion of one accidental meeting in the street, when he looked ill at ease whilst trying to address her with his former familiarity and kindness; and Mrs. Ryland had asked what she did with herself on Sundays, that she never went to see them. Lilly blushed, cast a confused look at Philip, and saying she was coming soon, abruptly broke away from them, which the moment after she deeply regretted. And she had reason to do so; for Mrs. Ryland, unable to comprehend this change in her manner, in conjunction with her continued absence, thought it indicated nothing good on the part of Lilly; and being a very rigid person in her notions, she was easily repelled by any appearance of an aberration from the straight course. An idea, too, glanced through her mind, extremely unfavourable to her former favourite. The alteration observable in Lilly's habits and proceedings was nearly simultaneous with a similar change in those of Philip; and as the young people had been extremely intimate and apparently fond of each other, she could not help combining the two circumstances, very much to the disadvantage of Lilly. So that the parting had been as cold on one side as it was abrupt on the other; and Mrs. Ryland had made no further advances towards a better understanding.

Thus, poor Lilly was cast out on all sides; she, who had lately thought herself so happy and so rich in friends!

One evening, however, as she was coming home from her work, she suddenly met Philip at the corner of a street. He was alone; and, with his hat over his eyes and his hands in his pockets, he was lounging along the pavement, with what struck her as an air of despondence. Had he looked gay and happy, she would have probably passed on with a slight recognition; as it was, she instinctively paused, and he stopped.

"Ah, Lilly, is it you?" said he; too much occupied at that moment with a trouble of his own, to think of her feelings or opinions of his conduct; and therefore not exhibiting the confusion he had lately evinced when they met. Nay, he even turned back with her, and walked by her side; but still slowly, despondently, and silently.

"How's Mrs. Ryland?" asked Lilly, who, having accommodated her pace to his, felt the silence awkward.

"My mother? Oh, my mother's well—quite well. And how are you, Lilly?"

"I am very well," answered she.

"So you are going to leave Mrs. Knox's?" said he; not speaking with interest or curiosity; but as of a matter already decided, and of slight import.

Lilly would naturally have said, "No, I am not;" for in fact she had no such intention; but she remembered what May had said, and, taken by surprise, she felt as if this were not a question, but an announcement of what must be; a sort of proclamation of May's high behest; and, setting apart the influence of habit, and of the impetuous will over the gentler nature, May's wishes in this instance she well knew would be omnipotent; for, as she was a very important person in Mrs. Knox's show-room, and Lilly of no importance whatever in any department, a word from the stronger would insure the dismissal of the weaker member.

"Well, Lilly," said he, "I hope you'll be happy, wherever you go; for I believe you're a good-hearted girl as ever lived. Perhaps, you may not care much for my opinion," he added, with a half smile; "but, you know, we're old friends, Lilly; and I've reason to know you better than most people."

This was a sort of sad, faint echo of the really serious, but, affectedly, jocular commendations he used to bestow upon her; and yet Philip had never been more sincere in the expressed opinion than he was at that moment.

His nascent love for her was extinguished by the blaze of his intoxicating passion for May, as a coal fire is dimmed by the noonday sun; and he had latterly avoided her, because he was conscious of this, and because he could not doubt that she was conscious of it too; nor did he doubt that she suffered from the change. But there was a tender sentiment towards her lingering at the bottom of his heart still; and he was by no means insensible to the instinctive delicacy and generosity, that had not only prevented her from speaking to his mother of his intimacy with May and his neglect of herself; but had also caused her to discontinue her visits.

But Lilly could say nothing to this; she only blushed and was silent. She was not experienced enough in the tactics of her sex to draw on an explanation from this favourable opening for one; so they walked on for another five minutes without a word. She half fancied there was something he desired to say to her— perhaps, he wished to speak of May! She hoped he would not, for she could not praise May now as she had always done before when her name was mentioned; not so much because her opinion of her friend was changed, as because her own feelings would not allow her. She would have been blind to May's faults, or have loved her in spite of them: but she was jealous; and although the beauty and fascinations of this Circe[83] seemed to her more potent than ever, for she witnessed their effects and magnified their power by her appreciation of what they had won from her, yet she could lift up her voice no more to sing the praises of those fatal charms.

Presently, a carriage passed with two footmen, whilst the lamps threw their glare on the brilliant figures within.

"What a strange world this is!" said he.

"Why?" asked Lilly, who was little given to moralize on affairs in general; and as to the question of what sort of a world it was, it was one that had never disturbed her.

"I mean, how different people's situation in life is," said he.

"Yes," answered Lilly; "there's rich and poor."

"Do you ever wish to be rich, Lilly?" said he.

"No," replied she; "I never thought about it; it would be no use."

"But that don't prevent one wishing for a thing. I wish it did. Can you help wishing for a thing because it's no use?"

"I don't know," replied Lilly; "only I never thought of wishing to be rich."

"So much the better for you, Lilly," said he: and then he relapsed into silence again.

---

83 Goddess of magic in Greek mythology. Daughter of the Sun God.

"How different he is to what he used to be?" thought Lilly; and she contrasted in her mind their merry walks and hearty laughs, with this lagging, aimless way of dragging himself along; and this disjointed talk. It was evident he was quite out of tune about something; but Lilly was too inexperienced in affairs of this nature to form any idea of what that something could be. It was in fact nothing more than a slight disappointment with respect to May. She was in the habit of walking with him every evening; but on the one in question an engagement had deprived him of her company. An acquaintance of Mrs. Knox's had given her two tickets for the pit of the Opera, and she had offered one to May; asking her at the same time if she could find any cavalier to accompany them. May said she could; never doubting that Philip would delightedly avail himself of the opportunity. And so he would have done, could he have commanded the money; but there was no ticket to be had under half-a-guinea, which was a sum he was not yet sufficiently mad to spend for such a purpose. Besides, he had it not; and the early habits and instructions of his youth were not so entirely obliterated as to allow him to borrow it of his mother or aunt under a false pretence.

But May could not understand such scruples, and had tossed her head with an "Oh, very well, if you don't wish to go, there are others that do!" And Philip had watched her departure, and had seen her, elegantly dressed, handed into the coach by a young man attired in a much more fashionable costume than he could boast of possessing. So that he had not only the mortification of not being able to accompany the mistress of his affections, but he was, moreover, jealous of the fortunate man that supplied his place. Added to this, he was suffering from a vexatious consciousness of his own poverty, a circumstance which till very lately had never given him any pain, but which he had now begun to look upon as a great evil.

In the intoxication of his early acquaintance with May, and the surprise and gratification of his vanity at finding himself an object of interest to so brilliant a beauty, he had thought of no difficulties, no impediments—love, the universal leveller, seemed to have smoothed them all. But several late circumstances had disclosed to him how much his happiness would be endangered by his want of means. How many things that the lover of so elegant a person should be able to do, were out of his power! He too should be fashionably dressed. His respectable suit of sables made by a country tailor was of a very different cut to the mulberry coat with basket buttons, and the pale canary-coloured waistcoat, of the happy Adonis[84] who was at that moment, probably, brushing May's cheek with his per-fumed curls, in the pit of the Opera! Then how could he accompany her to the play, or pay for her coaches, or present her with appropriate testimonies of his

---

84 Male God of beauty and desire in Greek mythology.

love? And, above all, how could he dare to ask her hand, or expect her to condescend to such appliances as he could offer? It was impossible! She must inevitably despise so shabby a fellow!

And yet, all this while, Philip, from this besetting weakness of mankind, which makes almost every body value themselves and other people according to what they *have*, and not according to what they *are*, was entirely mistaken in his estimate of his position in respect to May. She was, in fact, as much captivated by him as he was by her; only being older and more sophisticated, she had taken the *dessus;*[85] and made him her stringed instrument instead of her lord. If he were fascinated by her beauty and brilliance, and superficial virtues, she was no less so by his really handsome, manly person and genuine nature. He was a new character to her, and not the less irresistible for being so unlike herself and her previous admirers. She had never known before what it was to possess the ardent love of an honest heart; and though in the commencement of the acquaintance she had angled merely to catch him, she had ended by being caught herself; and if Philip, instead of succumbing to *her* nature, had been man enough to assert his own, he might and would have been her master; as it was, she was his.

And it is constantly thus in real life; these are the women that, by ruling men, have ruled empires. The true and noble woman disdains to rule, either as wife or mistress; she seeks a lord and not a slave. Her love must look ever upwards; and, except in the maternal relation, there can be no true love, from woman to man, that does not. There is another kind of woman that rules men too; the cold, calm, unexcitable, and ever-self-possessed; the woman that never forgets *herself.* We never saw such a one as a wife, that the husband was not, more or less, the subject of her will. In both instances, an intense selfishness is the predominant principle; in the first, combined with vanity; and in the second, with that, and a large portion of self-esteem, into the bargain.

In a true woman—and by a *true woman* we mean one in whom the nature of her sex is the most completely developed—candour will be the distinctive attribute; inasmuch as it is the distinctive attribute of the intuitive life which in her must prevail: but it is remarkable that these women, the true archetypes of their sex, are exactly those who have the least influence over men in general; for, to understand and appreciate such a woman, a man must be as noble and candid as herself. He must have *insight*—which few men have, for intellect does not give it; and, in the present stage of civilization, it is certain that men are much more governed by the vices and artifices of women than by their virtues. There is plenty of power to be had by bad means—by what are frequently called "the legitimate

---

85 The first step. In other words May has taken the initiative.

arms of the sex." Fie! we never see the *manège*[86] and the dexterities by which so many women retain their influence over their husbands, without feeling infinitely more contempt for her successful cunning, than we do for the poor spiritless un-resisting victim of a brute, who may be living next door.

The fact is, that few men know anything of woman's true nature—how should they? for what is more rare than a thoroughly genuine woman? And how are women answerable for this, when it has been for ages the business of society not only to repress and extinguish that nature wherever it appeared, but to educate its daughters out of it from their cradles; so that at this moment there can scarcely exist in any civilized country a woman in whom the germ has had so much vitality as to have resisted the external influences exerted to repress or pervert it, who does not feel herself in an ungenial atmosphere.

The usual light in which woman is considered is as of a being with a different physical organization to man; but in all other respects as of similar, but inferior, endowments—the essential distinctions, when observed, being set down to the account of eccentricity and aberration: and the education bestowed upon her has been in conformity with this view; that is, it has been, as compared with that bestowed on the other sex, an inferior sample of the same article—bad enough in the best—with a clumsy attempt to compensate for its inferiority by a few meretri-cious accomplishments. We humbly confess to a shrinking antipathy from what is commonly called an "accomplished woman." Let women draw, and sing, and play the harp—these things are good in their way—so are artificial flowers and French jewellery—but if these are their stock in trade—the armour with which they have been prepared to fight their battle and make their way through this life to another—we should think their outfit no more suitable, than we should their wardrobe, if its staple commodities consisted of the above mentioned pretty ap-purtenances.

Man having thus settled to his own entire satisfaction the question of the weakness and inferiority of woman, and every thing being done that training could do, to produce such results as confirmed his conclusion, it necessarily fol-lowed that she was unfit to cope with the world or resist the manifold dangers and temptations that surrounded her; and it was accordingly found necessary to hem her in by decorums and circumscribe her by conventionalities, which altogether precluded her from that self-education by experience which the more active life of man afforded him. Frightened at his own vices and the weakness of the creature to whose keeping he must needs confide his honour and peace, he saw nothing left for it but to turn the world into one large harem; perpetuating woman's slavery by perpetuating her ignorance; and teaching her, whilst he assumed a divine right

---

86 A place where horses are trained – or here lovers!

to despotic sway, that it was the worst of treasons to herself—that is, that it was *unfeminine*—to dispute his claims.

In short, he only discerned two functions for which woman could have been designed; namely, to be the slave of his passions, and the nurse of his babies in swaddling-clothes; and for these purposes, he sought to adapt her—he fitted her "to suckle fools;"[87] and verily he has his reward—for she has done it!

Thus, that the weakness and inferiority which they allege against us really does exist, we fear there is no mistaking. Let any woman to whom circumstances have been more favourable, or who, by the energy of her own will, has found a function for herself; and forced herself out of "the circumscription and confines,"[88] that custom had drawn about her, speak honestly the result of her experience and observation, in this respect. How many women could she reckon of her acquaintance, who have ever dared to think for themselves; or even, if they dared to *think*, would dare to *speak?* How many free souls could she count amongst them?

It is true, there is little real culture amongst men; there are few strong thinkers, and fewer honest ones; but they have still some advantages. If their education has been bad, it has at least been a trifle better than ours. Six hours a day at Latin and Greek are better than six hours a day at worsted-work[89] and embroidery; and time is better spent in acquiring a smattering of mathematics, than in strumming Hook's lessons[90] on a bad pianoforte. Then men have the benefit of rubbing against the world in their progress through it; they have mostly some definite pursuit or profession, within the domain of which they at least know something—and it is much to know something, though, like Walter Scott's companion in the stage coach, it be only about Bend-leather;[91]—and altogether, stunted though they be, they have been enabled to grow into more vigour, from not being so utterly repressed and stifled by the artificial restrictions and false delicacies they have entwined round the other sex.

It would be a consolation if, amidst all these disadvantages that have been heaped upon them, women could have preserved their candour, their simplicity, their singleness of mind; but they are so artificial, so conventional, so unreal, so afraid of being *themselves!* No wonder! For they have in ninety-nine instances out of a hundred been so frowned out of their individualities when they were young, that they have actually forgotten after what fashion God Almighty made them.

---

87 From *Othello*, Act 2 Scene I. Crowe is quoting Iago.

88 From *Othello* again.

89 Embroidery on canvas.

90 James Hook (1746 to 1827) was an English composer and performer. He wrote several instruction books for those learning the piano.

91 See *The Works of Sir Walter Scott*, Volume 20. Crowe's point is that it is better to know something than nothing.

Their minds have been compressed by tight stays, like their bodies; they have so entirely lost sight of Nature that they are positively shocked when she meets their view; and as soon as they get children of their own, they set about deforming her; squeezing, pinching, and paring, till, like the Flatheads or the Chinese,[92] they have reduced their offspring to the true standard of taste and gentility. Wo to any unfortunate little being, who should be found amongst the brood, in whom a strong nature prevailing over art will insist on asserting itself! Its mother will be as much astonished and dismayed as a hen that has hatched a duck's egg. The gods themselves know what an inane and insipid thing this eternal modelling, forming, and finishing, makes of society!

In what we have here said, we are very far from desiring to imply, that we think the intellectual faculty of woman, either in quality or calibre, equal to that of man. On the contrary, we are of opinion that the most intellectual woman that ever lived, be she who she may, has been far inferior in that region to the most intellectual man. This opinion we are aware will be very distasteful to some of the female champions of the cause we are advocating; but it is founded, not only on the records of the intellectual heroes and heroines of antiquity, but on observations and comparisons, made betwixt some of the most remarkable men and women of the present day. No female intellect that we have ever yet heard or read of exhibits any thing like the breadth, depth, and power of a noble, masculine, (honest) mind—for the degree in which the want of honesty cripples men's minds is past all calculation.

But what we wish to advance is, that, if allowed free scope and fair play, woman would be able to put forth, and make available, equivalent, though different endowments; which now not only lie fallow, but are actually in the process of extinction, from want of exercise; whilst, to most of those in whom the germ yet lives, it is, from the constitution of society and the restrictions placed on the sex, more a curse than a blessing. Nothing can equal the wretchedness of a woman, in whose bosom this lamp is pent, consuming herself, because not permitted to shed its ray upon the world. The utter hopelessness, the entire inanity of life, the sense of degradation, the wondering wherefore she was made, to bear all this and suffer to no end! Life all holiday, with nothing to do but play! And yet to break through this deadening charm that is flung about her, what "a downright violence and storm of fortune"[93] is most times needed! And how many, from the want of being guided to the true outlet and freer air, rush into perdition to escape it? Not because women of this temperament are vicious; exactly the contrary; they are the

---

92 Crowe is referring to the Salish Indian tribe who practised a form of head flattening, and to the Chinese practice of binding the feet of young girls.

93 From *Othello*, Act 1 Scene III.

least sensual of their sex; but because the living flame within must have something to pasture on. Denied to live their own life, and weave out their own destiny, they become absorbed in that of another; flinging themselves and their affections at the feet, not of a man, but of their own ideal—too often embodied in the form of some worthless idol, no more worthy of their faith, than the ill-carved stone that the poor Indian worships.[94]

If, as we believe, under no system of training, the intellect of woman would be found as strong as that of man, she is compensated by her intuitions being stronger—if her reason be less majestic, her insight is clearer—where man reasons, she sees. Nature, in short, gave her all that was needful to enable her to fill a noble part in the world's history, if man would but let her play it out; and not treat her like a full-grown baby, to be flattered and spoiled on the one hand, and coerced and restricted on the other, vibrating betwixt royal rule and slavish serfdom. In her childhood, woman is perverted by the ignorance of well-intentioned mothers and governesses, who view her, not as an independent soul, capable of the richest culture, and sent into this world for the purpose of qualifying herself to fulfil high duties here and higher hereafter, but as the appendage of some man, whose fancy she must first charm by her accomplishments, and to whose humours, for the rest of her life, she must afterwards conform; and it is lamentable to think that the great proportion of books now written on woman's duties, and put into the hands of young people, for their instruction, regard her in no other light. From first to last, she is governed by the pap-spoon[95] and the rod; and whilst, for his own selfish ends, man kneels at her feet and flatters her with mock devotion, he makes laws and enforces customs, that rob her of her free franchise, and of all the rights that God and Nature gave her.[96]

We have frequently of late heard the question asked, "Can woman regenerate society?" Really, we cannot see how that can be, till man regenerates himself. Till he elevates his own standard, it appears next to impossible for woman effectually to elevate hers: for prescription is on his side, might will be right, and he has so much the best of the game, that until by a nobler culture and the awakening of larger sympathies, his eyes are opened to his own injustice and his own loss, any

---

94 There was a popular perception that Indians were idol worshippers.

95 A spoon for feeding babies.

96 This note is in the original: "It gives us great satisfaction to learn that the women of Berne in Switzerland are at this time petitioning for equal rights; and that one of the American States is about to pass a law, giving females power over their own property". In 1847 a law was passed in Switzerland giving adult single women control over their own wealth without having to have a male guardian. In the same year the Married Women's Property Act passed in New York. In the United Kingdom, women would have to wait until 1882 for full control over their property.

material improvement in the condition of woman seems hopeless.

With all the independence, the freedom, the culture, the equal laws, the introduction into active life and employments, which we crave for woman, we still admit that man, through her heart and her affections, will be her lord; and should be, if he would raise himself to the standard that would entitle him to the fief.[97] There is nothing so elevating to a woman as the love of a truly great and noble man. The worship she pays him, whether it be that of friendship or of love, exalts her mind, and fills her soul with a holy joy; there is nothing so degrading, so crushing to the spirit, as to be the slave of a churl.

When men are better and wiser, they will be more just. When they are noble themselves, they will demand noble women to their wives; and for woman to be noble they will see that she must first be free. That so many amongst them do not desire to be so, is one of the worst symptoms of their condition.

CHAPTER XV

HOW ONE FALSE STEP ALWAYS LEADS TO MORE

May saw clearly the influence of Mrs. Ryland over her son—the influence of habit and of a genuine filial respect and affection—and she dreaded it. Her instinct showed her that she was not the wife his mother would accept for him; and although he had never distinctly told her so, she was well aware that their intimacy was carefully kept a secret from her. Lilly was therefore become to her an object of extreme apprehension and distrust. Yet, she knew her so well as to feel a tolerable degree of certainty that she would not betray them; that is, that she would not deliberately do anything that would be painful to Philip or herself, however provoked. Had she thought differently of her character, she would have treated her differently. She would have tried to win her by kindness and confidence, and sought to bind her by promises; but, as the best dispositions frequently encounter the worst usage, so, in this instance, she presumed on Lilly's gratitude and generosity to abuse them—treating her with coldness and disdain, and only implying her desire for silence with respect to Philip, by the extreme reserve she observed on the subject herself—in short, frowning instead of courting her to secrecy.

Nevertheless, she was not at ease; human nature is fallible; and even Lilly's devotion and generous forbearance might give way under temptation. Besides, it was extremely possible that Mrs. Ryland might interrogate her, and endeavour to extract what she knew with regard to Philip's late erratic courses; and she would not have given her worst shawl for Lilly's power of concealment, especially when

---

97 Chief or feudal lord.

questioned by one she loved; even supposing her faith remained incorruptible.

Then, again, her conscience told her that she was neither a worthy nor a fit object for Philip to centre his hopes and affections in. She was much more aware of their incompatibility than he was; for he saw her through a glare that dazzled his eyes, reinforcing and sustaining his own delusion by Lilly's former enthusiastic commendations. In concealing their intimacy from his mother, he was not actuated by any doubt of May's merits, but of his mother's capacity to comprehend and appreciate them. Her limited knowledge of the world, fixed prejudices, and provincial ideas, would render it impossible that they could ever amalgamate. How this difficulty was to be overcome in the future, he could not pause to consider; being too much engrossed and infatuated with the present. But May, though captivated and engrossed too, was older and clearer sighted. She knew herself, and she knew Philip—there was no difficulty in knowing him, for he "wore his heart upon his sleeve,"—and she was perfectly aware not only that Lilly loved him, and that he had, at the very least, been on the eve of loving her; but also that the ingenuous, pure, devoted, humble, true, and faithful girl, was a much more worthy partner for him, than she could ever be; and that if the glamour[98] were once off his eyes, he would think so too. It was therefore quite natural that she should fear Lilly, and equally natural that, fearing her, she should hate her, and desire to get her out of her way. What was to happen afterwards, she could no more pause to consider, than Philip could. How he was to be brought to marry her without his mother's consent; or how, if that came to pass, she was to conform to the mode of life that awaited him, she deferred to investigate. They were both carried away by the stream of their passions; and whether an abyss or a sunny haven, perdition or salvation, awaited them at the end of their course, they left it to the future to disclose.

In the mean time, Lilly, uncertain and irresolute, because not acting under an impulse, and too timid and inexperienced, and too much trammelled by her affections to form any deliberate plan for her own emancipation, hung on upon May still; though by a bond that she expected daily to see snapped. All that had rendered it dear was gone; all that had constituted her happiness within doors or without was ravished from her; her serfdom was no longer a joyous serfdom of the heart; yet, she toiled on as before; withholding no services, making no complaints. Now and then, May's good nature smote her, when she remarked the girl's patient sufferance; but the recollection of the mischief Lilly might do her if she chose, and of what a dangerous rival she would be if she were appreciated, hardened her heart. She feared the very virtues she was abusing; and the more clearly she perceived their beauty, the more clearly she perceived that they must not be allowed

---

98 Enchantment.

to come between her and her desires.

It is true, that she did not at all underrate her own charms and fascinations; and that she really had a profound contempt for Lilly's personal attractions, unadorned as they were by any aids of ornament; but she knew that Philip *had* once thought her pretty; and if she were allowed to be much in his way, he might some day return to the same opinion; which she now believed she had persuaded him out of; by convincing him that there could be no beauty worth looking at without what she called *style*—a proposition which Philip had not had courage to gainsay; and to which, indeed, his admiration of May's factitious graces had made him half a convert. But, however, people's passions and vanities deceive themselves or others, truth is there at the bottom all the while; it is only suppressed and stifled, not extinguished; and every now and then it flings out an unwelcome spark, throwing a very disagreeable glare into the secret places and tortuosities of the self-beguiling mind. Thus, in the midst of May's chimeras[99] and delusions, she was sometimes suddenly pervaded by an intuitive and extremely unpleasant suspicion, that the beauty of the ingenuous, pure, and candid soul that looked out of Lilly's mild eyes might possibly exert a more enduring charm than the bright gleams that shot from hers; and that the delicate features and smooth young cheek, which had yet not attained its ripest bloom, comprised in reality a much more perfect ideal of female loveliness than her more brilliant and developed beauty. A glance in the mirror was always, for the moment, sufficient to banish these intrusive whisperings of the spirit of truth; but they were nevertheless sufficiently alarming, together with her other sources of apprehension, to satisfy her of the prudence of getting Lilly out of her lover's way and her own, as soon as possible; and it was just when she was debating in her mind how this end could be best accomplished, that the devil—who we are told is always at our elbow watching his opportunity—seized the occasion to seduce her into an act of treacherous cruelty, that under any less potent influences than jealousy and fear she would have been incapable of. But fear is proverbially cruel; and jealousy, even to a good and generous nature, is the sorest of all temptations.

When Bet went home from Mrs. Knox's, and told her mother she was discharged, she omitted to mention the origin of the misfortune. She did not choose undeservedly to incur the suspicion of neglect or dishonesty, which she knew she did not merit, and to have avowed the truth would have been betraying May; for it was not to be expected that her mother would keep the secret. Hard working and willing, the poor girl tried to get some employment, which should furnish her bread, and her two shillings a week, which sufficed to pay her parents' rent, and was all she had had before; and for a short time she jobbed about from place

---

99 Here Crowe means something illusory that will never really exist.

to place: but failing to obtain any thing permanent, the day came that the rent, which was always demanded weekly, was not forthcoming; and the poor family was threatened with expulsion, if the debt were not speedily discharged. Then Bet, who was passionately attached to her sickly infant brother, began to waver; she could not allow the child and his mother to be turned into the street; yet it would cost her a great deal of pain to do her benefactress so severe an injury, for she was fully able to appreciate the fatal consequences that would result to May from the discovery.

At length, having duly weighed the *pros* and *cons* after her own manner, that is, not taking into consideration the moral view of the case, but only the balance of evils, she determined on the line of conduct which appeared to her the most advantageous; since, whilst it would probably restore her to favour, it might, at the same time, leave a loophole for May's escape. She accordingly presented herself before Mrs. Knox late one evening, when she knew the young people would have quitted work, and told her story.

On the following morning, after breakfast, Mrs. Knox took an early opportunity of taking May aside. "Have you ever had any suspicion of Miss Dawson's honesty?" said she.

"No," answered May; "I believe her to be quite honest."

"It is a very extraordinary thing!" continued Mrs. Knox; "but you remember about that white blond fall, that should have gone to Mrs. Wilmot's?"

"Yes," returned May, taking out her handkerchief, and violently blowing her nose, in order to account for the blood she felt rushing to her cheeks.

"Well, Betsy Barton has been here; she came last night, after you were gone, to tell me that she left that fall at your lodgings, with a bonnet of yours. She says that I put it into the wrong box. I don't think I did, by the by: and that when she went to your room you had not come in, but that she delivered them both to Miss Dawson. Did she take you a bonnet that night?"

"That night?" said May, pressing her hand on her brow, as if to summon her recollection; "she *may* have brought me a bonnet that night. I couldn't say she did not, because it must have been somewhere about that time I had my Tuscan cleaned and trimmed: still I don't think it was that week. But, to be sure, Bet may recollect the time better than I do."

"She says she is certain of it," returned Mrs. Knox, "but that she did not like to say so before, because Miss Dawson declared she knew nothing about the fall, and Bet was afraid she shouldn't be believed. However, I can't say I think that a very good reason, and that makes me doubt the whole story."

"I think Bet must be mistaken in the night," said May.

"She has never shown any love of dress—quite the contrary," observed Mrs.

Knox—"Miss Dawson, I mean. The fall could be of no use to her, unless she sold it."

"None!" answered May, whose brain was in such a whirl of uncertainty and confusion, that she could hardly command presence of mind enough to conceal it.

"And yet Bet declares she is positively certain of the fact, and that Miss Dawson must remember it; because, in taking out the bonnet, the paper the blond was in was caught by a pin, and when she lifted the bonnet the parcel fell on the carpet; and that she—that is Miss Dawson—picked it up and laid it on the table."

May remained silent, assuming an attitude of reflection, but in reality unable to collect her thoughts at all. She saw, at once, that if she disputed Bet's assertion with respect to bringing her a bonnet that night, some of the other young people, on being appealed to, might be able to substantiate the fact; and then the mere circumstance of the denial might point suspicion to herself. If, on the contrary, she countenanced the accusation against Lilly, the girl might be put on her defences. At that very moment the blond was lying concealed at the bottom of one of her own boxes; she could not be certain that Lilly was ignorant of this, and a search would be fatal to herself. Altogether, she thought it better to hint that she thought Betsy Barton was either mistaken, or that she had invented this tale, in the hope of recovering her situation.

"With respect to my bonnet," she said, "it very likely came home that night—certainly it was about that time; but it is very improbable that you should have put the fall in the wrong box. It is much more likely that Bet lost it; besides, why shouldn't she have said so when you asked her at first, before you questioned *us* about it at all?"

"There is one thing, however," observed Mrs. Knox, "that did strike me very much at the time, and that was Lilly Dawson's manner, I remember, indeed, I was so struck with it, that I was going to question her further, only that you remarked she had left work before the boxes went away. However, we'll have her in and question her at once;" and Mrs. Knox was about to open the door, for the purpose of calling Lilly.

"Stay," said May, seized with terror, "I think we had better say nothing about it to her till I have searched her drawers. If she has the lace, I shall find it; and if she has sold it, I shall find the money. If you will let me go home before her this evening, I may be able to discover something about it."

"Well, do," returned Mrs. Knox. "I dare say that will be the best way: and if you cannot make out anything, we will question her to-morrow."

Little dreaming of what was plotting against her, Lilly worked away; somewhat sorrowful, indeed, as she had been lately, from Philip's disloyalty and May's unkindness; but far happier than her brilliant rival. To the latter it was a fearful day—the most anxious she had ever passed in her life. She thought it would never be over, and that the hour of release would never arrive, when she might hasten home and thrust the cause of all this apprehension into the fire. There was no security for her now, but in burning the fall; and this she did the moment she reached her lodging. It was a moment of inexpressible relief to her when she saw the rich silk lace, the object of her eager desires, curling and crinkling in the flame.

So far, so good. But she was not out of her troubles yet. On the following day, Lilly was to be interrogated; and that, even though she wished it, she would be unable to disguise the truth, May felt assured. Lilly, with her tell-tale complexion and simple honesty, would be the last person in the world to baffle a cross-examination. Willingly or unwillingly, she would tell all she knew, and that in a manner that would probably command belief. She felt, from experience, that what Lilly affirmed it was not easy to doubt; so that, by her expedient of deferring the examination and burning the evidence of her guilt, she had only gained the reprieve of a day. There was more to be done yet; and now, the imminence of her own danger hardening her heart, she began to repent that she had burnt the lace. If she had been less precipitate, she might have taken it to Mrs. Knox and declared that she had found it in Lilly's possession; but her foolish haste had undone her, and some further expedient must be discovered for securing her own safety. After much deliberation, she could think but of one, and that was built on her knowledge of her friend's character.

"Lilly," said she, "come here; I want to speak to you." May was then sitting with her feet on the fender and her back to the light, which consisted of a single candle, standing upon a table in the middle of the room. Lilly had been working by it; but she now rose, and approached May. "Sit down," said the latter; and Lilly took a chair from the recess near the chimney, and, drawing it forward, seated herself just by the corner of the mantelpiece.

"Lilly," continued May, "I am in great trouble."

"Are you, May?" said Lilly. "What's the matter?"—"There's no money to pay the rent," thought she, knowing nothing of Mr. Cropley's twenty pounds.

"I dare say, Lilly, you think me altered lately: I know I am; I'm altered to you and to everybody. The truth is, Lilly, I'm miserable!"

"It's something about Philip," thought Lilly.

"Do you remember," said May, "about six weeks ago, that there was a fuss in the work-room about a blond fall that was to have gone to Mrs. Wilmot's?"

"Yes," replied Lilly, who indeed recollected it too well; the circumstance had never been out of her head since; and it had occasioned her the greatest uneasiness. As we have before hinted, Lilly, having no theory of morals, had hitherto been governed and guided wholly by her instincts, which, being virtuous, had kept her so; but the standard by which she judged the conduct of other people was quite unfixed, and much too lenient, especially if she loved them. She had never properly estimated the amount of ill-treatment she had received from her cousins; and she had never formed any just idea of the faults of May's character, although she was a constant victim to them. The selfishness, which had allowed her to live on Lilly's wages, and the dishonesty of prodigally spending money that she owed, had never been viewed in their true light: these were May's ways—ways which Lilly never thought of judging, till the amount of her own smart somewhat opened her eyes to their significance. She had not, comparatively, cared for her money, nor her labour, nor her self-denying meals—all these were sacrifices willingly made to her idol: it was not till May encroached on the domain of her affections, that Lilly began to judge her, and discerned that she cared for nobody's feelings but her own.

This discovery had given her great pain, every way; and by awakening her to certain reflections on May's character, it had prepared her to comprehend somewhat of the mystery connected with the blond fall; and many a time since she had thought of the circumstance with wonder, grief, and dismay. May was not the angel she had imagined her; her idol was a false idol; that was plain. The others had been true ones: Abel had been good; the Rylands were good; for, in spite of Philip's defection, she thought no ill of him. She too highly appreciated the amount of May's fascinations, and too humbly esteemed herself, not to excuse him.

"Well," continued May, "that fall has cost me more unhappiness than I ever suffered in all my life put together before! I dare say, you little thought, Lilly, when Mrs. Knox was asking Bet about it, that I could have told her where it was?"

"I knew Bet had left it here," returned Lilly, with her usual directness.

"You did!" exclaimed May, affecting considerable surprise. "Then that was the reason you looked so confused, and blushed so, when Mrs. Knox asked you about it?"

"Yes," answered Lilly. "I didn't know what to say, when I saw you didn't speak."

"I wish, with all my heart, you had spoken!" returned May. "What a deal of misery it would have saved me! Indeed, Lilly, it was very wrong of you."

"I wish I had," said Lilly, innocently.

"You see, when I took it into my room, I had no thought of what it was: I supposed it was my old lace come home from the clear-starcher," continued May, "and just threw it into my drawer, without ever so much as looking at it; and never, till two or three weeks after, did I discover what it was!"

"Then you didn't know about it when Mrs. Knox asked us?" said Lilly.

"No," answered May; for although she had just before implied the contrary, that was a mistake: "no; it was just an accident that I opened the paper one Sunday, and there I saw it. I'm sure you might have knocked me down with a feather!"

"And have you told Mrs. Knox?" inquired Lilly.

"No," replied May; "how can I? How can I expect her to believe me? If I had only had the courage to tell her last week! if I had only told her yesterday! But now it's too late!"

"Why?" asked Lilly.

"Because there's a stir about it again. Bet wants to come back again; and Mrs. Knox has been questioning her; and if they only remember about my bonnet, it will be all up with me. How can I say I haven't got it, if I am asked! And then, what is worse, how can you say it? and you will be asked to-morrow, you may depend upon it."

"I hope not," said Lilly. "I shouldn't like to be asked about it at all. But, if I were you, I'd just go and tell Mrs. Knox that I'd got it. It wasn't your fault, you know."

But May's conscience would not let her have done that, if she had had the fall still in her possession; however, she had now put it out of her power to do it, and so she told Lilly.

"I couldn't bear the sight of it," said she; "and, in my vexation, I threw it into the fire. But now, Lilly, you'll give me your word of honour you'll never tell."

"I'll never tell," answered Lilly. "I wouldn't for the world; but I wish you hadn't burnt it!"

"That's past praying for," said May. "But you won't betray me, even if Mrs. Knox questions you to-morrow?"

"I'll try not," replied Lilly; "but I know I shall colour up so!"

"Yes, you do colour so! That's the worst of it," returned May. "I'm sure, I can't tell what's to be done."

"I say, Lilly," said May, after a silence of some minutes, during which they both seemed to be cogitating on this unpleasant affair, "a thought strikes me. Suppose you were to stay away from work to-morrow! I can say you've a bad cold, you know."

"But then she'll question me the next day, you know," objected Lilly.

"Perhaps not," said May, "if I tell her to-morrow that you know nothing about it, which I will. Probably, the whole thing may blow over in a day or two."

Lilly by no means thought the expedient a good one; she would have much preferred risking all on a full avowal and a restitution. However, the latter being out of the question, she acceded to May's proposal, and the next day stayed at home.

"Well, have you found out anything?" inquired Mrs. Knox. "Where is Miss Dawson?"

"At home," answered May, with a very grave countenance, and at the same moment placing some money, wrapped in a bit of white paper, in Mrs. Knox's hands. "The truth is, there is some mystery between her and Bet that I cannot make out. But there is the price of the fall; and I should really take it as a favour if you would not press the thing further. That Lilly meant to be dishonest, I can't believe; but still there is something in the business I do not understand; but, however, whether it was an accident, or whatever it was, there's the money."

Mrs. Knox said it was very odd, and May agreed that it was; but, as she only spoke in innuendoes, she left the impression on Mrs. Knox's mind that she had designed, namely, that Lilly was, in some way, the guilty party; or, at least, if not a principal, an accessory to the misdemeanour, whatever it was.

Under these circumstances, she was not particularly desirous of having her back; nor was she at all surprised when May said, that she did not wish to return. On the other hand, Lilly was kept away without much difficulty. She had an intense dread of the impending interrogation; and, under all the circumstances of the case, would not have been at all sorry to leave Mrs. Knox, provided she were certain of employment elsewhere. When, therefore, May came home on the second night, and told her that, as the season was over, all the extra hands were to be discharged, Lilly's chief regret was, that she did not know where to look for a situation. But this May promised to find for her, against she herself removed to her new lodging; at which time it had been previously arranged that they were to separate.

May, however, since the alarm about the fall, was much kinder than before. She was more like what she used to be, in the early days of their acquaintance. But Lilly's feelings were not the same. She would not have been compelled to injure May for the world; and would much rather have resigned her place than run the risk of it; but she could not forget that May had superseded her in Philip's affections; and, without stopping to examine whether the fault lay with him or with her, she felt that she could not love her as she had done.

In the mean time, however, they continued on good terms together, Lilly keeping much by herself—avoiding Philip and his mother—and seeing but little of May, who, after she left work, always walked out with her lover. Lilly knew it; because, when they came home, she more than once heard him bid her good night at the foot of the stairs. Lilly was sadly in her way; but, however, the day was fast approaching when she was to move, and then she should be rid of her, and anxiously she expected it; for, besides the inconvenience of her presence, which impeded Philip's visits, she could not overcome her jealous fears. What, if urged by her own jealousy, Lilly should ever be induced to tell Philip about the blond!

The dread of this haunted her, and left her no hope of peace, till she had removed Lilly out of the reach of temptation.

CHAPTER XVI

LILLY AND MAY PART COMPANY

In the mean time, May had done as she had promised, with regard to finding employment for Lilly, with a friend of her own. "It is only temporary," said she; "but, if you'll just take her for a few days, and give her her living, I should be obliged to you." She also promised Lilly that she would look for a lodging for her, and get her more permanently settled; and Lilly's heart was half melted with all this kindness. May, after all, *was* very good, and she reproached herself for not being able to love her as formerly; but, when she saw her come home of an evening, after walking with Philip, radiant with joy, and when she heard how he lingered below, and what a long "good night" there was betwixt them, she felt that she could not.

As the time drew near that was to separate them, there was something about May that Lilly could not help observing, and which she attributed to a feeling of regret, and perhaps remorse, for some past unkindnesses. She seemed absent and depressed, and her conduct towards Lilly became capricious. When Lilly talked about the future, or made inquiries respecting her lodging, or expressed any apprehensions with regard to her chances of getting regular work, May always cut the conversation short; and any proposal of Lilly's to apply to Mrs. Knox for a recommendation was nipped at the onset. Yet, the variability of her demeanour was not calculated to inspire Lilly with confidence; and the latter was not without anxiety; but still, timid and irresolute, except when acting under an impulse, she waited on, from day to day, till the period for removal arrived.

"As I intend to move to-morrow, Lilly," said May, "I think you had better go tonight; and I have told the people to expect you."

"Where is it? and what am I to pay?" inquired Lilly, alarmed and puzzled; for she was at present earning nothing but her board.

"Never mind," answered May; "I'll look to that till you are settled somewhere."

"How kind!" thought Lilly again; and she made an attempt to express her thanks. But May cut short what she had to say, by observing, that it was late, and she must be off to her work. Lilly also went to hers; and the day passed as usual, except that she had a very unexpected alarm in the course of it, from seeing a man, whom she believed to be her cousin Luke, passing the shop window. It was only his side face she caught; for he was looking in another direction; but she felt pretty sure it was he; and it naturally disturbed her exceedingly. She felt that she should be afraid to pass through the streets, lest she should meet him; and, for the remainder of the afternoon, she avoided, as much as possible, showing herself in the front shop. When she went home at night it was dusk; but she had hardly courage to ring the bell when she reached the lodging—who could tell but he might be there waiting to clutch her—for she always felt as if he were a hawk, and she the poor partridge that he was stooping to seize. Luke, however, was not there; but she immediately communicated her alarm to May.

"I think it's very foolish of you to be so afraid of your cousin," said May. "Why should you be so afraid of a man that never did you any harm? He only wishes to marry you—and surely there's no harm in that."

"But I wouldn't marry him for the world!" said Lilly.

"But that's just a prejudice," returned May; "you know, Lilly, it's not easy for you to get your living by yourself, here in London—you are not fit to live by your-self, and that's the truth. You've done well enough while you've been with me; but, for my part, I don't see how you're ever to get on alone; and I do think it would be the best thing in the world for you to marry your cousin—I do, indeed. Then, you'd have a comfortable home, and somebody to take care of you."

"I'd rather starve than marry him," answered Lilly, with unusual energy. "I can't think how you can wish me to marry a person I hate so!"

"Well," returned May, "you must choose for yourself—only, I think it would be the best thing that could happen to you; that I tell you."

It was very easy for May to say all this, who had got Philip for herself, and who did not know what sort of person Luke was; but Lilly did not like it at all. She would not have relished such advice from any body; but, from the person who had superseded her in Philip's heart, it was bitter, indeed! And, although gentle-tempered almost to a fault, she could not help showing her dissatisfaction, by quitting the room.

It was about nine o'clock; and Lilly, having first indulged in a hearty fit of weeping, and since pinned up in a bundle the few articles of dress which formed her wardrobe, was endeavouring to persuade herself to return to May, and, for-getting her resentment, part in charity with one whom she had loved so dearly, and who had certainly done her many kind services, when her friend opened the door that divided the two rooms, and said, "Lilly, it's time to go!" Whereupon, Lilly rose, tied her bonnet-strings, put a pin in her shawl, and came out, with her bundle in her hand. She had had some idea of giving May a kiss, and thanking her for the home she had so long afforded her, before they descended the stairs; but she found that May was already half way down them; so she joined her in silence, and in silence they proceeded along the street.

"Is it far?" inquired Lilly.

"Not very," answered May; "but I'm not sure that I shall find the way without taking a coach; it's so dark;" and indeed it was a thick, misty night; and, although it did not rain, the streets were so greasy and slippery with mud, that Lilly was by no means sorry when May called "Coach!" to a man who was standing beside his vehicle, which was drawn up close to the pavement, at the corner of St. Martin's Lane.

"Open the door!" said she; and the man obeying her, the two girls stepped in; Lilly first; and May following, after making some observation to the driver, who then mounted his box, where another person was already seated, and drove off.

Not a word was spoken inside the coach, as they rumbled through the dimly-lighted streets. What May felt Lilly could not tell; but her own feeling was one of deep depression. The present was dark, and the future was dark; and she saw no ray of light to brighten the picture. She had never lived alone in her life, and she foresaw how dismal it would be; besides, her very means of subsistence were precarious. And then the void in her heart was so sad. Ever since her emancipation, and the awakening of her spirit, Lilly had lived upon love—but now she had no one to love—no one to serve—no one to sacrifice to. Poor Lilly! She was desolate without, and desolate within!

She was so occupied with these sad thoughts, that she did not know how long they had ridden, when the coach stopped, and the door was opened—that it was so, she rather heard than saw; for it was so exceedingly dark, that she could not even distinguish May, who sat opposite to her. "Go!" said the latter; and Lilly got out, assisted by the man, expecting May to follow; but, to her infinite surprise, her feet were no sooner on the pavement, than she heard the steps folded up, the door smartly shut, and the coach driven away; whilst the man who had assisted her to alight, still holding her by the arm, and saying, "This way," led her into the dark passage of a house.

"Is this the lodging?" asked Lilly, both alarmed and grieved. She had expected May to accompany her to her apartment, and introduce her to the woman of the house; and she had, of course, also expected that she would bid her *good by.* Such a parting, and such a reception, quite confounded her; and, little suspicious of evil as she was, she began to fear that some was intended her.

"Come this way," said the man. "It's rather dark; but I'll lead you."

"Is it high up?" inquired Lilly.

"On the third story," answered the man.

It was very odd; but still he did not speak uncivilly. As for his face, she could

not see it; perhaps there was no cause for alarm; it was doubtless a poor neighbourhood, and a poor house; what better could she expect? Indeed, she had charged
May to take for her but a single, low-priced room; and that the place should be
ill-lighted, or not lighted at all, was not surprising. But how dull it would be! and
how frightened she should be coming home at night from her work. All these
things she thought, as they groped their way up-stairs, her conductor still holding
her by the arm. When they reached the third story, he stopped.

"Is it here?" asked Lilly.

"All right!" said he, as he drew a key from his pocket, and opened a door. Lilly
turned quickly towards him, but she could distinguish nothing.

"Is there a candle?" said she.

"You'll get one presently," he replied; and, before she was aware of his intention, he had pushed her into the room, locked the door upon her, and she heard
his foot descending the stairs.

This action, conjoined to the words *"All right,"* were a revelation to her—she
felt assured that she was entrapped—May had delivered her into the hands of her
enemies! That expression, *"all right,"* was a slang one of Giles Lintock's; he used
it on all occasions; it had struck familiarly on her ear the moment he uttered it!
All was accounted for now: May's mystery—her vindication of Luke—the strange
parting and stranger reception—all was clear; she was betrayed, and May was the
traitor!—

CHAPTER XVII

THE HISTORY OF A NIGHT

The only light Lilly had, whereby to reconnoitre the place into which she had
been so strangely thrust, was that which struggled through the dirty panes from
the neighbouring windows. Exactly opposite, on the floor level with the room she
was in, there was a lamp, which, though not sufficient to illuminate the narrow
street below, did serve, in some degree, to dissipate the obscurity around her. It
sufficed at least to show her that she was in a tolerably-sized square room, in one
corner of which stood a four post bedstead, without curtains; that in the recess of
one of the windows there stood a small table; and she could also discern two or
three objects, which appeared to be chairs placed against the wall.

This was all the room seemed to contain—but the bed!—was there anybody
in that? What if Luke were there! Standing still on the spot whereon she found
herself when the door was closed behind her, afraid to move either way, she listened; but no sound reached her, except the low buzz from the street, and the

rolling of distant wheels. In this attitude she stood for upwards of a quarter of an hour, scarcely breathing, that she might hear the better; but all was so quiet, that she ventured at length to advance cautiously towards the bed, and, having listened till she was satisfied no breather was there, she put down her hand in order to ascertain if the bed was made. It was; and Lilly, whose trembling limbs could scarcely support her, seated herself on the edge that she might collect her thoughts.

That she was once more in the power of her cousin, she did not doubt. For what reason, she could not divine, May had delivered her into "the snares of the fowler."[100] It was a cruel thought—and as the conviction pressed on her, she could scarcely abide its bitterness. Poor Lilly had not believed in such a world—a world where what was fair could be so false.

Then she began to wonder what could be Luke's design in thus pursuing her. Why should he care for her so much as to give himself all this trouble—following her about the country, and employing Giles Lintock to entrap her? And how should he have known Giles? These were questions she found it impossible to answer. One thing, however, she was determined on, and that was, not to marry Luke. If he persisted in that scheme, she would do as Abel had advised her when first she met him; she would appeal to the clergyman, and tell him that she had never consented to the union, and that she would rather die than be the wife of Luke. Thank God, Abel had given her this advice! At that time, it would have been of no use to her, for she could not have dared to follow it; but now, she knew better—at least, she was bolder; she knew a little more of the world, though she did not know much; and besides, she had had her first lesson in love; and although Philip would never think of her again, she could never forget him; and if Luke, instead of being an ogre, as she thought him, had been a man, still she would have sought protection from him; she never would marry, whether by force or favour; on that point she was clear.

Then, she wondered whether he would intrude on her that night; and she listened anxiously for every sound; but though she sometimes heard doors clapping below, no one seemed to ascend so high as where she was.

Thus she sat for a long time, till, besides being very tired, she began to feel very cold.

Every now and then, in spite of her fears, she found herself dozing; and, at length, she thought she would slip into the bed, without undressing, and cover herself up with the clothes. It did not appear that any body intended to disturb her that night, and she would be in no more danger in the bed than out of it; but she resolved not to sleep, if she could help it.

---

100 Psalm 91:3.

She found it no easy matter, however, to keep herself awake; she tried and tried, but slumber would steal over her; and after many abortive efforts against it, she at length sunk into sleep.

She thought she could not have been long asleep, when she was awakened by a noise close to her. Her sleep had probably not been very sound either, for there was no forgetfulness; and her consciousness of where she was, and of the preceding events, was as clear and vivid when she opened her eyes, as when she closed them; and with this flash of recollection came the conviction that she was no longer alone—there was somebody in the room—and the faint light showed her a figure seated at the bottom of the bed.

To those who have ever felt what it is to fancy, in the dead of night, that there is some unknown being in the room, which they believed untenanted by any but themselves, we need not attempt to paint the thrill of terror that instantly pervaded Lilly's every nerve, nor how breathlessly she listened to the movements of this midnight visitor.

The first distinct sound that reached her after she awoke, seemed to be a convulsive sigh or sob; then there was another and another; in short, the person was evidently weeping: and she was soon satisfied that the mourner was a woman, and that the grief was of no gentle character. However, the discovery of the sex of the stranger somewhat reassured her; and she lay still, listening and wondering what was to come next. Perhaps, she had been put into a wrong room and the woman might be coming to bed; in which case there must necessarily ensue an explanation. Whilst debating whether to speak at once, or whether to wait the event in silence, she observed that this storm of grief was beginning to abate: there was a longer interval between the sobs; the breathing became more regular; the passion, in short, had apparently exhausted itself; and just as she was making up her mind to address her, the woman arose and quitted the room; closing the door, but not locking it.

Now, then, she might escape; at least, there was a fair chance that she might grope her way down stairs and reach the street; and she felt much disposed to try; but when the question occurred of what she was to do when there, she was at a loss to answer it. She did not know where she was, and would probably have great difficulty in finding her way to the part of the town known to her; and if she did, of whom to claim protection or advice, she knew not. Her thoughts ever recurred to Philip; but, after this experience of May's treachery, her faith in human faith was shaken—Philip and May were one. Besides, she could not persuade herself that any body could shield her from her cousin; he seemed to be possessed of some mysterious right over her person, which his unscrupulous nature would, sooner or later, find means to vindicate. She resolved, however, when the morning arrived, that she would make an attempt to escape; leaving the direction of her flight to be decided by circumstances.

She was still lying cogitating on these matters, when she was startled by the creaking of the stairs; and in a moment her ears were on the alert, and her eyes straining to the door—and presently the latch was very gently, but audibly lifted, and the door was slowly opened—then there was a pause; and then it was opened a little further; and some one entered the room, closing it very gently.

Lilly, at first, concluded that this was the woman returned, although the movements were certainly very different; for she had used no caution; whereas, this person seemed to be extremely fearful of disturbing her. A mother entering the room of her sick infant, on whose lids sat life and death, at issue, could not have moved more inaudibly. But as the figure advanced into the room and crossed the faint ray of light that still gleamed from the opposite window, where some low revellers of the night were congregated, she fancied that she could distinguish that this was the figure of a man. Be it what it might, however, it was moving towards the bed, and at length stood close beside her; and there it paused awhile. What mystery was this? Who was this midnight visitor, that trod with such a stealthy, noiseless foot, that she was satisfied he wore no shoes? Was it Luke? She thought it was; and during that fearful pause, what memories crowded on her! What had become of Mr. Ryland? What of Winny Weston's lover? What was the significa-tion of the scene in her dead uncle's chamber?

Whilst she asked herself these things, she perceived the figure stooping over her, bending gradually lower and lower, as if listening for her breath, which she endeavoured to the utmost to suppress; so that, apparently unable to ascertain by that means whether the bed were tenanted or not, a hand was gently laid upon the coverlet. This experiment seemed to satisfy the man, if man he were, and he immediately reassumed an erect position.

Then, there was another pause, during which Lilly, almost turned into stone with terror, lay as motionless as the dead, whilst there was some slight movement on the part of the man, which terminated in a faint sound, like the opening of a stiff clasp knife: the sound was familiar to her, because her cousins had such in-struments—strong knives, with horn handles, and two or three blades. Then she would have screamed; but she could not lift her voice; and at that instant she felt that something fell upon the bed: the man had dropped the knife; whereupon, he put down his hand to seek it; but it having fallen betwixt the folds of the cov-erlet, he could not find it. This Lilly understood from his actions; and apparently restrained from a more active search by the fear of awaking her, after a moment's hesitation, he turned about, and still with the same inaudible steps and cautious movements, he quitted the room.

The moment the door was closed, Lilly put out her hand and seized the knife, which, having fallen upon her, had slipped over to the inner side of the bed, which, by the way, we should have remarked, stood against the wall. She had not been mistaken: it was, as she had supposed, a large clasp knife, open. It was therefore plain that the man, whoever he was, had come to murder her; and doubtless, having obtained another weapon, he would return and execute his design. This one, however, she immediately thrust under the mattress.

What should she do now? Where cry for help? Whither seek protection? Who was in the house she knew not; perhaps nobody but this man and the weeping woman—but could she aid her? Wherefore had she wept? Perhaps for the victim that she could not save—that she had, may be, come to warn, but dared not. There was the window, and the light in the opposite room—there were livers there—and, trembling like a leaf, she got out of bed and crept towards it: first, she must throw it up—that would make a noise, and might be observed by the man below, and ere she could make herself heard by the neighbours, he would come behind her, and seize her, and drag her to the bed, and kill her there; it might only summon him the quicker to her destruction.

Suddenly, another thought struck her—she might get the key, and lock the door from within; that is, if she durst but open it—but what if he were standing on the other side However, this seemed her only chance, as it would give her time to open the window and call for help; so she turned in that direction; but before she reached it, she became aware that a foot was again approaching; and impulse now taking the command, and deciding for her in an emergency that left no time for reflection, she instantly retreated and took refuge under the bed, the only place of concealment that, as far as she knew, the room afforded.

She had scarcely reached her refuge, when, as she expected, the door opened, and the man, as she supposed, entered, but with less precaution than before. The latch was lifted, and the door was closed audibly enough; and the step across the room was audible too, till it reached the side of the bed.

"Now," thought Lilly, "he will miss me, and seek me; and he will find me, too, and I shall be dragged out and murdered." Her terror and agony were inexpressible. A space, however, of some six or seven minutes ensued—an age of anguish to her, when, to her surprise, she felt the bed shake above her; and it appeared that the person had stepped into it and lain down. How strange! Was this the man, or the woman, or some other visitor? She would have given any thing to know; but till they slept, at all events, that was impossible, without discovering herself, which she durst not risk doing; so, almost frozen with fear and cold, she remained quietly where she was, listening to the breathing of the person above her; which, very shortly, from the long drawn-out and heavy respirations, betokened that they slept.

And now Lilly debated what she should do next. If it were the man that was lying in the bed, she must either have mistaken his intentions, or he must have changed them; but, in either case, she so much dreaded being discovered by him, that, painful as her situation was, she would prefer remaining in it till he quitted the room again, to the risk of betraying herself. If, on the contrary, it were the woman, the best thing she could do would probably be to make her acquainted with the circumstance, and seek her protection or advice. Then again, if she were sure it was the man, now that he was asleep—if she were but sure of that—she might possibly creep out of the room and lock him in. But, amongst these difficulties and uncertainties, wrought up to a fearful pitch of agitation and terror by so many strange circumstances, it was not easy for a timid, irresolute, inexperienced girl to decide; so there she lay still, doubting and fearing, till the opportunity for action was lost.

Heavily slept the sleeper upon the bed; with a panting heart and straining ears for what should next ensue, watched Lilly under it; nor did she watch in vain; for now again the latch is gently stirred, and some one enters, slowly, softly as before. This was the man, she was sure; she recognised at once the difference betwixt his stealthy approach, courting concealment, and that of the woman, which sought none. He was, therefore, come back to murder her. Oh! the horror, the anguish of that conviction!

Silently and inaudibly as before, he advanced towards the bed. She rather *felt* than *heard* his foot; it was more the vibration of the floor than her ear that enabled her to count his steps. Now he is beside the bed—what will he do next?—ere he can do any thing, the woman wakes—he had placed his hand upon her face; and, whilst she seeks to put it away, she cries, "Who's there?"

There was no answer, but a sound betwixt a cry and a groan, for the breath seemed impeded, and the bed shook, as in a fearful struggle—there were efforts to speak, or to scream, on the part of the woman—and muttered curses on the part of the man—and still the struggle continued; till, suddenly, there was a strange, gurgling sound, and then it ceased, and there was silence. Some minutes elapsed; and then the man quitted the room.

With all the terror inspired by this frightful drama, the successive acts of which she had witnessed, up to the climax of horror accomplished in the last, Lilly's senses never failed her. She was one of those women who do not faint, though, having little courage, she could not make very available the senses she retained. She comprehended perfectly the deed that had been done, and knew that on the bed above her there lay a human being dying or dead—probably slain in her stead, for she fully believed that it was for her throat the knife was intended.

And she was not safe yet; for if the man should return with a light to look upon his work, he would discover his mistake, and she would still be sacrificed. Impressed with this fear, she durst not stir from her concealment; but, frightful as her situation was, she resolved to remain there till the light began to dawn—provided, at least, he did not return, which she scarcely dared to hope.

Oh, what long hours they were, till the light gleamed through those dusky panes! Previously to the appearance of its blessed beams, there had been an interval of utter darkness; for the candle in the opposite window had been extinguished, and the songs and shouts of the revellers, as they turned into the street, had ascended to that chamber of death and fear: whilst the pale stars that had witnessed that deed of blood had long veiled their faces. But red in the mist now rose the majestic Sun, to look upon his daughter Earth, glaring, as if in wrath, as he peered into her secret heart, and, one by one, brought out to light her sins of darkness. And now Lilly thought that she should make her effort to escape. But, oh, what an effort it was! She felt as if she would almost rather have died where she was, if they would leave her to die in quiet, than encounter it. But still it would be madness not to try; for she was sure now that Luke, if he caught her, would never rest till he had taken her life.

So, she softly crept out from the foot of the bed, and got upon her feet—she had resolved she would not turn her eyes towards the sight she knew was there; but there was a fascination in it—she felt she must take one look—and she did; and then she looked again, and again, and again; bending forwards to discern those ghastly features—for she recognised them—they were those of Charlotte Littenhaus!—

Luke had doubtless come to murder her; but, in her stead, had slain his sister!—

END OF VOLUME II

VOLUME III

CHAPTER I

LILLY'S FLIGHT, AND WHITHER IT CONDUCTS HER

Lamentable as was the spectacle of the murdered woman on the bed, Lilly was naturally too much alarmed for her own safety, and too anxious to provide for it, to spend much time in bewailing the fate of Charlotte Littenhaus. She did not doubt that if she were discovered there, she should share the same fate as her cousin, being now doubly obnoxious from the possession of so fatal a secret.

It was yet but the dawn of morning, and although sounds enough reached her, to tell her that life was stirring without, she heard nothing to indicate that any one was on foot within the house; so that if she could summon courage to open the door and descend the stairs, she might very possibly make her escape undetected. But it was a terrific enterprise to enter upon. The mere laying her hand upon the latch of the door, was fearful; and the slight noise she made in lifting it, seemed, to her excited ears, like an alarum that must infallibly arouse her enemy; and when she did venture to draw the door and slowly open it, it creaked—it had done so when the man entered, who had handled it with the same caution—and her breath stopped whilst she listened for the foot she every instant dreaded to hear. But all was still within; whilst the wheels of a hackney-coach that rumbled along the pavement without, redoubling her longing to reach the street where human life and help were stirring, she ventured on tip-toe to the top of the stairs and looked over the balustrade. She could see down one flight and part of the next; and so far the house was quiet and the doors on the landings were closed; but below that, all was dim, from the house being yet shut up, and her eye could not penetrate the obscurity, but there were no indications of any one moving; and time was so precious, that step by step she ventured to advance, holding fast the rail with her right hand, to compensate for the feeble pressure she permitted her feet to make on the uncarpeted stair, which, in despite of all her care, would still creak. Thus she had cautiously descended the first flight, with a light step crossed the first landing, and had nearly reached the second, when a door exactly facing her was opened, by a thin, sickly-looking man, in a shabby black surtout,[101] much too large for him, which was buttoned closely up to his chin, as if to conceal the want of other habiliments.

---

101 Man's overcoat.

As the opening of the door threw a flood of light upon the stair, these two early risers saw each other distinctly; and one seemed almost as much surprised and startled as the other. As for Lilly, her limbs gave way under her, and she was ready to sink into the earth, as she suddenly arrested her steps, uncertain whether to go backwards or forwards, and with pale cheeks, and white lips, and eyes expressive of the greatest terror, she stood staring at the man; who apparently equally irresolute whether to retreat or advance, stood also still with the door in his hand. However, seeing she did not stir, he made the first move, passed her, and descended, having carefully closed the door of the room he came out of; and after a moment's pause she followed him. It was clear, whoever he might be, he had no intention of impeding her escape. Indeed, he facilitated it considerably by opening the front door, out of which, without any further obstacle, she stepped after him into the street; up which he strode with great rapidity, never once, to her great satisfaction, turning his head to observe what course she took, which was the opposite one to his, for no other reason than that it was so; for she did not know in what part of the town she was; nor if she had known, could she have easily decided whither to direct her steps. Not to her former home, for there was May, who had betrayed her into the hands of her enemy; not to Mrs. Knox's, for there was May likewise. Nor to Mrs. Ryland, for she believed the old woman was no longer her friend; not to Philip—her soul recoiled from that; for he loved May, and would never conceal Lilly from her, nor be induced to believe her guilty of such cruel treachery. So she formed no plan, but that of getting as far from the scene of these horrors as possible; and fled forward as fast as her trembling limbs could take her, without knowing in what direction she was going.

Few people were yet about the streets, and they were such as cared little to notice her. They had most of them enough of their own to look to, so that she walked on unmolested through the wretched neighbourhood of squalor and poverty in which she had passed the night, till she found herself approaching a better part of the town, and presently she saw the river, which she crossed by Blackfriars Bridge. And now that the pressing danger was over, and she could venture to believe herself somewhat secure from the immediate peril of being overtaken and caught by Luke, she found time to be anxious about the future. And she slackened her pace from the consciousness that she had nowhere to go to, and looked anxiously in women's faces for pity and sympathy. And she might have won both if they could have read her story in her mild eyes. No money, no friend, no home! No roof under which she could claim shelter in all that large city! What a desolation it was! But still she walked on till she reached a place where the houses were less crowded together, and some had little gardens before them. There was something both cheery and sad to her in the appearance of these; for she had not seen such since her happy journey with Abel White, the dear, blind old man, never forgotten even in her happiest moments, and to whom she would long ago have written had she known how. But though her small stock of reading was somewhat improved, writing was an accomplishment she had neither had time nor opportunity to acquire.

It was still so early, that the shutters of most of the houses were yet closed; but there was one whose inhabitants seemed to be more alert. The lower windows were open, and a busy housemaid was seen bustling about the little parlour. Just as Lilly was passing, the door opened, and she came out for the purpose of shaking the hearth rug in the garden. As the sound had caused Lilly to turn her head in that direction, the two girls' eyes met, and they recognised each other.

"My! Lilly, is it you?" exclaimed Winny. "Well, better late than never, to be sure. I thought you never meant to come and see me at all. But, oh gracious! how ill you look! What *is* the matter?"

"I didn't know where you lived before," replied Lilly, evading the question.

"Well, but you've got a tongue in your head, and you might have asked. I should have come to see you long ago if I could have got time; but there's been a deal of trouble here, and now we're worse off than ever, so if you hadn't come I don't know when I could have got so far. But come in and sit down, do. I'm sure you must be fine and tired with such an early walk."

Lilly was fine and tired; not with the distance she had walked, but with anxiety, and, as she knew that Winny was no friend of Luke's, she thought she might venture to accept her invitation.

"And as soon as I've got a bit on with my work," continued Winny, "I'll get a cup of tea and a bit of breakfast for you; but I'm just over head and ears, for the girl we had to help is gone all of a sudden, and missus has not got any body in her place; so every thing's on my shoulders. That's the way I was up so early, for I've got their breakfast to get and every thing."

"Can I help you?" inquired Lilly.

"Well, if you're not too tired," returned Winny, "and I shall be sooner able to get you a cup of tea. If you'll finish this room, I'll go and set their breakfast things." So Lilly set to work at her old trade, and rubbed, and dusted, as she used to do at the Black Huntsman.

She was still busy, when a fine boy, about twelve years of age, came down from above, in his shirt and trousers, and entering the room, with his waistcoat in his hand, said, "I say, Winny, I wish you'd just mend this hole in my waistcoat, will you? Oh! it's not Winny," he added, perceiving his mistake. "What, are you the new servant? Well, *you* can do it, can't you?"

"Yes, sir, if I had a needle and thread," replied Lilly. "I'll go and ask Winny for one."

"Stop!" said he, "I'll fetch mamma's work-box, I know where it is," and presently he appeared with the box in his hand, and Lilly, helping herself to what she wanted, commenced repairing the damaged waistcoat, which was, however, in rather a dilapidated condition at the best.

"Mend it so that it can't be seen, will you?" said the boy, with some anxiety in his countenance, and Lilly did her best to conform to his wishes; whilst he, apparently attaching great importance to the operation, frequently rose and looked over her shoulder at the work.

"Thankye," said he, taking it from her and examining it when it was done; "that's better than Peggy used to do it," and seemingly relieved by the neatness of the performance, he skipped lightly upstairs again.

"That's Mister Fred, what's he been down for?" inquired Winny, who just then ascended from the kitchen.

"He wanted a hole in his waistcoat mended, and asked me to do it," replied Lilly.

"I'm glad he did," answered Winny; "for I'm not over handy with my needle. Peggy, the girl that's gone, did the mending. But now come below, and we'll have a bit of breakfast before they come down stairs. Well, and how's that good Miss Elliott?" continued Winny, as she poured out a cup of tea for her visitor.

"May's very well," answered Lilly, with a shudder, for that name suggested the memory of the cruel treachery which the horrors of the night, and the events of the morning, had somewhat banished from her recollection.

"But, lauk! Lilly, now I come to look at you again, you do look shocking ill!" exclaimed Winny; for, in fact, Lilly's face was blanched with the terrors and sufferings she had endured for so many hours, though the surprise of meeting with Winny, at so critical a juncture, had at first brought a little blood to her cheeks. "What's the matter?" said she; "has any thing happened?" for the subject was too much for Lilly's shaken nerves, and she burst into tears. "You haven't been having words with Miss Elliott, have you?"

But Lilly wept on, unable to answer; and her tears having once opened their sluices, poured down with a violence that quite alarmed poor Winny.

"What in the name of fortune *has* happened?" said she.

"I don't live with May now," answered Lilly, at length, speaking convulsively. "She's going into handsomer lodgings, and I——," and here she stopped; for she felt she could not narrate the events of the night; which, now that she was seated in this small, tidy kitchen, with the kettle singing on the fire, and the tea-things on the table, and Winny Weston opposite to her, seemed more like a horrid dream than a reality. There appeared to her something in the scene she had witnessed too awful and terrific to be made the subject of discourse. She could not have trusted her lips to tell it to any body but Abel White; he alone, with his sightless eyes and venerable face, seemed a fit confidant for such a tale. Then, the idea that the murderer was her own cousin, helped also to keep her silent. She shrank from bringing such an accusation against one that belonged to her, odious as he was; and she knew very well that at the smallest hint of such a thing, Winny would seize on the idea with avidity; and, perhaps, repeat the tale to others, and Heaven knows what might follow! She might even, through such means, be traced by Luke, and fall again into his hands; whilst all she desired was to be permitted to gain her living in safety and obscurity; for retribution or revenge she had no desire—indeed, the idea of either never occurred to her. Moreover, she did not wish to say a word to Winny about Philip; that was too painful a subject. She could not have told how her friend had betrayed her, and seduced her lover; nor have conveyed to any one else the grounds she had for believing he *had* been her lover, till he was captivated by the too seducing May. Altogether, poor Lilly could not tell her story; she could only weep, and allow Winny to draw her own conclusions, and compose a story after her own fashion; which she did.

"I see how it is," said she, "you've been having words with Miss Elliott, and perhaps she's got you out of Mrs. Knox's."

"I shouldn't like to go back to Mrs. Knox's," said Lilly.

"But can't you make friends, again?" inquired Winny. "If I'd time, I'd go and speak to her and tell her how sorry you are."

"No," said Lilly, confirmed in her determination of keeping her late adventure secret, "you mustn't; it would only make it worse. Besides, I don't wish to make it up, and I don't mean to go to Mrs. Knox's any more."

"Then, what in the world do you mean to do?" inquired Winny.

"I don't know," said Lilly, "I'd get a place if I could!"

"There's the parlour-bell for breakfast!" said Winny, rising and rushing up stairs with the tea-kettle.

"See, ma," said Frederick, when they met in the dining-room, "how nicely the new maid has mended my waistcoat. I'm so glad she can sew better than Peggy—Peggy always made such a botch when I asked her to mend my things, I was ashamed to go to school with it. Look, ma, isn't it?"

"Yes, dear boy," answered Mrs. Adams, "Winny seems to have put her best workmanship into it, for she's generally very awkward with her needle. I think much worse than Peggy was!"

"It isn't Winny that did it, mamma!" replied Frederick, "it was the new maid. I don't know what her name is."

"What new maid? We have no new maid, my dear," replied Mrs. Adams.

"There was a new maid doing the parlour!" said Fred.

"It must be some friend of Winny's that she's got to help her, then!" said Mrs. Adams.

"I'll ask her!" said Fred; and as soon as Winny appeared with the kettle, he put the question.

"She's a young woman from the place I come from," said Winny, "that called to see me; and finding me busy, she just put her hand to the dusting."

"Is she in service?" inquired Mrs. Adams.

"Not at present, ma'am; she's out of place," replied Winny.

"And is she a respectable person?"

"Oh, yes, there can't be one more respectabler. I've known her since she was that high, when she was living at home with her friends," returned Winny, holding her hand a yard from the floor.

"Then, perhaps, you might keep her here to help you a few days, till we get a servant," suggested Mrs. Adams. "Would she have any objection, do you think?"

"Not she, ma'am," answered Winny, who had been framing her answers expressly to attain this result. "She's the good temperedest girl ever I saw; and uncommon handy at her needle!"

"That she is!" said Fred., looking down at his waistcoat with complacence; "Ecce signum!"[102]

And as Lilly accepted the offer, she was immediately installed as Winny's assistant, *pro tempore;* and Winny being forthwith despatched into the neighbourhood to fetch a bit of mutton to make some broth, her first service was to carry up Colonel Adams's breakfast, who being an invalid, had not yet risen; Frederick accompanying her to show her the way.

It was a small house, with just two apartments on a floor, and he lay in the back drawing-room.

"Here's your breakfast, pa," said Fred, "and we've got a new maid!"

"Already!" said Colonel Adams, "where did you get her?"

"She came to see Winny; she's a friend of Winny's and came from her country; they've known each other ever since they were little; haven't you, Lilly?"

"Yes, sir!"

"Lilly!" echoed Colonel Adams, "is that her name?"

"Yes; Lilly—Lilly, what is it?" said Fred.

"Lilly Dawson, sir."

"Lilly Dawson—ah!" said Colonel Adams, with a sigh.

"Put the tray down here, Lilly," said Frederick, "and fetch pa's dressing-gown off that chair; and now you may go down, Lilly, and I'll call you to take away the

---

102 Behold the sign, or here is the proof.

things when pa's done. Isn't Lilly a pretty name, pa?" said Fred, "and she's like a lily; she's so white, poor thing! I never saw any body so white in my life. If she wasn't so white, she'd be very pretty."

"But has your mamma any character with her?" inquired the Colonel.

"Oh, Winny knows her very well, and all her friends; and I believe they're very respectable people indeed," answered Fred, unconsciously betrayed into a little exaggeration in his enthusiasm for Lilly; who had entirely won his heart by her dexterous darning. "And you can't think how nicely she does needle-work! She mended my waistcoat this morning, so that you can hardly see the place; and Peggy used to make such a botch, that I couldn't bear going to school with it."

"Is your waistcoat much worn?" inquired Colonel Adams.

"Oh, yes, pa; it's so shabby you can't think. Feel! there's a darn—and there's a darn—they're Peggy's. This is the one Lilly did; and you can hardly feel it."

"You must have a new waistcoat," said the father.

"But my jacket's almost as bad, pa; and my trousers, they're very bad indeed. There isn't one of the boys has such shabby clothes as I have; and they do quiz me so!—the ill-natured ones do."

"You must have new ones," said Colonel Adams gravely, whilst a spasm contracted his features for an instant.

Colonel Adams had been for some time in ill-health. He had first had a severe illness; and then a series of indispositions which had been both very painful and very expensive, reducing more and more his already reduced means; and he had now a malady in his eyes, which threatened him with blindness, if not taken great care of, and incapacitated him from bearing the light. He was, therefore, kept with his eyes shaded in a nearly dark room; whilst one member of the family, or the other, generally remained with him; Frederick or his mother when they could; if not, one of the maids. And it was on this account, they were obliged to keep two, which was more than their means well sufficed for. When he was taken into a light room, his eyes were entirely darkened; so that the dilapidations of poor Frederick's wardrobe, as well as many other matters, escaped his observation.

CHAPTER II

HOW MAY ELLIOTT PLAYS A DESPERATE GAME WITH HER OWN HAPPINESS

It is an undoubted fact, that apart from a positive disposition to dishonesty, there are many persons in the world, who have an entire incapacity for all pecuniary affairs. They are unable to calculate what money will do, and disliking poverty and privation as much as their neighbours, they are sure to run themselves headlong into both.

May Elliott was one of this class. In the commencement of her independent career she had no deliberate design of defrauding anybody; but the incapacity above alluded to, caused her to be always in advance of her salary; and as she had as little genius for self-denial as for arithmetic, she soon got into difficulties, which her principles were too unstable to battle with; and from being imprudent she became dishonest. This is the gently inclined-plane down which many a better nature than May Elliott's annually slides to perdition; a descent at once so easy and so fatal, that the first step towards it cannot be too carefully avoided. On the strength of Mr. Cropley's twenty pounds, and the extravagant hopes she built on his vague promises, together with a small increase of her salary, May had taken lodgings in Blenheim Street, to which she removed as soon as she had got rid of Lilly. She was influenced to this step by various motives. The desire to shake off Lilly without the odium of turning her out of doors, was one; her own pride and ambition furnished another; and her anxiety to dazzle Philip's eyes, and maintain her conquest over his heart, supplied a third.

A woman who has won the love of an honest, upright man, which she is conscious she does not deserve, is in the situation of a false gamester, playing with cogged dice;[103] her success may be as transitory as it is rapid; and when she is detected she is lost. May's own instincts told her that Philip's love for her was a delusion. She was fully aware of the influence that her fashionable dress and factitious airs of fine ladyism had on the mind of this inexperienced provincial Adonis; and in her anxiety to sustain and quicken his infatuation, she thought the style and situation of her residence not unimportant, and she was not altogether mistaken. Besides, she knew how to derive a double advantage from her new lodging, by shedding a grace over her motive for remaining in the old.

"What a nice lodging, and how beautifully it is furnished!" exclaimed Philip, whose taste in the matter of furniture had not been much cultivated.

"Do you think so?" answered May, carelessly, throwing her eye round the apartment, as if, after all, she thought it somewhat inadequate to her pretensions.

"It's a great deal nicer than the other," replied Philip, on whom her affected indifference had exactly the effect she desired; that is, it exalted his conception of her standard of excellence.

"Oh, yes," returned May, with a contemptuous little laugh; "I hope so! That was a horrid hole! I should never have lived there, you know, but for a particular reason."

"What reason?" inquired Philip. "To be near Mrs. Knox's?"

"Why, Lilly Dawson to be sure!" said May. "Of course you know two people's

---

103 Loaded dice.

living is more expensive than one—it makes a great difference, I assure you! and as Lilly isn't clever at all, her salary was next to nothing."

"Poor Lilly!" said Philip, "what is she going to do? Has she left Mrs. Knox?"

"Oh, yes," replied May, drily, "she has left Mrs. Knox; but what she's going to do is more than I know; only I should not be surprised if I heard of her being married!"

"Married!" exclaimed Philip, looking seriously astonished.

"Oh, I don't wish to make you uneasy," said May. "I didn't know you cared whether she was married or single."

"I don't care whether any body in the world is married or single, except one person," replied Philip; "but I am surprised, for I didn't know that Lilly had any acquaintance amongst young men."

"Well, we shall see," returned May; "time will show. I never pry into other people's secrets. I did all I could for Lilly Dawson, for I am sure I don't know what would have become of her if I had not stood her friend when I did; but, of course, people must do as they like, you know. I am the last person to interfere in any body's affairs; I've enough to do with my own."

"I always thought Lilly was very grateful," said Philip.

"Oh, I don't say she was not," returned May; "but Lilly has a will and a way of her own, like other people."

"I am sure she had cause to be grateful to you," said Philip; "for even by her own account, you've been a good friend to her. I'm sure, when first she used to come and see us, she couldn't say enough of it."

"Oh, yes, I dare say," returned May; "talking's easy, you know."

"But *has* Lilly behaved ungratefully to you?" asked Philip, finding a real difficulty in believing his old friend capable of what appeared so entirely inconsistent with all he had observed of her.

"*I* don't say she has," replied May as if either caution or generosity prevented her speaking out. "Lilly knows her own ways best; and I only hope she mayn't be worse off than she has been."

"I can only say, if she *has* been ungrateful, she deserves all she may meet with," returned Philip. "I should have very little pity for any body that could be ungrateful to you, May; you, that are so kind and good to every body."

"And pray, sir, how do *you* know I am kind and good to every body?"

"Why, you were kind and good to Lilly; and I'm sure you're kind and good to *me*."

"To *you!*—ah! more fool I."

"Don't say that, May; *I'll* never be ungrateful, depend upon it."

"Ah, all men say that. Promises are like pie-crust, you know."

"I don't know whether all men say it, May; but I say it, and mean it, too. If you don't believe me, you had better cast me off, at once, and have nothing more to say to me."

"And suppose I do," said May, "what would you do then?"

"Die," returned Philip, with an air of deep conviction. "I am certain I couldn't survive it."

"Pooh!" said May, "not you. You'd get another mistress in six weeks."

"You must have a very poor opinion of me, Miss Elliott," said Philip, really shocked, and half offended at the insinuation. "If that is the sort of person you think me, I am surprised you should have any thing to say to me."

"I dare say you are," returned May, with mock gravity.

"I only know *I* wouldn't have any thing to say to a person I had such a bad opinion of," rejoined Philip.

"But you can't expect every body to be as wise as you are, you know, Mr. Philip Ryland. You're a man, and I'm only a poor weak woman."

"You're an angel," exclaimed Philip, in a fit of gratitude and enthusiasm. "But tell me, May, have you such a bad opinion of me?"

"If I had such a bad opinion of you, do you think I should be so foolish as to care for you?"

"Then you own you do care for me, May?"

"Perhaps—a little."

"Is it only a little, May?"

"There, now; that's the way with men; they're always so unreasonable. Now, just tell me, Mr. Philip Ryland—"

"Don't call me *Mr. Philip Ryland,* May; I can't bear it."

"Why, didn't you call me *Miss Elliott,* just now?"

"Oh, well, never mind what I say. I'm a fool."

"Well, it's a good thing for people to know themselves. But just tell me whether, four months ago, you wouldn't have thought yourself a very lucky fellow if I had told you I cared for you?"

"Should I? to be sure I should. I couldn't believe it at first; and sometimes I can't believe it now. I can't think what you see in me, I'm sure!"

"I can't think either," said May, with an accent of *espieglerie,*[104] and an arch glance of the eye; "and yet you see you're such an ungrateful monster, that you're not satisfied, though you own you've got more than you ever expected, and a *great deal* more than you deserve."

"Ah! May, but you see as people get on they're always wanting more and more; when we've got one thing, we want another. At first I could hardly believe that you

---

104 Playful and charming.

could ever think of such a fellow as I am."

"Well, now what sort of fellow do you think you are?" inquired May.

"Why, to say the truth," returned Philip, "I had never thought about myself at all, till I knew you. I had never been in the way of knowing any girl but Lilly—"

"Oh, Lilly!" echoed May, contemptuously; "Lilly knows as much about a man, as about the figure on the top of the Monument."[105]

"But then, when I did know you, and when I began to love you, I said to myself how can the beautiful, elegant Miss Elliott ever think of looking at an awkward cub like me."

"Oh, so you think you're an awkward cub, do you?"

"I'm afraid so, May."

"Ah! ah!" laughed May, joyously.

"Why, don't *you* think so, May?"

"Oh, to be sure I do; you wouldn't have me differ in opinion with you, would you? I never contradict gentlemen."

"Then you do really think me an awkward cub?" said Philip, a little mortified that she did *not* contradict him.

"Now, suppose I was to tell you what I really do think of you," said May; "might not it do you a great deal of harm? Men can't bear praise—they're so shockingly prone to vanity."

"I hope not," replied Philip; "I'm sure I care very little what any body thinks of me, but you."

"Well, then, suppose I was to tell you that I think you a very nice, handsome young man?"

"Oh! handsome," said Philip, blushing like a girl; "I know I'm not handsome."

"Hold your tongue, sir, and don't interrupt me. A very nice, handsome young man—only—"

"Only what?" said Philip, anxiously.

"I shan't tell you," said May; "it's no use—you can't help it."

"What is it?" said Philip, colouring, and getting quite uneasy; "do tell me, May, and I'll try and mend it, whatever it is."

"You can't, Philip; I wish you could, for it's a great fault in a man, especially a young one," said she, with a sigh *obligato;*[106] "but men can't bear to be told of their faults."

"Tell me what it is," said Philip, earnestly, "and I swear I'll cure myself of it,

---

105 A Doric column in the City of London built by Christopher Wren and Robert Hooke to commemorate the Great Fire of London.

106 It appears that Crowe means that there is an obligatory sigh at this point in May's play to Philip.

or die."

"Why should *I* tell you of your faults?" said she, "they never can be any thing to me, you know."

"Indeed!" said Philip, "I thought they might have been something to you one day or other."

"No," replied May, in a subdued tone, and looking down at her work, "no, Philip, I am afraid you and I should never do together."

"Why, May?—for God's sake tell me why?" exclaimed Philip, getting quite excited. "You never said this before. What have I done? Is it this fault that you have found out in me?"

"Oh! I haven't found it out at all," said May, "it don't require finding out - any body may see it with half an eye."

"Then you own it *is* that, that makes you think we couldn't do together? What is it? I'll tell you what, May, if you won't tell me, I'll go away, and you shall never see me again. I'll leave London at once, and go back to the country. My mother's wishing to go, and it's no use my staying in a place where I see nothing but misery before me; and, indeed, I dare say it's the best thing I can do; and it will be the best thing for you, too; for then you'll be rid of me and my faults, too."

"There, now! Didn't I tell you you couldn't bear to be told of your faults?"

"Oh, May," said Philip, "this is very unkind! I *can* bear it;—I can bear any thing from you, but your not loving me—and here's something that prevents your loving me—and that makes you think we couldn't do together—and yet you won't tell me what it is."

"Well," said May, with apparent reluctance, "if I must tell you, I must. It is that—"

"Well," said Philip, eagerly.

"Well—it is that you're not like the London young men. You've no spirit—you're always afraid of doing this thing or that thing; and if it's to cost a few shillings, you're just in a perfect fright. Now, I like a man that has some spirit and spunk in him, and not one of your milksops[107] that's always tied to his mother's apron-string, and that durstn't say Bo! to a goose without her leave."

This was an accusation so much more severe and mortifying than Philip had anticipated, that he was quite taken aback; his face flushed, and he could not help feeling very angry; not so much with his mistress, however, as with himself; for grievous as the impeachment was to a youth that could hardly yet be called a man, he did not venture to doubt its justice. "Doubtless, his education *had* been very narrow; he had been brought up with very low ideas, and had seen nothing of what was genteel and fashionable, till he became acquainted with May Elliott.

---

107 A weak person.

What a difference she must see betwixt him and the London men! What a country booby he must appear in her eyes! those eyes in which alone he desired to shine!" It was a trying moment to poor Philip, and his countenance expressed all he felt.

"There now, I see you're angry; I told you you would be, you know; but you would force me to speak."

"I am very glad you have," said Philip, gravely; "and I don't wonder at all at your despising me. You have made me despise myself. I see that it is impossible you should ever think of marrying such a mean-spirited, shabby fellow as I must appear to you, and that the sooner I take myself off and make room for that Mr. Ferdinand Pycroft, that took you to the Opera, the better. He's much more suited to you than I am."

"Very well," said May; "of course, if you choose to do so you must. It's not I that'll ask any man to stay that wants to go."

"But it's you that wants me to go, May."

"I'm sure I didn't say so!"

"But you must! How can any girl like a man that she thinks mean and stingy?"

"Certainly, one can't like him as much," said May. "That isn't in human nature, you know."

"Then you own that you don't like me so well as that d—d Mr. Ferdinand Pycroft," said Philip, giving vent to his jealousy in a mode of expression quite unusual to him.

"I didn't say so, Mr. Ryland. Perhaps Mr. Ferdinand Pycroft don't like me!" But whilst May said this, there was a half smile at the corners of her mouth, intended to imply that she knew very well he did.

"Oh, I dare say!" said Philip; "you needn't suppose I'm as blind as that, Miss Elliott!" Now he had never seen this redoubtable Mr. Ferdinand in the company of his mistress but once in his life, and that was when he saw him hand her into the hackney-coach.

"As for his liking you, of course I can answer that myself," continued he; "but the question is, do you like him? Because, if you do, curse me if I don't blow his brains out, or my own!"

"I think he's a very nice young man," said May.

"You do?" said Philip, fiercely.

"Yes, I do; don't you?" answered May, with the most perfect sang froid.[108]

In spite of his anger and his jealousy, there was something in this question so irresistibly ludicrous to Philip, that he could not help laughing. "Oh, May, May!" he said, seizing her hand, "how can you torment me so? You know I adore you, and I can't bear to think of any body daring to love you but me; and if I but

---

108 Spoken with composure and as if unaware of the implications of what is being said.

thought you loved that fellow!"—

"I didn't say I *loved* him," returned May. "I only say that he is a nice, spirited young man, and that he has ideas like a gentleman. He wouldn't let Mrs. Knox or me pay sixpence towards the coach that night; and the other day, when I was at Harvey and Graham's—he's in the feather and flower department there—he invited me to go with him in the evening to Farrance's,[109] to eat ice, and—"

"And you went?" said Philip, growing fierce again.

"No, I did not," answered May; "I couldn't get away from work early enough; and he said he hoped I would do him the favour to accept a ticket some evening for Astley's,[110] and let him have the honour of escorting me. Now that's what *I* call behaving like a gentleman."

"If you wish to go and eat ice, or go to Astley's either," said Philip, "I should think I'd at least as good a right to escort you as Mr. Ferdinand Pycroft, and—"

"But you never asked me to do either," interrupted May.

"I know I haven't," answered Philip; "but I ask you now; and therefore, if, after this, you go with him, I shall know what to think, and shall act accordingly."

"Why, what shall you do?" asked May.

"Never mind what I shall do," replied Philip, in a tone that implied an inexorable determination to annihilate Mr. Ferdinand Pycroft, if he saw cause; "there's no need for you to know. All you have to do is to choose whether you like to go with him or with me I've no right to force your inclination, of course."

"Well, then," said May, "I'll go with you."

"And you promise me not to go anywhere with him?"

"Oh, I don't know about positively promising that," answered May. "He's a very polite young man, and in a very good situation, and I shouldn't like to affront him."

"Very well," said Philip, biting his lips.

"Besides," continued May, "I cannot do without some amusement, I've always been used to it."

"But you shall have amusement, if you can be satisfied with my company. If not, say so, May Elliott! Say so at once—let me know the worst, and—" Here the pride and the vengeance yielded, and the poor lad burst into tears.

"How foolish!" said May, though in her heart delighted at this evidence of her power. "I'm sure, Philip, I don't want to make you uncomfortable."

"Then why do you do it, May? You know, you know I can't bear it."

"Bear what?"

---

109 A confectionery and cook shop in Charing Cross. I cannot find reference to 'Harvey and Graham's' it is possible that Crowe means Harvey Nichols.

110 Astley's amphitheatre: the first circus to be opened in the late 1790s in Lambeth. It was later turned into a theatre.

"That you should go anywhere with that fellow."

"Or with any other fellow, I suppose?"

"No, May, no; why should you go with any body but me?"

"Well, but then you must invite me to go, you know; or else I see no choice but to go with Mr. Ferdinand or somebody else."

"I will invite you, May; and I know I've been very wrong not to have done it before, and I don't wonder that you thought it very mean of me; but you shall never have reason to think so again, May."

"Well," said May, "I'm sure I don't wish to think ill of you, Philip. I'm sure I've given you reason to think I like you."

"*Like* me! Is that all, May?"

"Why, what would you have?" said May.

"I'd have you *love* me," said Philip. "Will you, May, will you love me?"

"Lord! how unreasonable men are! Well, perhaps I'll try a little," said May, "a very little; that's if you behave well, though."

CHAPTER III

LILLY'S FORTUNES ONCE MORE SHOW SYMPTOMS OF AMENDMENT

Whilst May Elliott was playing this cruel game with poor Philip Ryland—and a cruel game it was, idly as the dialogue may read—a game in which both were sure to be ultimately losers, however well her cards looked in the hand, her former companion, Lilly Dawson was very differently engaged. If Fortune is blind and capricious, we, the subjects of her whims and blunders, are no clearer sighted. We cannot see an inch beyond our noses; and whilst we are for ever quarrelling with her best schemes, we are just as precipitate in applauding her worst.

Or, to take a more serious view of the case, is it not true, that through the gates of sorrow we enter into the palace of gladness; and that through the valley of tears we ascend to the hills of rejoicing? There seems to be one thing quite certain, namely, that there is no misfortune irremediable but vice and wickedness; and that, however darkly the clouds may have gathered above our heads, however ruggedly the path may seem to stretch interminably beneath our feet, if we can but keep fast hold of truth and integrity, we shall come to a gleam of light and a green sward somewhere—perhaps, in the most unexpected quarter. It was so with Lilly; when her fortunes were at the lowest ebb, and her little vessel of hope and peace seemed stranded, she had found a haven of shelter from the rude winds and the bitter waters, under the same roof with her old acquaintance, Winny Weston; and a more genial shelter, in her circumstances, she could not have found.

Charles Adams, the once gay young soldier, the now, though yet but in middle life, depressed and poverty-stricken invalid, was, at this period, almost wholly confined to the house. Though the climate of India had disagreed with him, and somewhat damaged his constitution, it was much less that, than the long dreary lawsuit, the pangs of poverty, and solicitude for his wife and son, that had ruined his health. Well born, accomplished, and amiable, the husband of a deserving wife, and the father of a noble and beautiful boy, he found himself, by the cruel facilities which the English Court of Chancery lends to malice, cast out of all the enjoyments of life, to which he and his family had been accustomed; deprived of the society to which every circumstance, but money, entitled him, and a prey to never-ceasing anxiety about the pettiest details of daily economy; with the superadded misery of not being able to give his son such an education as would best fit him to provide for himself, if need there was to do so; or becomingly fill his place in the rank he would be called to, should the suit be eventually decided in their favour.

That his daughter had been drowned, Colonel Adams never for a moment doubted; nobody did; not even the General, nor Cropley, nor the Chancery lawyers, however they pretended to do so. It was held certain that of the crew or passengers of the *Hastings*, no one human being had ever come ashore to tell the tale; and it was so improbable that the only survivor should be a feeble little child, that, had the parents entertained such a hope, it would have been pronounced, to the last degree, romantic and absurd. But nothing is too romantic and absurd to form the foundation of a lawsuit.

Deeply had the parents lamented their child, and deeply did Charles Adams lament his wife, when sorrow brought her to her early grave; but he was not formed to live alone, and he married again; being then possessed of a small patrimony,[111] which he inherited from his father, who, whilst in charge of Lilly, had perished by the hands of the assassins. But this, and his wife's little fortune, had been dissipated in the lawsuit, and now all was gone, but his half-pay; his health and vigour were fast forsaking him; and his eye-sight seemed going too. Poor Charles! His sun seemed to be setting in darkness, literally and metaphorically.

Long accustomed to affluence and elegance, it was very difficult for Colonel and Mrs. Adams to subside into all the *mesquineries*[112] of poverty: to be economical without being niggardly is a difficult art. The shifts of penury are unknown to the affluent; they must needs be learnt; and it is a learning, that experience only can communicate. Inevitably, therefore, the colonel and his wife, had got into difficulties, before they had reduced themselves to the low level of their means; and the struggle to keep clear of the *muddle*, inherent in an establishment served by a

111 Inheritance or legacy.
112 Meanness or pettiness.

maid of all work on low wages, was still maintained at more cost than they could afford. Peggy, the servant, whose sudden departure had made way for Lilly, was only a blowzy girl of fourteen; down to whom they had declined, through various gradations, from the neat respectable parlourmaid, with which they had set out, when they established themselves in a small house at Lambeth; and it was a matter of discussion betwixt Mrs. Adams and her husband, how far they were justified in engaging another in her place.

"Certainly, she was better than nothing," observed the lady, "though she was very inadequate to what we require."

"We must not look to have what we require," returned Colonel Adams; "that's out of the question; but really, Selina, I don't see how you can get on without a second servant of some sort or other; especially, now that I am confined so much to my room, and need such constant attendance—and I am afraid shall need more, ere long."

"It is difficult to get a girl of that description," replied Mrs. Adams, "I mean such a one as we could venture to take into the house. They are so ill brought up, and so ignorant and dirty; and frequently so immoral, about this neighbourhood, at least, that I am really afraid of them."

"I wish we could keep this girl, Winny's friend," said the colonel. "She seems quick and obliging; and Fred, has taken a great fancy to her."

"That's impossible, I fear," replied Mrs. Adams. "From her appearance, I suppose she would expect ten or twelve pounds a year. Mrs. Bates had a nice looking daughter that she offered to me before I took Peggy. I'll inquire if she is still disengaged."

The young damsel, however, had found another service; but Mrs. Bates mentioned a niece of hers that she thought would suit exactly, and who would be extremely glad of the situation; "She's just out for a week, ma'am, with a family in the Kent Road, as has got a daughter going to be married; but when she comes back, I'll send her to you, and I'm sure she's just the sort of girl you want, and I know she hasn't no engagement elsewhere."

As Mrs. Bates was a decent woman, the lady was content to wait for the niece, on her recommendation: but the marriage being delayed by some accidental circumstance, the girl did not return at the time expected. Meanwhile, Lilly continued quietly working on, as if she were a fixture in the place, though she did not know the day she might have to turn out to make room for Susan Bates. But week after week passed, and Susan did not appear, and at length one day, Mrs. Bates called to say, that the family she had been with liked her so well, that the bride had engaged her services for herself.

"So I don't know what we're to do, Winny," said Mrs. Adams, when she communicated this piece of intelligence, "for I don't remember any other girl fit for the place, do you?"

"No, ma'am, I don't," answered Winny. "You wouldn't like to keep Lilly Dawson, I suppose?"

"I should like it very much," returned Mrs. Adams; "but she would require more wages than I intend to give, I fear."

"I don't think she would," replied Winny; "if you please, ma'am, I'll ask her."

And Lilly, who was the least sordid of mortals, and would have been too happy to remain where she was even without any wages at all, immediately agreed to accept whatever terms Mrs. Adams chose to offer.

Nobody was better pleased with this arrangement than Freddy, who, as his father said, had taken an extraordinary fancy to Lilly; originating, in the first instance, in the darned waistcoat, but since confirmed, not only by repeated services of the same kind, but by other qualities that pleased him. Lads at that age are by no means insensible to beauty; and he thought her very pretty, since she had recovered her complexion and natural expression; which had been entirely disturbed, and, indeed, almost obliterated, for days succeeding that dreadful night. Then Lilly had very beautiful light brown hair, which, by imitating May, she had learned to arrange with great taste and elegance; and although it was not usual to see servants without caps, Mrs. Adams was not disposed to interfere with her new maid in this particular; especially as the neatness rendered the peculiarity inoffensive. Added to these recommendations, although her wardrobe was very scanty, and consisted of the most ordinary materials, she had acquired, whilst at Mrs. Knox's, the art of wearing her clothes to advantage; so that she was altogether a very nice, pretty-looking young woman. Then she was very quick and obliging; her natural humility, which was one of her most distinguishing characteristics, preventing her ever thinking any thing a trouble that she was asked to do; and finally she had taken as great a fancy to Freddy as he had to her.

Lilly was subject to *engouements*;[113] a weakness—we suppose, we must admit it *is* a weakness—which is very often the companion of many good and agreeable qualities; and it must be remarked that this disposition to form strong and somewhat sudden attachments by no means necessarily implies inconstancy. On the contrary, we have generally known such attachments extremely enduring, except where repulsion or unworthiness, on the part of the object beloved has broken the bond or destroyed the illusion; and even then a kindly feeling will long survive the warmer sentiment. Lilly's first passion had been Mrs. Ryland and Philip, her second Abel White, her third May Elliott, and her fourth was Fred Adams; but no one of these had driven out the preceding ones; and above them all, during these

---

113 Passions or infatuations.

successive dynasties, Philip Ryland reigned paramount. Next to him ranged Abel White; but they all lived in her heart together. Even May, ill as she had behaved to her, was not wholly banished; she could not bring herself to think as much evil of her as circumstances might have justified her in doing; and now that she was happier herself, she often felt more sorrow for the loss of her friend, than anger at her dereliction.

There is undoubtedly a great deal of pain incurred by this sympathetic adhesiveness. The cold-blooded members of society do not understand it; the hard ones despise it; the shallow and superficial livers, who do not look into the heart of the world, nor feel its pulses, laugh at it; and, unfortunately, the objects of these *engouements*, the fascinators themselves, not unfrequently belong to one of these classes. For it must be confessed, that occasionally, especially with the very young, these treasures of affection are sometimes sadly misplaced, as in the instance of Lilly and May Elliott. But on the whole, if there is much sorrow there is also much joy, and much genial cultivation of the heart to be derived from these natural fountains, which springing suddenly forth, make an Eden of a desert; and certain it is, that, if a fault it be, to be susceptible of, and to yield to, these strong sympathies, it is a fault of the most generous and candid natures. The unmerciful rigour, or contemptuous ridicule with which people who have reached what they erroneously suppose to be years of discretion, endeavour to nip and frustrate the blossoms of these flowers of existence, is as cruel as it is injudicious. They may give pain by compressing the lambent flame,[114] but it only burns the more vigorously; they cannot extinguish it. What they *can* do, and *do*, is to alienate affection from themselves, weaken their own influence, and fill young hearts with gall. Certainly, where *real* danger is espied, it must be guarded against; the nature of the peril must be indicated, and distinct reasons given for any authority that is exercised. But even then, unless the consequences apprehended are of a serious nature, though warnings may be highly commendable, authority is seldom wisely exerted. Impulsive natures *must* be taught at their own cost; that of others is of little or no avail to them; for the history of every heart, though alike, is different. They cannot stop to decipher a page which speaks not to their sympathies; nor examine a portrait presented to them as their own, where they find no resemblance. Their own suffering must be their teacher, the only and the best; and one lesson of experience is worth a thousand sermons.

The little sympathy of the old with the feelings of the young, is a great, though unavoidable evil; and by the old, we mean people of any age, whose hearts are old; people who never were young, as well as those who once were so, but have forgotten it. For it is the age of the heart that makes us old; and those in whom

---

114 Luminous or softly radiant.

years have not paled the vividness of their feelings and affections, are the ever-greens of the earth. But in order that these should retain their freshness in age, they must have been extremely vigorous in the outset; there must have been a great deal of fire, for the chill of the world not to have put it out; and we never see an enthusiastic, warm-hearted, impulsive young girl whom the prudent persons about her are accusing of "taking violent fancies to people," and other like mis-demeanours, without thinking what a delightful old woman she will make; and congratulating her children yet unborn. But to return to our story.

Winny Weston, too, was extremely pleased with the new arrangement. In the first place, she had had an opportunity of rendering back to Lilly the service the latter had done her in her need; and in the next, she had secured for herself a capi-tal helpmate; one who besides aiding her generally, could do all the needle-work, a department in which Winny did not by any means shine. Then, above all, she had got a companion to whom she could speak of her past life, her home, and her lost lover, the singular circumstances of whose disappearance had added a solemn, as well as a romantic interest to the memory of their attachment. She would talk to Lilly for hours and hours on the subject; indeed, it usually came in with the tea and bread and butter, and not unfrequently lasted all the evening. And it so hap-pened that this was a subject scarcely less interesting to the confidante than to the heroine of the tragedy herself; for whilst Winny eased her full heart by dilating on Shorty's love and virtues, and somewhat appeased the irritability of her protracted wonder and curiosity as to his fate, by suggestions and questions, whereby she hoped to extract some gleams of light or traces of evidence against the Littenhaus family, Lilly on her part listened with excited attention to all the details of an af-fair, which at the time it occurred, had made little impression upon her. But late events were beginning to cast a lurid light on earlier ones. Fearful suspicions were haunting Lilly's mind with respect to the doings at the "Huntsman," although precisely what manner of mischief was acted at that lonely inn she did not under-stand. But there was one circumstance, the memory of which pervaded her with a shuddering horror; and that was the scene that had been transacted when her uncle Jacob lay dead in his coffin, of which she had been an unseen witness.

Engrossed at the moment by the apprehension of being discovered behind the curtain, and too unsuspicious, dull, and unobserving, to draw conclusions af-terwards, she had never comprehended, or sought to comprehend, the mysterious proceedings of that night. Indeed her own illness first, and the many events that had subsequently occurred to her, had almost effaced the circumstance from her recollection. But what black deeds midnight may cover, she had lately learnt by frightful experience; and since she did not doubt that it was for her own throat the knife was intended, she could almost as little doubt that Luke was the murderer;

since she could not think of any one else who would be likely to seek her life. Besides, that she had been actually delivered into the hands of her cousins, she was assured by the presence of Charlotte Littenhaus.

Then, in pursuing her review of what she had witnessed that night in her uncle's chamber, she could scarcely help coming to the conclusion, that the body substituted in the coffin was that of Philip's father, the subject of so much grief and such anxious inquiry. Indeed, dull as she was, and attaching no particular significance to the transaction, the idea had occurred to her at the time she learnt from Winny the object of Shorty's nightly excursions; though the fear of Luke would have effectually prevented her giving utterance to the thought, even had she been certain of the fact. But if this were really Mr. Ryland's body, the question now naturally arose to her, how came her cousins in possession of it, and wherefore had they concealed it? Had they murdered him? The more she reflected on all the circumstances of the case, and the more distinctly she pictured to herself their strange mode of life, the stronger grounds she perceived for admitting this apprehension. Then, if they had taken Mr. Ryland's life, the belief that they had dealt in the same manner with poor Shorty, almost inevitably followed. Besides the various indications of the fact which she recalled, he must have been unconsciously rendering himself extremely obnoxious to them. There was reason enough for their wishing him out of their way.

It was a frightful thing for a young girl to believe herself a member of a family stained with all this blood; and except when her business diverted her thoughts into other directions, her mind was ever running on these problems, and endeavouring to solve them; so that Winny's never exhausted theme was one she was always ready for. Then Winny was rich in shocking stories of murders, especially those perpetrated by innkeepers; till by dint of collecting them, she had brought herself to look upon a road-side inn as a sort of slaughter-house; and she often made poor Lilly's flesh creep with the tale of Jonathan Bradford,[115] and others equally fearful.

She now too communicated to Lilly, that which on account of her youth, she had formerly forborne to tell her; namely, that on the night of his murder, for murdered she was sure he had been, her lover had appeared to her mother and herself.

There are few people in the world, if they had but courage to own it, who have not some instinctive persuasion that such apparitions are within the range of possibility; a persuasion against which they battle with all the force of their fallacious reason, which they erroneously suppose to be the surest guide, in a case beyond its province. Reason can tell us nothing of the invisible world; invisible

---

115 See note 70 on p.164.

to us, because the gross organs of this fleshly tabernacle in which we dwell on earth, are only calculated and designed to take cognisance of material objects. The possibility of the reappearance of the dead, that is of their rendering their presence sensible to us, who are yet in the flesh, is a question that can only be argued upon experience—all *à priori*[116] reasoning on the subject, being perfectly worthless—and the experience of all ages and countries is in favour of the fact; that is, if we are to believe the testimony of many credible persons, whose words would be received as a sufficient guarantee on any ordinary occasion. Under what peculiar conditions these recognitions take place, whether depending on the state of the seer or the seen, or the mutual *rapport* of both, we do not yet, and possibly may never know; but that such occurrences are more frequent than is commonly imagined, we are perfectly satisfied; although human pride and scepticism, and a reaction from the superstitions of a preceding age, caused them to be concealed, or denied, or explained away; but we trust the time is approaching, when this and similar subjects, the most deeply interesting that have ever yet been presented to the investigation of the human race, will receive the attention they merit, and be examined in that truly philosophical and liberal spirit, which can alone elicit truth.

But on this matter we shall say no more at present; as we propose very shortly to offer to the public our humble contributions to the as yet, in this country, scanty literature on the subject in question, in a separate volume, which we shall denominate "The Night-side of Nature."[117]

Lilly's mind was deeply stirred by this glimpse of tidings from the other world. If she had hitherto ever thought of death at all, she had looked upon it simply as extinction; she had seen nothing beyond the death of the body; that it was a translation—the mere act of passing from one condition of existence to another—had never occurred to her. It is true that Abel White had talked to her of a future state, and told her that the soul survived, and could not die; but her ideas of the soul, and the mode of its surviving, were much too vague to inspire her with any interest; or perhaps it would be speaking more correctly to say that she had no ideas on the subject at all; and in spite of all the teachings of the ministry, we fear Lilly's case is by no means singular. The human mind requires something more precise and tangible; that which it is unable to conceive of, produces little actual effect; and the notions of a future state generally presented by instructors, clerical or otherwise, are on the one hand too shocking to be believed, and on the other too insipid, and too far removed from our conceptions of what happiness consists in, to be very ardently desired, except it be as an escape from the opposite alternative.

---

116 Known before or innate.
117 Crowe's most famous book of 'real' ghost tales, published in 1848.

But this strong persuasion of Winny's, that she had seen her lover out of the flesh, awakened strange new thoughts in Lilly's mind. Once before she had had a momentary *feeling* that there *was* something beyond this material world; it was when Abel White took her to hear the cathedral service at E——. The solemn temple, and the young voices hymning forth the psalms, and sounding to her like the songs of angels, had touched and aroused her emotional nature; and it was then she first *felt* that there was a God; but her late course of life and companion-ship, had not been calculated to nourish this feeble germ, which had thus been overgrown and forgotten; nor had her church goings with Mrs. Ryland, nor the old lady's occasional Sunday catechisings,[118] been of any avail to revive it. Nay, even the long dogmatic sermons, and the chapters from the Bible, which were read of an evening, were neither showers nor sunshine to Lilly's arid faith. To say the truth, they were more like an east wind, drying and contracting the genial na-ture that might of its own accord have expanded into spiritualism; for she did not understand them, and they neither reached her intellect nor touched her heart; so that although after she met with the Rylands, till very lately, she had regularly attended the afternoon service, and spent the Sunday evenings after the most orthodox fashion, Lilly was in fact living as much without God in the world, as if she had been born and bred in a country where His name was not known, nor His being acknowledged.

But now various doubts were started; and her mind went through the whole-some process of wondering at many things that had previously excited neither observation nor curiosity; and many an hour she and Winny, after their own simple fashion, discussed such deep questions of theology and psychology as have puzzled philosophers of all ages; and it is extremely probable that the opinions they arrived at were of about as much value as most of those which have been so magisterially announced by their learned predecessors.

Howbeit, the exercise of thought and the excitement of wonder, were very wholesome processes to Lilly. People who do not live in a continual state of won-der in this world, are in a miserable condition; for where every object we behold, and every circumstance of our own being, and that of others, is properly speaking miraculous, those who can survey them with indifference, and feel no desire to penetrate into their mystery, must be either mournfully dull by nature, or griev-ously blunted by use.

So Lilly had lived; but so she lived no longer. She had arrived at that blessed knowledge, that there *were* "more things in Heaven and Earth than were dreamt of in her philosophy!"[119]

---

118 Christian dogma teachings.
119 From *Hamlet*, Act 1, Scene V.

CHAPTER IV

THE PAINS AND PERILS OF A BOY'S LOVE

There is nothing that confounds sense with insanity like jealousy; the mind of a person, under the influence of that passion, whilst it may be physically sane, is morally insane; and such had been the condition of Philip Ryland, when he undertook to supply May Elliott with those expensive gallantries, which she gave him to understand she could have commanded through the means of Mr. Ferdinand Pycroft. Whilst the words that bound him to this service were on his lips, he knew perfectly well that he had not wherewith to fulfil the promise he was making; but the intolerable pain he felt from the apprehension of losing his mistress, must be got rid of at any cost; nothing seemed so difficult, so impossible, as enduring that anguish; and, in the excitement of the moment, the most hopeless enterprise seemed easy, compared to the task of supporting life under its pressure.

But when he quitted her, the force with which the truth of his situation rushed back upon him, was dreadful. He knew very well that May would expect the fulfilment of his engagements, and that she was not a woman at whose feet he could throw himself, and confess the mortifying, degrading fact, that he had no money; for we are never so entirely deceived in people as we try to be; they deceive us less than we deceive ourselves. If we chose to open our eyes, we could generally see; but we do not; preferring to act on the maxim that "Where ignorance is bliss, 'tis folly to be wise."[120] The disenchantment comes at last; but, as regarded Philip, the period for that desirable consummation had not yet arrived; and in the mean time, the faith he had sworn himself to was, that May Elliott was an angel; and he did not choose to alter his persuasion.

But that terrible question, "Where is the money to come from?" which sits, like the Old Man of the Sea,[121] on so many people's shoulders, weighed heavily on his. For the part he took in the business, he had a small salary, together with board and lodging for himself and his mother; and in process of time, if he chose to remain with his aunt and cousin, he was to be taken into partnership; and it was at that period he looked forward to making May his wife; for the original plan of returning to the mill, which had been his mother's darling project as well as his own, whilst Lilly was in the ascendant, had since been relinquished, by himself at least; for he perfectly comprehended that the life of a miller's wife, on a bare common, six miles from any town, would never suit his intended bride. But the

---

120 Quote from Thomas Grey poem, 'Ode on a Distant Prospect of Eton College' (1742).
121 Greek God of the Sea; Nereus or Proteus.

partnership was yet a far distant hope; and one, indeed, that was never likely to be realised, if he did not give satisfaction during his years of probation; and to do this was not so easy as it had been before he became acquainted with May. Lilly led him into no expenses or irregularities; but now he thought it necessary to dress better than formerly; besides which, he was frequently later at night than the customs of the family authorised; and his Sundays were now invariably spent from home. His aunt and cousin, whose views of life were not so rigid as his mother's, scrutinised his conduct less narrowly; but she was very uneasy and very suspicious, and could not help communicating her apprehensions to them; so that it was to be feared Mrs. Dewar would not long continue indifferent to the alteration in his conduct. All this was upon his mind, and, together with his jealousy, and his scanty purse, formed a burden of care that rendered his life miserable. Yet, he could not extricate himself from it; nor would not, if some benevolent magician had offered him a Lethean cup,[122] that should have replaced him where he was twelvemonths before, and made him forget that such a person as May Elliott had ever existed in the world.

Most evils and sufferings people are glad to get rid of if they can; but for those caused by an imprudent passion, they are always determined to accept no remedy, even if one could be found.

In the mean time, his pride, his love, and his jealousy, all combined in urging him to act up to the promises he had made May; and there was but one way of doing this, and that was to help himself to some of the proceeds of the business, which passed through his hands. As nobody doubted his honesty, and as he kept the accounts, in a great degree, himself, nothing could be practically more easy; but the struggle with his own principles was a very different matter. It is difficult to conceive the agony of a young soul virtuously born and nurtured in such a strife as this. On the one hand, the madness of passion; on the other, the horror of crime; Oh! the sleepless nights and the anxious days!—The parched lips and fevered throat; and the burning brow, that made the pillow on which it rested so hot, that he was fain to fling it from under him. And then the necessity of concealing all this anguish from May, instead of finding in the bosom of his love, a generous sympathy, ready to share and lighten his burden!

The first question a man ought to ask himself before he allows his heart to become the thrall of a woman should be, "Is she worthy to be my friend?"

Philip would perhaps never have been able to bring himself to commit the act, had he not in some degree reconciled, or sought to reconcile, his conscience to it, by the sophistical argument, that he was only anticipating his salary; and

---

122 Crowe is again referring to Greek mythology and the River Lethe, one of the five rivers in Hades; the river of forgetfulness.

that thereafter, when he was received into partnership, he would replace whatever he appropriated. We know how many first steps in crime are made under some such delusion; and we know, too, how that first step, as well as some others, vindicates the proverb "ce n'est que le premier pas qui coute."[123] The pilfered money purchased the pleasure; the pleasure whilst it lasted, made him forget the pain; but when the pleasure was over, the pain returned with double intensity, and needed more pleasure to drive it away, and so he was hunted forwards by remorse and desire, till he had wandered so far from the straight path, that despair took up the chase, and urged him wildly on to desperate ruin. Then came his aunt's suspicions, and his mother's tears, and his young cousin's alienation; and, finally, detection; and then he forsook his mother and his home, and fled; intending not even to tell May whither he was going. With livid cheeks and haggard eyes, he one evening burst into her room, and said he was come to bid her farewell. At first she did not believe him; but when she became convinced he was serious, and that she was really about to lose him, her whole demeanour changed; she threw herself into his arms, and with passionate tears conjured him not to leave her; or if he would go, to take her with him. Here was a strange consolation in the hour of his deep woe! May, then, really loved him! All his jealousy, all his fears, had been groundless; her heart was his, and she was ready to share his desperate fortunes. How he had wronged her in concealing from her his poverty and his straits!— How he had wronged himself! And now adoring, and adored, he must leave her; for how could he stay, or how could he drag her into the misery and destitution that probably awaited him?

All these feelings rent his heart; but still in this delightful revelation of her love, there was such a balm that joy and sorrow contended in his breast for the mastery, and he felt almost inspired with a hope that all was not lost, and that he might save himself still. His prospects in the London business were blighted. Terrified at what had occurred, his mother would have been as averse as his aunt, to exposing him to further temptations; neither, indeed, could he have dared to encounter them himself; but his interest in the mill was not abrogated; his own family would desire nothing better than his reformation, and therefore would not expose his errors, and the motives of his leaving London would probably never reach the country. Might he not therefore return there and resume his former position under Luke, till the time arrived that would make him master of the mill, and then bring home his poor old mother, and marry May Elliott? For if she loved him enough to share his present wretchedness and disgrace, of course she would not hesitate to unite herself to him when his fortunes would be so much more prosperous. All this glanced through his mind, whilst she, in all the violence of

---

123 See note 80 on p.187.

surprise and disappointment, besought him with tears not to leave her.

"Oh, May!" he said, pressing her wildly to his heart, "why did you let me think you did not love me? Why did you make me jealous and mad?"

"I never thought you'd believe me," sobbed May. "I never thought you supposed I cared for Mr. Ferdinand Pycroft or any of them. But it isn't *that* you're going away for, is it?" said she, looking up at him, and suddenly ceasing to weep.

"No; it's because I'm in trouble, May, that I'm going; but it would break my heart to think that after I am gone you encouraged that fellow."

"I don't want to encourage him," replied May; "but you shall not go unless you let me go with you. What trouble is it that's making you go, Philip?"

"It's one I can't tell you, May; but you will promise to keep your heart for me till I can come and fetch you? Will you swear to love nobody but me, May? Will you?"

"No," said May, "I won't promise unless you'll take me with you; but if you will, I'll promise any thing."

"I dare not," said Philip, whose resolution was fortified by this display of attachment on the part of his mistress, for it inspired him with hope for the future, and with a more earnest desire to repair his fortunes and his character, in order that he might, under different circumstances, complete his own happiness and reward her fidelity. "Not for worlds would I drag my darling, beautiful May into the misery that probably awaits me for the next few years. Oh, May! if I were but a king that could lead you to a palace, and adorn you with jewels, and give you a hundred slaves to kneel at your feet and obey your looks!"

"But you haven't got a palace, nor slaves, nor jewels, either; but that's no reason why you should behave so ill to me! Why can't you stay in London? If you have quarrelled with your friends that needn't prevent your getting another situation. I can get you one. Besides, I'll speak to Mrs. Knox, and amongst the tradespeople she knows, I'm sure she could get you one. La, Philip! they'd be glad to have such a handsome young man as you are, at many shops; they always have handsome young men at Harvey's and Graham's. And then you must dress stylishly, like Mr. Ferdinand Pycroft, and you'll look a great deal better than he does, for you're a much better figure, only that his clothes are better made than yours."

"It cannot be, May," answered Philip half flattered and half vexed, but still sufficiently in his senses to know, that after what had happened, he must not attempt to take another situation in London; "It cannot be, though it breaks my heart to do it, I must leave you, for the present. But if you will be faithful, May, if you will but love me, and wait for me, we may be happy yet. Will you promise me?"

"I don't know," answered May, pouting. "If you won't do what I ask you, I don't see why you should expect me to do what you ask."

"But I can't stay, May. God knows, I would if I could!"

"Oh," said May, "where there's a will there's a way."

"There's no way but what will be my ruin, May; you wouldn't wish that, would you?" said Philip.

"Oh, nonsense, ruin! What's to ruin you? People get into difficulties, and get out of them again, without being ruined. Lord bless me! it's just because you're not used to any thing, that you're in such a quandary. If you're afraid of your mother, never let out to her where you are; and I'll recommend you to Mrs. Knox, and say you're my brother, or my cousin, or something of that sort; and she'll recommend you to Dyde's and Scribe's, or Harvey's and Graham's—"[124]

"I'd rather be shot than go to Harvey's and Graham's, to stand behind a counter with that fellow that I hate," said Philip.

"Well, it shan't be Harvey's and Graham's," said May. "There are plenty of shops that want handsome young men, besides theirs!"

But Philip understood his own situation too well to entertain the idea of remaining in London. Though guilty, he was not perverted; and no arguments of May's could have brought him to think lightly of what he had done. She might even, by irritating his pride and his jealousy, have urged him to a repetition of his offence; but she could not so far beguile his judgment as to make him look upon an act of dishonesty as a thing indifferent. With respect to May's loose principles and want of respect for truth, his judgment was less free. "Love was the cause of her folly;" and since he was the object of the love, her sins, "though they were as scarlet," never appeared to him of a deeper hue than pale pink; little peccadilloes, to be overlooked in so pretty and fascinating a woman.

"Then you are determined to go?" said May, almost sulkily.

"I must," answered Philip. "Oh! May, would I leave you if I could help it? But from this moment till you see me again, every thought and every hour shall be spent in the endeavour to bring about our union. If I can only once get a house over my head, that I can call my own, and be sure of the means of supporting you in comfort, I'll fly to London and carry you off, May, to my cottage, and there we'll live as happy as two birds in a cage."

We fear the simile was more appropriate than inviting.

"Oh, pooh!" said May; "when will that be? You may as well say, that when the sky falls you'll catch larks."

"Oh, May," said he, "don't discourage me! I need all the courage you can give me, to enable me to bear my own troubles, and this parting with you. You must strengthen me to meet all the miseries and the hardships I have before me, till I

---

124 Dyde and Scribe was a London department store in Pall Mall.

can conquer them, and call you my own; will you, May?"

"I don't know," said May, ungraciously.

"But, May, if you really love me,—and if you did not love me, you surely wouldn't be so anxious to keep me here—but if you do, you must wish that I should try to get into some way of business that may enable me to have a home for you. Now, I see but one way of doing this, at least I'm sure it's the shortest, and that is to go back to the mill; and—"

"To the mill! Is that where you're going?" said May, her cheeks turning crimson, and looking very much amazed.

"I did not mean to tell you," replied Philip, "but perhaps it's only fair that I should; only you must keep it a secret; as for the present, I don't want my mother nor any body to know where I am."

This was a piece of intelligence that quite confounded May, and baffled all her calculations. In order to remove Lilly, of whom she was quite as jealous as Philip was of the redoubted Mr. Ferdinand, out of her lover's way, she had, through the intervention of Giles Lintock, betrayed her into the hands of her cousins, and she did not doubt that Lilly at that moment was at the "Huntsman," either with or without her own consent, free or a prisoner; and now Philip was going to the very spot where he would not only be exposed to the charms of this dreaded rival, but where he would moreover learn what a false friend and a viper his lovely, angelic May Elliott was.

What was to be done now? The only feasible expedient that presented itself to May, was to go into hysterics, and she put it in practice immediately; the hysterics on this occasion being, as is frequently the case, partly real and partly factitious. The passion and the tears were perfectly genuine, for she was very much in love with Philip, and she saw that this scheme of his would be the means of awakening him from his infatuation, and be the destruction of her influence for ever; but hoping to overcome him by the magnitude of her despair, she could not forbear heightening the tone of the picture by a few touches of frenzy. And deeply was poor Philip moved by her anguish; but he held firmly to his resolution still, and to her surprise and dismay, she found that this young man, whom she had hitherto played on as a pipe, had a will of his own as strong as hers, when the antagonism of his nature was sufficiently aroused to exert it; and in the present instance, the agonies of shame, the dread of exposure, and the desire to reintegrate his character, and recover his self-esteem, sufficed to furnish the requisite energy. The truth was, that though a boy in years and in experience, Philip had the makings of a man in him; and although he had been led into error under the influence of a dangerous woman and an intoxicating passion, he had an honest and an upright heart, a love of virtue, and a fund of good feeling, that must have rendered him inevitably miserable as long as he knew himself unworthy.

Some of the finest natures existing amongst men, are those who, gentle and complying, almost to a fault, can yet show themselves possessed of an iron will, when an adequate occasion for firmness presents itself; and if Philip had studied as artificially how to enflame her love and deepen her regret, as she had done to get the better of his judgment, and shake his determination, he could not have adopted a more efficient means; for there is nothing more fascinating to women than such a display of character, where the circumstance justifies its exhibition. The more resolved Philip was to go, the more ardently she wished him to stay; and the more she saw how capable he was of keeping a resolution he had formed, the more clearly she perceived that if he once saw her as she really was, with all her faults and imperfections on her head, which now her beauty and the glamour she had cast over him concealed, he would probably be as inexorable in his deter-mination to fling her off for ever, as he now was to separate from her for a time. Whilst Philip, on his part—such are the cross purposes of intersecting passions—whilst he felt deeply for her affliction, found himself sustained and fortified in the sacrifice he was making, by her frantic efforts to induce him to forego it.

And so they parted; he swearing eternal fidelity, and endeavouring to recon-cile her to the present, by holding out vivid hopes for the future: she drowned in tears, yet angry and sulky, and mingling the most bitter reproaches with her entreaties and lamentations.

It was night when Philip found himself in the street after this interview, and with his heart somewhat lighter than it had been—for surely she would wait for him—she would be faithful—so much love could never die, he hastened to the office whence the coach started, and with his hat drawn over his eyes, and his coat buttoned across his chin, he took his seat on the outside; and in an hour after he had parted with May, he was whirling along with the Enterprize to Hotham.

If he could, by any possibility, have taken a peep into the room where he left her, he would have been entirely confirmed in the above satisfactory persuasion. For the first two hours, she lay stretched on the sofa with her face buried in the cushions, in convulsions of grief and despair; and when the violence of these demonstrations somewhat subsided, it was not because she was in any degree rec-onciled to her loss, but because the desire of finding some means of averting the misfortune, obtained the ascendency, in its turn: and under the influence of this new motive, she arose, dried her tears, and gathered her energies together, whilst with her lips firmly closed, and her arms crossed upon her breast, she paced the room from end to end, and set herself to think.

This was the first reality May had ever come in contact with. Life, to her, had hitherto been a masque, wherein she had played upon the feelings of others, her own unscathed; but the tables were turned now. She was wretched; and she bore her misery with all the impatience of an unsubdued temper, and an untrained mind: aggravated as it was, by the restless whisperings from within, reminding her, that her misfortune had its source entirely in her own unprincipled selfishness and folly.

CHAPTER V

LILLY IN HER NEW HOME

As Lilly was so handy with her needle, it was thought advisable to take this opportunity of refreshing and repairing the family wardrobe; and as Colonel Adams liked to have somebody always in his room, when his wife or son were not with him, Lilly sat there; he submitting to have his eyes darkened in order that sufficient light might be admitted for her to see her work. It was very natural that under these circumstances he should enter into conversation with her; and he began in the first instance, by interrogating her with respect to her own past life, where she came from, who she had lived with, whether her parents were alive, and so forth. But on all these points he found Lilly singularly reserved; insomuch, that he left off with little more information than when he began. But as this was the first day she had sat in his room, he thought she might be restrained by shyness and timidity, and so the thing passed from his mind. On the following day he desired her to read the newspaper to him, and as she mispronounced many of the long words and proper names, he took the trouble of correcting her. He also explained to her what he perceived, from the tone of her voice, she did not understand; and Lilly becoming more at her ease, they got on better together; whilst as he reverted no more to the subject of the first day's conversation, their intercourse at each visit grew less constrained. Too poor to take a newspaper, or to purchase books, he had nevertheless plenty of both, various old friends in different parts of the world sending him the former, and the latter being furnished by the clergyman of the parish, who had a very tolerable library. These in progress of time it became Lilly's almost daily business to read, as soon as it was found that she could do so sufficiently well to be understood; for Frederick attended a day-school, and Mrs. Adams was delicate, and could not read aloud without fatigue. Previously to this, Lilly had never read any thing in her life, except the Bible, and at first she found it rather an irksome employment; but now and then she would come to something that arrested her attention, or that would lead Colonel Adams to tell her a story, or give her some piece of curious information; till at length, little by little, she began to take up the books with a different feeling; her curiosity was awakened—she would venture to ask questions occasionally—which he always encouraged her to do; and, above all, she began to *think* of what she had read.

Humble, gentle, and obliging, with a sweetness of disposition that spoke in her tuneful voice, Lilly grew daily in the favour of her master. Besides, her name had a charm for him; it brought back tender memories, though they were sad ones; whilst the frequent attendance and the readings, and the instruction he gave her, endeared her to him so much, that he would generally address her as "Lilly, my girl!" or "Lilly, my child!" treating her with a degree of kindness and familiarity quite unaccustomed in their relative positions.

With Lilly's natural adhesiveness, it may be supposed that this sort of intercourse could not continue long without producing a very sensible effect upon her. Colonel Adams became her Abel White, whilst Freddy was her May Elliott. Towards the one, she felt a mixture of tenderness, reverence, and affection; towards the other, an enthusiastic love and admiration. He was her darling, beautiful Freddy! and she waited upon him as if he had been the heir-apparent, and watched for his comings in and goings out, as if he had been her sweetheart. To make a waistcoat for him out of one of his father's old ones, or to hem his new pocket handkerchief, she would sacrifice her night's rest with delight; and when he got his heel bitten by the milkman's dog, whom he had accidentally offended by running his hoop against him, she insisted on sucking the wound lest the animal should be mad.

In return for all these services, besides being very fond of her, Freddy rendered her one very great one; he taught her to write, lending her his own copy-books, and giving her a lesson every evening. Her deficiency in this necessary accomplishment, was very early discovered, by her being required to make out the weekly washing bills; and Freddy no sooner heard his mother lamenting her ignorance, than he joyfully undertook to become her instructor. A person at Lilly's age, who has tolerable intelligence and a desire to learn, may soon acquire the art of writing a legible hand, if not an elegant one; and as Lilly was very much ashamed of not being able to do what she found most other persons in her station could, she soon attained a reasonable degree of facility; and no sooner did she find herself able to write a letter, than she indited one to her old friend, Abel White, which she forwarded by the post; forgetting, however, to pay the postage in advance, so that poor Abel was nothing the better for it.

Lilly had thought herself very happy whilst tramping along the road with the old blind beggar; and still happier during her early days of housekeeping with May Elliott; but now she was happier than ever. It was a higher kind of happiness that she now enjoyed, and she was better able to appreciate it, for her mind was daily opening and ripening under these genial influences and generous tuitions.

It was not that she had forgotten Philip; far from it; not a day of her life passed that she did not think of him; but it was with a tender and unresentful regret. She had been too sensible herself of May Elliott's fascinations, to be surprised at their effect upon him and had too humble an opinion of her own attractions, not to find excuses for him. She often wondered if they were yet married; and this train of thought generally terminated in an ardent wish, that she might never be called upon to undergo the painful trial of seeing them together.

The recollection, too, of the dreadful night passed in the lodging, and the frightful death of Charlotte Littenhaus, frequently came over her with a shudder of horror; and it had been long before she had recovered her natural rest or the shock her nerves had received. The family had attributed her shaking hand, and pallid complexion, and uneasy, anxious look, to an ill-state of health; and as she gradually improved, they were naturally confirmed in this supposition. As for Winny, she ascribed the agitation and tremour in which she had first arrived, to her distress at quarrelling with May Elliott, and frequently she had proposed making an effort to bring about a reconciliation, which Lilly, however, always entreated her to forbear, assuring her she did not wish May to know where she was.

CHAPTER VI

PHILIP PUTS IN PRACTICE HIS GOOD RESOLUTIONS

Philip reached Hotham on the morning after he had started from London, and having taken some breakfast, he forthwith set out on foot for Combe Martin, or rather for Sir Lawrence Longford's; for to the baronet who had hitherto shown himself his fast friend, he intended first to present himself; but as he passed the "Red Lion," old Lacy, who was occupying his usual position at the door, hailed him with a "Hallo! young man! what tired of London, eh? Back to the old shop, I see."

"Yes," said Philip, "I *am* tired of London, and I don't care if I never see it again. Is Sir Lawrence at the Hall, do you know?"

"Yes, he's there," answered Lacy; "I saw your old master, Luke Littenhaus, going up that way, just now, in conversation with Mr. Cobb. We heard you was settled in London, and that Luke was to be *properioter*[125] of the mill after all; and I rather think that's what they've got in hand now."

"I'd better look sharp, then," said Philip. "How is the mill doing? and the 'Huntsman?' Just in the old way, I suppose."

"Much of a muchness, I fancy," said Lacy. "I sends them up a customer now

---

125 Proprietor.

and then, but I can't say as' ever I got a 'thankye' for it. Miss Charlotte, she's married, you know, to a Mr. Locksley; and gone away from here—but perhaps that was before you left."

"No," replied Philip, "it must have been afterwards. I think I remember once seeing a man of that name at the house—a seafaring man he was, I think."

"I don't know nothing on him," answered Lacy. "They wasn't married here; they went over to Hotham to get spliced; but I s'pose he was a man of fortin, at least; for Miss Grosset says, I'm told, that she had as fine silks and satins as Miss Longford herself. But they do dress surprising, to be sure! I often wonder where the money comes from."

"Well, I must be going," said Philip, who took no interest in the toilet of the Littenhaus ladies, "for I want to catch Sir Lawrence before he goes out."

As the servants all knew him, he had no difficulty in obtaining admittance to the baronet's study, where he found Mr. Cobb.

"Humph! That's odd enough!" said Sir Lawrence to the agent, as Philip was announced. "It seems to realise the old proverb! Why, Philip, what has brought you back so suddenly?"

"I don't think London will answer for me, sir," replied he, "and I wish, if you please, to settle at the mill again."

"You shall do that if you wish it, certainly," returned Sir Lawrence; "the promise I made you, I'll keep—I was just telling Luke Littenhaus so."

"Does he want the mill, sir?"

"Yes, he does; he always did, you know. But I told him that my engagement to you was still binding; and that if you came back to claim my promise, I must keep it. But what has brought you back?"

Philip blushed, and with some confusion, answered, "I don't think, sir, I'm altogether fit to live in London."

"Well, you must be the best judge of that," said Sir Lawrence; "and you are very right to leave it, if you think so. You will then stay the appointed time with Mr. Littenhaus, and at the expiration of it, he will resign the mill to you, if you think yourself able to manage it."

"I'll try to make up for lost time, sir," said Philip; and after some inquiries about his mother, Sir Lawrence bidding him good morning, he took his leave, and proceeded to the mill, in order to present himself to his old master. It is needless to say that he met no welcome—he did not expect one; but he had thoroughly made up his mind to have no quarrel with Luke; but as an expiation of his past offences, to bear patiently with his temper and his tyranny, till time should set him free of both. He now also wrote to his mother, avowing where he was. Ever since his interview with May, which had served as a safety-valve to his over-excited feelings, he had been calmer and more capable of reflection; and had consequently felt considerable remorse for the anguish he was sure his mother must be suffering on his account. He now thought he saw his way more clearly before him; he was able to look at the future; and he hoped, with the aid of May, and his own perseverance and stern resolution, to recover his self-esteem and the esteem of his friends, and to be able yet to work out his destiny with honour to himself and credit to them: and so he told his mother; adding, that whatever annoyances he might have to encounter on the part of Luke Littenhaus, he should look upon as no more than a just punishment for his errors.

At the "Huntsman," he found things much as formerly, except as regarded the absence of Charlotte, and the addition to the family of a young girl in Lilly's place. The sight of her rather affected Philip; for his own misfortunes had softened his heart, and he recalled poor Lilly's former kindnesses in his boyish, hungry days; her innocent joy when she met him and his mother in London; her gratitude and affection towards them; and finally, the neglect with which he had lately requited her services and attachment. Not that he knew exactly the extent of the latter, for no declaration had ever been made on either side; and therefore when his own affections veered into another quarter, he had no great difficulty in persuading himself that Lilly's sentiments had never exceeded the bounds of a sisterly regard. But even so, he felt conscious that he had not behaved well to her; and he resolved, when he wrote to May, to send her a kindly message and ascertain her present address.

On the whole, he now found his situation less unpleasant than it had been formerly; for though Luke was as disagreeable as ever, Philip was more of a man now, and was better able to cope with him. As for Ambrose, he had never shown any disposition to annoy him; besides, he had little to do with him; whilst Anna now evinced an incipient disposition to be his friend. The two years Philip had passed in London had produced a very considerable alteration in his personal appearance, and his love for May, and her elegancies, had softened and somewhat refined his manners. He was not a mere rustic Adonis now, but might very well, had he been ambitious, have aspired to be the Corypheus[126] of fashion in Combe Martin and the vicinage; with his handsome face, well-made person, and London cut habiliments. His very sufferings, too, had improved his appearance, by giving an expression to his countenance which it before wanted; so that, altogether, Anna Littenhaus was privately of opinion that he was "a very nice young man," and as she saw no reason for concealing her sentiments from the object of them, she began to testify her regard exactly in the same way that poor Lilly had

---

126 The leader of a Greek chorus. Meaning here, Philip could be a leader of fashion in Combe Martin and its environs.

formerly done—namely, by giving him large lumps of pudding and other edibles, by no means unwelcome to a youth who lived on a breezy common, close to the sea-shore. It is true, that for the first few days, his appetite was rather sickly; but hope and occupation, and the elasticity of youth, together with the satisfaction resulting from the consciousness of trying to do right, soon restored it, and rendered these solid gallantries of the lady very acceptable. When Luke was out of the way, she ventured on still further civilities, and not unfrequently favoured him with her conversation. On these occasions she would sometimes make references to Lilly and her mysterious disappearance, and being altogether unconscious that Philip had any interest in her, she was extremely frank in her communications on this subject.

"Lilly," she said, "had escaped in the most artful way in the world; satisfactorily proving that she had been acting a part, and was by no means so stupid as they had imagined. She never showed the least dislike to marrying Luke," said she; "indeed, we supposed she would have thought it a great rise for her, shouldn't you?"

"Perhaps she didn't like him," said Philip.

"Oh, she knew nothing about liking or disliking," said Anna; "at least, we thought so. Didn't you think her very stupid?"

"She wasn't very bright *then*" said Philip, suddenly stopping short with the recollection that he must not betray Lilly's whereabout by communicating the change that had taken place in her.

"No," answered Anna; "but she must have been deeper than she seemed, though. Think how cleverly she must have managed it, to get out of Hotham and leave no trace behind her."

"And did you never hear any thing of her afterwards?" inquired Philip.

"Yes, we have; Luke has been up after her twice; once to the west of England. He put an advertisement in the paper, and offered a reward—I'm sure I don't see why he should want to get her back, for my part; since she *is* gone, I'd let her go, if I were him. However, a man answered it, and Luke went to the place where he said she was, but she was off, nobody knew where, and they did say that she had committed a robbery, and then set fire to the house to conceal it."

"What a lie!" exclaimed Philip, involuntarily.

"Ah! you think she's not sharp enough," said Anna, "but she's sharper than you think; for since that, he heard of her again and she slipped through his fingers just as cunningly."

"Indeed!" said Philip, curious to know to what she now alluded; for as regarded her two first escapes, he had learnt all the particulars from Lilly herself.

"I don't know any more, for Luke, you know, is as close as wax,"[127] she replied,

---

127 Miserly.

"only that he got a letter—I believe it was from the same man, saying she was somewhere in London, and telling Luke that if he would go up, he would put her in his hands, and Luke went, but he came back without her, though."

"How was that?" asked Philip, whose curiosity was considerably excited.

"I don't know exactly," replied Anna. "Luke was very sulky when he returned, and never said a word to me on the subject; but Ambrose told me, whilst he was gone, that Lilly was to be taken to where Charlotte lodged. Charlotte married Locksley, you know—you remember Locksley?"

"I believe I've seen him," answered Philip, "a seafaring man?"

"Well," said Anna, not entering into further particulars about Locksley, "Charlotte, and he were in London, living somewhere near Smithfield,[128] and there Lilly was to be taken; but how Luke missed her I don't know, only she never came here."

"This must have been a great disappointment to your brother," observed Philip, wishing to discover the motive of Luke's perseverance in this pursuit of a person he had always seemed to despise; "he must, no doubt, be very much attached to her, to take such trouble about the business?"

"Attached!" answered Anna, laughing; "Luke attached to Lilly! Lord help you! he's no more attached to her than you are."

"What does he want to marry her for, then?" inquired Philip.

"Oh! he has his reasons, I suppose," said Anna; "but if he'd take my advice and Ambrose's too, he'd let her alone. Good riddance of bad rubbish, I say. But wilful men will have their way; so he must do as he pleases."

This information of Anna's with regard to Luke's unremitting pursuit of Lilly, and the circumstance of his having received some intelligence respecting her since her flight from Mrs. Ross's, surprised Philip a good deal, and inspired him with considerable alarm for the poor girl's safety. Lilly herself had told him every particular of her history, from the moment she quitted Hotham; so that he had no difficulty in fixing on Giles Lintock as the person who had hunted her up. Moreover, by further interrogating Anna, when she was in a communicative humour, he ascertained that this last visit of Luke's to London must have been contemporary with the separation of Lilly and May, since which he had never heard any thing of his old friend. It was very consoling, certainly, to learn that she had again eluded her pursuers; but the terror and anxiety she must have undergone, and the difficulties she might have been plunged into in consequence of this persecution, caused him serious uneasiness. He knew, too well, that she had no friend now to protect her. He ought to have done it, and might, if he had retained his own station and respectability; but he could do nothing now but warn and advise

---

128 A large meat market in the City of London.

her; and in order that he might do this, he resolved immediately to write to May, and inquire her address.

With respect to May herself, he was at this time not a little anxious; as she had never answered the letter he sent her shortly after his arrival. His apprehensions pictured her to his imagination ill and brokenhearted; the victim of love and disappointment; probably, confined to her bed, and unable to write, from the effects of grief; with nobody to tend and watch over her. This suspense was a great trial to poor Philip; and it required all the energy of his good resolutions, and the moral purpose that possessed him, to inspire him with courage to attend to the dull business of the mill; whilst his thoughts were for ever hovering around that visionary sick bed in Blenheim Street. He would have given the world to go to her; but he held firmly by his resolves; and only wrote and waited.

In the meantime, no particular incident occurred at the "Huntsman," except, one night, the arrival of a thin, sickly-looking man, dressed in a shabby black coat, whom he understood to be Locksley, the husband of Charlotte. For his own part, except from Anna's information, he never would have recognised him, so much had his appearance altered since he last saw him. He had formerly exhibited a healthy complexion, and had worn the garb of a sailor, and Philip could not forbear inquiring of Anna the cause of the change. Much, however, as she seemed disposed to favour him, it was not every question he asked that she thought proper to answer. On the present occasion she was somewhat reserved.

"After he married Charlotte," she said, "he went into another line of business, and she supposed the change had not agreed with him. In my opinion," she added, "my sister had better have stayed as she was, for they live together like cat and dog. Charlotte wanted to come back here with Luke, that time he went up to fetch Lilly; but he wouldn't agree to it."

"Who wouldn't?" inquired Philip; "Locksley?"

"No, Luke. He and Charlotte had had a good deal of quarrelling about the match, from the first; but now he said, that as she had been determined to have him she must keep him."

"And where is she now?" inquired Philip.

"In London, Locksley says; but I don't think they see a great deal of each other."

CHAPTER VII

PAST EVENTS

Ralph Locksley was the son of a London tradesman, and was brought up to his father's business, which in due time, at the death of the old man, he had succeeded to. It was a prosperous concern, and he might have done very well in it, as his parents had done before him; but Ralph was more fond of company than minding his shop; and moreover, in his mode of conducting the concern, was apt to wander from the straight way into tortuous bypaths, whose pleasant meanders too frequently conduct people to very unpleasant catastrophes. Ralph began with cheating the customs, in concert with some of the officials of that somewhat corrupt department of the public service; and he ended with cheating his customers, who did not like that proceeding so well as the first; but it was the former delinquency which led to the latter. Some large seizures embarrassed his circumstances; and he had recourse to dishonesty to repair them. This was discovered, too, and his credit being lost, and his business broken up, he not unnaturally had recourse to the line of life, at that period of our national history, so seducing and so profitable. He became a smuggler; a pursuit in which his acquaintance with the value of certain sorts of merchandise, was extremely available to his coadjutors, who, for lack of this knowledge, were not unfrequently cozened[129] by their allies on the other side of the Channel. It was in the prosecution of these enterprizes that he became acquainted with the Littenhaus family, who had long been engaged in the same traffic—a traffic infinitely more pernicious from its perverting influences than from its direct effects; the loss to the revenue being of slight importance, as compared to the injury done to the morals of the people.

Why he and Charlotte Littenhaus, after an acquaintance of some years, should have thought proper to unite their fates, it would seem somewhat difficult to decide. Perhaps, as far as regarded the lady, her inducements might be resolved into one; namely, the extreme *ennui* that pervaded life at the Black Huntsman. That is, female life; for the male part of the family made themselves enough to do. When they lived at the extreme west, as they now lived at the extreme east of the island, their situation had been different. Smuggling was there too common, and too many people took advantage of it to be regarded as a very heinous offence; and it was not till shortly before their removal, that they had been looked on coldly, and made to feel themselves outcasts, and of this misfortune Luke's savage disposition was the cause; he, who though the youngest of the family, from

---

129 Won over or persuaded.

his strong will, governed them all. Smuggling was one thing—a little peccadillo, which as we have remarked, was looked upon with indulgence; but direct robbery and murder were beyond the rubric; and some awkward circumstances had brought Luke under suspicion. Amongst these was the affair of the *Hastings*. It is true, that the circumstances of her loss and the fate of her passengers were never distinctly known, for none survived to tell them, but one, and her lisping tongue could not relate what the young eyes had doubtless observed; and ere she was old enough to translate her thoughts into intelligible words, the whole scene she had witnessed had become no more than a confused dream. But still there were indications that "a deed had been done." In the morning, early, some fishermen had visited the wreck, then fast going to pieces. The body of the murdered man had been flung into the sea, but his blood yet stained the planks where the waves had not reached them, whilst in the distance, the white sail of the smuggler's cutter had been seen steering away from the ill-fated ship. But the fishermen had no desire to quarrel with the smugglers; they did a little in that way of business themselves, sometimes, and they therefore brought no accusation against them. But still the thought circulated, and the word was given from one to another; and the Littenhaus family found it desirable to change their quarters. But this change was a melancholy one for the young women, whose handsome persons and fine clothes were entirely thrown away at the "Huntsman." They continued to enrich their wardrobe with varieties of "brave attire," because from indulgence, what was originally a propensity had grown into a passion, and like the miser and his gold, they had transferred their love from the use of the thing to the thing itself. They could not wear their fine clothes, but they could lay them in their drawers and look at them. Still, it was but a *triste plaisir*,[130] one apt "to pall upon the sense;"[131] so that it was not surprising some variety should be desired; and it was this weariness for change that had brought about the inauspicious union of Charlotte and Locksley. The scheme had been hers, and he consented to it induced by the prospects she held out to him, of what her brothers would do for her now, and in time to come. Amongst the rest, she and her husband were to set up a shop in London, which was to be furnished with such articles as the smugglers traded in, and betwixt the low prices at which they would thus be supplied with their goods, and the high ones at which they would sell them, she looked to make a considerable profit. Locksley himself was aware of the fallacy of many of her anticipations; but as it was likely he might make something by the arrangement, he acceded to it. They went to London, but the shop was never opened. The goods were disposed of for present necessities, and when they were gone her fine wardrobe went

---

130 Sad or dreary pleasure.
131 Quote from Alexander Gerard 'An Essay on Taste', 1780.

after them, till at length the newly-married pair were reduced to utter destitution. Under these circumstances, it may be imagined that their *ménage* was not the most harmonious in the world. They quarrelled, and occasionally fought, and Charlotte would have gladly taken refuge at her former home, if they would have received her; but Luke forbade it. She was consequently extremely miserable, and was fast falling into the habit of drowning her cares in Lethean draughts[132] when her sorrows and her vices found their earthly termination in a violent death; and this little sketch having brought us up to the date of Lilly's fearful adventure, we will take the opportunity of narrating out of what circumstances it arose.

When Lilly confided to May, that Giles Lintock was no stranger to her, and that she had a deep interest in keeping her abode secret from him, May had not the most distant idea of betraying her. Indeed, had the idea of such a cruel act of treachery been presented to her mind as possible, she would have disowned it with indignation. As little would she have credited, that Lilly could ever have become an object of jealousy to herself; yet both these unforeseen events had taken place; and we must do her the justice to say, that no weaker incentive than jealousy would have induced her to commit so barbarous a breach of faith. Moreover, we must premise, that the notion that Lilly stood in any danger of her life from her cousins, had never occurred to her; that she would be taken back into the country, and married to Luke, was the whole amount of evil she had anticipated. Thus, when she believed it indispensable to her own happiness to get her out of the way, she took the only decisive means she could think of; she betrayed her to Giles Lintock, who immediately transferred the information to Luke—not, of course, saying where she was to be found, but offering to put her into his hands on payment of the promised reward. Luke immediately came to London; but for some time they could not agree about the pecuniary arrangements. This matter settled, a scheme for delivering her up was devised betwixt the latter and May; but as Luke was anxious not to appear in the business till the last moment, lest she should see him, and, taking fright, escape again, the plan was formed which we have seen executed. The night for the enterprize being appointed, Giles was to be stationed in a certain spot, with a hackney-coach, so that there might be no necessity for any orders being given in Lilly's hearing, she thus remaining ignorant of the name of the street she was conveyed to. They then drove her, according to directions previously given by Luke, to the house where the Locksleys were lodging; and Giles receiving her at the door, conducted her up stairs to a room hired for the purpose, and locked her in, without saying a syllable that could enlighten her with respect to so strange a reception.

"Well," said Giles to Luke, who was waiting the issue of the adventure in a

132 Here Crowe means alcohol.

neighbouring eating-house, "the bird's caught and caged."

"And the door locked?" said Luke.

"Fast; and here's the key," replied Giles; "so if you let her slip this time, it's your own fault, and not mine."

"She shan't do that," answered Luke, quietly.

"There now, I should be glad if you'd come down with the shiners,"[133] said Giles, "for I want to be off into the country with the daylight; but perhaps you'd first like to see that she's safe there?"

"No," answered Luke, who, under the cover of the darkness, had watched the arrival of the coach, and seen Lilly conducted into the house; "I don't want her to see me till it's absolutely necessary. She may take fright, and scream, and raise the neighbourhood."

"That's not very unlikely," returned Giles, significantly, "for she seems to have but an indifferent opinion of you."

"How? What do you mean?" inquired Luke.

"I mean what I say," replied Giles, not sure how far it might be safe to go; for like every one else who came into contact, or collision, with Luke, he was afraid of him. "She don't like you."

"I know that" returned Luke; and he might have added, "nobody ever did. But what does she say?" he rejoined, firmly; "I'll thank you to tell me."

"Nothing to me," answered Giles, "but she's given some awkward hints to the people she's been living with, about your doings down in the country, there."

Luke made no response to this unpleasant piece of information, for he was a man of very few words. He inquired who those people were; but Giles had his own reasons for not telling him that; so the conversation terminated, and the debt being discharged, they parted.

But the impression this hint made upon Luke was much deeper than he chose to display. He had long apprehended that Lilly knew more than she should do, and this intelligence seemed to confirm it. In this conjuncture, what line of conduct might it be advisable to pursue? For about two hours, alternately biting his forefinger, or twirling the key slowly with his right hand round the thumb of his left, or rubbing his chin with the palm of his hand, he sat debating this question. It was certainly a very important one. At length, having apparently duly weighed it, he arose from his seat, and taking the key in his hand, he went to the house, the door of which stood open for the accommodation of its several inmates, and by the light of a small lantern which he carried, he ascended to the room in which Lilly was a prisoner and gently turned the key; but whilst his hand was upon the lock some sudden thought made him hesitate, and he paused, and finally, after

---

133 Slang for money.

locking the door, without drawing out the key, he descended the stairs again as quietly as he had ascended them; and entered an apartment on the first floor which appertained to the Locksleys, where he passed another hour, in walking up and down the room, with his hands behind him, listening and thinking.

In the meantime, the Locksleys, who had been out together, arrived at home in the very climax of a quarrel. They had both drank more than they should; and hard words and bitter reproaches, flew from one to the other as they came up the street. When they reached the door he savagely bade her enter, which it had been her intention to do; but, because he told her to do it, she refused, and turned up the street again, whilst he went up stairs to the room where he found Luke.

Amongst Luke's vices, intemperance did not reckon; on the contrary, he had an entire contempt for those who "put an enemy into their mouths to steal away their brains;"[134] he found too much use for *his* brains, such as they were, to be so prodigal of them. In consequence, therefore, of his habits of intoxication, rendering him an unsafe depository, he had ceased letting Locksley further into his confidence than was absolutely necessary; and, accordingly, he did not think it advisable to say any thing to him with respect to his intentions regarding Lilly. For sometime, Locksley entertained him with complaints of his wife, who he said he had no doubt would not be home all night; and, when weary of this subject, he stretched himself on the bed and went to sleep.

It was during this interval, that Charlotte, who had only pretended to turn up the street, from a spirit of opposition to her husband, had ascended to the room where Lilly was sleeping, and given vent to her misery and her passion in tears. The apartment had been engaged some days before for the reception of the expected prisoner; and, supposing it still empty, she preferred sleeping there, as she had done on the previous night, to sharing her husband's chamber. But "sorrow's dry,"[135] and after a hearty convulsive fit of weeping, she felt the necessity of some drops of consolation; and it was to obtain this solace that she quitted the room.

In the meantime, Luke, leaving Locksley snoring on the mattress, once more ascended to Lilly's room. When he reached the door, he set down his lantern, and taking a large clasp knife from his pocket, he entered the chamber. It was now the middle of the night and all was quiet; and Lilly, who was listening to his every movement, breathed so gently, that he almost thought Giles had deceived him, and she was not there. But he advanced to the bed, and felt that she was; nor did he doubt, so motionless she lay, that she slept. It was at the very moment that he was about to use his knife, that he dropped it. To grope about the coverlet for it might have been vain and dangerous; the sleeper might have awakened. Neither

---

134 From *Othello*, Act 2, Scene III.
135 This is probably a misquote from *Romeo and Juliet*, Act 3 Scene V, 'dry sorrow'.

did he wish to introduce the lantern. That, too, might have disturbed her sleep; besides, he consulted his own security in preferring the faint light from the window which sufficed to conduct him to the bed. He could accomplish his object quite as well; and, if she did wake before he had attained it, she would not be able to recognise her assassin.

It now became necessary, however, to provide another weapon; and with this view he quitted the room, and descended again to that of Locksley, where he hoped to find a razor, and where he ultimately did find one, but not immediately; since the dull light furnished by his lantern, and the disorder of the chamber, rendered it not very easy to find any thing. He finally, however, discovered the article he wanted, in a bundle containing some articles of dress belonging to Locksley, which was thrust under an old settee. Being now provided with what he needed, he ascended the stairs once more, and softly entered Lilly's chamber. But in this interval the tenant of the bed was changed—Lilly, his intended victim, lay trembling beneath it—upon it, in the heavy sleep of intoxication, was stretched his sister.

With one sudden and resolute grasp, he stopped her mouth with his left hand, whilst he drew the razor across her throat with the other. He then paused a minute, and stooped over the bed, to listen if she breathed; but he heard only the trickling of her life's blood; so he quitted the chamber and the house, well satisfied with his work; and immediately started on his way back to the country.

CHAPTER VIII

AN UNEXPECTED VISITOR AT COMBE MARTIN

Philip did not very often go to the village, except on Sundays, when he went there to church. It was on one of these occasions, that chancing to cast his eyes up to the gallery whilst the organist was playing the voluntary, he almost lost his breath with amazement, at seeing a head that he thought certainly belonged to May Elliott. The head happened to be turned in another direction at the moment; but for all that, the resemblance was so striking, and the bonnet and shawl so similar to the last new ones he had seen her wearing in London, that his heart beat high, till he reflected on the improbability of her making her appearance there. Added to which, the lady that had attracted his attention was sitting in a pew belonging to Sir Lawrence Longford, into which strangers of condition were usually shown; so it could not be May; it was only an accidental resemblance in dress and *tournure*. But still, although he rapidly arrived at this conclusion, he could not help watching for the turning of the head towards him—he longed to see the face that might resemble hers, too—and presently the head did turn, and the eyes were directed instantly to the corner where Philip sat, from which, indeed, they had only been temporarily diverted—and the face was the face of May Elliott!

Poor Philip! we need not say how his heart felt as if it were in his throat, and how the blood rushed to his cheeks, nor on what deaf ears, as far as he was concerned, the remainder of the service fell.

As for May, she stooped forwards, holding her pocket-handkerchief before her face, and he saw that she was laughing at the amazement his countenance expressed. She presently, however, collected herself into an air of mock gravity and composure, whilst he awaited the end of the service with restless anxiety. At length it terminated, and the rude voices of the village choir swelled on the ear, whilst the congregation slowly emerged into the open air, and then Philip went round to the door out of which May would necessarily pass, and awaited her at the foot of the stairs; and by and by, down she came, amongst the aristocracy of the neighbourhood, holding her head very high, and looking very demure. He allowed the great people to pass, and then he made an effort to join her, but she walked on with her head up in the air, affecting not to see him.

"It is her modesty," thought Philip. No, it was her pride. The inexperienced pew-woman, judging her by her silk bonnet and lace veil, and the rest of her fashionable attire, had called her *my lady*, and put her into the pew "with the gentlefolks," and she could not bear to undeceive the woman by joining Philip; and, indeed, could scarcely bear to be undeceived herself. So she walked on, he following her, till they found themselves alone.

"May!" he said, at length, when he was permitted to address her; "why, May! how can I believe my eyes?"

"Well, what is there so surprising?" she asked, dryly.

"Surprising! Can you wonder I'm surprised?" said he; "I am perfectly astonished! When did you come?"

"Last Wednesday," she replied.

"What! you have been here ever since Wednesday!" he exclaimed, "and never let me know!"

"Well, it's time enough isn't it?" answered May, pertly.

"And where are you living?" asked Philip, quite bewildered.

"I've got a house in the village," answered May; "but it's a poor, shabby place; and I shall look for a better."

There was something about the tone of this conversation that was perfectly astounding to Philip. May was so cold, her answers were so short and dry, just in so many words telling him what he asked, and no more; whilst she walked along, scarcely looking at him, that he could not conceive what it all meant; for if it were not for his sake she had come to Combe, what in the world could have brought her there at all. But the cause of her strange demeanour was one that poor Philip's mind, for an honest mind it was, in spite of his past errors, would never have guessed without assistance—the pew-woman had done it all. The "gentlefolks" and the "my lady," and the contrast betwixt a very elegant young man, a visitor at the Hall, who in the most graceful manner and with the whitest of hands, had opened the pew-door for her and picked up her pocket-handkerchief, and poor Philip, as he stood at the bottom of the stairs, waiting for her, was too much for her nerves. She was quite terrified lest he should betray her by addressing her familiarly in the presence of this exquisite person; and she had not yet forgiven him the fright. In short, although it was for Philip's sake she had resigned an excellent situation, and abandoned London, it most perversely happened, that at this precise moment she did not love him at all.

As Philip did not know what to say next, and as May did not seem inclined to say any thing, they walked on side by side, like two people that had quarrelled; he with his eyes on the ground, half affronted, and pondering what it could all mean; she looking straight before her, with a certain expression of injury and defiance on her countenance; which was produced by her consciousness that she was behaving extremely ill, and her determination, for the present, not to behave any better.

For the purpose of avoiding the eyes of the curious, she had led the way from the village instead of towards it, and as they had now walked some distance and nothing very agreeable seemed likely to result from this sort of conversation, she proposed turning back, and Philip acceding, they retraced their steps; he, now thoroughly offended, as well as considerably perplexed. So, as he was too angry to speak, and she was too proud, they walked back in silence for some distance, till they drew near the village, and then May suddenly burst out laughing.

"What a fool you are, Philip!" she said. "You take every thing so seriously! You're offended now, I really believe."

"I think I've no great reason to be pleased," replied Philip; speaking as dryly as she had done.

"Pooh!" said she, "you never *can* take a joke. I was only doing it to try you. Come, be a good boy, and tell me if it was not very good of me to come all the way to Combe to see you?"

But it was not immediately that she could restore her lover's temper and self-complacence, which she had very much ruffled and disturbed. To come into the country at all, was a very imprudent step; but to come there to quarrel with him and make him uncomfortable, was cruel and inexcusable. May, however, was now bent on appeasing him. It was a distressing fact, that she did not, just then, love him half so much as she had done when she left London, or, indeed, as she had done three hours and a half previously, but still she could not afford to lose him whom she had come so far to seek; and she was painfully aware, that probably, by the following Sunday, the pew-woman would not call her *my lady*, nor mistake her for a person of quality. So she tried to smooth poor Philip's ruffled feathers; and when they reached a neat cottage at the entrance of the village, she invited him in, and now she condescended to explain her plans to him.

"It's more than you deserve," she said, "but after racking my brains to think what I could do, it struck me that I might come here and set up a straw bonnet shop; so I've brought a few with me, and as I can turn and clean them, and know all about the business, I've taken this house, and to-morrow you'll see my name on a board outside—'Miss Elliott, straw bonnet-maker. N. B. Bonnets cleaned and turned.' What do you think of that?"

Philip did not know exactly what he thought of it. If she had received him warmly and affectionately, it is highly probable that he would have been so much flattered as to have thought very well of it; as it was, he did not feel so delighted as he ought to have been at such a decided proof of regard; and he accordingly suggested difficulties, and hinted his apprehensions that she might not make a living in so small and insignificant a village as Combe. This want of gratitude and enthusiasm on his part, now displeased her; and they were very near quarrelling again; but at length, seeing she had got so far wrong with him, that to get right it was necessary to touch his feelings, she had recourse to tears and confession. She declared, that the manner in which she had received him, was all a joke; but owned that she had carried it too far, never supposing he would be offended; but if he was not glad to see her, he had only to say so, and she could return to London again; and although she *had* given up Mrs. Knox's situation, and so ir-retrievably offended that lady, she should not be at a loss, as Harvey and Graham wanted a person for the straw bonnet department; and had made application to her, through Mr. Ferdinand Pycroft; to whom she could write on the subject that very evening.

This finale, which was in fact an *impromptu*, was a *coup de maitresse*.[136] At the hated names of Harvey and Graham, which instantly suggested to his imagination the dreaded Mr. Ferdinand, invested with all his dangerous fascinations, he felt his blood stirred, and by the time she had finished her speech, she had accomplished her end. Philip was jealous again, and from being jealous he grew to be repent-ant and loving, and May was once more in the ascendant and the queen of his destiny. So they passed the remainder of the day together; but certain it was, that May's feelings towards her lover were not so lively as they should have been. There are ebbs and flows in all passions, and these tidal variations frequently depend on

136 Master stroke, or here, mistress stroke.

very subtle causes. In the present instance, May could not herself perhaps, have told the cause of the chill that was over her. One thing was that the *grand coup de théatre*,[137] the first meeting, and Philip's surprise had gone flatly off, owing to the unfortunate interlude of the pew-woman and the *beau cavalier*.[138] Another depressing influence arose from the dulness of a village Sunday. Since she arrived, she had been too busy preparing for her little business, and anticipating the meeting with Philip, to feel weary; but now she missed the walk in the park and the thronged streets, especially as she did not choose to go to afternoon service with her lover. She could not consent to so soon undeceiving the pew-woman, or encountering the *beau cavalier* when arm-in-arm with a rustic, so that altogether this first day of rural bliss was but an indifferent specimen, and certainly not worth coming so far to fetch.

One piece of intelligence that Philip gave her did, however, both astonish and interest her, namely, that Lilly had again escaped the toils spread by her enemies; whilst he was equally surprised to find that she had wholly lost sight of her former companion. This circumstance of Lilly's absence, was also, perhaps, not without its effect, since it left her with nobody to be jealous of, and somewhat diminished the necessity she had imagined for her continued proximity and close supervision of his proceedings.

There are certain kinds of love to which a species of jealousy is absolutely necessary to give them a relish; and May's seemed to be of that quality.

CHAPTER IX

HOW MAY PLAYS AWAY HER TREASURE

Nothing could have been more injudicious than the tone May's pride and caprice had given to the first meeting with her lover. She had certainly honoured him with a considerable proof of attachment in leaving London; but to commence their new career with a quarrel, was tarnishing the glory and grace of the sacrifice. He had been extremely hurt by her behaviour; the more so, as he had a slight suspicion that the elegant stranger, whose horse and groom were waiting at the church-door, had something to do with it. It is true, that betwixt her tears and the judicious use of Mr. Ferdinand Pycroft's detested name, she had brought him round to a more satisfactory state; but, nevertheless, she had chilled that enthusiastic gratitude and devotion which her heroic exploit might otherwise have secured for her; and which, had their bright pure flames been allowed to burn unchecked, might have induced him to make a corresponding sacrifice. Even on

137 A surprising, dramatic event.
138 Handsome cavalier or man.

the ensuing Sunday, her vanity again got the better of her love; and she preferred passing for a lady of quality, and sitting in the well-lined pew in the gallery, to which the still deluded pew-woman conducted her, to accompanying Philip to his seat below. She made the best she could of it now, certainly, by confessing, frankly, that it pleased her to be taken for a fine lady; but this candour would probably have been more successful if she had practised it earlier. It could not now altogether efface the meanness with which she had disowned him on the first occasion. It was perhaps the unpleasant effect that this proceeding of hers had had on his mind, which enabled him to persevere, contrary to her wishes, in a plan he had formed for bringing his mother from London. Ever since she knew where he was, the old lady had been eager to return; and he had been looking out for some small place, consistent with her very narrow means, which she might inhabit till he became master of the mill.

"If your mother comes, I go," said May.

"I can't disappoint my mother," returned Philip; "she won't interfere with you. Besides, if you can't live in the same village with her, how will you live under the same roof?"

May might have answered that she never intended to live under the same roof; however, she had the prudence not to do so.

"That will be different," she said; "but now, you'll see, she'll take a dislike to me, and you'll repent it; mark my words if you don't. I know very well what sort of a person she is—Lilly told me."

"I don't think Lilly ever said anything against my mother."

"Oh, Lilly! no. Your mother's ways might do very well for Lilly, and Lilly's for her. Lilly could never say 'Bo!' to a goose, you know. But I'm very different. I have never been used to those stiff, stuck-up people; and I don't know how to behave to them. Besides, I'm sure London's a much better place for your mother."

"But, May," said Philip, "you didn't like staying in London after I had left it; and isn't it very natural my mother should feel the same. Besides, May, if you really love me, I should think you must respect my mother."

"Yes, at a distance," answered May; "but I'm sure if we come together we shall quarrel; and I think after I've given you such a proof of regard, you've no right to do any thing I don't like."

"I don't wish to do any thing you don't like, May," answered Philip; "but I can't disappoint my mother. I've made her very unhappy already, and she's not in good health, and says London does not agree with her."

"Very well," answered May, "then you may take my cottage for her, if you like; for I shall be off, you may depend upon it."

"I've taken a place for her already," said Philip. "It's a very poor one; but Sir

Lawrence says I may have it for nothing; and Westall, the wright, says he'll repair it, and make it habitable for her, without any charge, because it was my father that lent him money to set up in business."

"And where is it?" asked May.

"On the common, between the village and the mill. It's only a hut with two rooms; but it's dry, and there was furniture enough saved from the fire to fit it up."

This arrangement did not please May at all; she did not like the prospect of a divided influence; and she had seen very clearly, ever since she came from London, that Philip was an altered man. He loved her still; but he loved her more wisely—if it could be called wise to love her at all—in opening his eyes to his own faults he had become aware of hers too; and terrified at the degree, and the kind of influence she had exercised over him—though he blamed himself for it and not her—he was firm now in retaining his own will and self-respect, and in not yielding to her wishes against his judgment; and although he at first found considerable difficulty in resistance, it was a difficulty that diminished with every exertion of his resolution. In short, May and he changed places, in a great degree; and he took the ascendancy which his qualities entitled him to, and which he ought to have had from the beginning; but which his youth and inexperience, and her fascinations, had prevented his assuming.

The effect of this conduct on his part, as regarded May, was, that it disarmed her of her weapons. Her caprices, and her airs, and her hysterics, were of no use, their edges were blunted. The hysterics lasted longer than any thing else; for, like most men that are endued with a manly soul, Philip was soft-hearted to women, and exceedingly moved by their tears; but although, when he saw her in these convulsions he was very much distressed, and did his utmost to console her by tenderness, and convince her by argument, she by no means always gained her point—never, indeed, if he thought the matter one of importance. But still, though she became sensible of his power, and although these calm exhibitions of it enchained her fancy more and more, yet she had not the sense to see that her only chance of retaining his heart, was not to struggle for the ascendancy, but to yield a graceful and reasonable—we will not say obedience—but compliance.

So Philip worked on at the cottage, and with the assistance of the wright, made it tolerably comfortable; and when he thought it sufficiently aired, a precaution which he secured by lighting a fire, and sleeping there himself nightly, he sent for his mother, who, in spite of his great errors, was languishing to see him; errors which, to one who knew little of such syrens as May, or of the temptations of London to a youth plunged suddenly into them, had appeared to argue a more entire perversion than had really existed. But when she saw the preparations made for her, and how tenderly, in spite of his humble means, he had cared for her comfort, and when he fell upon her neck and asked her forgiveness—and then when, with a steady voice and earnest countenance, he told her of his good resolutions for the future, adding, "And I will keep them, mother, you may trust me now"—her soul rejoiced in him again, and the tears she shed were tears of sorrow no more.

May's threat of departure was not fulfilled; indeed, it was impracticable, for more reasons than one. In the first place, in spite of all her follies and faults, she was still in love with Philip; and although, when she fancied he was so much her slave, that she might venture to indulge her caprices, and do as she pleased with him, she frequently behaved as if she had no regard for him at all, yet the idea of losing him, or any coldness on his part, revived her passion in its full force; and actually leaving him, was a project she had never seriously entertained. In the next place, she had quitted London on the receipt of her quarter's salary, leaving her debts behind her, and to have appeared there so soon might have been inconvenient; but without this reason she could not have left him, unless there had been a railway station at Combe, and she had started in a fast train, within five minutes after a quarrel.

The Littenhaus family had now carried on their illicit trade for some years, without discovery or suspicion. They had not grown rich upon it; the frequent losses and the uncertain profits precluded that. Indeed, their means had multiplied very little; still they clung to it; it was the way of life they had been brought up to, and there was a fascination about it, like drinking or gambling, that prevented even Ambrose from relinquishing its pursuit, though he did sometimes wish his lines had fallen in other places. As for Luke, he was fit for nothing better; danger and crime were his proper elements.

But although no suspicion had attached to any parties in particular, at least to none connected with the Littenhaus gang, the height to which smuggling was carried had occasioned an increased degree of vigilance on the part of the government. A preventive station[139] was formed at Long Point, and several active men added to the force. With these men Philip became acquainted. Spirited fellows, that had seen something of life and adventure, their conversation and stories amused him much more than the gossip of the village population, who had grown up on the soil where they were born, and could talk of little but hoeing and dibbling, and the last Sunday's sermon. There was one amongst them, called Wybrow, who was a particularly fine young man, handsome in person and enterprising in character; agreeable, too, and good-tempered, provided his potations did not exceed small ale, but hot and quarrelsome in his cups. Aware of this failing, however, he rarely

---

139 A government centre and government officials charged with preventing smuggling and enforcing the payment of customs and excise revenue.

exposed himself to the danger; and Philip, who was sobriety itself, and who took a great liking to him, was at once his friend and his monitor, as well as the ready companion of his recreations. It was not to be supposed that so brilliant an apparition as May Elliott could fail to make a considerable sensation in the village of Combe. When she alighted at the "Red Lion," she was supposed to be a visitor on her way to the Hall; and Lacy had asked her if she did not want a post-chaise, or if the carriage would fetch her. When she took the cottage, it was concluded she was some fine lady, whom sorrow, or adversity, or a romantic taste, had driven into retirement. It was not till she had caused her name and calling to be inscribed over the door, that they brought down their excited imaginations to the plain fact, that this elegant vision made and cleaned straw bonnets. Even at the Hall, her advent was not unnoticed. First, Lady Longford's maid employed her to turn a bonnet for her, and next Lady L. herself bought a Dunstable,[140] which May trimmed so neatly and simply—for she had an admirable taste in such matters—that she was pronounced quite a treasure, and might possibly have obtained permission to add to her inscription, "Purveyor of bonnets to her ladyship." Altogether, she did not want custom; her neat cottage, agreeable manners, pretty person, and tasteful dressing, brought her both profit and patronage; and although the pew-woman left off calling her *my lady*, and putting her into the pew with the *gentlefolks,* she yet enjoyed deference and admiration enough to sustain her spirits and keep her in tolerable good humour.

Of course, this belle of the village was not unknown to the preventive men; and whilst they drank her health at their mess, they called Philip a lucky fellow. Wybrow, especially, admired her, and they sometimes accused him of wishing to supersede his friend; an imputation which he disowned, but which he did not altogether dislike. The truth was, that he was very much *épris*[141] with May; and although he had no deliberate intention of wronging Philip, he had loose notions on such subjects, and was moreover, from his nature, thoughtless of consequences; embarking in enterprises, whether of love or war, without reflecting much about what was to be their issue. Then May, who was equally thoughtless, could not help giving him some encouragement. She had no serious intentions of wronging Philip, more than Wybrow had; but it would have been contrary to her nature to have repressed the exhibition of the young sailor's admiration, and besides, she was of that class of women who consider a slight show of rivalry necessary to the maintenance of their influence. Mr. Ferdinand Pycroft was now *hors de combat*,[142] and this gallant young preventive man was an excellent succedaneum.[143]

---

140 A type of hat for older ladies.
141 Infatuated by or in love with.
142 Out of the action.
143 Substitute.

There was, however, an openness about Wybrow's character and proceedings that disarmed Philip's suspicions, and baffled his penetration, added to which, he had become so sensible of his boyish irritability about the coxcomb "in the feather and flower department at Harvey's and Graham's," that he had been admonishing himself severely against yielding to such follies for the future. He discerned, too, something of May's disposition to make him the toy of her humours; and resolved as he was, to act a manly part and redeem the past, he fortified himself to the utmost against idle doubts and jealousies. Had she not given him the most irrefragable proof of attachment by following him, and thereby showing that she cared nothing for the man she had almost driven him mad about? That Wybrow should admire her, was natural; that she liked admiration was her weakness; and his own part was to smile at both. Besides, if she really did not love him exclusively the sooner he knew it the better—much better before marriage than after. Thus argued Philip, under the influence of his reason and his firm resolve to be a man, and to act through life the part of one.

CHAPTER X

THE CONFESSION OF HANS PEFFER

It was a considerable time now since Mr. Cropley had been able to get, what he called *a new windmill*, for the general, and consequently the costs at the end of the year were not satisfactory. The starting a supposititious Miss Adams had not answered his expectations; the general had been too rash and May too restive. He found it a dangerous game, and prudently relinquished it before it had brought him into trouble. But something must be done; the cause must not be allowed to sleep; what should it be? It was whilst he was meditating on this curious question, that he received a summons to attend the general on particular business.

"Well, sir," said the great man, when Cropley was shown into the library. "Have you discovered any traces of my niece yet—Miss Isabel Adams?"

"No, sir," replied Cropley, who had, in fact, never sought for her, nor ever supposed that the general seriously intended him to waste his time in so ineffectual a pursuit; "I am sorry to say my inquiries have been quite unsuccessful."

"And how stands the suit?" inquired the general.

"They are still threatening to procure an order from his honour, the Vice Chancellor, for the production of the young lady in court, since we deny her being deceased; it was on that account, you recollect, I thought, last year, it might have been desirable to get some body to stand in the young lady's shoes; it could have been of no ultimate benefit; but it might have raised up difficulties and investigations, that your adversary could not have afforded to meet."

"I'll tell you what, sir," said the general, contemptuously, "you're like that man on the Manningtree Farm, that has been half ruining himself, digging for water whilst there was a fine spring close to his own door,—if he had only sought it in the right place—only, to be sure, the difference is, that he has been spending his own money, and you've been spending mine."

"You haven't really heard any thing to lead you to believe Miss Adams was not lost with the *Hastings*, sir: have you?"

"Yes, sir, I have heard something to lead me to believe Miss Adams was not lost with the *Hastings*," replied the general; who had indulged his vile humours till they boiled over on every unfortunate person that came within their scope, like Vesusius,[144] in an eruption.

"God bless me! That's very extraordinary!" exclaimed Mr. Cropley, unfeignedly surprised; and unfeignedly vexed, too, that the discovery, if it were to be made, should not have been made by himself. "I could never have thought it."

"No, sir, you would never have thought it; you were too much engaged in thinking how you could run up your bill of costs against Christmas, to think of doing my business."

"I'm sure, sir, I made every inquiry; but the thing seemed so entirely hopeless—but are you sure there is no mistake? No imposture in the case?"

"Read that," said the general, putting into his hand a very dirty scrap of paper, "and see what you can make of it."

Betwixt dirt, pale ink, bad writing, and worse spelling, it was not very easy to decipher the document; and whilst the general is walking up and down the room, and Cropley, with, a puzzled and mortified expression of face, is sitting in one corner of it, holding the paper extended before his eyes, and whilst trying to extract its meaning, at the same time racking his brains to determine how it would be most advantageous to himself to act in this emergency—whether to give in to the imposition—for such he had, no doubt it was—or vindicate his own fidelity and perspicacity by unmasking it—we will take the opportunity of narrating the history of this scrap of soiled paper to the reader.

It will be remembered, that amongst the early visitors to the Black Huntsman, was a man called Hans Peffer. Hans was a German by birth, and had once been a respectable man in a decent line of business, as a seller of tobacco in all its various forms, in Exeter. He had a wife whom he dearly loved—a beautiful young Englishwoman—and five children, two girls and three boys, on whom he doted. It might have been hoped, that such tender domestic relations would have been sufficient to keep Hans from risking the welfare of these beloved ones, by any rash, much less illegal, speculations; but, unfortunately, his very best feelings led

---

144 A volcano in Italy.

him into error. He was ambitious for his children, and wanted to do better for them than the limited profits of his little trade afforded. In an evil hour, therefore, he resolved to make a bold stroke for a fortune. He pulled down part of his house, threw out a handsome shop-front, laid in a stock of curious goods in his line, including sundry showy meerschaums and hookahs,[145] called his place an emporium, and advertised largely. But the unimpressible citizens of Exeter could not be brought to develop a true German relish for Hans Peffer's wares. They used no more snuff or tobacco than they had done before—at least, with the exception of a few foolish young men, who were ensnared by the strange sinuosities and the gold tassels of the hookahs and meerschaums. Hans got into difficulties, and as such traders were the natural allies of the smugglers, and *vice versa*, the gang of which old Jacob Littenhaus was one of the chief leaders, found him out, and, although unwillingly enough at first, he ultimately entered into dealings with them. But this expedient was a straw to a drowning man, and could not save him; he became a bankrupt—lost his character; and from one descending grade to another, fell at last to be a mere receiver and agent of these illicit traffickers. Still, in the midst of his depravation, his love for his wife and children continued undiminished, and he would risk any adventure, or undergo any privations himself, to procure them comforts. He was no sailor, but as he could speak German and Dutch, he was often taken to sea with them, because he was of use on the other side of the water; and it thus happened that Hans Peffer was in the cutter the morning that the smugglers boarded the wreck of the *Hastings;* but it had been a fearful night, the wind was scarcely lulled, and the sea was still flinging up its wild waves to the sky, and Hans, being a landsman, did not like the idea of approaching the sinking ship in the little cock boat,[146] that was tossing madly about on the raging waters below, and into which the smugglers were eagerly leaping. So he remained on board the vessel, but, unfortunately, for his own peace of mind, near enough to witness all that took place on the wreck. He saw the murder, and beheld, with a breathless interest, the debate about the child, the purport of which he easily guessed—especially, when he saw it terminated by old Jacob snatching her up in his arms, and leaping into the boat with her. It was the first and the last blood poor Hans had ever seen spilled, and it made an indelible impression on his mind. His humanity and his conscience took the alarm, when, by this instance, he perceived the crimes and barbarities to which he might be made a party, by the desperate band with whom he had allied himself, and from which he could not get disentangled without subjecting his wife and children to utter destitution. So he hung on to them, but timid, suspicious, and miserable; he

---

145 Pipes for smoking.
146 Small rowing boat.

shrank from joining their expeditions, and soon lost their confidence. Misfortune pursued him, too, in his domestic relations; his wife, and then his children died one after the other, two of the latter under very painful circumstances; and as he wept over the graves of these dear departed ones, Hans believed that they had died for his sins; and setting aside the poor father's theological view of the case, he was, probably, not far wrong; for, under happier external circumstances, these young vines, and their parent stem, might have lived and flourished. Reckless and hopeless now, Hans became indifferent to his own fate here, or hereafter. He sank lower and lower; sought to drown his cares in strong potations, and, betwixt that practice and much nightly exposure to cold and wet, he was seized with an illness that brought him into the Exeter infirmary, where he did not die, but so far recovered as to be dismissed and transferred to the poor house; and here, having lingered in weak health for some months, he expired after a few hours' suffering. It was almost in his last moments, when remorse and terror had full possession of him, that he communicated to a fellow pauper, named Abrahams, to whom the charge of watching him had been committed, some details of the boarding of the *Hastings* and the murder of the sole survivor found on the wreck, with the exception of a child, whose life had been spared, requesting him to give information of the circumstance to some person in authority. Intending to fulfil the injunction, the trustee of this important secret, as soon as he had an opportunity, noted down the particulars he had received, to the best of his power, but with the omission of dates, names, and localities, which had escaped his memory; so that when he presented himself before a magistrate with the intimation that he had something important to communicate, it was found impossible to make any use of the information. The man was dismissed, and no further attention paid to the subject.

But a bit of paper often survives through as many adventures and vicissitudes as might make a three volume novel; and the one on which the substance of Hans Peffer's confession had been noted down, was not destined to perish without fulfilling its mission; at least in some degree. Finding it ineffective to the purpose designed, and therefore not likely to bring him the handsome reward which he had expected, Abrahams set no further value on his manuscript, and it reposed in his pocket, unthought of, till he wanted a bit of paper to wrap some tobacco in—and this office it fulfilled for some time—till one day he tore off half of the sheet for Abel White, whose stock of that unfragrant consolation being exhausted, had begged him to accommodate him with a little for present use.

As people in poor houses have nothing to spare, Abel did not fling away the paper when its contents were exhausted, but smoothing and folding it, he kept it in his pocket till fortune might bring him a fresh supply of tobacco or snuff—and it so happened that one day, when his daughter was paying him a visit, he drew it out with his pocket-handkerchief. Martha picked it up, and seeing some writing on it, she spread out the paper on her lap, to read what it was about—and as her eye ran listlessly over the lines, it was suddenly arrested by the following words:

"Went away, and took child with 'em, cald her dawson, or lawson, can't remember wich—pertended she war ther cosin—and one on 'em marred her, or wanted to—supose to be sumbody of consekence cumd from Indy ship lost on—"

"Listen to this, father," said Martha.

"Where did you get that?" asked Abel, when she had read it; "what does it mean?"

"I don't know," replied Martha, "it's on the paper you just dropped. Where did *you* get it?"

"I got that from Abrahams," returned Abel, after feeling it to ascertain what it was. "Read it again."

"I should like to ask Abrahams about it," said Abel, when he heard the paragraph a second time; "when I see him, I'll speak to him about it;" for, like most blind men, Abel always talked of seeing.

"It made me think of Lilly," said Martha.

"I often think of her, poor thing!" said Abel, "and wonder what could have happened to her that night—some mischief, I'm afraid."

"Unless she really had set the room on fire, and then run away," said Martha.

"Not she," said Abel; "no, I'm afraid it was her money that got her into some trouble; and I've always thought that the girl we heard had been found in the river next day was she. I wish you had gone to look at the body."

"I was just too late," answered Martha, "they had just buried her."

"I have often thought there was something odd about those cousins of hers, from different things she told me," said Abel.

"Do you remember their name?" asked Martha.

"It was a foreign name," said Abel, "but I should know it if I heard it."

All that Abrahams knew, or could recollect respecting the contents of the paper, he willingly communicated to Abel, adding however, that from the imperfect information no use could be made of it. But by judicious interrogation, Abel extracted a sufficient portion of the dying sinner's confession to awaken in his own mind considerable interest. Abrahams remembered that it was to the effect that a child had been taken off the wreck of a ship supposed to be from India; that a gentleman had been murdered and robbed of jewels and money; that the pirates had removed and taken the child with them to a distant part of the coast—and on being asked if the name of Luke had been mentioned, he remembered that it had.

Now Abel had frequently heard Lilly allude to a long journey she had made with her cousins; and to some faint recollections she had of once being in a large ship; then the name of *Luke* and the marriage, were remarkable coincidences; so that on the whole he thought the matter sufficiently important to be communicated to somebody better able to weigh its significance than they were, and they naturally fixed on Mr. Ross, from the circumstances of Lilly's being known to him, and because he was the only professional person Martha had access to.

But poor Lilly's unfortunate *escapade,* and subsequent disappearance, had not prepossessed the family in her favour. Mrs. Janet had comfortably settled herself into the very worst opinion of her; and Mrs. Ross had never quite forgiven her the danger to which she had exposed her children. Mr. Ross himself knew nothing about her, but it was very natural that he should adopt the opinion of those that he imagined did; so that altogether he was by no means disposed to believe that his late under nursery-maid was a princess in disguise, or the heroine of a romantic tale of shipwreck and murder. Besides, Hans Peffer was dead, and could give no further information on the subject; probably Lilly was dead, too, as the girl found in the river had been buried unowned; and finally, so obscure an indication as *Dawson* or *Lawson,* amounted to nothing at all. Thus opined Mr. Ross; and there, to Abel's extreme disappointment, the matter ended for some time.

It was some months after this that Mr. Ross, being on his way to London, made arrangements for passing a night at the house of his former clerk, Mr. Treadgold, for the purpose of discussing some matters in which they were mutually concerned. "And how do you get on with my old client, the General?" asked Mr. Ross, as they sat after dinner with their bottle of claret before them.

"As well as can be expected," said Mr. Treadgold, with a laugh—"you know the general's wife is now the general."

"And some people say, dairy-maid though she was, that she is much more fit to be so than he," answered Mr. Ross.

"So she is," returned the other, "her temper is not of the best, certainly, but she has a great deal more principle than he has, and she has sense enough to see through him, and to despise him accordingly."

"And how goes on the grand suit?" inquired Mr. Ross laughing.

"Oh! I don't know," returned Mr. Treadgold, "I've nothing to do with that—I washed my hands of it long ago. It's a rascally business, I fancy."

"But does he go on with it?" asked Mr. Ross.

"Oh! yes, I believe so. Cropley conducts the cause, so you may judge what sort of a concern it is."

"But what is their plea? what do they allege against the will? I thought the verdict must have settled that for ever."

"So it did," returned Mr. Treadgold, "Colonel Adams left India in the full persuasion that he was about to take possession of the fortune; but he found himself out of the frying-pan into the fire."

"How so?" inquired Mr. Ross.

"Why, they raised up another question respecting the decease of the heiress—the child that was lost with the *Hastings*."

"But how can they maintain the suit on that ground? I thought it was satisfactorily proved that every body on board perished, crew and passengers."

"So it was always understood," returned Mr. Treadgold; "but a suit may be maintained to the day of judgment, when one party has no principle and the other no money. Betwixt folly and malignity, the General's half mad; and Cropley thinks of nothing but his own pocket; any scheme's good enough for him that will fill that. It isn't long since it was reported that they were actually bringing up and educating some girl, that they meant to produce as the heiress; but the scheme blew up, somehow or other."

"I wonder," said Mr. Ross, after a little reflection, "whether a thing that was brought before me lately, was any part of that scheme."

"I shouldn't wonder; for I believe there certainly was something of the sort in agitation."

"The thing I allude to was a bit of paper, purporting to be the dying confession of a pirate. It was to the effect that a child had been taken from the wreck of an India ship, and brought up as the relation of some of the gang, who had robbed and murdered the survivors or survivor, I forget which, that had escaped drowning."

"It looks very like it," observed Mr. Treadgold.

"It was brought to me," continued Mr. Ross, "by the daughter of one of the paupers in the poor-house, because I had had a girl in my service called Dawson, which was the name mentioned in the paper."

"The name of the girl?"

"The name the pirates were supposed to have given her."

"But what connexion could they make out betwixt your servant and the child found on the wreck?"

"Why, it seems that the people who recommended her to us, had met with her under some peculiar circumstances; and they fancied that there were some coincidences betwixt her history and the events alluded to in the pauper's confession. But, however, be that as it may, it's now, I fancy, of very little consequence; for Lilly Dawson, the girl who lived with us, turned out but so-so; she ran away, and, I suspect, threw herself into the river."

"Was her name *Lilly?*" inquired Mr. Treadgold.

"It was," returned Mr. Ross.

"That's odd, too," said the other; "for I perfectly well remember seeing a letter from Mrs. Adams, which arrived here before the loss of the ship was known in India, in which she called the child *Lilly.*"

"That has been part of the plot," rejoined Mr. Ross; "depend on it, Cropley knew that as well as you."

"Very true," replied Mr. Treadgold, who had been momentarily excited by the coincidence of the name: "no doubt he did; and it has been a deeper laid scheme than I was aware of."

And here would have ended all interest and inquiry about Lilly Dawson, had it not happened that our old friend Tom Watts, who, in the interim, had returned to the service of Mr. Treadgold, chanced to be putting some coals on the dining-room fire, at that very critical period of the conversation, when the disappearance and probable drowning of Lilly Dawson was mentioned by Mr. Ross.

Tom disposed the coals with careful exactness, and swept up the ashes with a degree of neatness quite exemplary, whilst he opened his ears to this discourse; hesitating, the while, whether to speak or not: but recollecting, that though in the room, he had no business to hear or understand the conversation of his betters, he forbore, and departed in silence. It was not in human nature, however, to keep such a secret; so he relieved himself by narrating below, how the gentlemen upstairs were talking of a girl called Lilly Dawson, whom he knew; and how, whilst they were supposing her drowned, she was working in London, at Mrs. Knox's; and how, moreover, that very girl had, on one of Mrs. Treadgold's former journeys, been her fellow-traveller to London.

We need not say that, in due course of time, this story reached the destination Tom intended it for; the housemaid told Mrs. Treadgold, whilst she was fastening her dress; and Mrs. Treadgold told her husband; but the latter was now so possessed with the idea of Cropley's scheme, and of this being a part of it, that he paid little attention to the information, till a slight corroborating circumstance directed his mind again to the subject. A suit, in which he was employed to obtain evidence respecting the sale of some property in Cornwall, at a former period, obliged him to refer to the newspapers of that date; and whilst looking over one, called "The Falmouth News-letter," his eye was attracted by a short paragraph to the following effect:

"It is reported that some fishermen who boarded the wreck of the *Hastings*, before she went to pieces, observed traces of bloodshed on the planks. This rumour has given rise to a suspicion that this unfortunate vessel may have been attacked by an enemy, before she entered the Channel."

Here was certainly a sort of corroboration of one part of the confession; namely, that the ship had been boarded by pirates, and a murder committed; and Mr. Treadgold thought it worth while to endeavour to obtain the paper Mr. Ross

had mentioned; which by the aid of the latter gentleman was soon in his possession; for Abel White, not being by any means fully satisfied that it did not refer
in someway to Lilly, in whom, whether dead or alive, he still felt a deep interest,
had carefully treasured it. It was this paper which, with such particulars as he had
collected, Mr. Treadgold had forwarded to the General, that the latter had now
placed before the astonished eyes of Mr. Cropley.

"A very strange, and I should say, suspicious-looking document," observed
the latter, holding the paper up to the window to examine the water-mark, by the
way of exhibiting great acuteness.

"What do you see suspicious about it?" inquired the General.

"The writing and the spelling are too bad to be natural," said Cropley.

"Nothing's too bad to be natural, sir," returned the General. "The worse any
thing is, the more natural it is," which favourite axiom of the General's embodied
his real opinion in regard to human nature, whilst it now conveniently served as
a sarcasm against Mr. Cropley.

"I should be very glad to believe that paper authentic, I am sure, sir," returned
the lawyer; "but what evidence is it? What's the use of it?"

"The use of it, sir, is to let us know that my niece was not lost with the ship—
that she survived the wreck; and that if we seek her, perhaps we may find her;"
and the General then proceeded to inform Mr. Cropley, though in the most ungracious manner, and mingling every sentence with bitterness and reproof, that a
girl called Lilly Dawson, whose history seemed to be enveloped in some obscurity,
had within a few years, been living in that part of the country. "And now, sir, it
remains to trace what became of that girl. Mr. Treadgold has ascertained that she
had left the place where she first found employment, but where she went afterwards, they do not know."

"It shall be my business, sir, to inquire," answered Mr. Cropley, perceiving
that whether Lilly Dawson were a real or fictitious personage, it was the General's
pleasure for the present to believe in her existence; and, at all events, the hunting
for her, might not be an unprofitable pursuit.

He, accordingly, went to London, and easily learnt all the Watts family or
Mrs. Knox could tell; and he also visited both of May Elliott's lodgings; at the first
of which he learnt, that Lilly had departed in a hackney-coach one night, with her
friend, and had never returned; but of her subsequent movements he could discover nothing. Neither could he ascertain what had become of May herself, after
she quitted Blenheim Street; nor was it likely, since she went away in debt, that
she intended to leave any marks by which to track her steps. This circumstance
rendered him delicate in his dealings with regard to her. It was not his interest
to offend or bring her into difficulties; for she knew of more things than one,

whereby she might have repaid his injuries with interest.

He, therefore, forbore to advertise her, a measure he adopted with respect to Lilly, though unsuccessfully; because nobody in the world knew any thing about her, but the family with whom she was living; and there none saw the advertisement but herself. As we have said, it was her office to read the papers to her master; and when she did so, it was rarely that either Mrs. Adams or Frederick looked at them. The former took little interest in any part of their contents except the fashionable intelligence, or the announcement of a new novel; and Freddy was too busy with his lessons to have much time for extraneous reading.

It was thus that the only person who both read the advertisements and was able to give the information desired, was the one most deeply concerned in the matter; but terrified at the sight of what she concluded to be a scheme of Luke's to get her again in his power, she took care to despatch the papers to their further destination, immediately she had read them; thus rendering Mr. Cropley's exertions unavailing, and inducing him to suppose that the girl who had appeared under the name of Lilly Dawson, was either no longer in existence, or that she had been an impostor, connected with some project of May Elliott's; who for aught he knew might have actually been acquainted with what she said she was, namely, who the parties were for whom he had been seeking a supposititious heiress.

CHAPTER XI

SYMPTOMS OF MAY'S LOSING THE GAME

It may be conceived, that the preventive force stationed at Long Point very seriously interfered with the convenience of the Littenhaus family. Amongst the rest, Wybrow was especially obnoxious to them by his activity; and it augmented Luke's hatred of Philip not a little, that these two young men should be so much together. Indeed, it was to him an exceedingly dangerous intimacy. A very slight hint from Philip might have put Wybrow on the right track for a discovery, which they were all seeking to make, regarding some late proceedings on that coast; and had Philip been more suspicious and observing, he could not have failed to make the discovery himself. From certain accidents that had occurred, Luke hardly knew how to believe in his ignorance, and had consequently actually grown to fear him so much, that he had been trying to conciliate his good-will by civility; though, in his heart, he detested him with a treble-distilled hatred, which every month that brought nearer the period when he would have a right to claim the mill, rendered more bitter.

In the meantime, although this circumstance was not yet known to Luke,

Philip and Wybrow were not altogether the good friends they had been. May had got piqued, at finding she could not make Philip jealous so easily as formerly; and in order to vindicate her power and her charms, she set seriously to work to render him so: and, unfortunately, in spite of his good resolutions, she succeeded too well.

"May," he said to her one day, after an exhibition of levity on the part of his mistress, that had awakened in his own breast a severe struggle betwixt his judgment and his infatuation—the former whispering him to be free, for that she was not worth the pangs she was inflicting, whilst the latter rendered him the chained victim of her tyrannous folly—"May," he said, "you'll be sorry for this some day; yet I don't know why I should say so—if you loved me enough to be sorry, you wouldn't do it."

"Do what?" asked May.

"Give the encouragement you do to Wybrow."

"I don't give him any particular encouragement," she answered. "I am not obliged to be rude to a man, because he admires me, am I?"

"Admires you, May? He thinks you a very pretty woman, I dare say; so, doubtless does that ragged boy that brought the firewood here just now; but is that any reason you should encourage him to tell you so?"

"But you don't compare Harry Wybrow to that wretch, do you?" said May. "Let me tell you, Harry's a very nice young man."

"I admit it," answered Philip; "but let me tell *you,* May, that to a woman who really and truly loves *one* man, the admiration of others, nice or otherwise, is of very little value, and certainly not worth angling for."

"I don't angle for it," she replied, sharply; "there's no occasion for that."

"You do all you can to excite, instead of repressing it," returned Philip. "I believe it's more thoughtlessness than mischief on the part of Wybrow," he added, "and therefore I don't want to quarrel outright with him, if I can help it; but—"

"Well, but what?" asked May. "You're going to threaten to swallow him up alive, I suppose?"

"Oh no, I'm not going to threaten any thing," said Philip. "If your own heart does not warn you, my threats would be of little use."

"Warn me of what, I should like to know?" answered May. "I don't see any thing so fierce about you, for my part, that I need be frightened at; nor Wybrow either, for that matter."

"Very well, May," returned Philip, turning very pale, "you must do as you please—may you never have cause to repent it!"

This is but a sample of the sort of scenes that passed between the lovers weekly, sometimes daily, and it would be doing Philip great injustice to say that they were without their effect. His reason was growing gradually stronger, and his infatuation weaker. He saw how base, how mean, how selfish a thing it was thus to indulge her vanity at his expense; and yet he pitied her too, for he did not believe she cared for Wybrow, and it was often less jealousy, than anger at this paltering with the truth—this mingling of a profane mask with so holy a thing as love—that irritated and vexed him; whilst, with respect to Wybrow himself, his feeling was not so much that of rivalry as of indignation, at his wantonly perilling a woman's happiness to gratify a passing fancy.

"Oh, May!" he said to her one day, "May you never live to feel the want of what now you don't know the value of!"

"What's that?" asked May; "a pretty face? Oh, I know the value of it very well, I can tell you; and I mean to keep it too, as long as I can."

"No, May," returned Philip; "it's what would have lasted you much longer than your bright eyes, or your silken hair, or your white teeth."

"Then you do admit that I *have* bright eyes, and silken hair, and white teeth," said May, smiling, more pleased with the compliment than impressed by the seriousness of his manner; "for I'm sure it's a long time since I heard you own as much. I wouldn't say thank ye for a lover that never pays one a compliment."

"The greatest compliment I could pay you, was to love you, May," answered Philip.

"And it's your love, I suppose, that I'm to regret the loss of?" she said, haughtily.

"It's the love of one honest heart, May, that I was hoping you might never live to feel the want of," answered Philip.

"Pooh!" said May, flinging away. "I hate people that are always preaching and threatening."

"Lilly would not have said that. Lilly would not have acted so," were thoughts that often glanced through Philip's mind now, as he sighed at the future that lay before him, and yet knew not how to break his chains; and it is probable that his heart would have returned much more decidedly to his first love had he not felt that with all the charm of Lilly's ardent affections and singleness of heart, there was a want of culture, nay, even of the commonest rudiments of education, that somewhat incapacitated her for being his companion, improved as he was himself; for his sufferings and his experience had awakened his intellect and developed his character; and even his intercourse with May—the constant abrasion of his mind against hers, had tended to ripen and strengthen his understanding. With respect to culture, properly so called, it is true, she had none; but she had the rudiments of education, and her natural quickness and independence of character, together with her knowledge of the world—in the common acceptation of that phrase—had served her in good stead with a man some years younger than her-self; and they might have served her still if she could have been true to her own affections; for Philip was right in believing that it was himself, and not Wybrow that she loved. But she played false with herself for her lover's heart, as many a woman does; the worst part of her nature against the best, and lost the stake.

In the meantime, Philip's mother in her lone cottage on the Heath, was hap-pier than she had ever expected to be again; for though very poor, being rent-free, she was able to live. Lady Longford did not forget her; old Lacy, the innkeeper would sometimes send her a little present of vegetables from his garden, and Philip was all attention and duty. May, even May, sometimes prompted by her better angel, would melt Philip's heart and banish her faults from his remem-brance by some little attention to old Rachel—old we call her, for though not so old in years, the misfortunes that had overtaken her, had broken her health and spirits, and she had become prematurely aged. It was scarcely possible that two people so antagonistic in nature as she and May, could like each other, or that they could have lived together a week in harmony. Philip had become fully aware of their utter incongruity, and had long demolished all the *châteaux en Espagne*[147] which he erected on so shallow a foundation, as the hope of May's conformity; but he had from his childhood entertained a devoted love for his mother, and nothing appeased him so quickly when he had reason to be displeased with his mistress, as any evidence of respect for the old woman. A straw bonnet of her own making, neatly trimmed with black crape, which she once presented to her, balanced and obliterated a whole month's ill-behaviour that had very nearly com-pleted Philip's alienation and offended him beyond redemption.

In spite of these little attentions, however, they were mutually too conscious of their unsuitableness, to seek each other's society. May in her heart disliked Mrs. Ryland exceedingly; and Mrs. Ryland both disliked and feared May—she feared her for Philips sake—for though he had never confessed it, she now believed her to have been the cause of all his errors; and although she saw clearly that that phasis[148] of her son's life was past, and that he could never again be so drawn aside from his true orbit by any erratic star, yet she foresaw either endless misery in a union with such a woman, if it ever took place, or great pain to Philip, and perhaps even to May, if it did not. But aware that these dangers are often rather expedited than averted by too much interference, and that bonds wrenched whilst there is yet life in them, will fester, she waited, hoping that their vitality being de-stroyed by time and circumstances, they might fall off by their own dead weight, and Philip find himself once more free.

---

147 Castles in the air.
148 An archaic word for phase.

CHAPTER XII

AN ALARM AT THE COTTAGE ON THE HEATH

Since the establishment of his mother in her cottage on the heath, Philip generally passed the night there. Occasionally Luke, for some reason or other kept him away—but these were exceptions—and on a Saturday evening Rachel always reckoned securely on enjoying his company to sup with her.

At the particular period we refer to in our present chapter, old Rachel was suffering some uneasiness about her son. She had clearly discerned that his mind was depressed and unhappy; or, at least, uneasy. He was less with her—seemed to seek solitude—and was often so lost in thought, that he was not aware when she spoke to him. But, influenced by the respect and consideration that his late conduct had inspired her with, she forbore to press into his confidence, and waited till he should be disposed to give it her of his own accord. The truth was, that poor Philip was in the heart of a struggle about May—a struggle with himself, not with her—for the last was a conflict in which, finding himself beaten, he had relinquished. But the question of the future was becoming imperative. Every day brought him nearer to that period which would see him master of the mill, when he had looked to taking home his wife and his mother. That the two were incompatible, he had long decided; and had May given him no cause for dissatisfaction in other respects, he would have abandoned the latter project for her sake; but it had now become an urgent question, whether the first part of the plan must not be resigned, instead of the last. May's unfitness to make him happy, or to be happy herself in the situation he would have to place her in, was so palpable, that not only for his own sake, but for hers, he saw the necessity of breaking off the engagement; but his honour and good sense made him feel acutely the deep responsibility of such an act, at least he could not do it lightly, nor without an entire moral conviction of the necessity of the step, as regarded the welfare of both parties. He knew that vows exchanged and promises given were holy things, even though yet unratified by the church, and he could not fling them to the winds with careless levity. He knew that *words* were *things* that cannot be trampled on without crushing life out somewhere. Trust dies, and our confidence in loyal human dealing perishes on the desecrated altar of human faith. Still, that there are occasions where the rupture of such an engagement is of less evil than the maintenance of it, he was well aware; and it was the careful weighing of his own particular case, impressed as he was with the deep responsibility of the decision that now so engrossed his mind; and it was scarcely possible for him to doubt that the moral defects of May Elliott's character would justify the disruption, both to his own conscience and in the opinion of his friends. So far for himself; but then when he thought of May, his heart misgave him. It was not only her disappointment, although he was well aware that, in spite of all her levity, that would be considerable, but it was the apprehension of what might be the effects of it on her subsequent career: there was no saying what follies and imprudences her wounded feelings and mortified pride might drive her into. This was the great source of his present anxiety and hesitation; for as regarded the immediate pain on both sides, he was clear that that was far preferable to the imminent risk of long years of future repentance.

It was on a dreary Saturday evening in the month of November, that old Rachel sat by her dim fire-light, thinking of these things, and wishing the conflict were over; whilst she listened for the music of his foot upon her threshold, wondering that Philip was not yet come, and what could have detained him. Her bit of supper was on the table, with one of her own white aprons spread under it for a cloth; and her candle was ready to light, as soon as she heard his hand upon the latch; for although, from economy, she sat in the dark herself, she always expended a candle when he supped with her, that she might enjoy the pleasure of beholding his young face. But he came not; and after waiting and hoping till ten o'clock, a late hour with her primaeval habits, she arose from her seat; and having first looked out upon the murky night, and listened, for some minutes, to the deep silence that surrounded her, she closed her door, removed her supper to the little cupboard that formed her larder, and retired disappointed to bed.

When she awoke again, it was still dark; nor did she very well know what it was that had awakened her, although she was conscious that her waking was not merely accidental; so that instead of instantly seeking to forget herself again in sleep, she rather sought to rouse herself into perfect wakefulness; and presently, whilst so doing, she heard a slight sound, as of some one moving outside her door. Perhaps it was Philip; and she was just stepping out of bed to admit him, when the recollection of her lonely situation, and the possibility that it might not be he, arrested her, and she paused to listen again; and now she was sure she heard receding footsteps; so that it had either been some one else, or he had gone away from the fear of disturbing her. She had half a mind to get up and call him back; but the apprehension that it might be some other visitor, deterred her; and so after listening a little longer in case he should return, she tried to sleep again; and she had partly succeeded in her efforts, when she was aroused by a sound like a dog scratching against the door.

"Who's there?" cried Rachel; no voice answered; but presently the scratch was repeated with a very low whine; and now the old woman, who did not want nerve, resolved to rise and penetrate the mystery. It might only be some poor animal in distress; but even so, Rachel was willing to give it shelter. Before opening the door she would have lighted her candle; but the fire was out, and to find her tinder-box and strike a light, was too tedious a process for her impatience, so she opened it at once; asking again, "Who's there?" But no one answered; and as there was not a gleam in the sky to penetrate the thick atmosphere, she could discern nothing; and she was just about to close the door again, concluding that it was some strayed animal that had wandered away again, when she felt something rubbing against her foot, and on stooping down to ascertain what it was, her hand alighted on a human body.

"Philip! oh, Philip!" she cried, for that it was her son she never doubted— "What has happened? Are you ill? Are you hurt?"

But there was no answer; and now with frantic eagerness, Rachel returned into the room and sought her tinder-box. How long it seemed till she could find it! How long, till the feeble spark sufficed to light her candle and she could inspect those features—those features that were dearer than all the earth contained to her? Was it he? Was it the pride of her happier days? The prop and stay of her adversity? No; the dead man, for so he appeared, wore the dress of a sailor; and the features were those of Wybrow, the young preventive man. Besides him stood a small terrier, which she had often observed crossing the common at his heels.

This was most strange! Wybrow at her door, dead! For though the body was still warm, and although she had certainly distinguished footsteps but a few minutes before, he showed no signs of life. He had either fainted or had expired. She fetched water and sprinkled his face, and lifting up his head poured some down his throat; but he neither stirred nor spoke. What was she to do? He might not be dead; and it was shocking to leave him there on the cold stone, even though she sat by and watched him: so she must try to drag him into the room; a feat which with some difficulty she accomplished; then she lighted her fire, and stretching him before it, she endeavoured by warmth and friction to restore animation, but in vain; and whilst she was busy about him in this way, she discovered the probable cause of his death or insensibility; namely, a fearful fracture on the back part of his head, which appeared to be quite beaten in, whilst the hair was matted by the blood that had exuded from the wound.

When Rachel was exhausted by her ineffectual efforts to revive the young sailor, she stretched him decently on the hearth, made up her fire afresh, and set herself down beside him, to watch and to reflect. Who could have done this murder?—and how came the victim to her door? Unless the injuries had been inflicted on him very near her cottage, it was not likely he would himself select so unhopeful a place for aid or protection; besides, on consideration, she could not believe that he had walked there; for if able to do that, he might have given some more audible signal of his presence. Moreover, she was satisfied that she had heard a footstep; not that of a dying man, staggering to her door, but a firm, heavy step, receding from it. Somebody, consequently, must have brought him there. Who? and for what purpose? In this inquiry she was lost. That Wybrow, or any other man in that service, should be murdered, was not perhaps very extraordinary. They must have enemies, who would be glad to put them out of the way; but she was not aware of any motive that could induce the assassin to bring his victim to her threshold. And thus wondering and amazed, beholding with pitying and reverent eyes the poor remnant of mortality that lay at her feet, with his dog, who had anxiously watched her proceedings, stretched beside him, Rachel sat till morning. When the dawn broke she arose, and having spread a sheet over the body, she put on her bonnet and shawl, locked her door, and started for the village, to give notice of what had occurred.

CHAPTER XIII

THE GAME LOST

It was a cold wintry morning; a thick mist hung in the air; and long before Rachel had reached the village, her clothes were as wet as if it had rained; but her mind was too intent on her errand to care for such matters; and she trudged on, assisted by her stick, as fast as her feeble limbs would permit. She had forgotten, however, in her eagerness, that being Sunday morning and very early, probably nobody would have risen; and she was only reminded of this by seeing that the shutters of every house were still closed. It was to Mr. Lacy that Rachel intended to apply for advice; but even the "Red Lion" showed no signs of life; and not liking to disturb the slumbers of the good man about a matter in which he had no concern, she resolved to go on to Mr. Blackburn, the surgeon, who resided at the other end of the village. Indeed, on reflection, it appeared to her that he was the most proper person to address herself to, as the sooner he visited the wounded man the better, in the case of life not being extinct; so thither she directed her steps.

As she approached the surgeon's residence, she found that the silence that pervaded all the rest of the village was far from prevailing in that quarter. The house was open; and before it stood two of the preventive men, and half a dozen other persons, men and women, who had turned out of the neighbouring cottages; they were all talking eagerly together; and ever and anon casting inquiring glances over to that side of the house where the laboratory was situated.

When they saw Rachel approaching, there was a general movement amongst them; they all simultaneously fell back and made way for her; and there was something in the manner in which this was done, that struck her with a sudden and undefinable presentiment of evil; insomuch, that that which had before filled her mind passed from it, to give place to other anxieties.

"Don't let her see it," said a woman to Walsh, the preventive man.

"What is it?—what's the matter?" inquired Rachel.

"I don't think it's any thing serious," returned one of the sailors; "there's no need to be alarmed; but you'd better go in and see him yourself."

"See who?" asked Rachel, staring at the man, with terror in her countenance.

"Don't you know that your Philip is in there with the surgeon?" returned the speaker, surprised at her question, since he naturally accounted for her appearance there, by supposing that she was come in search of her son.

"My Philip!" she exclaimed, as she turned to ascend the steps. "My Philip here!" she murmured to herself, "and Wybrow lying dead on my hearthstone!"

The laboratory door, which was on the right of the hall, being open, she entered at once; and there, sure enough, in a small room adjoining it, lay Philip on a sofa, pale, but quite sensible, and evidently very glad to see her. He had just been bled; and the surgeon was binding up his arm.

"Mother!" he said, with a faint smile. "How did you get here so soon?"

But poor Rachel was so overcome by surprise and consternation at this strange coincidence, that she was obliged to support herself against the counter, quite unable to speak.

"Give Mrs. Ryland a chair," said the surgeon to his assistant. "You have no cause for alarm," he added, addressing her; "it is only a contusion, and he will be quite well in a few days, I have no doubt."

But this information did not appear to afford Rachel all the consolation that might have been expected. She still sat speechless on the chair into which she had dropped, with her eyes expressing terror and inquiry, fixed on Philip's face.

"Don't be frightened, mother!" said he, in a low voice. "It's nothing at all."

"Nothing to create alarm, I assure you, Mrs. Ryland," repeated the surgeon; and he handed her a glass of water and some sal volatile.[149] "I must leave you now," said he, addressing himself to Philip; "but you had better lie where you are, for an hour; and then you can walk gently home, and keep yourself quiet till I see you again."

Even when they were alone she was so alarmed at the thoughts of what she might have to learn, that Rachel could not at first break silence.

"What's the matter, mother!" said Philip, looking at her with some surprise. "Sure, you may believe Mr. Blackburn!"

"How did it happen?" at length gasped out the old woman.

"It's a blow that Wybrow gave me," answered he. "We had had a bit of a quarrel, and he came behind me and gave me a savage blow on the head, with a

---

149 Smelling salts.

bludgeon."

"Oh, my God! I thought so!" exclaimed Rachel, flinging up her arms in despair.

"I believe he meant to kill me," continued Philip; "and if I hadn't had a pretty hard skull, he'd have done it, I fancy."

"And what followed next?" inquired Rachel, with trembling lips.

"I don't know very well," answered Philip. "Walsh and Harding found me lying in the lane where it happened, and brought me here; but Mr. Blackburn was away to Colston, and the assistant was doubtful what to do; and so they carried me to Seton's close by, and there I came to myself in time—but I mustn't talk so much, mother," he added, turning paler than before.

"One more question—one more," said Rachel, eagerly bending over him to catch his words, for it was not the apprehension of his present danger that terrified her—in that respect, she was content to risk something for an immediate answer. "Did you strike Wybrow?"

"No, I had no time to do it," answered Philip, speaking with difficulty; whilst his head, which he had partly lifted, fell back, and he became once more insensible. But Rachel was herself again; for she entirely believed him, however much appearances seemed to contradict his assertion; and having by means of the appliances that were at hand, somewhat revived this beloved son, she bade him remain quietly where he was till she returned; and immediately quitted the room in search of the surgeon, who was just then making his toilet; but presently attended her.

"This is a very awkward coincidence," said he, looking at her gravely, when he had heard her story.

"It is, sir, and I was very much terrified indeed at first, for I was afeard they'd been fighting; but Philip says he never struck him."

"There can have been no fair fighting on either side," returned Mr. Blackburn, "for according to your account of the other patient, both wounds must have been given from behind."

"It must have been a terrible blow, sir, that Wybrow got, whoever gave it," returned Rachel, "and though I'm afraid he's dead, wouldn't it be better you should see him?"

The surgeon agreed to accompany her, after taking a cup of tea to refresh himself after his night's fatigue; and as soon as he was ready, she started with him across the heath, leaving Philip to recruit his strength by resting where he was.

The young preventive man, with his dog beside him, lay on the hearth as she had left him covered by the sheet, on removing which Mr. Blackburn found that he was not dead, though in a condition rendering it extremely improbable that he would ever recover from his present state of insensibility. The first thing to be

done, however, was to remove him to a more convenient situation for the operation he intended to perform; and the station being at too great a distance, he was
carried into the village.

The sensation created in the neighbourhood by these events, and the gossip
and discussion they gave rise to, may be easily imagined. That the young men
had quarrelled seemed to be very generally known. High words had been heard
between them late on the Saturday evening, and many were ready to assert that
Philip had for some time been extremely jealous of Wybrow, and moreover, that
he had very good cause for being so. Then, the preventive men as soon as they
heard of their comrade's fate, became extremely angry, and were loud against
Philip; and in spite of one circumstance that appeared very much in his favour,
the affair began to assume a serious aspect as regarded him, provided Wybrow did
not recover, an event of which there seemed very small chance.

The favourable circumstance was, that a heavy stick, known to be Wybrow's,
had been found near to the spot where Philip was discovered, with which there
was every reason to suppose that the blow on the head of the latter had been
given. But, then, it was suggested that Philip might have brought away the stick
after assassinating its owner, for the express purpose of perplexing inquiry; as to
the blow he had himself received, some people went so far as to assert, that he
might have procured it purposely with the same view, by hitting the back of his
head violently against some hard substance; "And perhaps," said they, "he was not
actually insensible when he was found, but only pretended to be so." All these notions emanated chiefly from the preventive men and their adherents. There were
other parties who took a different view of the case. They admitted that Philip, as
well as another man, might kill his adversary in a quarrel, but they denied his being capable of the artful contrivance attributed to him. Those who knew him best
were the most stoutly sceptical on this point.

In the meantime, what was May Elliott doing? That was what nobody could
tell; for she did not go to church, nor appear outside her door, on the Sunday;
and on the subsequent days, her front windows and door which were towards
the street were closed. There was a door behind, however, which led into an old
orchard, belonging to Sir Lawrence Longford; for hers was the last house in the
village, and stood just on the borders of his enclosures: and some persons, curious
in such matters, and prone to recondite investigation, took the trouble of making
a little circuit, for the purpose of ascertaining the state of the back premises. By
these enterprising discoverers, it was reported, that the windows were open behind; and that the girl whom May kept, as partly servant, and partly assistant in
her work, had been seen twirling a mop at this same back door.

Certain it was, that she made no effort to see Philip, though he lay ill at his mother's for several days. He was not simply ill from the blow, though its effects were aggravated by his having been in a very excited state of mind when he received it; but the moral conflict he had been sustaining for sometime, and the painful scene in which it had at last terminated, had otherwise deranged his health; and these things, added to the pain and anxiety consequent on Wybrow's danger and the mystery that hung over the whole affair, had quite overthrown him. Even if Wybrow recovered, he was not at all sure that he would not accuse him of his being his intended assassin—very possibly he would think he was; and how he was to disprove it he could not tell. Besides, he was not long left in ignorance of the reports that were circulated to his disadvantage; and he felt so painfully that he was lying under suspicion, that he told his mother he should "have no peace till he went and gave himself up to a magistrate."

Of course, betwixt himself and her, and the friends that adhered to them, the question of who had struck Wybrow, was a constant subject of discussion. That he had been very active lately in tracing some clue, which he expected would lead him to the discovery of the smugglers, Philip was aware; and it might have been in the pursuit of them that he had fallen into danger. With respect to the injury he had received himself, he could suppose no other, than that Wybrow had inflicted it. They had quarrelled, and May had been the cause of the quarrel. Dissatisfied with the evident alienation, which she could not but perceive on the part of Philip, instead of seeking to recover his affections by reforming her errors, she sought to re-animate his passion by exciting his jealousy. This is the ordinary expedient of foolish women, who do not perceive that the frequent administration of this sort of stimulant, is apt to produce a very sedative effect. They blow the fire till they put it out. On the Saturday evening in question, Philip had gone to spend an hour or two with his mistress, before he went to his mothers; determined, to represent to her the crisis they were approaching, which must either terminate their connexion or unite them for ever. He had maturely deliberated on what he should say to her, and going charged with this thought, was naturally very much annoyed at finding her *tête-a-tête* with Wybrow. Formerly, the young sailor used to give place to Philip, as the accepted lover; but now he not only occupied a chair by May, which kept Philip at a distance from her; but he seemed determined to sit him out; whilst she, instead of evincing her disapprobation, took care to let her lover see that she enjoyed his discomfiture; and Wybrow partly with the view of recommending himself to her, by braving his rival's wrath; and partly because his natural recklessness was a little augmented by a few extra glasses which he had been taking, for the purpose of inducing another person, whose secrets he wanted to get at, to do the same—was foolish enough to aggravate the mischief by taunts and sarcasms, indirectly administered, but readily appropriated by an irritated man. At length, on the occasion of something particularly smart, said by Wybrow, at which May laughed heartily, Philip suddenly started to his feet, and advanced as if going to strike him; but seeming to recollect himself, his arm fell; and taking up his cap, he hastily quitted the room. But this was going further than May wished; there was something in his demeanour that whispered to her, "If he goes now he returns no more!" and springing past Wybrow, she flew after him to the door. "Philip!" she cried, "Philip! come back and forgive me, and I'll send Wybrow away directly. Pooh! you're not offended?"

"Oh, no," said Philip; "no, not offended!"

"Come back, then!" said May, flinging her arms about his neck.

"Never!" replied Philip, in a calm, firm voice; "never. Lift your arms from about me, May, and let me go, before worse comes of it."

"No, no," she answered, passionately, for she saw he was in earnest; "no, no; I'll go this moment and send Wybrow away. You go into the other room and wait till he is gone;" and opening the door on the opposite side of the narrow passage, she tried to lead him to it.

"No, May," replied Philip, firmly; "I might go in there and deceive you; but my last words to you shall not be a lie. It is all over, May; we are parted; I leave you this night for ever."

"Oh, Philip! oh, Philip! forgive me!" said May. "It was all nonsense, all a joke, just to tease you—it was, indeed!"

"Yes, it was to tease me," answered Philip; "but if you ever win the heart of another man, don't think he will love you for teasing him, May."

"I don't want to win the heart of another man," said May. "Come, forget and forgive."

"It is easy to forgive," answered Philip; "and I will not deceive you, I shall try to forget—not only your faults, but—" And here his voice faltering, she thought he had relented.

"But my virtues," said she, with her accustomed levity. "But you can't, you see; so now come back, like a good boy, and I'll go in and send Wybrow off."

"Never!" said he, "never, so help me God!" and stepping from the door, he walked rapidly away.

CHAPTER XIV

THE QUEST OF MAY ELLIOTT

Giles Lintock had never been acquainted with the particulars of Lilly Dawson's history. His wife and her father had long ceased to hold any friendly or familiar communion with him; he took no interest in their affairs, nor they in his; and where he went or what he did, had no further concern for them, than inasmuch as they always lived in the fear of his doing something that might bring their names into disrespect. But, nevertheless, he had long suspected that there was some mystery connected with Lilly, from the importance Luke Littenhaus had attached to her recapture. There was no appearance that the link that had united him to her had been affection; it must therefore, concluded Giles, be interest, though of what nature he could not guess, nor had he much curiosity to know. Since the night in which, by the assistance of May Elliott, he had delivered her into the power of her cousin, and received the stipulated sum for his service, he had ceased to think about her. He had only been waiting in London with a view to that enterprise, which being completed, he immediately quitted the city in pursuit of other objects.

Since these events had occurred, two years had elapsed; in one shape or another, Giles had been concerned in many a raid on the purses of the king's lieges in the interval. One favourite scene of his forays, in this kind, was the race-ground; and latterly, the only periods at which he was seen in the neighbourhood of his former home were the race-weeks, which annually recurred. It was on one of these occasions, that, whilst watching the vicissitudes of a gaming-table, he felt himself tapped on the shoulder; and on looking round, he perceived Mr. Cropley. Giles fell back, and touched his hat; for, however little respected in his own class, Cropley was a gentleman to Giles, in his fallen condition.

"Lintock," said Mr. Cropley, "I have been wanting to see you for some time. Come this way, will you? I sent a letter for you, some weeks since, to your wife; but she said she didn't know where you were."

"No, sir, I don't think she did just then," returned Giles, following him out of the crowd.

"Well, I am glad I have found you. I want to speak to you particularly. You are acquainted with May Elliott—Elliott the horsekeeper's daughter—you found her out for me some time since."

"Yes, sir."

"Well, I want you to discover her for me again. Do you think you can do it?"

"I've no doubt of it, sir," replied Giles, who believed May still to be employed at Mrs. Knox's.

"Do then, and you shall be well rewarded for it. Have you ever seen or heard of her since that time?"

"No, sir, I only went to her on your business," answered Giles, who did not wish to diminish the value of his services, by intimating that he already knew what he was to be paid for finding out; whilst Mr. Cropley, on the other hand, forbore for the present to inquire if he ever had heard of such a person as Lilly Dawson, because he wished to keep the whole inquiry in his own hands as much as possible, fearing, that if Giles got a hint of the important secret, he might anticipate him. So they parted, Giles promising to forward the desired information without delay.

For this purpose, it being understood his expenses were to be paid, he took the opportunity of an excursion to London, though he had no doubt at the time that a letter addressed to Mrs. Knox's would have answered the same end. But to his surprise, on his arrival he found that he should have to earn his money more honestly than he had anticipated. May Elliott had disappeared, leaving no clue whereby to track her flight.

At her first lodging, the woman said that she had left a trunk full of clothes as security for the part of her rent that remained unpaid, promising to send the money, and redeem the things. At the second lodging she had been less considerate; for she had left nothing whatever. She had removed much of her property, which consisted wholly of articles of dress, by degrees, and unobserved; and on the last day a man had fetched away a large trunk, on the plea that he was going to repair it. In the evening she had walked out, and never returned. Further they knew not, and the angry woman said she "Only wished she could catch her!"

This was perplexing—and Giles, having interrogated the young girls at Mrs. Knox's, and every body he could hear of as likely to give him the desired information, was at a loss in what manner to direct his inquiries, when he was advised by Mrs. Knox to call at Harvey's and Graham's, and ask for Mr. Ferdinand Pycroft.

"He's attached to the feather and flower department, in the inner shop," said she, "and he's a very genteel young man, and I know May had an inkling to him. Indeed, to say the truth, when she disappeared in that strange manner, I thought they had gone off together; and I went to Harvey's and Graham's to inquire, for she was a great loss to me. Mr. Ferdinand pretended he knew nothing about her; but he looked as if he wasn't speaking the truth, and I've a great notion that he does. At all events, you can try."

So Giles went, and Mr. Ferdinand answered him exactly as Mrs. Knox had described; declaring he did not know where she was, but allowing his looks to contradict his words. The truth was, that he was as ignorant of her proceedings as other people were; but he had no objection to its being supposed that the lady had fled from the world and her friends for love of him.

"But it's no joke that I am come about, I assure you," said Giles, "and if you've any regard for May Elliott, you had better tell me where she is, or how a letter can be sent to her."

Mr. Ferdinand swore that he had an immense regard for her, but 'pon honour he did not know the lady's address.

"It's something very much to her advantage, I assure you," said Giles, at a venture, "and very much to the advantage of any gentleman that might be connected with her."

"I wish I knew," replied Mr, Ferdinand, with more appearance of sincerity than he had spoken before.

"But you do know?" said Giles.

"I don't, upon my soul!" said Mr. Ferdinand—"but my idear is, that, she's gone off with a young feller that used to be follering her about, that she called *Philip*; but who Philip was, or where he came from, hang me if I know!"

Having by further interrogation satisfied himself that this was really all Mr. Ferdinand could tell him, Giles returned to the lodgings, where he easily ascertained that a young man, so called, had been in the constant habit of visiting her. Moreover, the landlady in Blenheim Street seemed to entertain the same suspicion as the shopman.

"That young man, sir, went away to the country, and it's my belief that she went after him. The last evening he was ever here, the girl that lived with me then, told me that she heard them talking about it; and that Miss Elliott never went to bed that night, but lay on the sofa crying, and there she found her asleep in the morning."

"And what was his name besides Philip?" inquired Giles.

"Well, I never heard his name," answered the woman, "but there's a book here that she left behind her, that the maid said was his—and there's a name in it. This is it," said she, taking a book off a shelf— "it's 'Gulliver's Travels,' you see, and there's 'P. Dewar, Castle Street,' in it. Well, sir, when she went off in that there manner, I went to Castle Street, and found the shop easy enough—they sell meal and seeds, and things of that sort—and there I saw an elderly, decent woman and a young boy, her son—but they both declared they'd never heard the sound of her name for six months, and that they'd never seen her in their lives. A girl that used to go there, they said, had known her; but more than that they couldn't tell, or they wouldn't tell, sir, Lord knows which."

With this clue, and the book in his hand, Giles proceeded to Castle Street, where he had no difficulty in procuring an interview with Peter Dewar. Of May Elliott, the boy knew nothing; "But that is my book," said he; "and it was my cousin, Philip Ryland, that I lent it to."

"And where is he?" inquired Giles.

"Down in the country," answered the boy, "at Trentesy Mill."

Where Trentesy Mill was, and whatever else it was necessary to know, Giles found no difficulty in extracting from Peter; and to proceed thither was his immediate determination; not doubting, that wherever this Philip Ryland was, there was May Elliott also.

So writing to Mr. Cropley, that he had found the track of the fugitive, he proceeded to the coach-office, and, like his predecessors on the same route, he, too, started by the "Enterprise" for Hotham.

CHAPTER XV

GILES LINTOCK VISITS COMBE MARTIN

Having duly reached the end of his journey, and refreshed himself with a good breakfast, Giles Lintock started for the mill, whose sole tenant, when he arrived there, not a little to his amazement, he found to be his former acquaintance, Luke Littenhaus; for the correspondence that had passed betwixt them had been conducted with such peculiar precautions by Luke, that Giles had never had an opportunity of learning his real address.

The surprise on the part of the mill-owner appeared no less than that of his visitor, though of a much less agreeable nature.

Whilst Giles's countenance brightened with satisfaction, Luke's increased pallor, and the anxious inquiring expression of his eyes, denoted that he had no desire to renew an acquaintance formed under such peculiar circumstances.

"Well, this *is* luck!" exclaimed Giles, with what he designed to be a hearty smack of mutual congratulation on the hand of the miller, which generous intention, however, failed, from the lax manner in which that unwilling hand was extended. "Who'd ha' thought it?" continued he, unabashed by his cool welcome; "hunting a rabbit, I've caught a hare."

"What do you mean?" asked Luke, with a savage expression of countenance, and putting himself on the defensive.

"No harm, old fellow," said Giles: "I'm only joking. The truth is, I'm in search of a young woman, called May Elliott; and hearing that there was a young fellow in these parts, of the name of Ryland, that she was fond of, I ran down to see if she wasn't here along with him."

"They're both here," returned Luke, much relieved. "But what do you want with her?"

"It's not I, it's Mr. Cropley, a lawyer, in our parts, that wants her; for what purpose, I don't know. But where's she to be found?"

"In the village," returned Luke; "they'll show you the house—she makes women's bonnets."

"That's she," said Giles. "What the deuce brought her here?"

"Exactly what you suppose, I believe," answered Luke. "She came after young Ryland; but she'd better have stayed away. He has got into a quarrel about her, with one of the preventive men here; and he's in custody for knocking out his rival's brains—or something like it."

"Well," said Giles, "I suppose my old acquaintance, Miss Dawson, is Mrs. Luke Littenhaus by this time?"

"I know nothing at all about her," returned Luke, drawing in again. "She's too cunning for me, and slipped through my fingers, as she had done before."

"The deuce she did!" exclaimed Giles, immediately anticipating the chance of earning a little more money by hunting her up again; "I'll get her for you, I'll answer for it."

"You needn't trouble yourself; I don't want her," returned Luke; "she's not worth the pains I took about her."

"Well, I always thought so," returned Giles. "But it's a capital joke, to be sure," and he rubbed his hands, chuckling at the idea of having pocketed the reward, though the object of his employer had failed.

Promising to call at the mill again, a favour Luke could well have dispensed with, Giles next departed for Combe, to seek out May Elliott, whose cottage he easily discovered.

The girl said, Miss Elliott was ill and could not see any body; but on his name being announced to her, May's curiosity was so far excited, that she consented to admit him.

"What's the matter?" said he to her, after the first salutation; for she was sitting in an old arm-chair, in a half-darkened room, with her person neglected—an indubitable symptom of something being very far wrong with May Elliott—and a general air of depression, that he at once attributed to the situation of her lover.

"It's nothing to you," said she, "you can't help me. What's brought you here?"

"To look for you," returned Giles. "Cropley wants you again."

"He may want then," said May.

"But I dare say it's something to your advantage, as they say in the advertisements," returned Giles. "You'd better go."

"No, I sha'n't," said May. "Not a step; and so you may tell him."

"Very well," said Giles, after some further vain entreaties; "I'll write and tell him so; and he can come and see you himself if he likes. I've found you; that's all I promised to do."

He then attempted to turn the conversation on Philip; and his present situation, as he had gathered it from Luke; but on this subject, she could not be induced to speak. He next tried that of Lilly Dawson, inquiring if she had ever seen her since.

"Never," replied May. "When I came down here, I expected to find her with her cousins; but I hear they know nothing about her."

"Where do they live, these cousins?" inquired he. "I saw nothing but a mill and a shed."

"They keep an inn about three-quarters of a mile from there," replied May. "It's called 'The Black Huntsman'—a dismal place; and they're so uncivil that nobody goes to it."

"*I* shall go to it," said Giles. "I shall certainly honour them with my custom; for I must stay here till I can get a letter from Cropley; and that won't be till the end of the week, at soonest.

In accordance with this determination, Giles retraced his steps, and presented himself as a lodger, where he was by no means desired. However, they had no choice but to admit him; and there he established his quarters to wait for the lawyer's answer.

In the meantime, Wybrow was considered *in extremis*,[150] and Philip, urged partly by his own feelings and partly by the resentment of the dying man's comrades, had anticipated the authorities, by giving himself up as soon as he was able to walk as far as the magistrate's house. His mother was, naturally, suffering great anxiety, though perfectly convinced of his innocence; and May, the guilty May, was broken-hearted with remorse; and the consciousness, that be the issue of the affair what it might, she had lost Philip's heart for ever. Moreover, she was not equally assured of his innocence; she had had no opportunity of hearing it from his own lips, and having witnessed the feelings with which he quitted her house, that he should seek to revenge himself on Wybrow, appeared to her extremely natural. The moment Philip left her she had ordered the young sailor away, disgusted and angry with him and with herself; but with what had happened afterwards she was unacquainted, except from such reports as reached her through the girl who lived with her. From these it appeared, that the two men had been observed wrangling together, and Philip had been heard to use some opprobrious language towards the other. Be the particulars what they might, however, well she knew

---

150 In this case, close to death.

that the fault was all her own, and that but for her wicked levity, for such levity *is* wicked, Philip would never have had a word with his friend, and she would still have been the mistress of his affections. But it was all over now; and it was the struggle betwixt her pride and her love, embittered as the pangs of both were by remorse, that was rending her heart-strings.

Whilst these things were doing and suffering in the country by those who had been once so dear to her; and whilst the General was fretting and Mr. Cropley was fidgetting because no tidings of her reached them, Lilly Dawson had been keeping on her even way; loving and serving, hoping and praying, for she, who had always known how to love and serve where love and service were accepted, had now learnt to offer up the sacrifice of humble hope and earnest prayer, where these were rejected never. Docile, tractable, singleminded, and true; and though without any great capacity, yet with a heart that informed her mind, the two years she had passed in the house of Colonel Adams, had wrought an astonishing alteration in her. Her gentle and unselfish nature had always been favourable to her manners, but her ignorance had formerly been unmitigated. We are very far from meaning to imply that she was now an accomplished young lady or a well-educated woman; far from it. Lilly was a servant, and she had no acquirements beyond what might have fitted her to be a lady's maid, or at the most, a nursery-governess for very young children. She could read and write with ease; was clever at her needle; had perused a good many books of various sorts, chiefly novels, voyages, travels, and light historical works; her manners were modest and inoffensive, her person pleasing; and she had an internal consciousness of God, and an innocent piety, little perplexed by creeds or dogmas, together with a reverent faith in the unseen, and an eager wondering over the strange and impenetrable mysteries of life and death, that made her walk ever holily through her daily path, enriching her simple mind with many a high, pure thought, and rendering her to those few with whom she could talk unreservedly, far from an uninteresting or unprofitable companion.

The person who profited most by these qualities and endowments, was Freddy. With Colonel Adams, she was rather a hearer than a speaker. She listened to his comments on the books they read, and occasionally asked questions, which he always encouraged her to do: to Mrs. Adams, she was only a very clever, valuable servant; to Winny, she was a pleasant companion and often an instructress; but to Freddy, she was more than all this—she was his friend and confidante; he told her all his own troubles, and all the family troubles; and she told him more of her past life and sufferings than she had done to any body else, Winny not excepted: and not only their facts, but all their hypotheses and speculations, upon all manner of subjects, were freely communicated to each other. Mrs. Adams sometimes told her son that he made Lilly too much of a companion; but his father always took his part; urging, that from their peculiar situation, the boy lived more alone than he should do, and that he would never learn any harm from Lilly. So their fresh young minds were allowed to mingle; and many a bright dream of the future Freddy would weave in his hopeful moods, in which visionary dramas Lilly had always an important part assigned her.

"If papa wins that horrid law-suit, we shall be very rich, and I shall some day have a great fortune, you know, Lilly; and then you shall always live with me; and if I have any children, you shall take care of them; won't you?"

"Yes; I should love them dearly, for your sake," answered Lilly.

"Isn't it a shame my uncle's not letting papa have the fortune that Mrs. Adams meant for him?"

"It seems to me very wicked," answered Lilly.

"If my sister was alive, of course it would be hers, and we should never wish to take it from her; but it's very hard, when she was drowned, not to let *any* body have it."

"Should you like to have a sister, Master Freddy?"

"Yes, dearly, if she was a nice, good-natured girl. I've heard that poor little Isabel was very good-natured, and very pretty too; and she was so fair, that every body called her *Lily;* and I think that's one reason papa took such a liking to you at first, because your name's Lilly. How came you to be called Lilly? Is it because you're so fair?"

"I don't know, I'm sure," said she; "I don't know who gave me the name."

"Then you don't remember your papa and mamma?"

"No; I only remember having a grandpapa; but I don't think I ever saw him again, after I went to live with my cousins."

"Then you didn't always live with your cousins?"

"I don't know; I don't recollect," answered Lilly; "but I don't think I did when I was very little."

It was during a similar conversation to the above, that Lilly, who was walking in the little garden behind the house with Frederick, felt her gown pulled; and looking round, she saw Winny holding up a letter.

"What's that?" said he; "what does she want?"

"She wants me to read her letter for her, I suppose," said Lilly; "she can't read writing very well;" and, so saying, she followed Winny into the kitchen.

CHAPTER XVI

A LETTER FROM COMBE MARTIN

When Giles Lintock received Mr. Cropley's answer, he was exceedingly surprised to learn that all this stir about May, in reality, regarded that very insignificant person, Lilly Dawson; and he now felt convinced of that which Luke's anxiety with respect to her had formerly suggested; namely, that there was some mystery attached to the girl, and he felt extremely sorry that he had not known it earlier; for in that case, he would have played his cards very differently. However, as it was, he saw a prospect of making himself useful; since it seemed probable that he was possessed of as much information with regard to Lilly as any body; and to this effect he wrote to Mr. Cropley, promising to lose no time in tracing her further.

The next consideration was, how to deal with Luke; whether to tell him the real object of inquiry, or not? And there was another question—did Luke, or not, know any thing about Lilly? It was difficult to say; for he might know a great deal and not choose to tell it—no one could look in his face without seeing that he was one who had heavy secrets on his soul—and it seemed somewhat marvellous to Giles, that after all the precautions they had used, she should have escaped again. But to extract a secret from Luke against his will, was a hopeless task; and from his reiterated assurances whenever the subject was introduced, that he knew nothing, it was clear that either the assertion was true, or that what he knew he did not intend to tell. But although Giles obtained no positive information from those repeated questionings, yet there was one valuable conclusion he arrived at—namely, that for some reason or other the subject was a very unwelcome one to Luke, whilst to the rest of the family it seemed one of nearly indifference. That they were ignorant of all that concerned Lilly, he had little doubt, but that Luke was better informed, he was satisfied—and he began to foresee the probability of his being obliged to turn "approver"[151] against his own ally. But wishing to avoid this in the first place, and also not knowing how far Mr. Cropley's affair might be calculated to bear the light, he resolved to try other expedients before he resorted to one so inconvenient. His next step, therefore, was to commission a crony of his in London to call at the house in West Smithfield, and to endeavour to ascertain if any thing had been seen or heard of the girl after he had locked her up in the room and delivered the key to her cousin. The answer which reached him in a few days, filled him with dismay, and even with horror—for there are degrees

---

151 An informer.

in wickedness, and Luke had taken a much higher one than Giles. It was to the following effect:

"Dear Gill,—The woman you want, according to date given, was murdered that same night, nobody knows how. She was found dead next morning. There was a great rumpus—I remember hearing of it—but nobody was nabbed for it, that I ever heard.

"I wish you wouldn't send a fellow on such unpleasant errands! The people stared at me, as if they thought 'I did it,' as the man says in the play—and I shall take care not to walk through that street again t'other side Christmas.

"Yours—C.B.

"*Nowhere*, Nov. 20th."

Giles's opinion of his friend Luke had not been of the highest before—but this letter really astounded him—and he felt somewhat at a loss how to proceed upon it. He did not doubt that Luke was the murderer, and it appeared to him that he should be taken into custody at once—but these were unpleasant matters, with which he did not like to meddle. Besides, he had neither authority nor proof to adduce; so he contented himself with sending the intelligence of Lilly's death, with an outline of the circumstances connected with it, to Mr. Cropley; concluding his letter by saying that he should wait that gentleman's further instructions, and meanwhile keep an eye upon the suspected person.

Amongst the many disagreeable epistles that Mr. Cropley had received in his time, few had contained information more disagreeable than this. As regarded the unhappy fate of the young heiress, it was bad enough; but as it regarded the interests and credit of Josiah Cropley, it was a great deal worse. What would the General say? What would the world say? The former, whose pocket he had been picking for years, on the strength of this suit, which might apparently have been satisfactorily terminated any day, by a little more honest activity on his part; and the latter, who thought him—at least, he flattered himself that a section of it did—the most diligent, acute, and far-seeing of the sons of Themis![152] He was so confounded, that, not daring to present himself before the General, he wrote to Giles, instantly to apply to a magistrate, and procure the arrest of Luke, whilst he himself proceeded to London, for the purpose of investigating the truth of the sad story, which he found too surely confirmed, both by the police reports and the people of the house to which Lilly had been carried.

Having then written to Mr. Treadgold, detailing the whole affair, and deferring to him the painful task of communicating the event to the General, he

---

152 Themis: Greek Goddess of divine or natural law.

himself, accompanied by Ledbetter, a London officer, able in detecting criminals, and worming out their tortuous paths, proceeded, without delay, to the scene of action; and whilst he is on his journey, we will return to Lilly, whom we left just as she was summoned by Winny Weston, to decipher a letter for her; a service which she had been for some time in the habit of performing with very particular zeal. The truth was, that Winny herself was an extremely indifferent scribe, and, until Lilly had become qualified to act as her amanuensis, her correspondence with home had been limited to a letter once a year; on which occasions she used to get a few lines written by whom she could; and in due time an answer would reach her, signed by her mother, to whom her own epistles were addressed; but written by the hand of no less a person than her cousin Bob Groby; who still filled the honourable situation of ostler, at The Black Huntsman, old Deborah not being more expert with her pen than her daughter was.

It was by means of one of Bob's letters, that Lilly learnt some news that went very near her heart; namely, that Philip Ryland had returned to the country, and that he had a sweetheart in the village, called Miss Elliott, a beautiful young lady from London; and that Mrs. Ryland was living in the old cottage on the heath, which Philip had repaired and furnished for her.

What strange news this seemed to Lilly! There they were all, who had been once her friends—all united and happy together; and she, who had loved them so much, was shut out from their hearts, and forgotten! She wondered whether all love was as hollow as theirs had been to her; and whether Freddy's would prove as unstable! She was happy now in her new attachments, but still she could not forget her old ones; and a secret instinct, which whispered her that May, who had been so false to her, could never be true to Philip, rendered her doubly anxious and curious to learn something of their proceedings; and Winny, aware of the interest she had in these letters, was very willing to gratify her. The correspondence became, therefore, rather more brisk. Lilly wrote the letters for Winny; and Bob Groby the answers for Deborah Weston; but not the most distant hint was ever given to the old woman, of the name of her daughter's amanuensis and fellow-servant. So, that whilst Lilly was pretty well acquainted with what was doing at Combe Martin, the good people there were entirely ignorant of her fate, and had, most of them, ceased to remember her existence.

"Come here," said Winny; "here's such a long letter from mother; and I can read your name in it, and Philip Ryland's; do see what it's all about."

The letter, which was rather obscure, from the circumstance of the writer's habit of confounding his own personality with that of whoever he represented, ran as follows:

"Dear Cousin Winny,

"I hope this letter finds you well, as it leaves me at present, except my cough, which is worse since the foggy weather, and the rheumatis in my nee; but I must expeck that at my time of life, which is 63. There's been a power of things happen here since I wrote last. Philip Ryland and Miss Elliott fell out about Frank Wybrow, the preventive man, and they fought and kill Wybrow, though he's not quite dead yet. Miss is in great trouble about it; and Philip's in prison; and Mrs. Ryland very bad with rheumatis and the trouble both together.

"You remember Lilly Dawson, as use to live up at the 'Huntsman,' where I live now, but shall leave, 'cause I don't like their doings; and I'd promised to tell Wybrow about some things, but he's dead, or as good as, so I shall say nothen to nobody, but keep out such doings myself. There's a man here come down from Lonnon to look for her; and they say she's done something very bad indeed. He's been to Miss Elliott and Philip Ryland about her, and axes Mr. Luke more questions than's agreeable, and he looks as black as thunder. Cousin Winny, if you could get me a place as ostler in Lonnon, I would come up, or groom, to ride behind a gentleman. The washing from the castle's been very heavy lately, for the company they've had; and I'm quite lame standing on my legs ironing my Lady Albina's smocks and petticoats, and wish you'd come home again. Cousin Winny, if you can get me a place, as above, to ride, or drive, or look after osses, pray do, and I am,

"Your affectionate mother,

"Combe Martin, Deborah Weston.

"Nov. 17."

Here was a budget of news that filled Lilly with amazement. Philip and May had quarrelled, and apparently killed somebody between them—Philip was in prison, May in trouble, and Mrs. Ryland in sorrow and sickness. Then there was somebody there seeking her, and there appeared to be some accusation brought against her. What could it be? The only thing she could imagine was that it might be something connected with the events of that fearful night she had passed in the unknown house. A paragraph she had seen in one of the papers some months before, had occasioned her some uneasiness at the time, because it struck her as referring to that event. It was to the effect that, "The hackney-coach-man who had driven two women to the house in West Smithfield, where one of them was found murdered the next morning had been at length discovered; but that he denied knowing any thing of the parties, who had taken him off the stand. He asserts that only one of the women entered the house conducted by the man who had engaged him, whilst the other desired to be driven back to where he had taken her up, which was near Long Acre, and that she left the coach there after paying him his fare, and walked away."

This seemed to indicate that she was supposed to be dead; but, on the other hand, the circumstance of somebody going from London to seek her at Combe, appeared rather to imply that she was suspected of being concerned in the crime; and on the whole, it did not seem to her very unlikely that if there were any stir about Charlotte's death, Luke might endeavour to shift the guilt from his own shoulders to hers.

All these matters gave Lilly a great deal of uneasiness, and afforded her subjects for very serious consideration. She was not now the silly child she had been. She wished to avoid Luke as her enemy, and one who would give her annoyance; but she was now aware that both law and custom would protect her from him, and it was therefore not so much fear for herself as the dread of being obliged to become her cousin's accuser, that rendered her unwilling to betray her own secret or come forward at all. But, on the other hand, it was both a painful and a dangerous thing to suffer herself to lie under a suspicion, which the lapse of time might render it very difficult to clear satisfactorily away. Then Philip was in prison, and Mrs. Ryland in trouble, and altogether that which she had never imagined could happen had at length actually occurred, namely, that Lilly Dawson longed once more to behold that dreary Heath which she had hoped never to see again; and when she laid her head on her pillow that night it was not to sleep, but to ponder on these things.

CHAPTER XVII

THE EXAMINATION

The magisterial functions for the village of Combe and its neighbourhood, were discharged by Sir Lawrence Longford and his colleagues, in what was called the large room, at "The Red Lion." They held regular monthly sittings, which were found quite sufficient for this quiet district; but on the 27th of November, 18—, they were called together upon a special occasion. Messrs. Cropley and Ledbetter had arrived, and Luke Littenhaus was to be brought before the justices and examined, with respect to the murder of Lilly Dawson; in which crime he was supposed to be either aider and abettor, or principal. Amongst the witnesses to be called were the family of the suspected person; Philip Ryland, May Elliott, Giles Lintock, and also his wife, and her father, Abel White; who, at the General's desire, had accompanied Mr. Ross to the spot; these last having only arrived on the morning that the sittings commenced. The General himself was also present, very loud, very lofty, and very full of malice; his private idea being, or, at least, it was the one he chose to insinuate, that his grand-daughter's own nearest connexions had been, in some way, privy to her long, inscrutable concealment, and her final making away, in the hope of enjoying her fortune themselves; a nefarious scheme, which he congratulated himself as having completely defeated.

Never was there such a sensation in the village of Combe before or since, as this strange affair created. The whole neighbourhood was astir; business was neglected, work laid aside; people were staring out of the doors and windows of every cottage; and the street in front of the "Red Lion," was so thronged, that the two constables of the district—very great men in their way—were obliged to exhibit their staves, and exert the whole weight of their authority, before way could be made for Lady Longford's carriages to drive up to the door. The magistrates themselves having ridden to the scene of action, their horses' heels cleared theirs without much help.

The next difficulty was to keep too many people from rushing into the room; which, after all precautions, was crammed to suffocation. Amongst those who did get in, however, was Bob Groby; whilst his mother and his aunt Deborah, through his interest in the household, of which he had formerly been a member, were privately admitted through a back door, before the rush from without had choked up the passage.

Of course, there was a great deal of pushing for places, and talking, and buzzing, and calling of silence, before silence could be obtained; but at length, all being reasonably quiet and orderly, the first witness was called; this was Ambrose Littenhaus, who presented himself with a countenance in which anxiety and confusion were very legibly written. There was also an air of considerable depression in his whole person and demeanour; and a wildness in his eye, which wandered inquiringly from face to face, as if in search of some sustaining glance or friendly smile; and "poor fellow, if there's any thing wrong, it's been his brother that's led him into it," was the general sentiment with which this appeal was answered. It was remarked that he never looked towards Luke, who, with the collar of his great coat so raised, that it almost concealed the expression of his mouth, sat motionless; and as far as could be discerned, with an imperturbable countenance, in the place assigned him.

As it would occupy too much space were we to give in detail the whole of the examinations, we must content ourselves with a succinct compendium of the evidence in general; only dilating on particular passages where it may appear necessary.

Ambrose Littenhaus, the eldest son of Jacob Littenhaus, formerly of Fowey in

Cornwall, said, that his father kept a small Inn there, called "The Mermaid;" and that having been bred to the sea, he sometimes went out with the fishing boats; that on one occasion, he and some others had boarded the wreck of a large vessel, on which they had found a little girl, apparently about four years old; and that they had brought her ashore, and out of compassion kept her with them, as if she were a relation of their own; they had always told her she was so, considering it better that she should believe it to be the case. When they came to their present residence they had brought her with them.

She had always been very happy and contented; and when she grew up to be about seventeen, his brother Luke wished to make her his wife, and she had been taken to Hotham to be married, and they had been asked in church; but for some reason or other which they had never discovered, after having yielded her free consent to the union, she had run away; and though, alarmed for her safety, they had made great inquiries after her, it was a considerable time before any tidings of her reached them. They had at last, however, received a letter from a stranger, named Lintock, informing them that she was residing in the family of a solicitor in Exeter; whereupon Luke had immediately gone to that place; but found that she had disappeared from Mr. Ross's, and nobody knew what had become of her. Once again, they had heard of her from the same man, who said she was in London; and his brother had gone there to fetch her; but he returned alone, saying that she had escaped again, and that he should take no more trouble about her.

On being asked if he had boarded the wreck with his father, he answered, that he had not; being at that time ill with a fever. Being asked if his brother Luke had been there; he answered that he did not know.

The evidence of Anna Littenhaus was, as far as she knew, to exactly the same effect as her brother's. It was not she, but her sister Charlotte who had accompanied Lilly Dawson to Hotham. Charlotte had since married a Mr. Locksley, and lived in London; but she could not tell her address.

Mrs. Ryland and Philip were then examined as to seeing Lilly at "The Black Huntsman." The old woman and her son both looked grave, pale, and ill; but their evidence was given with perfect composure and self-possession. They coincided in the opinion, that Lilly Dawson had not been well treated at "The Huntsman;" she had been over-worked; and her education and her health neglected. Neither could they have considered her by any means happy. Philip remembered her being taken to Hotham. She had made no objection; she was pleased to have some change; and with respect to marrying Mr. Luke, he did not think she well understood the nature of the contract she was about to form. She certainly did not like Mr. Luke—she was afraid of him; but she was extremely ignorant.

Mrs. Hobbs next made her appearance with Sally, her daughter, now a stout, ruddy lass; whilst the clerk of the parish, certified to the fact of Luke Littenhaus and Lilly Dawson having been asked twice in church.

Mrs. Hobbs confessed that she had advised "the poor thing to go out and fetch a walk;" for that it made her heart ache to see how she was shut up in the house, when Miss Charlotte, her cousin, went gadding about everywhere. What had become of her she never could make out. She had never heard of her from that time; and supposed she had gone away "to get quit of the marriage." Miss Sally did not recollect much about the matter. She only knew that she had been playing with some other girls at "Thread-my-needle," when Lilly, who was to have taken care of her, went away and left her. She had never heard of her since.

Then came Abel White, the old blind pauper—blind and a pauper still, and looking much older and more broken, both in mind and body, than when we met him last. As the particulars of his evidence must be already familiar to the reader, we will not detail it; but the poor old man was exceedingly affected whilst he gave his testimony, for he fully believed, as did every body else, Luke Littenhaus not excepted, that Lilly was dead; and the thoughts of her lamentable end brought the big tears from the sightless eyes of her aged friend. He spoke in the highest terms of her character and disposition, and dwelt in pathetic tones and language, on her gratitude and affection towards himself: whilst all he asserted was entirely corroborated by his daughter Martha.

Mr. Ross next related how Lilly had lived in his family as under nursery-maid for six months, and described the unaccountable manner of her departure, and the unfavourable suspicions to which that circumstance had given rise; adding, however, that his wife had previously been very well satisfied with her; but that they had always remarked that she wanted gaiety, and was extremely ignorant and inexperienced for her age. Jane Watts, who had been sent for by Mr. Cropley, next described the journey to London; and clearly accounted for Lilly's flight from Exeter; by saying, that she understood it to have proceeded from some alarm at the prospect of falling again into the hands of her relations, who had not treated her well. A piece of information that exceedingly puzzled Giles Lintock, who, being a great man on the present occasion, and the ally of Mr. Cropley, sat there listening with considerable personal interest to the narrative: and wondering by what means Lilly had become acquainted with his scheme for entrapping her.

After Jane Watts had retired, May Elliott was called forward. Unhappy as she was, it was not in May's nature, on a public occasion like the present, to neglect her person. She was accordingly attired very elegantly, in a green silk dress, white Norwich shawl,[153] and straw bonnet trimmed with pink ribbons; the whole worn

---

153 A type of shawl at the height of fashion in the mid-nineteenth century.

with that good taste and grace, which were her peculiar distinction, and which caused a murmur of approbation to be heard when she made her appearance.

The first part of her evidence was simple and straightforward enough. She had become acquainted with Lilly at Mrs. Knox's, and finding she had no friends, had taken her to live with her. When the interrogatories turned on the mode of their parting, however, there was evidently some mystery to be cleared up. Lilly, she said, had confessed to her that she had run away from her friends; and learning from Giles Lintock that they were still in search of her, she thought it was the best thing for Lilly to deliver her over to them, especially as she did not consider her able to take care of herself. She had delivered her up to Giles at the door of a house where she understood her cousin was waiting to receive her. She had imagined he would marry her, according to his former intentions, and had expected to find her in the country. On the whole, she made out a tolerably good story for herself, which answered well enough for every body but Philip. When *he* heard that she had confessed to having betrayed Lilly into the hands of her enemy, he was inexpressibly shocked; the more so, as he did not discern that she had been actuated by jealousy.

Then came Giles Lintock, who admitted all he had done in the business, making it appear that he thought he was doing no more than his duty, in restoring a runaway to her own family, who were affectionately seeking her.

At length Luke was called upon to answer for himself. He began by corroborating the story told by Ambrose, with respect to finding Lilly, and confessed that he had been with the crew that had boarded the wreck of the *Hastings*, but alleged that he had remained in the boat. He believed all the rest of the party were dead, having lost sight of them. He knew nothing of any body being found on the wreck, except the child whom they had brought away. Supposed she might have belonged to one of the sailors. Her dress furnished no indication with respect to her condition, as she had nothing on but her night-clothes at the time, and was wrapt in a blanket when brought ashore. On being questioned as to his motive for desiring to marry her, he answered, that he had no motive but to afford her protection; and he had taken so much pains to recover her, because he considered her not fit to go about the world alone. He had always thought her rather weak in her intellect. With regard to the last time that Giles Lintock had undertaken to deliver her to him, he declared positively, that when he went to the room, he found the door open and the bird flown. He had himself then quitted the house and the town, and had never made any further inquiries about her. Wherefore she had returned to that room, or who had taken her life, he could not conjecture. On being asked if he were sure she was not in the room, he said that he did not see her there, but she might have concealed herself in some closet, or under the bed; he had not thought of looking since the door was unlocked. He had always supposed Giles Lintock had deceived him, in order to defraud him of the reward. Here Giles affirmed that he had delivered the key to Luke; but that the latter denied.

Ledbetter, the London officer, then testified to a young woman, with fair complexion and light brown hair, being found murdered in the house and chamber to which it appeared, by the evidence of Lintock, that the young person known by the name of Lilly Dawson had been conveyed; and that body, he said, had never been claimed. The people of the house, who were of the worst description, declared they knew nothing of her; that room, and another on a lower floor, being taken only two days before, and the parties having all disappeared before the following morning.

Here terminated the first day's examinations, and various were the opinions with which the company dispersed. The villagers and people about Combe all suspected Luke to be the criminal; but the General expressed great doubts on the subject, and intimated that they had not got to the bottom of the plot yet. He, and Mr Ross, and Mr. Cropley dined at the Hall with the magistrates, and from the baronet's table to the inn kitchen, nothing was talked of but Lilly Dawson, and her melancholy fate.

On the ensuing morning it was understood that the session would commence a couple of hours later than usual, as a witness was expected from London by the coach, whom Ledbetter had gone over to Hotham to fetch. Of the arrival of this witness Luke Littenhaus knew nothing till he saw him enter the room, and in spite of his caution, the effect of this unexpected visitor was very visible. He was a pale, sickly man, suffering from asthma, and evidently on the brink of the grave, he wore a shabby black coat, which hung loosely upon him, and seemed to be buttoned up to his chin for the purpose of concealing the absence of other habiliments. This person was Laban Locksley, whom the London police had hunted up and sent away just in time for the occasion. He admitted that he had been acquainted with the Littenhaus family for several years; he was married to Charlotte Littenhaus; and well remembered Lilly Dawson, whom he had always understood to have been taken off the wreck of the *Hastings*. He had seen her acting as a servant at the inn, and had heard that she had run away because Luke wanted to marry her. He had expressed his surprise that Luke should have desired the union, but the latter had never explained his reasons—he, Luke, was never in the habit of explaining his reasons for any thing. Locksley had never seen the girl, to his knowledge, for several years; but he was aware that Luke came to London to fetch her about two years since, and he had himself by Luke's desire taken rooms in West Smithfield, to which place she was to be conveyed. He had himself only remained there two nights, and had left very early the second morning. His wife and he having quarrelled, he believed she had only been in the house once; and he had himself left the place secretly, for the purpose of getting rid of her, as she led him a very unhappy life. He had not seen Lilly Dawson on that occasion; but he understood from Luke that she was there, locked up in a room above stairs. Luke had told him so; and that she was asleep in the bed. He, Luke, had sat with him sometime, and had then gone up stairs, during which interval he had thrown himself on the bed and was going to sleep, when he heard Luke enter the room again, and rummage amongst his, Locksley's, things. He did not speak to him, being sleepy. Luke then went away, and he afterwards heard him there again, washing his hands. He had been asleep in the interim; but the noise awoke him. However, he soon dropped off again; and knew nothing more, till he arose in the morning, when he observed the water in the basin was tinged with blood. Being alarmed, he had thrown it into the street and rinsed the basin clean. It occurred to him then, that Luke had murdered the girl, and this hastened him away. He saw nobody but a young woman, whom he met on the stairs—there were several people lodging in the house. He had not spoken to her, nor she to him. He thought by her appearance she was a shirt-maker. He had afterwards missed his razor, and he believed that Luke had taken it away. He had since inquired of Luke about the girl, but had never obtained any satisfactory answer. On being shown the clasp knife which had been discovered amongst the bed-clothes, he could not say he had ever seen it before; but a razor which had been found upon the floor, he recognised as the one he had missed. He had read in the papers, that a young woman had been found murdered at that time; and he had never doubted its being Lilly Dawson. The motive for the act, he could not divine.

Here the evidence closed, and Luke was asked if he wished to say any thing further. "I only wish to say," he answered, "that the evidence of the last witness is false from first to last. He married my sister against my inclination; and because he has treated her ill, and forced her to leave him, we have quarrelled, and he is taking this opportunity to be revenged on me."

Whilst the prisoner was proceeding in this strain, a murmur amongst the people was observed at the lower end of the room, and the magistrates called silence more than once; but the noise continuing, Ledbetter moved down, to inquire the cause of the disturbance, and soon returned, accompanied by Bob Groby, who, on being asked what he had to say, answered, that he believed he could tell who that clasp knife belonged to, if he were allowed to look at it. He thought it was one he had bought himself at Hotham, at Mr. Luke's desire; if so, the name of *Crane* would be found on the blade. He had bought it at Mr. Crane's, the cutler, in Fore Street.

On examination, the name was there; and this circumstance seemed so clearly to bring the crime home to Luke, that not one in the room entertained a doubt of his guilt; he, however, declared that he had long lost the knife, and that he had always suspected Locksley of having stolen it.

It was whilst he was standing in front of the Bench, making this defence, that a door, situated immediately behind where the magistrates sat, was gently opened—it was the one at which they, and afterwards the witnesses, had entered—and there appeared at it a tall gentlemanly-looking man, wearing a blue military coat, and a green shade over his eyes, accompanied by a handsome boy about fourteen, apparently full of eagerness and animation. Suddenly Luke, the hardened and impassible, was observed to change colour—he stammered in his speech—his eyes stared wildly—he paused—his mouth gasped—his under jaw fell—his features became rigid, and he sank insensible to the ground.

Whilst they were assisting him and carrying him into another apartment, the two new comers, accompanied by two young persons, neatly attired in dark linen gowns and black straw bonnets, advanced into the room, followed by several of the witnesses who had been congregated in the room through which this party had passed. Foremost was Abel White, led by Martha; and behind came Jane Watts, Mrs. Hobbs, and her daughter Sally. Over their heads were seen the faces of Philip Ryland and his mother, who, on account of their own unpleasant situation, remained modestly in the rear.

"What is this interruption?—who are these?" inquired Sir Lawrence.

"It's Lilly Dawson!" answered those behind the Bench; "and the other's Winny Weston!" responded those in front of it.

"And this is Colonel Adams, and this is his son," added Mr. Ross. "Colonel Adams is the father of the young lady, whom we supposed to be dead!"

The sensation, or rather the uproar, in the room, may be imagined. Every body talked, nobody listened; and as any further explanations or elucidations were not to be expected under such circumstances, the magistrates rose and quitted the room, followed by all who were entitled to accompany them; whilst the crowd rushed pell-mell[154] into the street, and gave three cheers under the windows.

CHAPTER XVIII

THE CONCLUSION

Never was so blessed a village as Combe Martin! What a gossiping there was that day! What a standing before doors! What a setting of arms a-kimbo![155] What a

---

154 In a hurried, confused manner.
155 Hands on hips.

congregation of topers[156] in the beer houses! What toasts were drunk! What disputes! What arguments! What bets were made with respect to the true interpretation of this strange story! Had Luke Littenhaus murdered any body? and, if he had, who was it? How had Miss Adams escaped? and how had she discovered, or been discovered by, her parents?

These were, indeed, perplexing questions; all but the last of which, however, we think the reader can answer for himself, and with respect to that, the solution is very simple. When the General received Mr. Cropley's information, he desired that no communication on the subject should be made to the adverse party, as he called the Colonel; and Messrs. Ross and Treadgold received the same injunction, and obeyed it; thinking it useless to agitate the father with vain hopes and agonising fears. But the General's influence over his wife, was not sufficient to keep her silent; and she whispered the thing to one or two particular friends, who confided it to one or two more, till at length, it reached the ears of an acquaintance of Colonel Adams, who immediately wrote and told him that his long lost daughter was surviving, under the name of *Lilly Dawson;* adding a few more particulars which rendered the identification perfectly easy.

What was the joy, we will not attempt to paint, and least of all Freddy's, who almost kissed the skin off her lips, and never ceased calling her, sister Lilly. The next news that reached them from their friend was, that Lilly was dead, and that the General was gone down with Mr. Ross to seize the assassin. Four horses and a post-chaise resolve the rest of the mystery, and there was Lilly dining at the "Red Lion," with her father and brother, whilst the General was dining at the Hall; hinting, that he believed she was an impostor, and that it was all a plot of the Colonel's; and Winny, meantime, was telling the whole story in her own little home, to her mother, and as many as could crowd in to hear it; and Luke was carried to "The Huntsman" and put to bed, whilst Philip was conveyed to the prison from which he had only been taken to give his evidence.

On the following morning, the General started for London; determined, as he announced, to expose the imposition, whilst Colonel Adams and his daughter were closeted for some hours with Sir Lawrence Longford and the other magistrates. The results of which interview were manifold. In the first instance, it led to a great deal of inquiry and investigation, and examinations of various persons regarding the Littenhaus family, followed up by a search of their premises, and the opening of the coffin, supposed to contain the remains of Old Jacob, the father of these hopeful children; and the final issue of all these proceedings, the details of which would fill three more volumes, was, that Philip was released, and honourably discharged of all suspicion; and that the Littenhaus people were found to be

---

156 Hard drinkers.

members of a dangerous gang of smugglers. It was also discovered that they had murdered Mr. Ryland, because he was in their way; and poor Shorty, Winny's sweetheart, because they imagined he was spying their proceedings.

With respect to the affair of Wybrow, it appeared that, after quitting May, Philip had seen him flirting with another girl in the street; and, enraged at his wanton trifling with the happiness of others, had called him *a blackguard.*[157] This had led to some further words, which, having been overheard by Luke, had inspired him with the idea of getting rid of both; a scheme which he had executed with his usual determination and astuteness. But he did not live to suffer the punishment of his crimes. The shock he had received on the sudden appearance of his supposed victim, had been considerable; that, however, he would have recovered; but when he learnt that it was the life of his own sister he had taken, horror seized him, and, monster as he was, he showed some traces of human feeling. He had not loved her living; but when, by the examination of the remains, the fate of Charlotte, as described by Lilly, was confirmed, the effects were so terrific, as to render it necessary to convey him to an asylum, where he finally terminated his most wretched existence.

It would be wasting words to say, that all who had befriended Lilly in her evil days, were kindly cared for, and placed above want; especially Abel White, who had a comfortable cottage assigned him on her estate in Hertfordshire, where he terminated his days, peaceably, with his daughter and her children.

On the same estate, which was called Elmswood, Philip Ryland, to whom, after all that had occurred, the neighbourhood of Combe Martin would no longer have been agreeable, had a considerable farm given to him, on such advantageous terms as enabled him to prosper on its produce, and afford his mother a comfortable home.

When the bustle and confusion at Combe had somewhat subsided, and people had time to look about them, it was discovered that May Elliott was gone, nobody knew whither. The last we heard of her was, that she had married Mr. Ferdinand Pycroft, and that that name had appeared pretty frequently in the "Gazette."

But what became of Lilly herself? Lilly was now Miss Isabel Adams, with a father and a brother, and a large fortune, and, of course, hosts of friends; but before she could be introduced into the world in her true character, much was required. What accomplishments were needed! What improvements in manners and habits, in walking, in standing, in sitting, in eating, in drinking; in every thing, in short, were indispensable.

For the purpose of supplying all these deficiencies, a house was taken in the

---

157 A scoundrel. A man who behaves in a dishonourable way.

neighbourhood of London, whence masters of music, dancing, French, &c., paid daily attendance; whilst an accomplished governess was engaged to superintend the other departments. But Lilly, though she liked very much to listen to the organs in the street when they played some familiar air, found Hook's lessons insupportably dull, and made very little progress with them. With respect to French, she felt considerable difficulty in fashioning her mouth to pronounce the words; and she suggested, that as there was such a number of English books that she had not yet read, she thought there could be no hurry about French at the present. She would have liked dancing very well, if she had not been obliged to hold up her frock and point her toe, and execute her steps with so much precision. In her opinion, these particularities marred the whole pleasure of the exercise. Grammar, she thought a bore; and the "use of the globes,"[158] intolerable. Geography, provided Miss Vincent would describe the countries she named, and the way the people lived in them, she thought not amiss. On the whole, however, it appeared to Lilly, that the processes necessary to fit a young lady to fill the part of an heiress, were a considerable drawback to the enjoyment of the fortune. She found in herself no aptitude whatever for these things.

However, she hammered away at them for two years, supported through her difficulties by her affection for her father and her passionate love for Freddy, who, both, of course, lived with her; whilst the only pleasure she seemed to derive from her wealth, was in lavishing all manner of benefits and luxuries on them.

At the termination of these two years of wearisome study, Lilly could play an easy tune on the pianoforte, and could understand a very easy French book. She could dance well enough, and she was sufficiently educated not to *appear* ignorant; and this point being attained, it was thought advisable to let her visit her estates in the country, for the purpose of giving her a little change of scene and air. So she, and Freddy, and Colonel and Mrs. Adams, accompanied by a due number of attendants—and amongst them, Winny Weston, who was her own maid—quitted their house at Richmond, and started on their tour.

Lilly thought her country residences, with their green fields, and smiling meadows, and smooth lawns, and fine old trees, much the most agreeable appendages to her wealth she had yet been introduced to; but it grieved her much to find, that she had three houses, all uninhabited except by servants; and she observed, that as she could only live in one of them herself, that it would be better to let somebody else have the use of the other two; but Miss Adelina Fitzherbert, who was paying her a visit, told her, that when she was married, her husband would require them all, at the different seasons of the year, for shooting, hunting, &c. But Lilly blushed at this suggestion, and said she did not intend to marry,

---

158 Geography.

to which Miss Adeline answered "Pooh!" and hinted, that she hoped she did not intend to be so cruel to her poor brother, Sir Everard, who, she must see very well, was breaking his heart for her; which astonished Lilly, who had not been at all aware of his danger.

At last, the course of their journey brought them to Elmswood, and what glad hearts there were to meet them there, may well be imagined. There was old Abel, with his blind eyes and shaking hands, leaning on his stick, at the door of his cottage, when the carriage drove by; and worthy Martha, with her daughter, now a well-grown girl, beside him, wiping away the tears that stood in their eyes, for joy; and a little further on, stood Rachel Ryland, at her garden-gate, dressed in her neat widow's cap and white apron; evidently, ten years younger than when we last saw her. Lilly looked out, and kissed her hand; and her eyes wandered from the gate to the house, and from thence to the farm-yard; but there was no one else there.

So, on they drove, with their four horses, the postilions cracking their whips, and the servants following in another carriage, till they reached the lodge; and Lilly looked again; but there was nobody there, except the old woman that kept it; and so away again till they swept round the lawn to the front entrance, and there on the terrace were assembled the tenants, ready to receive their young lady of the manor. Amongst them there was one handsome young face with a thoughtful pair of dark eyes, and rich brown hair curling over the clear, high forehead, and a half-melancholy smile upon the lips. The owner of it dressed in a black velvet shooting jacket and white trousers, stood modestly in the rear, looking as if he wished to see, but not to be seen.

And then there was a loud cheer, and Lilly, bowing to her tenants, was led into the lofty marble halls of Elmswood.

It was a beautiful place, this Elmswood; the finest and largest of her estates; and it was a great delight to Lilly, who had never lost her early acquired habit of rising almost with the sun, to wander through the glades and shrubberies, and rich pastures where the sheep were feeding, whilst the dew was yet upon the grass; and Winny was always her companion, for Miss Vincent, born and bred in London, could not encounter the fatigue of these matinal[159] excursions; and the beloved Freddy was at Eton. Mrs. Adams rather disapproved of these rustic propensities, and expressed great apprehensions of the effect the bright morning sun might produce on Lilly's complexion; but the Colonel thought she had been too much confined to her studies for the last two years, and suggested, that as she was to come out during the following season, it was desirable to fortify her constitution against the fatigues that awaited her.

---

159 Morning.

So passed the Autumn; and when the Winter came, if it did not rain, Lilly still took her early walk, whilst the rest of the family were in bed, and her father pointed out to his wife how much it agreed with her. Lilly was so well, so bright, so rosy, so cheerful—and so passed the Winter; and the Spring arrived, and the London season drew nigh, and it became necessary to engage a house, and there was great talk betwixt Mrs. Adams and the ladies that visited her about white crapes and organdies, and presentation *toilettes*,[160] and Monsieur le Roi, *artiste célébre*,[161] inimitable for putting in feathers; and there were interminable discussions on the subject of corsets and cosmetics, for, unfortunately, Lilly's waist, not having been early compressed,[162] was too large for the fashion, and her hands had never recovered the scouring and scrubbing at "The Huntsman."

It was to be hoped, however, that all these things would come right in time, and in that hope preparations were made for the removal of the family to London; and Miss Adelina Fitzherbert wrote that her brother, Sir Everard was anticipating the meeting with inexpressible delight.

One morning, however, a circumstance was discovered that baffled all their calculations and disappointed all their plans—Miss Isabel Adams did not appear at breakfast, and by and by, a letter was sent up, which had been left at the lodge, addressed to Colonel Adams, and on opening it, he found at the bottom the signature of *Isabel Ryland.*

"The life of a fine lady," said the writer, "does not suit me. I am not fit for it, nor it for me. I should be often forgetting my part; and you would be ashamed of me, and I should be ashamed of myself. Having had no habits of early application, I cannot attain sufficient proficiency in the accomplishments I have been taught, to take any pleasure in them; and I cannot sufficiently accustom myself to the society of people of rank, to feel at my ease in it. Still less could I ever think of becoming the wife of a person in that station—I should be constantly miserable, from the sense of my own deficiencies.

"For myself, I prefer the amusements and occupations of humbler life; and a very moderate portion of the wealth Providence has bestowed on me, will suffice for all my wants; whilst you, my dear father, and my darling Freddy, will spend with credit and pleasure the fortune which I have, by deeds now in the hands of Mr. Dalton, my agent, made over to you.

"Finally, my dear father, I love, and have long loved, Philip Ryland, who is now my honoured husband, and I never could have been happy as the wife of any other man."

---

160 Dressing or grooming.
161 Fêted or famous artist.
162 Referring to the use of corsets.

No doubt, every body was very much shocked; and Colonel Adams and Frederick were, at first, a good deal grieved; but when they saw how happy Lilly was—Philip always called her by that name—and how well he merited her affection, they became reconciled to what could not be helped, and she and her brother were ever the dearest of friends.

How the courtship had been carried on nobody could ever guess except Winny Weston; but certain it is, that though Lilly had made a great many strange disappearances, this was her last. She lived a happy wife and a fond mother, and died at peace with God and man; and the simple epitaph that was engraven by Philip on her tomb-stone, ended with these words—

FOR LILLY'S LIFE WAS LOVE.

THE END

APPENDIX A - CROWE'S BREAKDOWN

The following extracts and letters relate to a breakdown Catherine Crowe suffered on 26th February 1854. It was first reported in the mesmeric journal *The Zoist,* edited by Dr. John Elliotson, in April 1854 and the report or rumour circulated quickly and widely. There is much dispute about the nature and severity of the episode. It is undoubtedly true that Crowe was hospitalised in Hanwell Asylum, but only for a very short time and it appears that she completely recovered.

Letter from Charles Dickens to the Rev. James White, 7th March 1854, (*The Letters of Charles Dickens*: Volume 7, 1853-1885, Graham Storey, Kathleen Tillotson and Angus Easson, Eds, Oxford: Clarendon Press, 1993, p. 285).

Mrs. [Crowe] has gone stark mad – and stark naked – on the spirit-rapping imposition. She was found t'other day in the street, clothed only in her chastity, a pocket-handkerchief and a visiting card. She had been informed, it appeared, by the spirits, that if she went out in that trim she would be invisible. She is now in a mad-house, and, I fear, hopelessly insane. One of the curious manifestations of her disorder is that she can bear nothing black. There is a terrific business to be done, even when they are obliged to put coals on her fire.

Letter from Charles Dickens to Emile de la Rue, 9th March 1854, (Ibid, p. 288).

The spirit rapping rottenness is fading away, after having done a world of harm, and driven divers and sundry out of their five wits. There is a certain Mrs. Crowe, usually resident in Edinburgh, who wrote a book called the Night Side of Nature, and rather a clever story called Susan Hopley. She was a Medium and an Ass, and I don't know what else. The other day she was discovered walking down her own street in Edinburgh, not only stark mad but stark naked too.

She said that the spirits had informed her that if she walked out with a card in her right hand and her pocket handkerchief in her left – and nothing else – she would be invisible but she was not surprised (she added) to find herself visible, because she remembered that in opening the street door, she had changed the card into the left hand and the pocket handkerchief in the right! She is now under restraint of course.

The Zoist, April 1854, number XLV, p. 33 - *Another person insane through spirit fancies – Second Postscript.*

We have raised our voice from the first against the folly and insanity of ascribing natural phenomena of any kind, and therefore against ascribing those alleged phenomena of the motion and sound of inanimate bodies through an occult living influence, if such table-moving and rapping, independent of muscular agency, be a fact, to supernatural means, – to the agency of spirits, good or evil. We have denounced these outrages upon common sense and upon piety in the strongest manner, and again and again. What would chemists say to a man or woman who ascribed the decomposition of a compound: what would electricians say to a man or woman who ascribed the electrical sparks and snaps: what would the astronomer say to a man or woman who ascribed the motion of a comet or any other heavenly body, the descent of an areolite or the appearance of the meteors which we behold in such numbers twice a year, to the agency of spirits? They would call either a blockhead, for a blockhead he or she must be. We have also given examples, alas! too numerous, in our last Number, of insanity produced by these ignorant fancies: and now we have to record another in the person of a well known authoress, who always had indulged in such superstitions and has of course adopted all the recent spirit fancies. She has gone stark mad and stark naked on the spirit rapping. She was found the other day in the open street, as her mother bore her, except that she had a pocket handkerchief in one hand and a card in the other. She said the spirits had informed her that, if she walked out so prepared, she would be invisible. She is now in a madhouse.

Daily News, 29th April, 1854. CRUEL RUMOURS ABOUT AN AUTHORESS.

The public will be glad to read the following letter from the pen of the authoress of "Susan Hopley," in reply to certain unmanly statements quoted by the *Times* from a mesmeric journal:

TO THE EDITOR OF THE DAILY NEWS

I am very sorry to trouble the public about my private maladies or misfortunes, but since the press has made my late illness the subject of a paragraph, stating that I have gone mad on the subject of spirit rapping, I must beg leave to contradict the assertion.

I have been for some time suffering from chronic gastric inflammation; and, after a journey to Edinburgh and a week of considerable fatigue and anxiety, I was taken ill on the 26th of February, and was certainly for five or six days – not more – in a state of unconsciousness. During the aberration, I talked of spirit-rapping, and fancied spirits were directing me, because of the phenomena, so called, have been engaging my attention, and I was writing on the subject; but I was not – and am not – mad about spirits or anything else, thank God! Though very much out of health and exceedingly debilitated. I have been residing in London for the last five weeks; and I am now at Malvern trying what hydropathy[1] will do for me.

I should feel greatly obliged by your insertion of this letter; and also, if those journalists who have aided in spreading the erroneous impression will assist in disseminating this corrected statement, which I should have made earlier, but the paragraph did not meet my eye till do-day.

I am, sir, your obedient servant,
CATHERINE CROWE

Letter from Harriet Martineau to Frederick Everard Hunt, (Editor of the Daily News), 30th April, 1854.

Gallant Mrs. Crowe! She <u>is</u> one of the honestest and bravest of women. You see she has actually seen the paragraph. Every other woman would have hid herself behind the body of 'authoress', but she, for our sakes, (I am very sure that is her reason) signs herself 'Catherine Crowe' at full length. Now I am all vindictiveness towards Elliotson. His rest ought to be broken for a night or two, – as he has broken a good many other people's. If I were not, in a manner, concerned, I would write him such a letter!

(Catherine Crowe Archive, University of Kent, Canterbury).

The Zoist, 12th July 1854, pp. 174-180. IV. *More insanity from Spirit-rapping fancies.* **By Dr. ELLIOTSON.**

Gentlemen Editors, I have a crow to pluck with you. You ought to be ready to give the name and address in private of the parties of whom you write. But in your account of the lady who went into the streets stark mad and stark naked through her spirits, you make no such offer to your readers. The consequence of which is, that, as you do not mention the lady's age nor even her country, whether England,

---

1 A natural therapy involving the use of water for physiotherapy.

Scotland, Ireland, or Wales, a lady has been fixed upon, and has fixed upon her-self, who perhaps never was mad for an instant in her life, nor ever listened to spirits commanding her to sacrifice her modesty for the good of her soul; and poor I, though I did not write one word of the description, have been fixed upon and abused as if I were the real culprit. First came a letter from Mrs. de Morgan, giving me her unasked-for opinion, and containing the following passages, which, in justice to Mrs. Crowe, and to shew you what my sufferings under such remon-strances must be, I am bound to send you for publication.

"I cannot help expressing my regret to you that an article should have a place in *The Zoist* calculated to give much pain to the subject of it – my friend, Mrs. Crowe, who is no doubt the person referred to. This lady had, it is true, an attack of cerebral congestion about five weeks ago, in consequence of want of attention to her health. She was looking out for a lodging – got her meals ill cooked, or did not get them regularly – had a young and heedless servant, who did not perceive the feverish attack coming on, and in consequence was seriously delirious for two days. The attack was removed by a very simple dose of medicine; but in the mean-time, some of her friends believing her to be permanently insane, had her brought *up by a night train* to Hanwell. Dr. Conolly soon saw that she was not a fit inmate for his place, and assisted her in extricating herself. She is now in a lodging at the west end of London, where I saw and bad a long talk with her a fortnight since. She was twice at the play the week before last. You have probably heard all this already, but I send it on the chance."

[…]

But the great letter to me is from Mrs. Crowe herself.

"Dr. Wilson's, Great Malvern,
May 3rd.

Sir,– I think before you inserted that 'unmanly' paragraph (as the *Daily News* justly calls it) in *The Zoist,* which has been thence copied into the newspapers, you should have taken the trouble to ascertain the truth of the statement. A little en-quiry would have enabled you to learn that I was not mad about spirit-rapping or anything else; but that I had been since the 26th of February, and was still, very ill, and that when the magazine was published, I was residing in London for the ben-efit of medical advice, and had been so since the 14th of March. Since during the whole of my stay in London, I was in the daily habit of visiting, and being visited by, many of your acquaintance, the fact would have been easily ascertained. The world has been ready enough to call you mad for your heterodox beliefs, and if I did believe in the spirits it would be no proof of madness: as it happens, my judgment is yet suspended on the subject; but as I happened to be investigating the phenomena at the time I was taken ill, in the aberration of mind that accompanied the illness I fancied myself haunted by spirits. I did not know till a few days since that you had done me this friendly turn. I should have thought your own experience would have made you more just and merciful to others: I have always been indignant at the persecution you have sustained; but since you are so ready and eager to persecute others, you thoroughly deserve what you have met with.

CATHERINE CROWE."

Now I really had no desire to make enquiries of Mrs. Crowe's friends: nor was I aware that I knew even one of them. I recollect the good lady at an evening party at Mrs. Milner Gibson's, and at another at Mrs. Monckton Milnes's; and perhaps at one or two others, but where I forget. People go to evening parties continually who can hardly be said to have any acquaintance with those whom they thus visit. I should never have thought of enquiring of either lady about her: and till now I was not aware that she was acquainted with Mrs. de Morgan, even should their investigations and convictions be identical. I really know nothing more of Mrs. Crowe than that I am informed she wrote a book of which I never read nor am likely to read a line, and which I never saw. Why should the world fancy that Mrs. Crowe was the lady? Your sole object was evidently to stay this plague: and I will aid you to the utmost of my poor power. Who Mrs. Crowe's friend in the office of the *Daily News* is, I am not aware. But this is certain, that the *Daily News* some months ago did not refrain from publishing a list of persons, with their names and residences, who had gone mad through spirit-rapping.

I hope she will give the results to the scientific world of her investigations into this recondite and doubtful matter of true science: and when she writes to me again will not aim at surpassing the very pretty little bit of Christianity which closes her epistle.

APPENDIX B - CROWE'S POLITICS

The following extracts are taken from a range of sources and illustrate some of Catherine Crowe's political ideas. The pieces show that she was opposed to slavery and vocal about issues around women's education and animal rights.

Catherine Crowe, 'Amicable Intervention in the Question of Slavery', *The Ladies Cabinet of Fashion*, January 1853.

We apprehend that most of our readers observed the report of a recent meeting at Stafford House, and have felt interested in the movement which has then emanated. The subject appears to us so essentially a womanly one that we are tempted to devote a little space to its consideration, and shall endeavour so to do in a manner as dispassionate as possible.

For long years past every thoughtful, true-hearted woman in Christendom must sometimes have sorrowed over the frightful question of negro-slavery; and it seems to have needed only such an impulse as Mrs. Stowe's book has given, to kindle deep smouldering feelings into one persistent glow. [...] But a new crusade is long in the preaching; and it was because minds were already informed on the horrid subject, and hearts open to receive faithful impressions, that the pathos of those scenes, written as it were in human tears, so quickly fulfilled its office. Mere sympathy, however, is of little avail unless it prompt to action; yet the idea that Englishwomen could *do* anything towards the abolition of slavery must at first have appeared preposterous. Still, a very vague idea, by tossing about in the mind, often acquires consistency, and probably something of this sort took place in the present instance. [...]

The following extracts comprise a report of the meeting, and a copy of the address, which is now in course of receiving signatures.

On Friday 26th of November, a meeting of ladies was convened at Stafford House, to consider the expediency of addressing a memorial from the women of England to the women of the United States on the subject of slavery. The ladies being assembled, the Duchess of Sutherland read the following paper:–

'Perhaps I may be allowed to state the object for which this meeting has been called together; but very few words will be required, as all, I am sure, assembled here must have heard and read much of the moral and physical suffering inflicted on the race of negroes and their descendants by the system of slavery prevalent in many of the united states of America. Founded on such information, a proposition appeared a short time ago in several of the newspapers,[1] that the women of England should express to the women of America the strong feeling they entertained on the question, and earnestly request their aid to abolish, or at least to mitigate, so enormous an evil. [...]

There are many reasons why this address should be presented rather by the women than by the men of England. We shall not be suspected of any political motives; all will readily admit that the state of things to which we allude is one peculiarity [sic] distressing to our sex; and thus our friendly and earnest interposition will be ascribed altogether to domestic, and in no respect to national, feelings'.

[There follows a list of names of ladies appointed to the sub-committee (amongst the list of august ladies is – a little further down- the name of Mrs Charles Dickens). This is followed by the Address itself.]

'THE AFFECTIONATE AND CHRISTIAN ADDRESS of many thousands of women of England to their sisters, the women of the United States of America:—

"A common origin, a common faith, and we sincerely believe, a common cause, urge us, at the present moment, to address you on the subject of that system of negro slavery which still prevails so extensively, and, even under kindly-disposed master, with such frightful results, in many of the vast regions of the western world.

We will not dwell on the ordinary topics – on the progress of civilization – on the advance of freedom everywhere – on the rights and requirements of the nineteenth century; but we appeal to you very seriously to reflect, and to ask counsel of God, how far such a state of things is in accordance with His Holy Word, the inalienable rights of immortal souls, and the pure and merciful spirit of the Christian religion.

We do not shut our eyes to the difficulties, nay the dangers, that might beset the immediate abolition of that long-established system; we see and admit the necessity of preparation for so great an event; but, in speaking of indispensable preliminaries, we cannot be silent on those laws of your country which, in direct contravention of God's own law, "instituted at the time of man's innocency," deny in effect to the slave, the sanctity of marriage, with all its joys, rights and obligations; which separate at the will of the master, the wife from the husband and the children from the parents. Nor can we be silent on that awful system which,

---

1 In a letter to *The Times,* Nov. 5th, from the Earl of Shaftesbury.

either by statute or by custom, interdicts to any race of man, or any portion of the human family, education in the truths of the gospel and the ordinances of Christianity.

A remedy applied to these two evils alone would commence the amelioration of their sad condition. We appeal to you, then, as sister, as wives, and as mothers, to raise your voices to your fellow-citizens, and your prayers to God, for the removal of this affliction from the Christian world. We do not say these things in a spirit of self-complacency, as though our nation were free from the guilt it perceives in others. We acknowledge, with grief and shame, our heavy share in this great sin. We acknowledge that our forefathers introduced, nay compelled, the adoption of slavery in those mighty colonies. We humbly confess it before Almighty God: and it is because we so deeply feel, and so unfeignedly avow, our own complicity, that we now venture to implore your aid to wipe away our common crime and our common dishonour'.

We hope our readers have perused the above 'affectionate and Christian' address with the attention it deserves, because it so happens that a number of worthless objections have been raised against it. One party says that it will be extremely offensive to the Americans; while another blast is blown from the opposite point of the compass, and declares that the draft of the address does not originate from our countrywomen at all, but has been smuggled over from the other side of the Atlantic. A very noisy host cry out from all sides, 'Look at home, and before you rebuke the slave-holders, reform the condition of your own poor, of your starving, ignorant children, your hungry needlewomen, your hardly-used servants, even of your ill-paid *dis*respected governesses.' Now it may very safely be asserted, that the ladies whose names have just been quoted, are of those who do thoughtfully consider, and to the utmost of their abilities, alleviate the misery which surrounds them; for true Christian Charity is like human knowledge – the more widely it is extended the more perfect is it likely to be in its details. [...] Besides, this address is but a very gentle, meek, sisterly expression of an Opinion, which will surely fall pleasantly on the ears of those who sympathise with it. [...] There is no appeal for money – that wondrous touchstone of feelings – only the influence of opinion and discussion is desired; though surely were this a case in which money were required it would largely be forthcoming; for the condition of the slave, distinct from every other lot of misery and degradation in the world, while it robs him of the rights of man in the country where he toils, renders him a brother and a citizen in every other land where Christianity prevails: and oh, may not England be pardoned if she do speak warmly and decidedly on a subject in reference to which she herself acted so worthily! In all her glorious past there is nothing that shines out more nobly than the abolition of her own slave trade.

After all, we need only ask our readers to think for themselves, feeling well assured that few truly womanly hearts will hesitate about signing the address. The doing so takes no mite from nearer claimants; it is but the emphatic expression of an opinion, and a gentle affectionate entreaty for sister Women to use their influence in ameliorating the worst horrors of slavery. The argument that we have evils in England which ought to be remedied before we notice foreign evils, is so trivial and inapplicable to the question, that it would not be worthy consideration, but for a sort of surface speciousness that makes in dangerous. True, we have oppression and undeserved suffering among us; but instead of these cases being upheld by law, and made part of a national system – as Slavery is in the Southern States of America – we have political economists, legislators, and philanthropists, toiling together to unmake bad laws, and remove the occasions of injustice. Rich in her charities beyond all comparison with any other nation, England has asylums for infants, and almshouses for the aged; hospitals for the sick, and workhouses for the destitute: her great difficulty is doubtless the brutal ignorance and degradation of the scum of her great towns, who are incapable it would appear, of helping themselves out of the slough into which they have fallen. But who shall say that generous helpers are not many and active? And surely the lowest form of human misery in England has one feature which distinguishes it from the condition of slavery. The poorest hind, the most toil-worn drudge, is free to better his lot, if his abilities and opportunities permit. The slighted and underpaid governess is not constrained to endure insult longer than the doing so appears a less evil that the want of employment. If more just and kind patrons present themselves, she is free to change her employment; and if fortune smiles on her family, and relieves her from her position of dependence, she is not serf to be controlled by a tyrant. Servants who are ill used 'better themselves' the first opportunity, occasioning a discomfort to unreasonable mistresses, which is satisfactory to contemplate. And when poverty and misfortunes, or even prudential motives, induce near relations to separate, they part with a hope of reunion; with a belief in achieving some future good that will compensate for present sufferings [...]. With the wretched slave there is no natural adjustment of this kind. A people proverbially affectionate and attached are ruthlessly separated, their fondest ties sundered at the will of another; their whole human nature corrupted by the laws of the country, and themselves taunted for a degradation that is inevitable, from the wrongs to which for centuries they have been condemned. Even the knowledge of a Redeemer, are in the majority of instances denied them; and secular learning is kept far away, lest knowledge should indeed prove to be power. But though the arguments which might be brought forward – to show that the sufferings of the negroes differ from any misery to be found in England – are well night inexhaustible, they are familiar to every thoughtful mind, and rise up in all their convincing truth, at the mere mention and contrast of the two words Freedom and Slavery!

Crowe on Science and the Supernatural: Extract from the introduction to *The Night Side of Nature*, (1848).

To minds which can admit nothing but what can be explained and demonstrated, an investigation of this sort [into the supernatural] must appear perfectly idle; for whilst, on the one hand, the most acute intellect or the most powerful logic can throw little light on the subject, it is, at the same time though I have a confident hope that this will not always be the case equally irreducible within the present bounds of science; meanwhile, experience, observation, and intuition, must be our principal, if not our only guides. Because, in the seventeenth century, credulity outran reason and discretion; the eighteenth century, by a natural re-action, threw itself into an opposite extreme. Whoever closely observes the signs of the times, will be aware that another change is approaching. The contemptuous scepticism of the last age is yielding to a more humble spirit of enquiry; and there is a large class of persons amongst the most enlightened of the present, who are beginning to believe, that much which they had been taught to reject as fable, has been, in reality, ill-understood truth. Somewhat of the mystery of our own being, and of the mysteries that compass us about, are beginning to loom upon us as yet, it is true, but obscurely; and, in the endeavour to follow out the clue they offer, we have but a feeble light to guide us. We must grope our way through the dim path before us, ever in danger of being led into error, whilst we may confidently reckon on being pursued by the shafts of ridicule that weapon so easy to wield, so potent to the weak, so weak to the wise which has delayed the births of so many truths, but never stifled one. The pharisaical scepticism which denies without investigation, is quite as perilous, and much more contemptible than the blind credulity which accepts all that it is taught without enquiry; it is, indeed, but another form of ignorance assuming to be knowledge. And by investigation, I do not mean the hasty, captious, angry notice of an unwelcome fact, that too frequently claims the right of pronouncing on a question; but the slow, modest, painstaking examination, that is content to wait upon nature, and humbly follow out her disclosures, however opposed to preconceived theories or mortifying to human pride. If scientific men could but comprehend how they discredit the science, they really profess, by their despotic arrogance, and exclusive scepticism, they would surely, for the sake of that very science they love, affect more liberality and candour. This reflection, however, naturally suggests another, namely, do they really love science, or is it not too frequently with them but the means to an end? Were the love very different fruits to that which we see borne by the tree of knowledge, as it flourishes at present; and this suspicion is exceedingly strengthened by the recollection, that amongst the numerous students and professors of science I have at different times encountered, the real worshippers and genuine lovers of it, for its own sake, have all been men of the most single, candid, unprejudiced, and enquiring minds, willing to listen to all new suggestions, and investigate all new facts; not bold and self-sufficient, but humble and reverent suitors, aware of their own ignorance and unworthiness, and that they are yet but in the primer of nature's works, they do not permit themselves to pronounce upon her disclosures, or set limits to her decrees. They are content to admit that things new and unsuspected may yet be true; that their own knowledge of facts being extremely circumscribed, the systems attempted to be established on such, uncertain data, must needs be very imperfect, and frequently altogether erroneous; and that it is therefore their duty, as it ought to be their pleasure, to welcome as a stranger every gleam of light that appears in the horizon, let it loom from whatever quarter it may.

But, alas! Poor science has few such lovers! Les beaux yeux de sa cassette, I fear, are much more frequently the objects of attraction than her own fair face.[2]

[...]

With respect to the evidence past and present, I must be allowed here to remark on the extreme difficulty of producing it. Not to mention the acknowledged carelessness of observers and the alleged incapacity of persons to distinguish betwixt reality and illusion, there is an exceeding shyness in most people, who, either have seen, or fancied they have seen, an apparition, to speak of it at all, except to some intimate friend; so that one gets most of the stories second-hand; whilst even those who are less chary of their communications, are imperative against their name and authority being given to the public. Besides this, there is a great tendency in most people, after the impression is over, to think they may have been deceived; and where there is no communication or other circumstance rendering this conviction impossible, it is not difficult to acquire it, or at least so much of it as leaves the case valueless. The seer is glad to find this refuge from the unpleasant feelings engendered; whilst surrounding friends, sometimes from genuine scepticism, and sometimes from good-nature, almost invariably lean to this explanation of the mystery. In consequence of these difficulties and those attending the very nature of the phenomena, I freely admit that the facts I shall adduce, as they now stand, can have no scientific value; they cannot in short enter into the region of science at all, still less into that of philosophy. Whatever conclusions we may be

---

2 Attracted by the money, rather than by the beauty.

led to form, cannot be founded on pure induction. We must confine ourselves wholly within the region of opinion. if we venture beyond which, we shall assuredly founder. In the beginning, all sciences have been but a collection of facts, afterwards to be examined, compared, and weighed by intelligent minds. To the vulgar, who do not see the universal law which governs the universe, everything out of the ordinary course of events, is a prodigy; but to the enlightened mind there are no prodigies; for it perceives that both in the moral and the physical world, there is a chain of uninterrupted connexion; and that the most strange and even apparently contradictory or supernatural fact or event will be found, on due investigation, to be strictly dependant on its antecedents. It is possible, that there may be a link wanting, and that our investigations may, consequently, be fruitless; but the link is assuredly there, although our imperfect knowledge and limited vision cannot find it.

And it is here the proper place to observe, that, in undertaking to treat of the phenomena in question, I do not propose to consider them as supernatural; on the contrary, I am persuaded that the time will come, when they will be reduced strictly within the bounds of science. It was the tendency of the last age to reject and deny everything they did not understand; I hope it is the growing tendency of the present one, to examine what we do not understand. Equally disposed with our predecessors of the eighteenth century to reject the supernatural, and to believe the order of nature inviolable, we are disposed to extend the bounds of nature and science, till they comprise within their limits all the phenomena, ordinary and extraordinary, by which we are surrounded. Scarcely a month passes, that we do not hear of some new and important discovery in science; it is a domain in which nothing is stable; and every year overthrows some of the hasty and premature theories of the preceding ones; and this will continue to be the case as long as scientific men occupy themselves each with his own subject, without studying the great and primal truths what the French call Les vérités meres[3] which link the whole together. Meantime, there is a continual unsettling. Truth, if it do not emanate from an acknowledged authority, is generally rejected; and error, if it do, is as often accepted; whilst, whoever disputes the received theory, whatever it be we mean especially that adopted by the professors of colleges does it at his peril. But there is a day yet brooding in the bosom of time, when the sciences will be no longer isolated; when we shall no longer deny, but be able to account for phenomena apparently prodigious; or have the modesty; if we cannot explain them, to admit that the difficulty arises solely from our own incapacity. The system of centralization in statistics, seems to be of doubtful advantage; but a greater degree

---

3 The mothers or origins of truths.

of centralization appears to be very much needed in the domain of science. Some improvement in this respect might do wonders, particularly if reinforced with a slight infusion of patience and humility into the minds of scientific men; together with the recollection that facts and phenomena which do not depend on our will, must be waited for that we must be at their command, for they will not be at ours.

Catherine Crowe on animals: Extract from *Ghosts and Family Legends*, (1859).

There are few friends so sincere as the animals who have love us, and none that I, for my part, more earnestly desire to see again. I have had two dogs, in my life, who contributed much to my happiness while they lived, and never caused me a sorrow till they died. Besides, there is a deep mystery in the being of these creatures, which proud man never seeks to unravel, or condescends to speculate on. What is their relation to the human race? Why are these spiritual germs embodied in those forms and made subject to man, that hard and cruel master! who assumes to be their superior, because he is endowed with some higher faculties, the most of which he grossly misuses. How beautiful are their characters when studied? How wonderful their intelligence when cultivated? How willing they are to serve us when kindly treated? But man, by his cruelty, ignorance, laziness and want of judgement, spoils their temper, blunts their intelligence, deteriorates their nature and then punishes them for being what he himself has made them. Well might Chalmers exclaim, All nature groans beneath the cruelty of man. Why are these creatures, sinless, as far as we see, placed here as the subject of this barbarous unthinking tyrant? That has always appeared to me a solemn question.

APPENDIX C - CONTEMPORARY REVIEWS

The Critic, 13 March 1847, no. 115; pp. 205-206.

There is a charm about Mrs. Crowe's novels which all feel, but nobody can describe. Professional critics, the mill-horses of the press, who can acknowledge excellence in nothing that comes not within their own narrow circle of conventionalisms, shake their heads at her and point to faults in plot or composition; and "the silver fork school" turn up their noses at maid-servant heroines and adventures of low life. But still the non-critical reading public, caring nothing for reviewers, and content to be pleased in spite of most unanswerable arguments why they should not be pleased, persist in reading, and as they read, unanimously they feel deeply interested, and thenceforth "*Susan Hopley*" and "*Lilly Dawson*" become, not merely memories of tales that were told, but being whom the reader has personally seen and talked with.

What is the secret of this charm? What are the characteristics of these fictions which baffle the sagacity of the self-appointed judges of literature?

Is there among the books most honoured in the library, most universally loved, any that resembles Mrs. Crowe's fictions in its quiet command of the reader's fancy – in its power of self-embodiment, and the hold it takes upon his curiosity? Yes, there is one such book – "*Robinson Crusoe*" – and comparing its effect with the like effect produced by the novels of Mrs. Crowe, it may not be hopeless to trace the cause.

That charm, then, is not in the story, nor in its personages, but in the truthfulness of manner in the telling of it. It is seen not only in "*Robinson Crusoe*" but in all the narratives of Defoe. Who does not find it difficult to believe that "*The History of the Plague*" is fiction? It requires more effort to convince oneself that Robinson Crusoe's adventures are inventions, than to assure oneself that the records of history are truths. Probably this is not the result of art, but an unconscious faculty in the writers, by which they are enabled so completely to realize their ideas, that the pictures rise up in the mind perfect in the minutest details; whereas the imaginations of ordinary writers are rather outlines than pictures.

[…]

This, then, is the secret of Mrs. Crowe's popularity. This was the charm that riveted the reader's attention from the first to the last page of *"Susan Hopley,"* and left him in doubt whether it was fact or fiction that had engrossed his fancy. The same quality pervades this new *"Story of Lilly Dawson."* Like its predecessor it is a tale of low life, the adventures of a girl brought up in a smuggler's family, and spectator of their crimes, which, beginning with defrauding the revenue, end in murder. It is a fearful tale, wrought with extraordinary power, abounding in scenes that hold the breath in suspense, and in hairbreadth 'scapes that keep the curiosity continually upon the stretch. They who remember *Susan Hopley*, and who does not? will readily understand the effect with which our authoress works up situations of this sort. We will not mar the absorbing interest of the story by anticipating it; it will be read, and it deserves to be read, by all who ever indulge in a novel. It will not be less popular than its predecessors, whether in its present form, or moulded into a drama, as doubtless it will be ere long.

***The Literary Gazette: A Weekly Journal of Literature, Science, and the Fine Arts*, 6 March 1847: Issue 1572, pp. 187-8.**

NOVEL IN LOW LIFE

Susan Hopley made herself great fame, especially with the lower orders, not only as a story of tragic incident in the original form, but when dramatized and set upon the stage. Lilly Dawson, being a bird of the same feather, may doubtless anticipate a similar success.

[…]

The characters have the merit of force in their drawing, and the difference between the commission of crime and the immediate consequences, among the lowest classes and those of a superior station, are delineated with much talent. [...] We accordingly avoid that morbid dwelling upon the minutiae and balancings of conscience, – which we fear, offer no beneficial lessons to mankind, – and have little more than the naked facts of throat-cuttings to lead us on through the series of villainies, and their final retribution.

[…]

Luke Littenhaus is the remorseless ruffian and assassin of the piece. His accomplices are well diversifies, and admitting, for argument's sake, that the tale is unobjectionable in base materials and brutal atrocity of action, it must be conceded that Mrs. Crowe has exhibited much skill and ability in its construction and development. We see tolerably well how it is to terminate, and yet she has wrought up most of the details with such fearful interest, as to hold the curiosity in a condition of excitement till the result is made known.

The Morning Post, 10 April 1847, Issue 22885, p.6.

In "Susan Hopley" Mrs. Crowe may have done something for the numerous and much-neglected class, domestic servants; but in "Lilly Dawson," we have personages and scenes which, if any such ever existed or happened at all, can never occur again, and which can therefore afford no guidance and suggest no instruction to any class. [...] We recommend Mrs. Crowe in future, to select better materials, and to keep nature and probability more in view; she may then, with her admirable style of composition and undoubted powers of description achieve *a good novel.*

The Lady's Newspaper, 13 March 1847, Issue 11, p. 256.

Rather would we be the writer of this tale of real life than a score, at least, of fashionable novels. The history of one true heart, amidst temptation, weariness, distress, peril, hope, and final happiness, is as a "cordial comfort" to the soul, and contrasts strangely and triumphantly with the pasteboard figures which so often fret and strut before us – the very wires by which they are moved being clumsily unconcealed. [...] We have no fear for the popularity of "Lilly Dawson" – it is so intelligible, so earnest, and exemplifies so admirable a moral.

New Monthly Magazine and Humorist, April 1847, Issue 316, p. 532.

The story of "Susan Hopley" at once raised its authoress, Mrs. Crowe, into the first rank of domestic novelists, and "Lilly Dawson" has sustained the pre-eminence so deservedly gained. [It is] in the consummate art with which a character itself not very prepossessing is invested with interest, in the power with which the gradual awakening of sense and intellect, from the prostration of servitude and tyranny is portrayed, and in the life and character which is impressed upon each accessory character, rather than in the mere incident and narrative, that lie the chief merits of this truly clever and able performance. It belongs to that class of story which, since the days of Fielding and Richardson, has been the most enduring of all works of fiction.

The Mirror of Literature, Amusement, and Instruction, 1 April 1847, pp. 70-273.

It is now becoming very much the fashion to introduce, for a heroine into a novel, no woman of dazzling beauty and winning loveliness, but little plain children, who pass quietly into beauty as they grow in years. We are far from intending to deprecate this practice, but our attention is naturally attracted by the continual fluctuations which are observable in the taste of writers of fiction. At one time the fashion is for sylph-like heroines; and at another, for pale, tall, intellectual ladies. Now, however, the heroine is generally introduced as a child, around whom, though, at first described with characteristics and peculiarities little calculated to meet our attention, we feel the interest of the story is nevertheless destined to centre. We perceive, that the large dark, though heavy eyes, and the pale cheek, are intended to ripen into something far more attractive. Lilly Dawson, the heroine of the three volumes which no claim our attention, belongs to this class. She is introduced at a very early period of her life, under somewhat unfavourable circumstances, or, we should rather perhaps say, auspices, as drudge in fact to a family who kept 'the Huntsman,' one even of a suspicious character, and who affect to be her cousins. The reader, however, alone perceives that Lilly Dawson is no relative of the smuggling gang. Her mode of life while living with these people, is very admirably described, and some peculiarly striking scenes are here introduced. Mrs. Crowe displays considerable ability in treating this portion of her narrative. She brings the characters and actions she is engaged in describing with startling reality before us. Her pen represents in vivid colours, the events of which she intends the reader to be the spectator; and, even while our judgment compels us to find fault with the improbably nature of two or three of the scenes, we cannot at the same time fail to admire the energy of the writer who depicts them. She makes no attempt at over-strained sentiment, but takes life much as it is found, and gives us its smiles and its tears, its lighter and darker shadows, with its moderate and truthful language. [...] No one, however, in perusing the tale of 'Lilly Dawson,' can fail to be struck with one or two glaring defects in the conduct of the tale. In the first place, the incidents are pushed too far forward, so that the middle of the tale seems in fact, only to be arrived at in the commencement of the third volume. This necessarily leaves the authoress little space in which to develope [sic] the circumstances connected with the denouement, which is therefore rather hurried.

[...]

'Lilly Dawson' will prove a source of considerable interest to all who delight in ably-written, stirring narratives, in effective scenes, and in infinite variety of character. With such attractions the story of 'Lilly Dawson' abounds.

John Bull, **15 March 1847, Issue 1370, p. 169.**

We have read this work with deep interest; an interest derived from the nature of the incidents, the character of the principal personages, the clear, forcible style of the writer, and her occasional reflexions [sic] upon motives if human conduct. In all these requisites of a good novelist Mrs. Crowe excels. She possesses, also, another quality of scarcely inferior importance, that of making her characters tell their own tale, instead of telling it herself. The progress of the story, consequently, has all the rapidity and individuality of a dramatic piece; and, as the incidents are numerous and striking, all have the power of continued action, instead of being languidly moved forward by description. Some of the characters are delineated with striking fidelity, and a thorough acquaintance with human nature, and the passions that shape its destiny. Among the most successful of her efforts in this way are Abel White, the blind beggar, May Elliott, a sort of *Milwood*, Luke Littenhaus, Philip Ryland, and the heroine herself, Lilly Dawson. The last of these, Lilly Dawson, is a creation not unworthy of Scott. [...] Every portion of the work, indeed, indicates powers of no common order. Nothing is forced for the sake of effect; nothing is out of nature, except, perhaps, the sanguinary crimes of Luke, which seem to want sufficient motive for their perpetration. But their improbability is so well managed that the reader's assent to their probability is given without much difficulty. [...] As a whole the *Story of Lilly Dawson* will place Mrs. Crowe high among the living writers of fiction.

Victorian Secrets

Sowing the Wind by Eliza Lynn Linton
edited by Deborah T. Meem & Kate Holterhoff

St John Aylott's life is in turmoil. With his social status already under threat, even his virtuous wife Isola is questioning his authority. Influenced by her tomboyish cousin, journalist Jane Osborn, who provides female solidarity and strong opinions, Isola fights to assert her subjectivity over a tyrannical husband; meanwhile Jane is forced to adjust to the masculine world of work on a daily newspaper.

Sowing the Wind was Eliza Lynn Linton's first critically successful novel. Written during the breakdown of her marriage, it is openly, and often painfully, autobiographical. With its themes of inheritance, concealed identity, madness, and domestic violence, Linton's novel epitomises the sensation genre.

The *Athenaeum* reviewer concluded: "The primary idea of the book is ingenious, and it is consistently kept in view throughout the narrative. We recommend readers in search of an uncommon novel to send for *Sowing the Wind.*" The *Saturday Review* was terrified by the "dark hints of what would happen if women, instead of men, had the making of the laws".

Includes critical introduction, explanatory footnotes, contemporary reviews, and extracts from relevant texts.

ISBN: 978-1-906469-51-1

Available in paperback and Kindle editions. For more information, please visit:

www.victoriansecrets.co.uk

Victorian Secrets

Victorian Secrets is an independent publisher dedicated to producing high-quality books from and about the nineteenth century, including critical editions of neglected novels.

A City Girl by John Law (Margaret Harkness)

All Sorts and Conditions of Men by Walter Besant

The Angel of the Revolution by George Chetwynd Griffith

The Autobiography of Christopher Kirkland by Eliza Lynn Linton

The Beth Book by Sarah Grand

The Blood of the Vampire by Florence Marryat

The Dead Man's Message by Florence Marryat

Demos by George Gissing

East of Suez by Alice Perrin

Henry Dunbar by Mary Elizabeth Braddon

Her Father's Name by Florence Marryat

The Light that Failed by Rudyard Kipling

A Mummer's Wife by George Moore

Not Wisely, but Too Well by Rhoda Broughton

Robert Elsmere by Mrs Humphry Ward

Selected Stories of Morley Roberts

Sowing the Wind by Eliza Lynn Linton

Thyrza by George Gissing

Twilight Stories by Rhoda Broughton

Vice Versâ by F. Anstey

Weeds by Jerome K. Jerome

Weird Stories by Charlotte Riddell

Workers in the Dawn by George Gissing

For more information on any of our titles, please visit:

www.victoriansecrets.co.uk

CPSIA information can be obtained
at www.ICGtesting.com
Printed in the USA
LVOW04s1506291015

460297LV00024B/1094/P